RELATIVE CRUELTY

"Take her and that filthy suitcase to her room, and show her what her duties are."

"Yes, Mrs. Dallas," said Señora Rosario.

"I won't tolerate another lazy Mexican in my house or on my grounds," my aunt said, and started to turn away.

I quickly spoke up in my newest English words.

"Thank you, Mrs. Dallas. I'm pleased to be here and grateful for all you are doing for me," I said.

She spun around, her eyes wide. I held my gaze. I would not be treated as if I were no better than a *cucaracha*, something to be crushed and swept away. Then she marched out of the living room, her high heels tapping the travertine floor in a rhythm of rage. It was as if my very presence infuriated her. If this was so, why did she send for me? If she still hated her family so much, why did she want a living reminder of it right under her nose?

Something told me that I had seen only the tip of the flame. There was quite a fire burning in her chest, a fire started years ago back in our village. Would it consume me, or would I snuff it out before it could?

V.C. ANDREWS®
DELIA'S CROSSING

V.C. Andrews® Books

The Dollanganger Family
Flowers in the Attic
Petals on the Wind
If There Be Thorns
Seeds of Yesterday
Garden of Shadows
Christopher's Diary:
    Secrets of
    Foxworth
Christopher's Diary:
    Echoes of
    Dollanganger
Secret Brother

The Audrina Series
My Sweet Audrina
Whitefern

The Casteel Family
Heaven
Dark Angel
Fallen Hearts
Gates of Paradise
Web of Dreams

The Cutler Family
Dawn
Secrets of the Morning
Twilight's Child
Midnight Whispers
Darkest Hour

The Landry Family
Ruby
Pearl in the Mist
All That Glitters
Hidden Jewel
Tarnished Gold

The Logan Family
Melody
Heart Song
Unfinished Symphony
Music in the Night
Olivia

The Orphans Series
Butterfly
Crystal
Brooke
Raven
Runaways

The Wildflowers Series
Misty
Star
Jade
Cat
Into the Garden

The Hudson Family
Rain
Lightning Strikes
Eye of the Storm
The End of the Rainbow

The Shooting Stars
Cinnamon
Ice
Rose
Honey
Falling Stars

The De Beers Family
"Dark Seed"
Willow
Wicked Forest
Twisted Roots
Into the Woods
Hidden Leaves

The Broken Wings Series
Broken Wings
Midnight Flight

The Gemini Series
Celeste
Black Cat
Child of Darkness

The Shadows Series
April Shadows
Girl in the Shadows

The Early Spring Series
Broken Flower
Scattered Leaves

The Secrets Series
Secrets in the Attic
Secrets in the Shadows

The Delia Series
Delia's Crossing
Delia's Heart
Delia's Gift

The Heavenstone Series
The Heavenstone
    Secrets
Secret Whispers

The March Family
Family Storms
Cloudburst

The Kindred Series
Daughter of Darkness
Daughter of Light

The Forbidden Series
The Forbidden Sister
"The Forbidden Heart"
Roxy's Story

The Mirror Sisters
The Mirror Sisters
Broken Glass
Shattered Memories

The Girls of Spindrift
Bittersweet Dreams
"Corliss"
"Donna"

Stand-alone Novels
Gods of Green
    Mountain
Into the Darkness
Capturing Angels
The Unwelcomed
    Child
Sage's Eyes

V.C. ANDREWS®

Delia's
CROSSING

POCKET BOOKS

New York London Toronto Sydney New Delhi

Pocket Books
An Imprint of Simon & Schuster, Inc.
1230 Avenue of the Americas
New York, NY 10020

Following the death of Virginia Andrews, the Andrews family worked with a carefully selected writer to organize and complete Virginia Andrews's stories and to create additional novels, of which this is one, inspired by her storytelling genius.

This book is a work of fiction. Any references to historical events, real people, or real places are used fictitiously. Other names, characters, places, and events are products of the author's imagination, and any resemblance to actual events or places or persons, living or dead, is entirely coincidental.

This Pocket Books paperback edition June 2017

V.C. ANDREWS® and VIRGINIA ANDREWS® are registered trademarks of Vanda Productions, LLC

POCKET and colophon are registered trademarks of Simon & Schuster, Inc.

For information about special discounts for bulk purchases, please contact Simon & Schuster Special Sales at 1-866-506-1949 or business@simonandschuster.com.

Manufactured in the United States of America

10 9 8 7 6 5 4 3 2 1

ISBN 978-1-5011-6222-0
ISBN 978-1-4165-9407-9 (ebook)

Prologue

It was my grandmother Anabela who came to get me at school. Through my classroom window, I watched her charging up the broken cobblestone street, occasionally coming down awkwardly on a crumbled section, nearly twisting her ankle and struggling to keep her balance, her roller-pin arms out as if there were an invisible person on each side of her to keep her steady. She was, after all, close to ninety.

Age had not diminished *mi abuela* Anabela as it had so many other elderly people in our Mexican village. Time had shrunken most of the grandmothers and grandfathers of my classmates. They were now not much heavier or larger than their grandchildren. Some were not much taller. I sometimes thought of them as children who had aged quickly far beyond their years. Many younger than my grandmother and far less fortunate with their health had to be wheeled about and fed like infants. They sat with empty faces on their tile patios, staring out blankly as if they were stunned with the realization that they had suddenly grown old. It was as if they had gone to sleep at eighteen, and when they awoke, they were eighty. It put them into a daze.

But not Grandmother Anabela. Her stubborn body refused to weaken or acknowledge time. She had thick ankles and calves, wide hips, and a rear end that ballooned out and kept the hem of her skirt an inch or so higher in the back than it was in the front. Despite her age, she still had strong shoulders and arms, first from a lifetime in the soybean fields and then, after she was married, from vigorous housework in her own home and in the homes of rich people. No one got down on her knees and scrubbed tiles as clean as my grandmother scrubbed them. My father always said she could easily sterilize a hospital operating room all by herself. From the way *mi abuela* Anabela described it, hard work had been her steadfast companion from the day she could wash a dish or sweep a floor.

"Childhood is a luxury only the rich can enjoy," she told me. "When I was barely eight years old, I was working alongside my mother in the fields and was expected to do adult work and not complain or cry."

Maybe that was why most of the people in our poor village looked older than they were. They had little time to be children. Tiny shoulders bore heavy weight. Ten-year-old boys had calluses on their palms and fingers as hard and as big as those on their fathers' and grandfathers' palms and fingers. Laughter and giggles were lost and forgotten like memories too deep to be found even in sleep.

Grandmother Anabela would look at her old friends, shake her head, and say, "*Lo que pronto madura poco dura,*" which meant "What ripens fast doesn't last."

"I have seen too many pass on before their time, Delia, like oranges dried out in the hot sun."

Watching her now through the classroom window, *mi abuela*'s round face with her puffy cheeks reminded me of the face of a doll on a spring in the rear window of a car. It bobbed and shook as she took her choppy steps. However, nothing seemed capable of discouraging her from moving forward. She never left our *casa* with her silky gray hair loose and untied, and she never stepped out into the village streets still wearing her apron. Something very serious was propelling her along and making her move like a woman half her age.

Grandmother Anabela's wrinkled skin was leathery, and she had some age spots sprinkled on her cheeks and forehead and down the right side of her neck, but the only place I found she really looked her years was in her eyes. No matter what time of day, those dark pupils were tired, and those eyelids hovered so close to shutting that it was sometimes hard to believe she could see. I used to think the world surely looked so narrow and small to *mi abuela* Anabela that it must be like peeking at it through a keyhole.

I was about to learn why the world looked horrendous to her today, as it soon would to me as well, even though just yesterday my family had celebrated my *quinceañera,* my fifteenth birthday. We had begun the celebration with a *misa de acción de gracias,* or thanksgiving mass. My mother had tailored one of her most beautiful dresses for me, and my grandmother had created a matching headdress for me to wear at the mass. With my parents beside me, I had sat at the foot of the altar through the entire service, and at the end, I had placed my bouquet on the altar. Following that, we had a fiesta at our *casa*.

Abuela Anabela had cooked all the day before and early in the morning had created an orange-almond cake so moist it melted in your mouth. We had a wonderful party. My mother sang for us. Everyone, especially my friends, wanted her to sing. Abuela Anabela always said, "Even the birds are jealous of your mother's voice. *Ella canta como un ángel.*"

"No," my father said, looking lovingly at my mother. "She doesn't sing like an angel. She sings better than an angel."

My mother was always embarrassed by compliments. She was modest, even though I felt she was the most beautiful woman in our village. I know my father believed that.

"*El sapo a la sapa la tiene por muy guapa,*" she would say whenever he heaped compliments upon her. "The toad believes his woman toad is beautiful."

"Never mind toads. I know what I know," my father insisted. "And don't call me a toad."

"What should I call you, then?"

"I'm sure," he said, smiling, "you can come up with a better name."

How my mother laughed. Watching the two of them fence with their eyes and their lips, hold on to each other when they walked and blew kisses across a room or a street whenever they were to be apart even for only a short time, made me feel witness to something very special.

After my fiesta, my mother took me aside. For us, the *quinceañera* was a cross between a Sweet Sixteen and a debutante's coming-out party. I knew for most it signified reaching maturity and being of a marriageable age. However, my mother had other ideas for my future.

"You know, Delia, you are now no longer a child. You are a woman, but I do not see you getting married quickly and having children. You are a very good student. I want more for you. I want you to have more than I have. Do you understand why this is so important to me?"

"Yes, Mama."

"I know you do," she said. "You woke up a child, and now you go to sleep a woman, but you are a woman with a bigger future. I am sure of it." She said it with such certainty that I believed her, and for some reason, it frightened me. I was afraid I wouldn't live up to her expectations. The greater the love, the bigger the expectations, I thought.

I went to sleep every night thinking I was very lucky to have such a family, especially the night of my wonderful birthday. I went to sleep under a blanket woven of kisses, hugs, and good wishes. I was content. I felt safe in my wonderful fortress of love.

Now I wondered, can you really be punished for being too happy? Señora Porres, one of *mi abuela*'s friends, believed in the *ojo malvado,* the evil eye, some dark power that watched for people who were too happy or bragged too much about their good luck. She actually searched the streets, windows, and alleyways looking for signs of the *ojo malvado.* Her face, with her wide and deep black eyes always looking shocked and surprised, haunted me in dreams about the evil eye. In them, she was hurrying down the street and periodically pausing to look behind herself as if she were positive she was being pursued by the *ojo malvado.* She had me on the lookout for it sometimes, especially when I was very happy. I'd stop and freeze a smile, hold my breath, or abort a laugh.

I was thinking about all that this day as *mi abuela* Anabela stepped into the schoolyard. Something had to be terribly wrong. She had never come to the school. I saw her pause, hold her hand over her breast, look up at the sky, mutter a short prayer, take a deep breath, and head for the entrance. A thin, high-pitched ringing began in my ears. It sent an electric alarm down to my toes and through my hands to the edges of my fingers.

Señora Cuevas turned abruptly when *mi abuela* opened the classroom door without knocking. Our teacher hated any interruptions. We had no doubt she would ignore an earthquake if she were in the middle of giving instructions or asking questions. Her long, thin face seemed to stretch around the corners of her mouth as her thin orange lips leaked into her cheeks. Her eyes, the color of *cajeta,* a caramelized brown candy, brightened with hot fury like the tips of candle flames and were usually enough to bring the class to attention with, everyone becoming as quiet as a sleeping *burro.* Even the flies stopped buzzing.

The sight of my grandmother standing as firm as a statue in the doorway took Señora Cuevas by surprise, however, and her anger quickly subsided. Her shoulders, which had been hunched up like a hawk's in preparation for her pecking snappy, angry words at the intruder, sank.

"*Buenas días,* Señora Yebarra, how can I help you?" she asked.

My grandmother simply shook her head and searched the room until her eyes found me.

Then she started to cry.

Even without knowing why she was crying, I began to cry myself. All of my classmates were staring at me, their faces now filling more with fear than curiosity. Abuela Anabela held out her arms toward me, beckoning with her long yet still full fingers.

"She must come home right away," my grandmother said. "*Venga*, Delia."

I looked at Señora Cuevas, who was now overwhelmed with curiosity and concern. She nodded at me, and I rose slowly, afraid that the fear seizing my body would turn my legs to jelly. I scooped up my books and only then ran to my grandmother's arms. She clamped them around me as quickly as a tarantula seized its prey and held me in the doorway, pressing my body to hers as if she thought I might run away. My heart was pounding. I didn't know what to do or say. Had she gone mad? I had heard that older people could wake up one day and be so unhinged that they didn't know who they were or where they were anymore.

"What is wrong, Señora Yebarra?" Señora Cuevas asked. "Why must you take Delia from her classroom before school is finished for the day?"

"There has been a terrible truck accident this morning, Señora Cuevas." She paused to draw in a deep breath and then said, "Only a short time ago, *el policía* came to *mi hijo*'s *casa* to tell me Delia's *madre y padre están muertos.*"

It was as if the whole class, Señora Cuevas included, had one mouth and together uttered the same gasp. My grandmother turned me with her, her right arm clasped tightly around my shoulders. In tragedy and grief, we indeed had become attached. She led me away. I glanced back once and saw Señora Cuevas make the sign of the cross and then close the classroom door slowly, as someone would close the lid of a coffin, her head and shoulders weighed down with sadness.

I did not know it yet, but I would never enter that classroom again.

This walk I began with my grandmother was the start of a long journey that would take me from my home and my friends in ways I could never have imagined.

I was kidnaped by cruel fate and condemned to be a prisoner of destiny beyond my control. Even the simplest choices would be denied me. I would lose everything, *todo que poseí,* including most of my meager wardrobe and one pair of my two pairs of shoes. Essentially, when I left here, all I would have would be my name, Delia Yebarra, and even keeping that would become a challenge.

It was truly as if I had been in the pickup truck with my parents and had died as well.

1

A Message

As we walked away from the school, I clung to *mi abuela* Anabela's hand like someone afraid she might drown if she let go. It did feel as if we had been tossed into a sea of sorrow. She had stopped crying, but she was chanting, "Oh, *Dios mío,* oh, *Dios mío,*" with every step she took.

When we reached the town square, she paused as if she had heard God's voice. Our church loomed at the center, its tall, slender bell tower never looking more important to me. I had to confess that as a little girl, and still today, I believed that all of the prayers uttered and all of the songs sung inside the church traveled up through the ceiling and through the tower directly into the ear of God.

Perhaps Abuela Anabela wanted to go inside and pray that what had happened did not happen, I thought. She lingered and gazed reverently and hopefully at the church, gazed past the curious eyes of those who had not yet heard the terrible news, the elderly sitting on benches in the shade of our immaculately pruned ash trees supposedly as old as the village, reading newspapers, drinking coffee, and talking softly. No one seemed to raise his or her voice in the presence of the church, but later in the early evening, there would be music and laughter and dancing. Street vendors would come out to sell their tacos, grilled meats, and steamed *tamales*.

I couldn't help looking covetously at Señora Morales, who was eating a chocolate-dipped *churro*. She pushed it into her mouth like someone pushing a carrot into a grinder and then licked her fingertips. In the middle of all of this misery and shock, I was hungering for a fried strip of chocolate-covered dough. The irony didn't escape me, nor did my sense of guilt. I shifted my gaze quickly to the church, as if I expected to see Father Martinez in the doorway shaking his head and waving his right forefinger at me, making me ashamed.

Our meditative moment was crushed by the loud-speakers on the truck passing by, announcing a sale of washing machines. It stirred little interest. I gazed at my grandmother. She crossed herself again and muttered a quick prayer before putting her head down and continuing our journey through the village.

We hurriedly passed the small *menudo* shop where I saw two of my grandmother's friends, Señora Paz and her sister, just sitting down to have a bowl of warm, mushy tripe soup. When they saw us, they both crossed themselves. They had obviously heard the horrible news. I looked back, my grandmother tugging me along, but neither one of the Paz sisters smiled at me. They saw us in a dark shadow, and it frightened them.

I was still too much in shock to cry or speak. It all seemed more like a dream, like being dragged through someone else's nightmare. I felt suspended, hanging like a puppet on dead string.

My parents were dead, gone? I had just seen them that morning. My mother had kissed me good-bye and had reminded me to come right home to help my grandmother with dinner. She was always worried that I would loiter at the square with the other girls my age, some of whom had already gotten themselves into trouble with older boys.

How could she be dead and gone, and my father, too? This couldn't be so. In a moment, I would snap awake and be back in my classroom. Señora Cuevas would bawl me out for not paying attention. I closed my eyes and opened them quickly, but that didn't happen.

We turned down the dusty dirt street on which was our adobe house with its sheet-metal roof. Our *casa* was considered one of the better ones in the village, because it was large enough for us to have three rooms. The kitchen, as in most *casas* here, was simply a lean-to built of poles and corn stalks against the outside wall; however, we were able to have a separate bedroom for Grandmother Anabela and me and one for my parents. We were one of the few families that had a television set, but its picture was so powdery we often couldn't make out what was happening, and very often we would lose our electricity. Once, we didn't have any for nearly two weeks.

There was no lawn or even any grass in front of our *casa,* just some shrubs, stubble of grass, stones, and the remnants of a faded pink and white fountain that no longer had water running through it unless it rained hard, but we didn't sell it or remove it, because it had an angel at the top, and *mi abuela* Anabela believed that if you had a replica of an angel in or around your house, real angels would stop to bless you.

Despite what my grandmother had told Señora Cuevas, I half expected to see my father's pickup truck in front. He and my mother worked for Señor Lopez on his soybean farm not quite ten miles from the heart of the village. He had lost his wife five years ago to a blood disease. His daughters had married and moved away, and he had no sons. My mother cleaned his home every morning and prepared all of his meals, and my father oversaw his laborers.

For the moment, my grandmother's solution to our great tragedy was to prepare food for the expected visitors and comforters. I was brought home from school quickly so I could help. There was almost no time for tears. She went about her work diligently, grateful for everything she had to do: chop the chicken and the cheese to include in her wonderful tortillas, and prepare her salsa and beans. We had little dishware to speak of, but we had a carton of paper plates and plastic knives and forks my mother had been given by Señor Lopez. She told me to get it all out, and then I was given the job of preparing the salsa and beans.

Early that morning, *mi abuela* Anabela had made some of her bread, her *pan hecho del rancho,* a recipe she said had been passed down through generations. She always knelt down barefoot to knead the dough, because that was the way her mother made it, and her mother's mother. To Abuela Anabela, traditions were as holy as scripture.

Many times I had worked alongside her like this, but never with this sort of frenzy. Tears streaked down her face. However, she didn't make the sound of a single sob. I was trembling inside, still too much in shock to realize what was happening, but I did feel as if, at any moment, I might shatter like some clay pot and fall in pieces to the floor.

Just as my grandmother had expected, the villagers began to appear when the terrible news spread, most bringing food and drink. The wailing and shaking of heads began soon afterward. I could never remember how many times I was held and kissed and told to be strong. I was spun around to be embraced and comforted until I was so dizzy I nearly fell.

It wasn't long before the crowd of mourners became thicker, finally spilling out to the front of the *casa*. People stopped noticing me. They were heavily into remembering their own sad tales, weaving a net of tragedy to cast over the entire gathering and hold everyone in sorrow's grip. Old wounds were opened. We were having our own private Day of the Dead.

When Father Martinez arrived, the crowd quieted down and then parted like the Red Sea for him. He comforted *mi abuela* Anabela, and then he came to me, took my hands into his, and looked at me with such sad eyes I finally started to cry very hard. He said some prayers over me and then headed for the food.

I caught my breath and retreated outside to sit on a rock in a shady area, where I often sat to wait for my parents' return from work when I was younger. Despite the people, the prayers, the tears, and the grief, I still had trouble digesting the news of their deaths. The few details I had overheard inside the *casa* regurgitated. An *hombre borracho* driving a dump truck hit them head-on while they were on their way to work. It was hours and hours before any medical help arrived, and by then it was too late. As was often the case with drunks who cause the deaths of other people on the roads, he was barely scratched. Anyway, nothing done to him would bring back my parents.

The villagers streamed by, shaking their heads at me with faces filled with so much pity that it finally occurred to me that I should be wondering what would happen to me and my grandmother now. My own welfare had never seemed as important or as much in jeopardy. My uncles, aunts, and cousins in Mexico were spread far and wide, and none but my aunt Isabela in the United States had as much as or more than we had. Most were far worse off. Uncles worked in the United States and rarely saw their own families these days. Who needed another mouth to feed, another young girl to worry about?

Despite her ability to work in our kitchen, *mi abuela* Anabela couldn't earn enough working for a restaurant or any wealthy person now. No one would hire someone her age. The most she could hope for would be taking in someone else's wash or selling some of her wonderful chocolate *mole* whenever she had a chance to make some. It would provide only a piddling income.

Maybe I would have to stop attending school to go out to Señor Lopez and take my mother's place. Because of my grandmother having me work beside her in the kitchen and because of what she had taught me, I could prepare many meals myself, and I could certainly clean and keep up his house. Many girls my age were already working full time, and some of them were already married, but my parents were determined that I remain in school, something my mother had reinforced just last night after the *quinceañera*. I had always done well in my studies, and my mother especially had hope that I would be something more. I had no idea what, but as she often said, "*La esperanza se encienda mañana.*" Hope lights tomorrow.

Suddenly, I saw Señor Orozco, our postmaster, come running down our street, his skinny legs kicking up a trail of dust that lingered in his wake like a low-lying clay fog. His nearly shoulder-length white hair flew about him as if the strands wanted to break free of his scalp. He was in a frenzy, looking as if he might explode with excitement. When he saw me, he came to a dead stop and pulled back his shoulders, brushed back his hair, and hurried into the house.

I rose to follow and see what had brought him with such urgency. Was there some miracle? Did they find out that my parents were alive? Had the tragic news simply been a terrible misunderstanding? I hoped we would hear that it wasn't my parents in the accident after all but some other people in a similar pickup truck. Was it sinful to wish it on someone else? And would I be punished for it?

"Señora Yebarra," he called to my grandmother. She pulled herself away from her comforters and stepped forward to meet him.

"Your daughter-in-law's sister, she has called back and been given the terrible news," he declared. His body stiffened with his sense of importance as he pulled in his stomach and pushed out his chest to deliver the message.

The remaining mourners grew still. All eyes were on him. The tragedy had reached into California, and in no time, there had been a response. Despite this being the age of computers and satellites, some still saw such communication as an amazing and miraculous feat. It was as if we lived in a place on the earth that revolved at a slower place, crawling through history, decades behind the rest of the world.

"And?" my grandmother asked Señor Orozco. Death and mourning had made privacy quite unnecessary. Everyone was listening keenly. I held my breath.

"She said she is unable to attend the funeral," he said. "She will send some money for the funeral costs and money for the church."

Heads shook in disgust and disbelief. My aunt was unable to attend the funeral of her one and only sister? Many looked at my grandmother with pity. Everything was falling on her tired, old shoulders. She did not wince, however. She sucked in her breath and lifted her shoulders like someone recuperating from another blow.

"And?" Grandmother Anabela asked again. What more could there be?

He turned, his eyes searching the crowd until his gaze fell on me. Everyone else looked my way as well.

"She said you are to pack whatever *su nieta* has, everything that is . . ." He paused and added, "That isn't full of lice, and prepare her for the trip. She has decided to take her into her home."

Someone clicked her lips, but no one spoke. Everyone's eyes remained on me for a moment before turning to my grandmother to see her response.

Grandmother Anabela looked up and whispered something to God. It looked to me as if she was giving thanks. She was always having private conversations with the Almighty. Until now, I believed that her special conversations with him had protected us. What had we done for him to turn a deaf ear even to *mi abuela* Anabela, who was to me truly what a saint should be?

Slowly, she lowered her head, and then her eyes locked on me.

She didn't have to say anything. I could read it in her face.

Delia, I cannot take care of you. I am on death's doorway myself. Your uncles and aunt in Mexico have their own overwhelming burdens. This is the best solution and your best hope.

In less than a day, you lost us all, your parents and me. You will pack a small bag, but in your heart, you will carry the heavy burden of great sadness and loneliness. You might carry it for the rest of your life.

I shook my head. It was raining sorrow too hard and too quickly. Yes, I was drowning in this sea of sadness. Maybe it was my fault. Maybe I had done something. Maybe I had opened the evil eye to look our way.

My terrified eyes fell on Señora Morales, and suddenly, all I could think of was that chocolate-dipped *churro* that she had slipped past her lips.

I turned and ran from that image as much as from anything else that haunted me this terrible day.

2

Good-bye

Any memories I had of my aunt Isabela were as vague and indistinct as the faded old sepia pictures in our chest of family photographs, the images evaporating with time. *Mi tía* Isabela drifted in and out of my thoughts so rarely, I often forgot my mother had an older sister. We had a few snapshots that were still quite good, but they were taken of her and my mother when they were little more than children. There were no photographs of her children or her husband, who I knew had died. He was much older than Tía Isabela, actually close to twenty years older. I had seen her only once, now more than ten years ago, when my maternal grandmother passed away. She hadn't come for her father's funeral, but she had come for her mother's. When she had defied my grandfather and married her much older American husband, he had disowned her.

To me, the story was almost a fairy tale or our own

family soap opera. I couldn't help but be curious about every detail, but I always would hesitate to ask too many questions, because I could see it saddened my mother to talk about her sister and what had happened. Nevertheless, the whole story had trickled out over time until I now understood this much.

Tía Isabela had matured into a beautiful young woman early in her life, and by the time she was twelve, she was attracting the interest of men twice her age and older, because she looked twice her age. No one, not my father or my mother, would come right out and say it, but from what I heard in their voices and saw in their faces, I could see they believed Aunt Isabela was quite a flirtatious *muchacha*.

"She had a way of looking a man up and down that stirred his blood," *mi madre* told me once, when she was more relaxed about discussing her sister. "I'm not even sure she was fully aware of what she was doing, but I'm sure to most men, it looked like she was sending some kind of invitation."

My mother paused and looked at me. I was only ten myself when she was telling me this.

"*Entiendes,* Delia?"

I nodded, even though I wasn't sure I fully understood. What sort of invitation was it? To a party? To a dinner? How could you send an invitation with your eyes?

"Men," she told me, leaning down to speak more softly and more privately so neither *mi abuela* nor *mi padre* could hear her, "are too quick to read what they want to read, see what they want to see. *Recuerda eso,* Delia."

She didn't have to say it. I wouldn't forget anything she told me in such confidence with her eyes so big and dark. She so rarely talked about the relations between men and women that whenever she did, I was mesmerized.

According to what my mother had described, no matter what Tía Isabela did, it displeased my grandfather. She was rebellious, disobeying him almost from the moment she awoke every morning. He didn't like the way she dressed for school or her putting on lipstick before she was eleven. He did all he could to stop her from doing these things, even when he caught her in the village and wiped her lips with the sleeve of his shirt. The second he was gone, her lips were red again.

"The more your grandfather punished Isabela, the more defiant she became. She was a wild thing, *una cosa salvaje,* no tamer than a coyote."

"A coyote in heat," my father added, overhearing our discussion as he passed by.

My mother glared at him, and he turned away quickly. For a reason I would come to understand, talking about Tía Isabela was not something they would do in each other's presence.

My mother was very upset about all of it and somehow blamed herself for what happened between *mi tía* Isabela and their father later on. It was a family mystery, why she would blame herself, a skeleton in one of our closets, but I sensed now that it wouldn't be much longer before I opened that closet, saw those dangling old white bones, and found out why. Was I better off never knowing?

"*Tu abuelo* thought *tu tía* was headed for lots of trouble," my mother said. "They were always at each other. I did what I could to help her, make excuses for her, protect her, but nothing I would do or *tu abuela* would do mattered. If your grandfather confined her to the house, she snuck out. If he dragged her home kicking and screaming, she would turn and run off. He was at wits' end and finally gave up trying. At one point, both he and my mother were considering sending her to a nunnery, but they decided not to put such a burden on the sisters.

"She quit school at your age and went to work at a hotel on the beach, first as a housekeeper, and then she was trained to be a waitress in the restaurant. Two years later, she met Señor Dallas. We did not know she was seeing him romantically. He returned to the hotel many times for vacations. We didn't know he returned solely because of her, but then, one day, she announced he had proposed to her and she wanted to marry him. We knew nothing about him, of course," my mother told me.

"At first, *tu abuelo* and *abuela* were cautiously happy about it," she told me, and smiled. "After all, someone else was going to take responsibility for their *cosa salvaje,* but when they met him and found out more about him, they were very disapproving. He was nearly twenty years older than she was, not a Catholic, and an American who barely spoke Spanish.

"Even though she did not do well in school, she was not stupid, my sister Isabela. When she put her mind to something, she did it or learned it, and learning English was very important to her. The faster she learned it, the more responsibility she was given at the hotel, responsibility and opportunity. It made her feel superior. In fact, whenever she came home from the hotel, she would avoid speaking Spanish and pretend she didn't understand anyone who did, which infuriated my father even more. She put on airs and made it seem as if she was better than the rest of us.

"They forbade the marriage. I should have suspected something when she didn't argue. She left one night, and we heard nothing from her until we received an announcement of their wedding in Palm Springs, California. My father burned it and went through the house tossing out anything that reminded him of her, all the clothes she had left behind and especially pictures.

" '*Ella está muerta a mí.* I wipe her from my memory!' he cried. My mother was very upset. For days afterward, it was truly like someone in the family really had died. We didn't speak at our meals. My father went to work in silence, and my mother sobbed in the corner whenever anything reminded her of Isabela. He would get so angry if she cried in front of him.

"We heard very little about or from her for some time, and if anyone did bring any news here, my father would refuse to listen to it. The mere mention of her name burned his ears.

" 'I have only one daughter now,' he would say.

"I went to the pay phone at the post office and called her when our father died. She told me he had died years ago and hung up. When our mother died, as you know, she came to the funeral, but I wished she hadn't," she added. "You were too young to remember it all. She arrived in this limousine as long as the street, just in time for the church service. Bedecked in jewels, with her hair full of diamonds and her face caked with makeup, she was dressed as if she were going to a ball and not a funeral. Her husband wasn't with her. He was already quite ill. And neither were her children. She brought a personal secretary instead, a personal assistant, a fragile young woman following at her heels, holding an umbrella over her as if she had become supersensitive to sunshine. The poor girl was terrified of missing a step or a word of her commands.

"Your aunt behaved as if she were a foreigner, too. Her English was surprisingly perfected by now. She was a true *norteamericana*. Again she acted as if she didn't understand a word of Spanish and forced Father Martinez to speak in his broken English. All she talked about was her wonderful home, the places she had traveled, her army of servants, her cars and jewels and clothing. She bore no resemblance to the young girl who had grown up here.

"She left a sizable donation at the church and was gone practically the moment the coffin was lowered into the ground. She spent no time with us and told me the first thing she would do when she returned to Palm Springs was take a bath.

" 'I'll have to soak for hours to get this dirt and filth out of my skin,' she said.

"We haven't heard a word directly from her since, but she makes sure we know about her wealth. You have two cousins: Edward, who is two years older than you, and Sophia, who is a month younger than you. She had sent us announcements of their births but no pictures, and she had no pictures to show your father and me when she came to the funeral. She didn't care to talk about her family with us. She was truly like a stranger. If our mother hadn't died before, she would have died then."

I recalled these conversations with my mother and thought how strange that this sister she had described with such pain was the woman who apparently wanted to claim me, to provide for me and be my legal guardian. If she had no interest in her family all these years, why would she care now? She wasn't embarrassed about not attending her own father's funeral, and she wasn't embarrassed about the way she had behaved at her mother's funeral, and now she was not embarrassed about not attending her sister and brother-in-law's, either. Why would ignoring me even after all these family tragedies embarrass or bother her at all? If her own parents and my mother weren't that important to her, why would I be?

Was she trying to make amends, repent, and using me as the way to do it?

Did she regret the way she had behaved, and was she so sorry about it that she wanted to lavish her wealth and kindness on me as part of her redemption?

Should I be more grateful and happy about the possibilities than sad and afraid?

What awaited me?

And what about my cousins? I hated to think of anything good coming out of my parents' deaths. No matter what that good was or how much better off I might be, I would never be happy knowing why I had it all, but wasn't it good to get to know them and for them to know me?

Right now, I couldn't think about it. For our small village, the prospect of a double funeral draped the streets and houses in a dark, dreary shadow, even though the March sun was shining brightly. The very sight of the two coffins side by side in the church was devastating. It was difficult for many, not only me, to believe this was actually happening, that my young and beautiful parents were gone in seconds, their lives snuffed out like two candles. People were either hypnotized by the sight or avoided looking and kept their heads bowed. Even the babies on their mothers' hips looked subdued and mesmerized by the deeply mournful atmosphere.

Mi abuela clung to me almost as tightly as I clung

to her. She had seen much sorrow in her life. Besides her own parents, she had lost a younger brother in a farm accident with an overturned tractor. He was barely fifteen. She told me her father never stood or walked straight after that.

"He looked like a broken corn stalk, his shoulders turned inward under the weight of his great grief."

Everything stopped in our village for my parents' funeral. A parade of mourners followed the coffins through the village in a procession that seemed it would take the rest of my life. The sky should be gray, I thought. The world shouldn't look so bright, but the heavens had already shed all the tears the night before in a downpour that created streams carving grooves everywhere in the old roads. It was truly as Señora Morales told my grandmother as they went around the puddles. *La muerte tuvo que ser quitada.* Death had to be washed away.

And then there was Señora Porres nodding at me, confirming in her mind that the *ojo malvado* had indeed visited our small village and chosen my parents. Her eyes were full of "I told you so." She gave me the chills. Perhaps the *ojo malvado* wasn't yet satisfied.

There were even more people at the cemetery than there had been at the church. Some had just gotten off work. Señor Lopez had brought many from his soybean farm to attend, the men fumbling nervously with their hats in their hands, all of the women dressed in black, surrounding us in an inky pool of grief. Everyone looked devastated, not least of all Señor Lopez.

"They were truly like my own children," he said. *"Mi hijo y mi hija."*

He gave my grandmother some money and shook his head as if his tongue had died in his mouth. There were no more words, no Band-Aids, no soothing balms, no remedies to help cure this sorrow. Only time would make it possible to continue.

According to what I had been taught, there were three types of death, and now we had gone through two. The first death occurred when your body stopped functioning and your soul departed. The second occurred when you were interred in the earth. And the third death occurred if and when you were no longer remembered by anyone. I was determined not to permit my parents to suffer this final death.

"My heart must look like a spider's web with all the scars that have been carved in it," my grandmother told her friends. She battled to keep the final death away from so many departed loved ones.

I sobbed softly, but for the most part, I think I was still too much in shock to cry my heart out. All I wanted was for it to end. The silence that followed us afterward was as deep and as hollow as the tunnel to hell. That's what *mi abuela* told me.

My departure for America was to be immediate. It was almost as if my grandmother were afraid my aunt might have second thoughts and decide not to take me.

I pleaded softly for her to reconsider. All of her siblings were gone now, her other sons working in America. I was the closest family she had left to be beside her, and she was my closest, too, I realized.

"You would have no chance here, Delia. You would grow old quickly, as I did, maybe even more quickly. Your parents wouldn't want this. Think of all the men and women who would love to have your opportunity. You will eventually become a citizen of the United States! You will get a better education and everything you need to stay healthy and strong, and you know how much your mother wanted you to have an education. Maybe you will go to a college, too."

"But Isabela was not good to us, Abuela."

"What she was she was. What she is she is now," she replied, and waved her right forefinger. "Remember, Delia, *hasta el diablo fué un ángel en sus comienzos.* Even the devil was an angel when he began. It's not too late to change."

I thought she recited it all more to convince herself than to convince me, or perhaps to make herself feel better about her inability to keep me with her. I couldn't continue to contradict her, for fear I would make her feel even more terrible than she already felt. There was nothing to do but nod and smile and accept.

"You will return to visit soon," she continued. "You will come back in fancy clothes and in a fancy car. Everyone will be envious of you."

I turned away so she wouldn't see my face, the great pain and the terrible doubt. I looked down at the small suitcase we had packed for my trip. The fastener no longer worked. It had to be tied with one of my father's old belts.

Señor Orozco had delivered my aunt's warning about bringing along lice, and that had frightened us into limiting what I was to take. I packed only my newest garments, and my grandmother had washed them even though they did not need to be washed. What I had wouldn't have filled more than two suitcases anyway.

"I'm sure she means to buy you many new things," my grandmother told me. "She didn't intend to be nasty about lice. It's simply that she wouldn't let you wear old clothes in her beautiful new *hacienda.* You are her niece.

She won't want you to look any worse than her own children. Isabela was always concerned about the way she looked. Appearances are very important to her."

I glanced at *mi abuela*. She was struggling so to make my future look rosy. I knew she didn't believe these things. She, like most everyone else, was not approving of Isabela's worship of wealth.

"I don't care about beautiful clothes," I said.

"Oh, sure you do. You will. Why shouldn't you? You are a beautiful young woman, the most beautiful in our family on both sides. Would you put a dirty, old, ugly frame around a beautiful painting? No."

She made me smile.

"I'm not a beautiful painting, Abuela Anabela."

"*Sí,* you are, God's beautiful painting," she said, stroking my face and smiling. "Don't fill your heart with too much pride, but don't regret yourself," she advised, and kissed me on the forehead.

And then she shook her head and muttered to herself. "I lived too long to have lived to see this."

Finally, she went off to be alone, shed her tears, and talk to God.

I sat waiting and wondering why all of this had happened. What had we done to bring such tragedy down upon us? Father Martinez's explanations in church seemed hollow and inadequate to me. God had brought them to his bosom? Why would God want to take my parents from me? Why would he be so selfish? I would have to go elsewhere to understand, I thought, and I might spend my whole life getting there.

The car sent for me arrived surprisingly early in the morning the next day. I didn't remember my aunt's car when she came to her mother's funeral as well as some of the other people in the village remembered it, but I couldn't imagine a more luxurious-looking or bigger automobile. She had hired the driver and the car out of Mexico City. Everyone who saw it approaching came out to watch the driver, who was in a uniform and cap, take my small bag and put it into the cavernous trunk, where it looked about as insignificant as it could, like one pea on a plate. It didn't occur to me until that very moment how quickly it was all happening. *Mi tía* Isabela had practically pounced on me the moment the news had arrived in Palm Springs, California. Again I wondered, was that good? Why had she decided so quickly?

There was no longer any time to think about it. *Mi abuela* Anabela followed me out to hug me and say a prayer over me. She kissed me and made me promise to say my prayers every night, for myself, yes, but for my poor departed parents' souls as well.

"And for you," I added.

"*Sí, y para mí,*" she said, smiling. "You will do well, Delia. You have a heart big enough for many who need love. I am sorry I can give you nothing more than my prayers."

"It's enough," I said, holding back my tears.

I looked at our house, our stubble of grass in front, and the old fountain. I was sure it wasn't much of anything compared with where I was going, but it was all I knew as home. In this poor house, we had laughed and cried, eaten our meals, and slept through our dreams. We had celebrated our birthdays and holidays and talked into the night, with me mostly listening and my parents and grandmother remembering. It was through them that I had grown to know my extended family and my personal heritage, and now that was all being left behind.

I might as well be shot into outer space, I thought when I turned to get into the limousine. Where I was going was just as far away as a distant planet, not in miles so much as in customs, language, and lifestyle. Without my ties to my family here, I would be like someone floating through space, untethered to anything, alone, hoping to land on a warm star.

Grandmother Anabela kissed me and held me tightly for a moment, before she sighed deeply and let me go.

"No more good-byes," she said, and urged me to get into the limousine.

I paused to look at our neighbors and friends. I could see the pity for me in their faces, even though I was getting into this expensive automobile and heading for the United States, a world of endless promise and wealth, from which so many *norteños* sent back remittances that were enough to make eyes bulge and put smiles on hungry faces of despair. The committees of *los norteños* sent back funds that helped restore our church and plaza, repair roads and sewers, and make our village more livable. The United States was a well of opportunity into which I would have the privilege of dipping my hands.

And yet they didn't envy me. They saw how lost and alone I was, and despite their own poverty and limited futures, they would not trade places with me. In fact, they stepped back into their doorways or into the shadows, as if to avoid being contaminated by the tragedy that had befallen me. Some wouldn't even wave good-bye. Some wouldn't even nod. They stared, and some crossed themselves and moved closer to their loved ones.

Good-bye, Delia, I could hear them think. *Adiós pequeña muchacha. Vaya con Dios.*

I got into the limousine. The driver, who had not introduced himself and who barely looked at me with any interest, closed the door. I moved quickly to the window, already feeling like someone being locked away from all she loved and knew. *Mi abuela* Anabela smiled and pressed her right hand to her heart. She nodded and looked up to mutter a prayer.

I put my fingers against the window, as if I could somehow still touch her.

"Don't smudge up the windows," the driver muttered sharply. I pulled my hand away instantly.

The limousine started away, its tires unhappy about the potholes deepened by last evening's downpour. The broken street bounced and tossed the automobile as if it were a toy. The driver cursed under his breath and then accelerated, spitting up some dirt behind us, enough to create a cloud of dust, dust through which *mi abuela* Anabela grew smaller and smaller, until she was gone, and I was carried off and away, my tears as hot as tea streaming down my cheeks.

We drove on, the scenery turning into liquid and floating by as the road got better and the driver could accelerate even more. He didn't speak or ask me any questions to pass the time. He listened to his radio as if he were all by himself. It was the way I felt. Why not him?

In a little more than one hour, I was traveling through places I had never been. Looking back, I saw nothing familiar. It was truly as if God had snapped his fingers, and *poof,* like magic, my life and my world were gone.

3

Nothing Familiar

At no point during my journey was my aunt there to greet me. Whatever her reasons for not coming to the funerals, I nevertheless kept anticipating her, envisioning her standing there with my two cousins, all of them anxious about meeting me. After all, I was as much a stranger to them as they were to me, but I hoped they were eager to help me recover from such a catastrophic blow. I imagined their eyes would be filled with pity, and they would overwhelm me with their kindness and warm welcome.

Perhaps my cousin Sophia, close to my age, would see me more as a sister than a cousin. Since we were close in age, maybe we were close to the same size. We would share so much. After all, I had been an only child and had no brothers and sisters, even though my parents had tried to have more children. I longed for such a sister, someone with whom I could trust my intimate thoughts and feelings and share the confusion and wonder that came with growing up. I would have so much to tell her about our Mexican heritage, and she would have tons to tell me about Palm Springs and the United States. Eventually, I would have to learn more English, of course. I knew some, but I was sure there were dozens of expressions that would confuse me at first. It would be necessary, but also it would be fun to learn them.

I also looked forward to hearing music and going to movies and parties like the ones I occasionally saw on television or heard about from people who had been in the States. They described working at fiestas with more food than could feed our village for a week. The people were dressed like royalty, with diamonds glittering and gold dangling from their necks and wrists. There was lots of live music. I was told that every party, no matter how small the reason, was like a Mexican wedding. There was such abundance. Dogs and cats in America ate better than people ate in most underdeveloped countries.

Thinking about entering such a world both frightened and excited me. How long would it take for me to get used to it? Would I ever get used to it? I would have so much compared to what I did have. How soon would I be able to send things to *mi abuela* Anabela? Would I indeed have a bedroom almost as big as our *casa*? And would there be a wardrobe of new clothing awaiting me in that bedroom?

I tried to shoo away all of these hopeful fantasies, feeling terribly guilty about imagining anything wonderful and good resulting from my parents' unfortunate deaths, but it was hard not to think about all of it as I traveled from the limousine to the airplane and then another limousine.

I pretended that I had been in an airplane before, in order to bolster my own courage, but anyone could see both my fear and my wonder. The flight attendant kept looking at me, smiling, and asking me if I was all right. Maybe I looked as if I would throw up. My stomach was doing flip-flops. I was given the paperwork to show at customs in Houston, Texas, but the scrutinizing eyes made me so nervous I was sure I looked as if I were smuggling in something illegal. My bag was searched. I boarded my second flight, which was in a smaller plane. No one paid much attention to me this time, and the gentleman beside me slept almost the whole trip.

When we arrived at the Palm Springs airport, I saw my name on a big card being held by a stout-looking, somewhat gray-haired man in a uniform even more impressive than the one worn by the driver who had picked me up in Mexico. This man had gold epaulets on his shoulders and wore white gloves.

"*Soy* Delia Yebarra," I said, approaching him. I looked past him, hoping to see my aunt and cousins waiting or sitting in the seats behind him.

"How many bags you got?" he asked gruffly.

I shook my head. I didn't understand. Bags? Why did he want to know about bags?

"Bags, suitcases!" he practically screamed at me, and then pretended to hold one.

"Oh. *Uno,*" I said, holding up one finger.

"Good. C'mon," he said, gesturing, and led me to the baggage carousels, where we waited for my small suitcase to come around.

He looked at me and squinted. He had big, pecan-brown eyes and a face that looked chiseled out of granite, the lines cut deeply and sharply around the corners of his mouth and at his eyes. He even had lines cut into his chin. I imagined his face suddenly shattering.

"*No sabe usted hablar inglés?*" he asked.

I shook my head.

"Jesus, you don't speak any English at all?"

"*Poco,*" I said, afraid to say I spoke or understood more. Whoever spoke to me would expect me then to understand. I thought about reciting some of the words I did know, but he grimaced and shook his head.

"Yeah, a little. Little good that will do you with Mrs. Dallas."

I perked up at the sound of my aunt's name and looked around again.

"Don't worry. She ain't here. *No aquí,*" he said. "Like she would come to an airport to greet anyone," he muttered.

He pounced on my bag when I pointed to it, practically ripping the handle off when he grasped it.

"It's amazing this piece of junk lasted," he said, tugging on my father's belt.

I knew he was making fun of my suitcase. I wanted to explain. After all, none of us ever traveled in an airplane, and whenever we did go on a trip, we put things in cartons. Before I could say a word, however, he turned quickly to march out of the airport. I had to walk very quickly to keep up with him. He led me to the parking lot, where a car that looked as if it were made of gold was parked. Later, I would learn it was a Rolls-Royce. The backseat was even more roomy than the limousine, but it also looked spanking new, not a smudge or anything on the windows or seats.

As we drove away from the airport and headed for my aunt's *hacienda,* my face was practically glued to the window. I was amazed at how well kept and new everything looked. The streets were so wide, and there were no potholes and cracks. Everyone seemed to be driving a brand-new automobile, too. The palm trees, varieties of bougainvillea, flowers, and even the grass all looked unreal. The mountains in the distance seemed more like scenery built for a movie.

When we reached a side street and I saw gardeners working, I suddenly became very homesick. They paused in their work to look at us as we passed by, and I thought they surely thought I was some rich American girl safe in her fishbowl. If they only knew who I was and where I had just come from and why, they wouldn't even bother turning in my direction.

Of course, I was prepared to see a big house with a nice lawn, but I had no idea my aunt really lived in a palace, or at least what looked to me like a palace. There was a very tall chocolate-colored entry gate with elaborate scrolling that had to be opened first for us to enter the property. It swung in slowly, as slowly as the gates of heaven. I imagined the sound of trumpets.

The driveway to the main house seemed as long as the road that had brought us from the airport. To the left of the main house were two smaller buildings, and farther in the rear I saw tennis courts and a very large swimming pool, as large as, if not larger than, most hotel pools I had seen. A small army of gardeners was cutting grass, pruning bushes, and trimming trees. Just to the right of the house was a four-car garage, but the driver, who had yet to tell me his name, stopped at the front of the main house.

"This is it," he said. "*Vámanos.* Out." He waved, and I opened the door while he went around to the trunk to get my suitcase.

I waited, looking up at the grand front door. It looked as if it were made of copper or brass, and it had the emblem of a lion embossed on its surface.

The driver charged past me to the door and pressed the buzzer. He looked back at me and shook his head. Did he pity me or disapprove of me? Why was he so annoyed? Had he been pulled away from some far more important work?

An elderly lady in a maid's uniform, not much taller than I, opened the door.

"Here she is, Mrs. Rosario," the driver told her, and nodded at me. "She don't speak much English at all," he added.

Mrs. Rosario nodded. She had soft eyes sunk in a round face with plump cheeks and a small mouth with puckered lips. Her complexion wasn't quite as dark as mine, and there were strands of gray woven through her tightly brushed black hair pinned back into a bun. A small silver cross rested just below the base of her throat.

"*Venga adentro,*" she told me, and stepped back.

The driver handed me my suitcase, and I entered the grand *hacienda.* Señora Rosario closed the door, and I stood there gaping at everything. There were statues of two half-naked African women facing each other, with large, colorful tapestries above each that nearly reached the high dome ceiling. The floor was dark marble with white spots that looked like milk dripped over it. It led down a short stairway to a living room the size of our *casa* back in Mexico, if not bigger. The ceiling was as high as a church ceiling, and there were embossed elephants, birds, and tigers. I couldn't drink it all in quickly enough.

All of the furniture must have been built for a family of mythological giants, I thought. The sofas were long and thick, and there were oversized chairs that I was sure would swallow me whole if I sat on them. There was a very long and wide center table with carvings in its wood frame and other matching marble tables beside the chairs and sofa.

Artwork of every kind was everywhere I looked, from grand paintings of what I imagined were scenes of world-famous cities to busts on pedestals, more tapestries and glass-doored armoires filled with crystal figures, as well as other kinds of collectibles. Everything appeared sparkling clean and new.

Large area rugs were set over the travertine floors. Across the room were tall glass doors that opened to a grand Spanish tiled patio. I could see a large pink fountain, more statuary, and pretty turquoise, red, and yellow outdoor furnishings. The patio led down to a walkway through gardens, more fountains, and beautiful beds of flowers. I felt certain that the president of Mexico didn't live any better or in a grander *casa* with as many servants. When people back in my village said Americans lived like kings and queens, they were surely thinking of people like *mi tía* Isabela.

"Put your suitcase against the wall," Señora Rosario told me, and nodded to my right. She spoke in fluent Spanish. "And go sit on the sofa on your left and wait. Don't touch anything. Señora Dallas will be here soon."

I did what she asked and then walked into the living room. The richness of everything and the way everything glittered and sparkled made me feel as if I should tiptoe and be extra gentle. As I had envisioned, when I sat on the sofa, I felt lost, as if I could drown in gold. Señora Rosario watched me absorbing the richness and wealth. Finally, she softened her lips. It wasn't quite a smile, but it was on its way. I wondered if she had reacted in a similar way when she first had entered this *hacienda*.

"*Como se llama?*" she asked.

"Delia," I told her.

"Señora Dallas *quisiera que usted me llama* Señora Rosario, but," she added, still in Spanish, "when we're alone, you can call me Alita, but never, never in front of Señora Dallas," she emphasized.

"It's so beautiful here," I told her.

She nodded like someone used to hearing it. "It's all very expensive. Almost everything is imported from one place or another."

"It's like a museum."

She smiled fully this time but then quickly erased it.

"Don't say that to Señora Dallas. She thinks it's a home."

She told me she was going to let *mi tía* Isabela know I had arrived and left to do so.

I sat stiffly, afraid to move or touch anything. I was so nervous that I felt faint. When would I meet my cousins? I wondered. Judging from all of this, my room must be as beautiful and as big as Abuela Anabela predicted. Just the thought of having my own room was exciting enough, but looking at all this, I couldn't help but let my imagination run away with itself.

There was a clock placed in what looked like an oval-shaped piece of black marble on the mantel of the milk-white marble fireplace, a fireplace that appeared never to have held a spark, much less a fire. It was as clean within as any other part of the room.

After more than ten minutes, I let myself relax and sit back on the sofa. It was very quiet. I didn't even hear anyone's footsteps. Where was my aunt? Why hadn't she come quickly? I took a deep breath. The traveling had been more tiring than I had thought it would be, despite the luxury in which I was transported. Tension, fear, and confusion had worn me down. I couldn't help but close my eyes. I fought back, but my eyelids were determined, and in moments, without my realizing it, I fell asleep.

I woke up to what sounded like someone screaming at me.

"How uncouth, unwashed, and impolite! Look at her!"

I opened my eyes quickly and sat up. Glancing at the clock, I saw that I had been there nearly an hour waiting. The woman I knew had to be my aunt stood before me, her hands on her hips. An older man with thick, well-trimmed gray hair and slightly bulging dark brown eyes stood beside her, smiling at me.

Of course, I had seen stately, elegant-looking women in magazines but never one in person as regal in appearance as *mi tía* Isabela. She was taller than my mother, full-figured in a form-fitted, sequin-covered dress the color of alligator. The V-neck collar dipped well down into her cleavage. Her ebony hair looked too rich and bright to be natural. Everything about her was somehow emphasized. It was as if she walked about under a magnifying glass that highlighted her eyes, her lips, her body, and her complexion. Nothing was out of place. There wasn't a crease or a blemish. She was like one of her statues come to life. I could only gape in wonder, and as I focused in on her, she appeared to grow taller.

Of course, I was desperately searching for more resemblances to my mother, but except for the curve of her chin, which was as smooth as my mother's, the color of her eyes, and a similar diminutive nose, I saw nothing to convince anyone beyond a doubt that they were sisters.

The gentleman beside her wore a gray sports jacket and slacks with what looked like tennis shoes. All of his facial features were a bit too large, starting with his protruding nose and thick lips. His chin was sharply rounded, with a slight cleft, and when he smiled, he revealed big teeth as well. Not quite my aunt's height, he was slight of build. I saw that he had long, thin fingers that looked more like feminine than masculine hands. Those hands never did any hard labor, I quickly thought. They never opened a tightly closed jar. It was how my father would have characterized them.

"Look at how she's gaping at us. Tell her to sit up straight," my aunt said. "Especially when she is in my presence."

"*Siéntese derecho, señorita joven, especialmente en la presencia de su tía,*" the gentleman told me like an obedient translator.

Why did my aunt need him to translate, and why was she speaking to me now only in English? She must know I had a very limited understanding of the language, I thought. This was no time to put on airs. Besides, she didn't have to do anything more to impress me.

I sat up as straight as I could. She beckoned for me to stand, and I did. Then she walked around me, looking me over. Suddenly, she put her hands under my breasts and lifted them.

"Why aren't you wearing a bra?" she asked. I knew what she meant.

"No lo tengo," I told her, and she made a face.

"See how they live, John."

"Your daughter doesn't wear a bra most of the time," he told her, and she spun on him. I picked up a word or two, and from the smirk on his face, I thought he was referring to my cousin.

"She does when it's proper to do so, John. It would have been proper for her family to have her wear a bra the first time she met me."

"But her parents were killed," he said.

I understood that he was defending me. Why was she so angry?

"Her grandmother should have had the . . . oh, what the hell am I talking about? They don't know anything about social etiquette back there. Tell her I'm having a bra sent to her room, and I want her wearing it all the time."

He did so, still smiling at me. I thought it was time to tell her or ask her to speak to me in Spanish.

"I don't know little English," I said. "Please. Talk *español.*"

"How idiotic she sounds. You want me to speak *español*?" she asked sweetly.

I nodded.

Without any warning, she brought her hand up and slapped me sharply across the face. The blow spun me around, and I had to catch myself on the arm of the sofa.

"Never! Never tell me what to do!" she shouted. "Tell her, John."

He spoke quickly in Spanish, looking as terrified

as I was. My eyes filled with tears, but I trapped them quickly. I would not cry. I held my palm against my cheek. It still stung.

"Sit down!" she shouted, pointing to the chair, and I did so. She strutted about a moment with her arms folded under her breasts and then began dictating to the gentleman, who told me the following.

"My name is Señor Baker. I've been Señora Dallas's daughter's tutor on and off for years, and now, anticipating your arrival after your family tragedy, she has hired me to tutor you in English. You are permitted to speak Spanish only with the servants and never in front of Señora Dallas and never again to Señora Dallas unless she so permits.

"Furthermore, Mrs. Dallas wants you to forget your Mexican background immediately. Never talk about your family or the . . . slum village you come from. It is an embarrassment to her to have any reminders of it or of your family. Your cousins don't speak Spanish very well, so don't hope for that.

"Eventually, Señora Dallas will make your adoption formal, and you will become a legal American citizen, but until then, you are to earn your bed and board here just like any other servant. Señora Rosario will show you where you sleep and will tell you what your duties are. You are not to wander about the property without permission or go into anyone else's room without permission. You are to do your work properly and efficiently, and you will be held accountable for anything you break or damage."

"What about school?" I asked him.

"Until you learn enough English to get by, you will not attend public school here. Those are your aunt's

specific orders. For the time being, until otherwise instructed, you are not to tell anyone that you are Señora
Dallas's niece."

What?

I looked at her. Of course, she understood everything
he was saying in Spanish, but she kept her face un-
changed and stared at me.

"*Por qué?*" I asked. I had to know why I couldn't do
that. She was my mother's sister. We had the same blood.

She muttered something to him that I couldn't hear.

"Señora Dallas is a woman of high regard in Palm
Springs. She is very well respected and admired. She
would find it an embarrassment for people here to know
that she has such an uneducated, unwashed relative living under her roof."

"Unwashed?"

"She doesn't mean you're dirty. It simply means unsophisticated, uneducated."

"I'm not uneducated. I go to school," I said.

"It's not the same thing. Don't worry. I'll be teaching
you all about social etiquette. I'm very good at what I
do. I'll have you ready for school in no time, if you listen and do what I tell you to do," he added, smiling and
drawing very close to me.

He's the one who looks unwashed, I thought. His
teeth were yellow, and now that he was close to me, I
could see he wasn't very careful about how he shaved.
There were tiny pockets of stubble along his jaw bone.
He put his hand on my upper left arm.

"Repeat after me, Delia, in English. Thank you, Mrs.
Dallas. I am pleased to be here and grateful for all you
are doing for me. Go on." He winked. "She'll like that."

He repeated it, urging me strongly.

I turned to her and said it.

"See how easy that was?"

"Well, John," my aunt said, relaxing her posture, "if anyone can turn her into something at least tolerable, it's you, I'm sure."

"I might need to spend a lot more time with her," he said, scrutinizing me as if he were going to adopt me and not her. "I'll let you know when we begin and I see how much we have to do. I have no idea how quickly she can learn."

"Spend as much time as you want. She has no important appointments at the moment," she added, and they both laughed. I knew the words *spend* and *time* and *important*. I could figure out that they were making fun of me.

"Dare I say I see some resemblance between you?" Señor Baker asked her, pointing to me and to her.

"No. She looks more like her father than my sister."

"Your aunt says you look like your father," he told me. I took it as the first sign of familial warmth, but when I looked at my aunt, she seemed even angrier. I was afraid to say anything or even smile.

I glanced at the front door. The thought crossed my mind that I should pick up my suitcase and walk out now, but how would I get back to Mexico? I had no money, and I didn't even know the way back. Abuela Anabela would be so disappointed, too, even if I did find my way home.

My aunt saw the look in my face and the direction of my gaze.

"Tell her she can leave anytime she wants and go back to that squalor she calls home," she told Señor Baker, who translated for me.

I looked directly at her now. I would not speak through him.

"I am here," I told her in Spanish. "I will do what I must to make you happy, and in the end, you will be proud to have people know me as your niece."

She nearly smiled and caught herself. "Tell her I didn't understand a word she said," she told Señor Baker. He started.

I smiled and looked away, daring to mumble, "*Sí*. Yes, you did."

She heard me, and it reddened her cheeks and put the fire back into her eyes.

"Mrs. Rosario!" my aunt screamed.

Señora Rosario appeared so quickly that it was obvious she was waiting just outside to be called.

My aunt pointed to my suitcase.

"How could you permit that dirty thing to be brought into the main house?"

"I . . . she had . . ."

"Never mind. Take her and that thing to her room, and show her what her duties are. Don't treat her any better than anyone else, and let me know the moment she fails to do what you say."

"Yes, Mrs. Dallas."

"Mr. Baker will be teaching her English whenever her work is completed. Do whatever is necessary to make him comfortable in the library."

"Yes, Mrs. Dallas."

"Get her moving. I won't tolerate another lazy Mexican in my house or on my grounds," my aunt said, and started to turn away.

I looked at Señor Baker and quickly spoke up in my newest English words.

"Thank you, Mrs. Dallas. I'm pleased to be here and grateful for all you are doing for me," I said.

She spun around, her eyes wide. I held my gaze. I would not be treated as if I were no better than a *cucaracha,* something to be crushed and swept away. She glanced at Mr. Baker, who dared a short laugh and shrugged.

"She's got spirit," he said. "She's more like you than you think, perhaps."

She paused and stared at me a moment. I held my gaze on her, my self-pride still firm.

"We'll see," she said, and then marched out of the living room, her high heels tapping the travertine floor in a rhythm of rage, rage I neither appreciated nor understood. It was as if my very presence infuriated her. If this was so, why did she send for me? Why did she want me in her home? If she still hated her family so much, why did she want a living reminder of it right under her nose?

Something told me, warned me, however, that I had just seen only the tip of the flame. There was quite a fire burning in her chest, a fire started years ago back in our village. Would I ever understand it?

More important, would it consume me, or would I snuff it out before it could?

"You can get more with honey than with vinegar," my grandmother used to tell me. "Anger is easy. Kindness is harder but more rewarding."

I had seen the anger.

Now I wondered, where was the kindness here?

4

Cleaning for Sophia

Señora Rosario told me to pick up my suitcase and follow her. I was surprised when she took me out a side door and led me to one of the buildings away from the house. I was anticipating going up the beautiful stairway to my room.

"*Adónde vamos,* Señora Rosario?" I asked.

"In this building is a room for you," she said as we walked toward it. "You will be responsible for cleaning up after yourself and keeping your things in order. You will share a bathroom with Señor Garman, Señora Dallas's driver. I can tell you now that he is not happy about it. He's never had to share his bathroom before, so don't dilly-dally whenever you're in there, and be sure you pick up after yourself, and never, ever touch any of his things."

So, that's why he was so upset, I thought. There were so many bedrooms and so many bathrooms on this property, probably, and he had to share his with me. I wondered if Señora Rosario slept in this building, too, but before I could ask, she told me that she and the other servants lived in their own homes. Señor Garman and I would be the only servants sleeping on the property.

Of course, I never considered that I was being brought here to be another servant. This was my family. Supposedly, I was going to have an aunt for a legal guardian, not an employer. I looked back at the beautiful *hacienda* longingly. I was not to have a grand room to myself after all. There was no way I could think of myself as part of this family now. In fact, I had just been warned that I couldn't let anyone know I was related to Señora Dallas and her children. She had slapped me only once, but her words were far more stinging anyway. I was sure my ears were redder than my cheek.

At least I no longer had to feel guilty about my parents' deaths bringing me wonderful new opportunities. I felt more like a starving girl standing outside a restaurant, watching other people gorge themselves on rich and delicious foods. My suffering hadn't ended. It might only have just begun.

Now that I was closer, I could see that the building where I was to sleep was devoid of any style or character. It looked as if it had been thrown together in a rush, the dull brown stucco smeared quickly over the squared structure. It had a very ordinary front door and a dark, dank-looking, narrow hallway that took us to what would be my room.

I stood there staring in at it. Ironically, I had enjoyed a bigger room with my grandmother back in our humble *casa* in our Mexican village. This room was stark and had only a single window. The floor was charcoal-painted concrete, cracked and pitted, with a rusty drain at the center. It wasn't meant to be a bedroom, I thought. To the right was a single bed which now had a naked, stained mattress and a pillow without a pillow case. The bed had no sides, no headboard. It had been pushed against the wall. I saw spiderwebs in every corner, and the window looked as if it hadn't been washed since the day the building had been constructed. There was a strong, stale odor that reminded me of dead fish.

"I'll show you where your bedding is," Señora Rosario said. "You make your own bed, of course. There's a blanket and a pillow case. You should strip it down and wash everything once a week. The room needs a little dusting as well," she added, gazing about.

A little? I thought. As my grandmother might say, there was so much dirt in here I could plant flowers.

The room had no closet, just an old wood armoire with one door open. I would discover that it wouldn't close. To the right of that was a small dresser of lighter wood. There was a lamp on the dresser and a naked light fixture at the center of the ceiling dangling on a wire. That was it. This was my new room. Could a Mexican prison be any worse? How surprised and disappointed *mi abuela* Anabela would be if she saw this, I thought. I would never tell her. It would break her heart to hear about it and to hear the things *mi tía* Isabela had said and done to me.

"Follow me," Señora Rosario said.

She led me farther down the hall to show me the bathroom. It had a tub and a shower with a faded yellow plastic curtain, a sink with a small cabinet above it, and a toilet. The toilet seat was up and had urine stains all over it. The floor was a chipped and cracked pale white linoleum, and the walls looked as if they had never been repainted or, on closer inspection, ever painted.

All of the fixtures were old and rusted, and there was a long rust stain at the bottom of the tub. She opened the cabinet. The four narrow shelves were crowded with Señor Garman's things. There was no place for anything of mine.

"Um," Señora Rosario said. "There is no room. You'll have to bring your things in and out every time you use the bathroom. Sorry."

She continued down the hallway a few more feet to a closet and showed me my bedding.

"You have no time to start all this now," she said, "but later, this is where you will come for your things."

"No time now?"

"No. You need to go directly to Señorita Sophia's room and start on the bathroom. Señora Dallas so instructed before you arrived."

"But after all this traveling? I'm not to be given any chance to rest?"

She looked at me as if I had asked the dumbest possible questions, and then she took an apron off a bottom shelf and handed it to me.

"You are to wear this over your clothes always when you are here on the property. There's another in here so you can wash one and have a spare. Don't ever let Señora Dallas see you wearing one that's dirty. You saw how clean the house is kept. She has a thing about seeing any dust or smudges and can get very angry about it. Put it on now," she ordered.

I did so. It was starch white with a hem that was somewhat frayed. It nearly reached my feet.

"Pull it higher and tighten it around your waist, or you'll trip over it," she instructed. "Okay, let's go."

I followed her out of the building. She led me through a rear entrance of the main house this time, to familiarize me with the pantry that had all of the cleaning utensils, soaps, rags, and pails. She told me what to take. It was so much I almost dropped some of it as we made our way from the rear of the house to the stairway. I glanced about to see if my aunt was nearby but neither heard nor saw anyone.

"Señorita Sophia and Señor Edward are still at school. They attend a private school," she told me as we started up the carpeted stairway. She glanced at my feet. "Be sure you never track anything onto these carpets. If you work quickly, you will be finished before Señorita Sophia arrives. She doesn't like any of the help in her room when she's there. Her room, her bathroom, her clothes are all now your responsibility.

"However," she added at the top of the stairway, "that's not all you will have to do here. You will help serve the meals and clean the kitchen and the bathrooms downstairs. Señora Dallas calls them powder rooms, so if she says that, you should know what she means."

"Powder?"

"Just remember it," she snapped. Either she was impatient with me now or with *mi tía* Isabela's assigning her to supervise me. Before I had even set foot on the property, my aunt's main employees resented me, I thought.

The upstairs was just as beautiful as below. The floors had thick light blue carpets, and there were big teardrop chandeliers all the way down the hall. The windows were stained glass, and there was more statuary, busts on pedestals, and great pictures in gilded frames.

We paused at a double doorway.

"This is Señorita Sophia's room. Even though she is not here, knock. We might be mistaken, and she might be here. Sometimes she comes home earlier from school or doesn't go and we don't know it. You are never to go in there without first knocking. Understand?"

I nodded.

She knocked and then waited to demonstrate or drive the point home, because she had already told me she was sure my cousin was still at school. Why knock? Did they all think I was that stupid just because I had just arrived from a small Mexican village and they had to demonstrate such a simple thing? How sad that a Mexican would think that of another.

She opened the door.

I was not prepared for such an overwhelmingly grandiose bedroom. At the center was an enormous four-poster bed with a canopy and a headboard that had two great butterflies facing each other. Their eyes were filled with emeralds or stones closely resembling them. The bedspread looked softer than a cloud, and the pillows were enormous. The pink rug was so thick I felt as if I were truly walking on air when we stepped into the room.

Above the bed was a ceiling I didn't understand. There were hundreds of tiny lights. Señora Rosario saw how I was staring, my head back.

"Mr. Dallas designed this room for Señorita Sophia before he died. He created a night sky in the ceiling."

"Night sky?"

"Those little lights look like stars, and to the right up there, they form the Milky Way. There are other constellations as well. Do you know what that means?"

"*Sí,*" I said. "Stars shaped as things. Aquarius, Cancer."
She looked surprised that I knew so much.

"*Mi padre* loved to tell me about the stars," I said, and
for a moment, I saw some pity and sadness for me in her
eyes, but just as quickly, as if she were afraid she would
be caught showing kindness, she blinked it away.

To the right, I saw the closet door was open, but the
closet looked as big as my room, if not bigger. I could
see the shelves were stacked with shoes, and there was
a very long rack of dresses with blouses and jackets on
the other side. At the end of the closet were a dressing
table and a full-size mirror. There was even a small
television set in the wall. Why would someone want to
watch television in a closet? I wondered.

"Everything is supposed to be organized in that
closet," Señora Rosario said, smirking, "but never is, no
matter how well it's kept. Nevertheless, you are to put
everything back where it belongs as best you can. You
see where the dresses belong, the blouses and shoes. Just
around the door, there are five bathrobes on hangers."

"Five?"

"Some were presents, and some were just . . . some
presents," she added, holding her smirk. "Don't ever
hang a bathrobe where a dress goes," she warned.

Glancing through the bathroom door, we saw a pink
silk bathrobe on the floor. There was a slipper near it
and another just outside the bathroom.

"She's not in the habit of picking up after herself,"
Señora Rosario muttered, picking up the slipper outside
the bathroom.

When I entered the bathroom, my mouth dropped
open. Not in the habit of picking up after herself?
That was an understatement. Besides the wet towels

and washcloths on the floor, there was a sanitary pad beside the garbage can, at which it had been tossed perhaps. The roll of toilet paper was unraveled on the floor. There were two sinks side by side, and both were streaked with makeup and toothpaste. The mirrors were smudged, and the shower doors were streaked with shampoo residue. Everywhere I looked, something was left open. Drawers were open as well.

Señora Rosario checked her watch.

"You have less than a half hour to do this and straighten out the closet and the bedroom, so work quickly, and don't dilly-dally. When you're finished, come down to the kitchen," she said. "And don't leave any cleaning supplies behind in the room. She hates that."

I wanted to ask how a girl this young had so much authority and could put so much fear into the servants, but I didn't have to ask. Señora Rosario saw it in my face.

"Señorita Sophia and Señor Edward are owners of the estate and of the family's financial holdings. It is in the will their father left, and they have let everyone know it. Stay out of her way, and you'll be all right," she added.

How do I stay out of my cousin's way? I wondered. What did that mean, anyway?

I began to clean up the bathroom. I had everything picked up and the tub and sinks washed down before I started on the shower stall. I had taken off my shoes and socks and had gone into the stall to wash down the tile. Time was never something I paid much attention to when I worked with *mi abuela* Anabela in our *casa*. I was determined to do a very good job and impress my aunt Isabela, so I lost myself in the work.

Squatting to get at the lower tiles in the shower, I had my back to the stall door and did not hear anyone enter the bathroom. Suddenly, a downpour of ice-cold water crashed down on my head and shocked me so much that I lost my footing and fell back onto the shower floor. The water rained down over me, soaking my clothes, my apron. I heard laughter and turned to see my cousin Sophia standing in the doorway.

As quickly as I could, I regained my balance and turned off the shower faucet. Dripping wet, I looked at her. Her smile evaporated, and her face filled with rage.

"How dare you go into my shower with your filthy, diseased feet?" she screamed. I understood *filthy* and *feet* and figured out the rest.

In Spanish, I said, "It was the best way to clean it."

"I don't speak Spanish, you idiot. Mrs. Rosario!" she cried. "Mrs. Rosario!"

Her screams echoed in the shower stall. I actually felt myself trembling. Mrs. Rosario came running to the bedroom.

"Look at where she is!" Sophia told Mrs. Rosario, and pointed at me.

"Why are you soaked?" Señora Rosario asked me in *español*.

I explained what had happened, and she shook her head. She spoke softly to my cousin, trying to calm her down, but my cousin fumed and folded her arms under her breasts.

Sophia was *un pollo regordete,* a plump chicken, as *mi abuela* Anabela would say. Her cheeks were bloated and looked as if she had a mouth full of walnuts. They diminished her dark brown eyes, which were her best feature. Her nose was just a little too long, and the nostrils flared like the nostrils of a small bull. She had twice the size bosom I had, but her hips were wider, and her arms were puffy all the way to her shoulders. I noticed she had fat fingers, too.

I thought, considering her round face, that her walnut-brown hair was cut too short. It emphasized the fullness in her cheeks and the slightness of her small mouth, which she seemed capable of stretching like a rubber band when she shouted. She turned back to me.

"Can't she speak any English?"

"*Un poco,* a little," Señora Rosario quickly corrected. "She just arrived from Mexico."

"Why did my mother want such a servant in our house? Don't we have enough Mexicans?"

"She's a good worker," Señora Rosario said. She didn't know what else to say. "She went right to work as soon as she was brought here."

"More reason for her not to be in my shower. Did she bathe first? Did you bathe first?" she asked me.

Señora Rosario explained what she had said and what she wanted to know, but I already understood what she was implying. My grandmother or my mother wouldn't let me out of the house with as much as a pin stain on my clothing and never before I washed and had my hair brushed.

"I'm clean," I told Señora Rosario. "Cleaner than she is, I'm sure."

"What did she say? Did she say something mean? What did she say?" Sophia demanded.

Señora Rosario made up something satisfying, because it seemed to calm Sophia down a bit. Then she pointed to me again and shouted, "Get her out!"

I quickly put on my shoes and socks, gathered up my

pail, washcloths, mop, and cleaning fluids, and started out of the room.

"Why did you take so long?" Señora Rosario asked me in the hallway. "I told you how much time you had. I told you not to be in there when she returned from school."

"I was trying to do a good job. It's so dirty and messy," I explained. "That was a mean thing for her to do to me."

Señora Rosario sighed deeply.

"Welcome to La Casa Dallas. You'll go back later and finish up," she said. "In the meantime, go change out of your wet clothes. You might as well make your bed and get yourself organized in your room. Then come to the kitchen," she told me.

I started down the hallway.

My aunt Isabela stepped out of her bedroom just as I reached the stairway and shouted at Señora Rosario.

"Why is she soaked? Why is she tracking water down the hallway?"

Señora Rosario hurried to her, urging me behind her back to continue down the stairway and out of the house as she passed me by. I looked back and saw her explaining desperately. My aunt glared after me, her eyes so red with fury and anger that I couldn't move fast enough to get out of their range.

As I hurried from the main house, I saw two gardeners looking at me and laughing. I tried to ignore them, but one shouted, "Señorita, *usted se cayó en la bañera?*"

"No," I shouted back, "I did not fall into the bathtub, but looking at you, I would advise you to fall into one."

They both looked shocked and then roared with laughter.

I charged into the help's quarters and went to the

bathroom, dried my hair, and gathered up the bedding for my bed. Then I hurried to my hole-in-the-wall room, where I quickly stripped off my wet clothing and began to dry my body. Moments later, I heard someone coming down the hallway. There was a knock on my door.

Señora Rosario isn't giving me much time, I thought. Why did everything have to be in such a rush here? I held the towel over my breasts and opened the door.

Standing there was Señor Baker. He had two books in his hands and a brassiere. His gaze moved quickly down to my feet and then slowly rose up my body, bringing a deep, wide smile to his face. I felt the heat of a deep blush come into my own.

"I thought you were Señora Rosario," I told him.

"It's all right," he replied. "Don't be ashamed. I'm your teacher," he added, as if that meant he could see and do whatever he wanted when it came to me. "Mrs. Dallas wanted me to give you this right away," he said, holding out the bra. "I bought it for you myself. I think it's the right size."

The sight of a strange man holding out a brassiere for me brought even more heat to my neck and face. He laughed.

"I have good language books for you," he said, and offered them to me as well.

It was difficult to hold on to my towel and reach for everything, but he didn't seem to care. I tried taking it all quickly, and part of the towel fell away. I brought my hand back and covered myself.

"Why are you changing your clothes now, anyway?" he asked.

"I . . . had an accident," I said, thinking that was the easiest way to explain.

He nodded but didn't turn away to leave. Instead, he leaned to look past me at my room.

"This isn't very nice," he said. "We've got to get you into nicer accommodations. Once you learn English, Mrs. Dallas will move you to a nicer room, I'm sure. We'll figure something out."

Why would my learning English have anything to do with that? I wondered, but didn't ask.

"Is there anything you need now?" he asked.

"No," I said. "I have to change quickly, make my bed, and get to the kitchen."

"Really? Put to work so soon? I was hoping to start your first lesson," he said. "I'll have to have a conversation with Señora Dallas about you," he added, and walked right past me into my room.

I had no way to cover myself from the waist down. I lunged quickly for my dry dress, scooped it up, and charged out of the room, wrapping as much as I could around me. I was sure I looked very foolish.

"I'm going to the bathroom to change," I cried, and continued down the hallway, but when I got to the bathroom, the door was closed. Señor Garman was inside.

Señor Baker came out of my room and looked down the hallway at me.

"You can change in your room," he said, laughing. "I'll wait outside if you like. Come on," he said, beckoning.

I heard Señor Garman flush the toilet. When he opened the door and saw me standing half naked, holding a towel against myself and my dress around my waist, he grimaced.

"What is this?" he demanded. He looked down the hallway at Señor Baker.

"She went to change in the bathroom," he called back. He spoke in Spanish and then realized it and repeated it in English. "She's just very confused."

"Why don't you use your own room for that?" Señor Garman asked me angrily.

"He wants to know why you don't change in your room," Señor Baker told me, laughing. "Come on back. Change in your room, you silly girl."

I gazed at Señor Garman, who was still grimacing angrily, and then hurried back to my room and closed the door. I could hear them both laughing in the hallway. I could barely keep my tears under my eyelids.

Señor Baker knocked on my door.

"Aren't you ready yet?" he asked, and then he opened the door before I could respond. I had just buttoned my last button on the bodice of my dress. "Fine," he said, entering. He stood there looking around a moment and then smiled at me. "Your aunt was right, Delia. You should wear a bra. You have a very nice figure, and you should be very proud," he said.

I couldn't speak. No man ever spoke about my body like that. Boys made remarks, but no grown man ever did in my presence, at least. Was this common in America?

"Okay, why waste an opportunity? Let's have our first English lesson," he said.

"But Señora Rosario wants me in the kitchen."

"Don't worry about it. Señora Dallas thinks this is more important. We'll begin by identifying things," he insisted. "When I point to them, I will give you the word in English, and you repeat it, understand?"

I nodded, and he put his hand on my bed.

"Bed," he said. He went through my room, identifying everything from the floor up. I knew many of these words already, but then he surprised me by turning to me to identify the parts of my body.

He took my hand.

"Hand," he said. "Arm."

He touched my face, and I repeated every English word: *eyes, nose, cheeks, forehead, mouth, chin.*

Then he stepped back and tested me by pointing to everything he had translated. I was very nervous and trembling so much inside I had trouble speaking, but he was impressed with my memory.

"Very good," he said. "You have an ability for language, and you are motivated to learn. We will be very successful very quickly. I feel confident I can help you. It's good you know some English already. Were there many American tourists coming to your village?"

"No, only a few and not to the village. They stayed at the hotel where my aunt used to work, but they came to the square or to the farmers' market sometimes."

"Your aunt worked in a hotel? I didn't know," he said. "She never told me much about her youth or her life in Mexico. Most people think she came from somewhere else in America."

I said nothing, afraid that I wasn't supposed to tell, and now she would have another reason to be angry.

"Oh, well. It's not important. What's important is your learning English well enough to get along. I want you to start with this primer," he said, picking up one of the books. "I'll be working with you right after you serve breakfast every day and attend to Señorita Sophia's room. Don't waste time, because you'll be wasting my time as well as your own," he warned. "And besides, the faster I get you into some basic English, the faster things will improve for you. Understand?"

I nodded.

"I don't know," he muttered in English, and then looked at me and shook his head. "She wants you to learn English practically overnight so you can attend school. I don't see how catching you between your chores is going to work for either of us, but don't worry. I have an idea."

He smiled again and stepped closer to put his hand on my cheek.

"You're a very pretty young woman," he told me. "You will do very well once you learn English. Before you know it, you'll have *todos los muchachos* eating out of your hand. Did you have a boyfriend back in Mexico?"

"No," I said.

"A real virgin, then?" he asked.

I did not reply. My father would whip him to an inch of his life for talking to me like this, I thought. With an aunt who wasn't sympathetic, servants who seemed to resent me, and a cousin who mocked me, I was totally unprotected.

Suddenly, he brought my hand to his lips and kissed it.

"Welcome to America, Miss Yebarra," he said.

He held my hand and smiled.

"You say thank you."

"Thank you."

"You could also say, 'I'm pleased to be here.' Go on," he urged, and I said it. Then he nodded and released my hand.

"It's a nice way to say hello to people or even good-bye," he emphasized. "You have to learn the social graces," he told me, pretended as if we had just met, and did it again.

"Oh, I can see it won't take us long to get you up and running in English if I can have enough time with you," he said, his face so close to mine I could see the pores in his cheeks, some filled with what looked like soot. His breath was a mixture of onions and cigarettes and made my stomach churn, but I was afraid to move or insult him.

"Your aunt wants you to do more than learn English, Delia. She wants you to learn how to be in society, how to be a lady. I'll show you how to walk, sit at a table, even how to eat, so that when people meet you, they will think you came from a quality home."

"I did come from a quality home."

"Yes," he said, laughing, "but not quite the level of quality your aunt appreciates. Believe me," he said, "you've crossed more than a border. You've crossed into a new life. That is why she wants you to forget the old."

I started to shake my head.

"At least, pretend you have," he warned.

Finally, he said good-bye and walked out of my room.

I stood there, feeling as if my chest were filling with air, and any moment I would simply explode.

This was my welcome to my new life? To forget the people I loved?

I gazed around my tiny, dark room and wondered what we had possibly done to anger God so much.

5

Edward

I didn't meet my cousin Edward until I helped serve dinner.

He sat across from Sophia and was dressed in a dark blue sports jacket and a light blue tie. He had long, dark brown hair tied in a ponytail, which surprised me. Unlike Sophia, he was slim, with a long, narrow face and a nearly square jaw. His eyes were more narrow and a lighter shade of brown. He had a thin but small nose and full, almost feminine lips. He smiled the moment I appeared and then looked at Sophia, who was staring down at her plate.

Mi tía Isabela was at the head of the table. There was a tall, light-brown-haired man sitting across from her at the other end of the table. He wore a beige jacket and a dark brown tie. He fixed his bright blue eyes on me and smiled. I quickly looked away. I was bringing out a tray with four bowls of French onion soup. It had a deliciously strong aroma. My stomach churned with hunger. I had yet to eat anything since my arrival. The main dish, or entrée, as Señora Rosario called it, was a delicious-looking poached salmon. My aunt had a chef, Señor Herrera, who, I learned, had been the head chef on a luxury cruise ship. My aunt had been on the ship and had stolen him away.

I picked all of this up by listening to the tidbits of gossip while I worked in the kitchen alongside Señora Rosario and another maid, a Mexican girl who had been born in America, Inez Morales. She didn't look much older than I and was barely my height, thinner, with eyes that revealed a catlike timidity. She hovered over her work as if she thought someone would steal it and therefore her reason to be there. I could see she was looking at me suspiciously, perhaps thinking I was there to be trained to take her place.

I found out she was in her midtwenties and had been married but deserted by her husband after she had twin boys. Her mother cared for her children while she worked. She worked for my aunt six days a week, alternating her day off between Saturday and Sunday every other week, depending on my aunt's schedule and needs. She was there from six in the morning until ten at night, which didn't leave her much time to spend with her children.

When I entered the dining room, I wondered if my aunt would say anything more to me about what had happened in Sophia's bathroom. She glared at me and then smiled at the young man across from her. I wondered who he was. He seemed much younger than she was. Could he be another relative I had not met or even knew existed?

I placed the first bowl in front of her. I had been given instant instructions about how to serve at the dinner table, but Señora Rosario was there overseeing it all. I glanced at her, and she nodded as I moved toward Sophia.

"I like your new help," the young man said, still smiling at me. "Welcome . . . what's her name?"

"She doesn't understand that much English yet, Travis," my aunt told him before I could even think of responding. "I'm having her tutored to get her up to speed quickly."

"Oh. Let's see . . . ah, *recepción* a America . . . what's her name? How do you say that in Spanish, Isabela?"

"I forget."

"Forget? How could you forget that?"

"Easy," she muttered.

"Well, what's her name? You must know the name of someone you just hired."

"Delia," my aunt said, almost under her breath.

"Delia," he repeated. "Hi, Delia."

I looked at the young man and returned a smile. I started around Sophia, but I didn't see she had turned just enough to bring out her foot. I stumbled over it, and the tray slid from my hand, the two remaining bowls of soup flying off and onto the table, splashing over everything.

My aunt screamed and pushed herself back. My cousin Edward leaped out of his seat. Some of the soup hit Travis and spotted his jacket. I caught myself from falling altogether and immediately started to clean up the mess.

"Get her out of here!" my aunt screamed.

Señora Rosario seized my arm and pulled me back from the table. Sophia was smiling up at me.

"*Dios mío*," my aunt screamed, looking at the table. She realized instantly that she had spoken in Spanish and slammed her chair against the table. Her face was pepper red. I held my breath. "Get this table cleaned up and reset immediately, Mrs. Rosario. Get her out!" she said, pointing to me and then to the kitchen door. Although I didn't understand all of the words, her rage was terrifying, and it was all clearly aimed at me.

"Isabela," Travis said, wiping down his jacket. "It's not the end of the world."

"Don't tell me what it is and isn't."

I looked at my cousin Edward. He wasn't smiling. He was glaring at his sister and shaking his head.

Señora Rosario practically dragged me out of the dining room.

"You had better go to your room," she ordered.

I glanced at Señor Herrera, who was confused.

"*Qué sucedío?*" he asked.

Inez, who had seen it all, now looked at me with pity and no longer suspicion while Señora Rosario explained.

"How could she . . . how did you stumble? *Tropezó?*"

I wanted to tell him how Sophia had tripped me, but instead, I started to cry and ran out of the kitchen, through the pantry, and outside. I started across toward the older building and then stopped. Above me, a thousand stars blinked as if tears had crossed each and every one of them. Could there have been more of a horrible finish to this horrible day? I sucked in my breath, looked back at the main house, bright and warm, and then headed for the dark building and my small room, tears now flying off my cheeks.

When I got there, I sat on my bed and stared down

at the cold concrete floor. I hadn't closed my door. I sat there with my arms around myself, swaying back and forth, wondering if I would be sent home right away. At the moment, I was wishing for that.

Suddenly, I felt a shadow fall over me and looked up at Edward standing in my doorway.

"Hey," he said, stepping in. "Are you all right?" I stared up at him. "Oh, I guess I have to practice my broken Spanish." He pointed at me. "Okay, *sí?*"

I shook my head and looked down and then up again at him.

He pointed at himself. "Edward," he said.

"Edward, *sí.* Edward."

"I saw my sister trip you." I shook my head. "*Mi hermana . . .*" He stuck out his foot.

"*Sí,*" I said, nodding.

"She's an idiot," he said. "So, you don't speak much English? *No habla mucho* English?"

"No," I said, shaking my head. "*Poco.* A little. I understand . . . from television . . . a little school . . ."

He nodded and stared at me. "Why did you come here? Why . . . *por qué . . . aquí?*"

I sat back. Why here? I pointed to myself.

"*Sí, sí, por qué aquí?*"

I stared at him. Sophia didn't know who I was, and now it was clear that he didn't, either. I wasn't permitted to tell anyone who I really was, but did that apply to my cousins as well? Right now, I was so angry, I didn't care if my aunt found out I did. Besides, he should know who I am, I thought, and then wondered how I should explain all this. Just come right out and say it, I thought. I was still hoping to be sent home, and perhaps doing this would speed that up even faster.

I pointed to him and then to myself.

"*Primo*," I said.

"What?"

"*Primo.*"

He shook his head. "My mother made me take French. The only Spanish I know, I know from the workers," he said.

I started to explain that I didn't understand that, but he held his hand up to indicate that I should wait, and then he went out of my room and out of the building. I stood up and looked out the window. I could see him walking over to a man who was washing down an outside patio. He spoke to him and then turned and looked at my building, spoke to him again, and then slowly started back.

I turned when he returned to my bedroom door. He just stood there looking in at me strangely.

"You," he said, pointing at me, "*es mi prima*?"

"*Sí*," I said, smiling, happy he finally understood. But why hadn't *mi tía* Isabela at least told him and his sister? She implied that if and when I learned English well enough to go to school, she would let people know, or was that just another lie, an empty promise? How did she explain my appearing here to the other help? Maybe she didn't feel she had to explain anything to anyone, except Señor Baker.

He shook his head.

"*Cómo?*" he asked, stepping into the room.

"*Cómo? Mi madre es la hermana más joven que su madre.*"

"*Más joven?* Oh, but I thought . . . we thought . . ." He pointed to his temple. "*Su madre ha muerto.*"

"*Sí, muerto*," I said, and he shook his head, now

looking even more confused. Again, he put up his hand and went out. I returned to the window. I saw him get the worker and start back with him. The two returned to my doorway.

"Mr. Edward is confused about you," the worker said in Spanish. "You told him you were his cousin, daughter of his mother's younger sister, but he was told she died when she was a child."

Now I was more frightened. Maybe I would be forgiven for telling my cousin who I really was, but here I was telling one of the workers. Maybe my aunt wouldn't send me back to Mexico. Maybe she would do something worse. How should I balance the truth with my own safety?

"Lies multiply like rabbits," my grandmother used to say. "No matter how small they seem."

I hadn't been here a day, but I was already tired of living a lie.

"No," I said, shaking my head. "This is not true. My mother and my father were just recently killed in a car accident with a truck. This is why I've come here to live."

He translated for me, and Edward's eyes grew wider. He wanted to know if his sister knew who I was.

"No. If she does, she pretended not to know," I added.

He told the worker to tell me he would return, and he left. The worker, who introduced himself as Casto Flores, wanted me to know that this family, the Dallas family, was *loco*. He had been an employee of the Dallas family for nearly twenty-five years and had liked Señor Dallas, but, he said, Señor Dallas took ill not too long after he married my aunt Isabela. The other workers thought she was too much for him, he added.

I understood that he meant too much woman. He said she made him age quicker, and soon an illness took him over and turned him into an invalid. He said there were long periods of time when he didn't see Señor Dallas at all. He was a prisoner of his illness.

"Señora Dallas did not let that stop her from living a full life," he added. I was not too young to hear what he was saying between the lines.

He wanted to know what exactly had happened to my family in Mexico and why I was there. I told him everything. I could see he felt very sorry for me. Before he left to return to work, he asked when was my day off, and I realized I had never been told I had a day off. He said he would speak to Señora Rosario about it, and when I had a day off, perhaps he would introduce me to his daughter Nina, who was about my age.

"You're not going to school here?" he asked.

I told him what I had been told. First, I had to learn enough English, or I couldn't be admitted to the school.

He shook his head.

"Not so," he said, but I could see he didn't want to say too much more.

It wasn't until he had left and Edward had left that I remembered I hadn't eaten anything. The tension and the disaster at the dinner table had taken my mind off my own pangs of hunger, but now that I was more relaxed, they returned with a clamor. I was very thirsty, too.

I wasn't sure what I could do about it now. I was afraid to return to the main house kitchen. The only solution, I thought, was to try to sleep, so I prepared myself for bed. There was no sign of Señor Garman in the building. When I went to the bathroom to take a shower, I realized there was no lock on the bathroom door. Consequently, I showered and got into my one nightgown faster than ever.

However, when I returned to my bedroom, I was surprised to discover Edward had returned again. This time, he had brought me a plate of food. In what he had obviously just learned and memorized from one of the other Mexican employees, he recited the following: "*Sabía que usted tendría hambre y hice que el cocinero preparar este plato para usted.*"

He knew I'd be hungry and had the chef prepare the plate for me.

I thought he had pretty good pronunciation. I wanted to tell him that no matter what his mother wanted, he couldn't disguise his Latino heritage, but I knew he wouldn't understand, so I just thanked him and took the plate. He stood up and watched me eating.

"How old are you?" he asked. "*Años?*"

I flashed my hand three times.

"Fifteen? You're Sophia's age."

I nodded. I remembered my mother once telling me I was about the same age as my cousin Sophia.

"I heard Mr. Baker is helping you learn English . . . *hablar inglés* . . . Baker?"

"*Sí.*"

My smile faded.

"You don't like him? Er . . . *no le gusta?*"

"No," I said emphatically, and he laughed.

"Me, neither," he said, shaking his head and pointing to himself.

I didn't realize I had been gobbling my food until I looked down and saw it was nearly all gone.

"You were definitely hungry," he said.

He just stood there staring down at me. It wasn't

until then that I realized I was just in my nightgown. Although it wasn't sheer, it was slight enough to bring a flush of red heat into my neck and face, especially when I traced his gaze to my breasts. I put down the plate when I finished and folded my arms over myself.

He smiled. "Enough? *Más*?"

"*No más, gracias.*"

"Okay, I'm going," he said. "I'm sorry about all this. *Mi hermana* is an idiot, and *mi madre* . . ." He shrugged and shook his head. "I will talk to her. I will *habla mi madre*."

I smiled. He was the only member of the family who had been nice to me.

"*Buenas noches,*" he said.

"*Buenas noches.*"

He nodded and left. I went to the door and watched him leave the building, and then I looked up through the cloudy pane and stared at the stars. These were the same stars above my house back in Mexico, where *mi abuela* Anabela was probably preparing for bed. All my life, except for when I slept in a cradle in *mi madre*'s room, I shared this bedroom with my grandmother. Together, after we had both prepared for sleep, we would recite our prayers, and she would say a prayer for me at my bedside, praying for me to have a long and healthy life. She was the last person I spoke to before I went to sleep and the first one I spoke to when I woke in the morning. She was there for my nightmares and there to nurse me when I was sick, and now, she was sleeping alone in the house. Despite where I was in this two-by-four of a cold, stark room, I felt sorrier for her.

Surely, the house back in Mexico was full of echoes, memories that had begun to haunt her. How much despair could her aged heart withstand? Did she feel betrayed, lost, and alone? What would drive her to care about the next day, about rising to clean the house, wash clothes, prepare food for herself? How many times would she look at my empty bed and think about me?

And what of the son she had lost, his life snuffed out like some small flame that had promised to burn brightly and keep us all safe and warm? How severe her mourning surely had become. The echoes of yesterday weren't only the echoes of my voice, my footsteps, and my laughter through the house. I was sure she was fixed on her memories of my father as a young boy, fixed on her memories of holding him, protecting him, feeding and clothing him. The little boy fades into the man, and the man fades into his old age, *mi abuela* Anabela would tell me, but the images remain, lingering like smoke in your mind, bringing smiles back, old smiles, old laughs from time past.

When I had first set out for *mi tía* Isabela's *hacienda,* I envisioned her enabling me to keep in contact with my grandmother, perhaps making a phone call that the postmaster would receive, and then, perhaps, she would be able to call me. My letters would go out to her, and her letters would come to me here. Now I wondered what, if anything, my aunt would do for me. I had left Mexico clinging to the belief that I would somehow return to see my grandmother again, clinging to the belief that this wasn't a final good-bye.

However, I felt more like a prisoner trapped on this estate of my aunt and cousins. Not only was I being treated as if I were just another immigrant worker, but my identity was being taken from me. I was truly turned into an orphan, someone without any familial past.

Being forbidden to mention any of it, it was erased. Who was I now? Who would I become?

I couldn't help but wonder if my cousin Sophia would have treated me any differently if she had known we were related. Would she have been as cruel? Look at how kind my cousin Edward was even before he knew we were cousins. There was hope in all of that, I told myself, wasn't there? Now that Edward knew the truth, perhaps he would get my aunt to change the way she was treating me, and perhaps Sophia wouldn't be so antagonistic and mean.

Clinging to that tidbit of optimism, I said my prayers and got into bed. Everything had a starchy machine smell. The sheet and the blanket must surely have been in that closet for a very long time, I thought. And of course, this room, with its one window, was dank and stuffy and still smelled like old fish. I almost decided to sleep outside but then thought that might attract more negative attention to me and make my aunt even angrier.

I closed my eyes, but opened them moments later to listen to the heavy footsteps in the hallway. Who was coming now? I couldn't lock my bedroom door, either. The footsteps went by my room, so I imagined it was Señor Garman. I heard a door close and then the sound of water running. Other than that, it was very, very quiet. After I heard him go into his room, the stillness felt like a heavy blanket thrown over me.

I folded myself into a fetal position and tried desperately to fall asleep. Minutes after, far more exhausted than I had imagined I was, I did tumble into a twisted tunnel of nightmares, with flashes of my aunt's angry face and my cousin Sophia's sneer appearing on the dark walls. I careened into one long, screaming descent and broke out into sunlight when the morning light flowed through the window and snapped me into reality, a reality that wasn't much better than the nightmares I had just escaped.

I groaned and turned on my narrow bed, grinding the sleep out of my eyes just as my bedroom door opened and Señora Rosario looked in at me.

"Why aren't you up and dressed already?" she demanded.

"What time is it?"

"It's six forty-five. I told you to be in the kitchen at six-thirty. There are preparations to be made. Señorita Sophia and Señor Edward go to school at seven-thirty unless Señorita Sophia oversleeps."

"Señora Dallas still wants me to serve?"

"You are to be given another chance for that, but in the meantime, you are to bring Señorita Sophia her breakfast every morning."

"You mean to her room?"

"Of course. Where else do you think you'd bring it? There is much to do, and Señor Baker wants you to meet him in the library at eight-thirty, I am told. You have to clean Señorita Sophia's room as soon as she leaves, change the sheets and pillow cases. They are changed every day."

"Every day?"

"Don't keep questioning what I tell you. Just get yourself up and come to the kitchen," she snapped. "I'm in charge of the domestic help here, and I get blamed for anything stupid someone working under me does. I don't intend for that to happen. Get up!" she snapped, and closed the door.

I rose quickly, gathered my clothes, and headed for

the bathroom, but when I got there, the door was shut. I knocked. Was Señor Garman in there, or was the door just closed? I started to open the door.

"*Espere hasta que me acabo!*" I heard Señor Garman shout. He was in there, and he was telling me to wait until he'd finished.

"But I have to get to the kitchen," I told him in Spanish.

"Get up earlier," he told me.

Get up earlier? I had no clock to wake me. How was I to know what time to get up?

He didn't come out. I heard his electric shaver going and decided to dress without washing. I returned to my room, dressed, and ran my brush through my hair. Then I hurried out the door, my heart pounding. I didn't want to do anything to rile up my aunt today, especially since I was being given a second chance. Perhaps she realized what Sophia had done and how what happened wasn't really my fault. Perhaps Edward had defended me. Things could now get better, I thought hopefully.

Or perhaps Sophia would be angry that she was blamed and would be only meaner toward me and think of other terrible things to do to me. I could see now why Inez looked as if she were walking on a floor of shattered glass. They must all be paid well to put up with such tension. No one, I gathered from listening to Señor Flores, liked this family or respected it. How different this was from the way Señor Lopez was thought of by my mother and father and his workers.

I was still waiting to see what, besides the wealth, was better in America.

The two Mexican gardeners who had been there

yesterday after Sophia had soaked me turned to watch me rushing. They laughed, and one shouted, "What, no falling into the bathtub this morning?"

No, I thought, I've fallen into something far worse: my own private hell.

6

English Lesson

Both Señor Herrera and Inez were working frantically in the kitchen when I arrived. They glanced at me, and then Señor Herrera began dictating orders. I was told to make some toast for Señorita Sophia's tray and warned not to burn it. He was preparing some scrambled eggs and bacon. Inez was working on setting the breakfast table for my aunt, her guest, and my cousin Edward. I was told to pour coffee into a container that would keep it hot, and then Señor Herrera set up the tray for me to bring up to my cousin Sophia. The plate had a silver cover, and the cream, butter, and cheese were all in silver as well. Inez put a fresh rose on the tray before I picked it up.

"If you forget the flower, she'll send you down for it, even though she just throws it into her garbage can," Inez told me.

"Careful, don't spill anything," Señor Herrera warned

me. "She'll send the tray back if there is even a drop of something out of its container or off its dish."

"And don't look like you're breathing on anything. She hates that," Inez added.

I waited a moment to see if there were any other warnings.

"Go on, before it gets cold," Señor Herrera said.

Slowly, I started out and up the stairway. As I ascended, my eyes glued to the tray so I wouldn't spill anything, Edward came out of his room and paused at the top of the stairway. He was dressed in a jacket and tie and had his hair tied back the same way. He smiled at me.

"Morning," he said. "*Hola.*"

"*Hola.*"

"I'll see you later," he said. "We have a lot to talk about."

I shook my head. I was so involved in carrying the tray carefully that I wasn't paying attention. He pointed to himself and then to me and said, "*Tarde.*"

"Oh. *Sí, tarde.*"

He continued down the stairway, and I went to my cousin's door. It wasn't until then that I realized I would have a problem knocking on the door, opening it, and holding on to the tray. I had to put the tray down on the floor and then knock. I heard nothing, so I knocked harder.

The door was jerked open so hard the air nearly sucked me in and over the tray. She was standing there in her bra and panties.

"Jeez," she cried. "I'm not deaf, you idiot. Put the tray on my desk," she added, pointing to the desk.

I knelt down, picked up the tray, and went to the desk. She gazed at herself in the mirror and fluffed her hair. I saw that her bra was tight, and the fat around the back of it rolled over and formed folds beneath as well. She had a roll of fat on her hips, and her rear end sagged over her heavy thighs. She spun around on me.

"What are you looking at?" she asked. "You're not queer, are you?"

I shook my head. She was speaking too fast, and I didn't understand the question.

"I'm sorry. I do not understand so well yet," I said.

"Oh, jeez. How am I supposed to deal with someone who can't speak English?" She smirked. "Edward says you're our cousin. I think he's just kidding me, right? You're not really our cousin, are you?"

"Cousin. Oh, *sí, prima, sí,*" I said.

"I don't believe it. My mother hasn't said anything that stupid to me yet."

She walked over to the tray, lifted the cover, and inspected the eggs.

"You can go," she said, waving at the door. "*Vamos* or whatever you say. Go!"

I started out.

"Wait!" she screamed. I turned back. "This coffee is cold. The coffee," she said, holding up the cup, "it's cold . . . cold . . . what's the word? *Frío?*"

I shook my head. I saw Mr. Herrera pour it into the container steaming hot. It couldn't be cold.

"Don't tell me. It's cold. Get me hot coffee *pronto . . . caliente.*"

I went back, took the coffee container, and left her room. When I got back to the kitchen, I explained to Inez, who poured it into a cup and shook her head.

"We'll teach her," she said.

She poured the coffee into another container and put

it into the microwave oven. The steam flowed up as she poured it into the container again, and I took it back upstairs quickly, practically running up.

Sophia had put a tight thin blouse over herself and was slipping into a skirt. She watched me bring the coffee to the desk, and then she poured it into a cup. The steam rose. She felt the cup and made a face.

"By the time this cools down, I'll have to leave. Forget it," she said.

I didn't understand but figured from her gestures that she wasn't going to drink the coffee now. I saw she had eaten everything on her plate. I picked up the tray, shrugged, and left.

"Right, just go," she cried after me. "Idiot Mexican. How could you be our cousin?"

Idiot Mexican? You're half Mexican, I thought, but imagined that, like her mother, she was in denial about it. Nevertheless, I smiled to myself and went downstairs. As soon as Sophia and Edward left for school, Señora Rosario was on me to go up and start cleaning Sophia's room.

"Quickly," she said. "Do it well but quickly. No daydreaming."

"What would I dream of here?" I muttered. "Except to escape." I thought I saw her smile.

The bathroom was in the same terrible condition I had found it in when I first tried to clean Sophia's suite. This time, I did work faster, and I didn't spend any time scrubbing down the shower stall or the floors. I turned my attention to her bedroom instead and began scooping up clothing and hanging things up in her closet. For a few moments, I was in a daze. I couldn't believe how many blouses, skirts, pairs of pants, drawers of socks, undergarments, and shoes she possessed. There was more in this closet than in most stores in my Mexican village or even the bigger nearby villages.

Once the clothing was picked up, I turned to the bedding. When I took off the blanket, I was shocked to see the bloodstains on the sheet. Didn't she know she was going to have a period or remember she was having one? Didn't she care? For a moment, it nauseated me, and then I quickly ripped off the sheet. To my surprise, there was a rubber cover over the mattress. It was as if she was known to pee in her sleep as an infant might. I washed it down quickly, dried it, and put on a new sheet and new pillow cases. I was just finishing up when Señora Rosario came by to tell me I had ten minutes to go get myself some breakfast before I had to meet Señor Baker in the library.

She showed me where to put all the dirty laundry, and I hurried down to the kitchen. Laughter coming from the dining room made me pause. I glanced in and saw my aunt and her guest, the young man named Travis, at the table sipping their coffee. My aunt was still wearing her negligee under her red silk robe. The robe was open, and she was leaning so close to Travis their lips were just touching. She suddenly stopped and turned to the doorway, where she saw me gaping.

"How dare you spy on me!" she screamed. Travis laughed. "Get back to work!"

Her shouts brought Señora Rosario downstairs quickly. She ordered me into the kitchen, shooing me with her hands. Terrified, I hurried. Both Señor Herrera and Inez stared in amazement.

"What happened now?" Inez asked me, and I told her I had done nothing more than just glance into the dining room at Señora Dallas and her guest. When I said he looked young enough to be her son, she smiled at Señor Herrera, who laughed and set out a bowl of oatmeal for me with a glass of juice and a cup of coffee.

"Sit," he said, pointing to the chair by the kitchen table. "Eat."

I sat and started, feeling Señora Rosario behind me, rushing me along with her hot, condemning eyes.

"Señora Dallas does not want you to be late for your English-speaking lessons," she said.

I gobbled down my oatmeal.

"Let the girl eat," Señor Herrera said. "She's wolfing it down like a dog."

"You want to go tell Señora Dallas that?" she fired back at him. Now that I thought about it, I was surprised they all were speaking Spanish rather than English. Why wasn't my aunt insisting they speak English if she was demanding it so of me? They were all able to speak English.

He made a face and turned back to his preparations for lunch and dinner.

Inez left to start cleaning the house, every room except Sophia's. I was to be the fortunate one as far as that suite was concerned.

I gulped my juice and stood up.

"Where is the library?" I asked Señora Rosario. I really hadn't had much of a tour of the house.

"This way," she said. I followed her out, glancing back at Señor Herrera, who threw me a comforting smile.

As we walked down the hallway, I noted that practically all of the available wall space was covered with paintings or pictures. There were many pictures of my aunt taken with people I would later learn were celebrities, politicians, or simply very, very wealthy businessmen. In time, I also would learn that many officers of charities would court her to have her name on their programs.

When I reached the library, I saw a table filled with trophies and awards given to her by this charity or that. Except for a half-dozen pictures and the large picture of her with her husband in the library above the fireplace, there was no other evidence of her husband in the house as far as I had seen. There were no trophies or plaques with his name on them. Wasn't he as generous, or did she simply remove anything that didn't favor her solely? In every picture I did see, he looked as if he could have been her father.

Señor Baker was sitting behind the desk in the library when we arrived. He started to smile and stopped the moment I walked through the door.

"Where are the books I gave you?" he demanded.

"Back in my room," I said.

"Run, don't walk," he ordered. "Go!" he said, waving his hand at me.

I glanced at Señora Rosario who gave me a look of chastisement and then turned and hurried down the hallway. I didn't actually run until I was out of the house. By the time I returned, I was gasping as much out of fear as anything. With all that had happened, I had completely forgotten about the books. I never even opened one.

"How could you forget your books?" Señor Baker practically shouted at me when I returned to the library. Señora Rosario was gone. "Haven't you opened any and started to read?"

I shook my head. "I have not yet had the time."

"Haven't had time? Don't you want to get to go to

school? Don't you want Señora Dallas to like you? Well?"

"*Sí*," I said, choking back my tears.

"*Sí, sí* . . . no more *sí*. Say yes or no, understand? Yes or no."

"S . . . yes," I said.

"How good is your memory?" he asked, and came around the desk. "Let's find out. Give me the English words for what I showed you."

I recited the words.

"That's good," he said. "You'll make me look good," he added. He told me to sit on the long, dark brown leather sofa. He sat beside me and opened my book. "Let's begin," he said, and I started to read the Spanish and struggle with the English translations, with him correcting me. He was so close that I could feel his breath on my neck. He had a sour mouth odor that came from coffee and cigarettes.

Suddenly, *mi tía* Isabela was in the doorway. She was still in her robe, but she was alone.

"Well?" she asked. "What is your prediction about her ability to learn? Should I bother wasting your time and my money?"

"Oh, she's a good student," he told her, looked at me, smiled, and repeated in Spanish what he had said. "But with her spending so much time on housework and me traveling back and forth, it's going to take a while, Isabela. She's very distracted concentrating on pleasing you here. There's so much competing for her attention. She hardly has time to study and read. I can't perform miracles."

"What do you suggest, John?" she asked him, smirking.

He shrugged and looked at me again. "I could do wonders with her in two weeks if . . ."

"If what, John?"

"Well, I favor the Helen Keller method when it comes to a situation like this," he said. "Someone who can't speak our language, comes from a place that's like another planet, someone like her," he said, turning to me and nodding, "is really like someone deaf, dumb, and blind. She needs to be dependent on me to learn quickly. She then learns out of the need to survive as much as anything, but that obviously speeds things up. Unless you don't mind how long it takes, of course."

"Of course, I mind it. Do you think I want her here like this forever?" she snapped back at him. "Look at how much she has embarrassed me just in the past twenty-four hours. My sister probably got herself killed deliberately just to make me suffer."

Señor Baker smiled.

"Go on, laugh. You don't know what I went through before I escaped that world."

He shrugged again. I wished I understood more of what they were saying. I did understand that she was complaining about me. I was struggling with the few words I understood. Was all this anger caused by my forgetting my books? Señor Baker turned to me.

"Then I'm not proposing anything you'll think terribly unfair or cruel."

She stared at me, making me feel uncomfortable.

"If you feel her grandmother wouldn't approve . . ." he continued.

"I don't care what anyone back in Mexico thinks!" she cried.

He nodded. "Delia," he began in Spanish, "how would

you like to stay with me for a while and just spend all day and night learning how to speak English? No more housework for now."

I looked at my aunt and then at him and then at my aunt and shook my head. I didn't fully understand yet, but staying with him? Did that mean moving into his house?

"She doesn't like the idea," my aunt said, smiling coolly. "No?" she asked me, her smile still unnerving.

"No, *por favor*," I said.

"No, please," Señor Baker corrected. "Please. Say please."

"Please."

"See?" he told my aunt. "Imagine my being able to do that day and night for two weeks."

"Yes," she said. "I see what you mean. You're right. Besides, I'm not interested in what she wants and doesn't want. She's already opened her big mouth and told Edward she's his cousin." She glared at me. "After I specifically said not to mention that to anyone!"

"It had to come out sooner or later, Isabela," Señor Baker said.

"Later would have been better. Mrs. Rosario!" she screamed. She went to the doorway.

I looked at Señor Baker. He was staring at me strangely. It made me feel naked.

"*Todo será bien,*" he said, trying to calm me down, assuring me that all was going to be just fine.

I looked at my aunt again. She shouted once more for Señora Rosario, who came hurrying down the hallway.

What did he mean, everything would be fine? What was happening?

My aunt spoke quickly to Señora Rosario and then turned back to Señor Baker.

"However, now that I think of it, it might attract too much unnecessary attention if you return to your condo, John."

"What do you suggest?"

"I have that house for rent in Indio. It's furnished. Take her up there for two weeks. No one in that neighborhood will notice or care. Half the people living up there were probably brought here last night by a coyote. I will expect that she'll be quite different when you return," she added in a threatening tone.

"Oh, she'll be like brand new," he said, looking at me and smiling. "She'll be a Mexican American and not just a Mexican."

"Good," my aunt said. "Do you want Mrs. Rosario to go along to help you set up?"

"Oh, no," he said. "We don't want her to have anyone near her who can speak Spanish. That's the point. She will need to remember what I teach her to survive."

"You'll have to keep her under lock and key up there, then, John."

"No problem," he said, and smiled at me again. "It'll be like *My Fair Lady*. I'll be Professor Higgins."

"Yes, only don't expect her to turn into Audrey Hepburn, John."

"She'll come damn close to it," he vowed.

My aunt laughed.

What was going on? They were speaking too quickly, and the words I caught and understood just confused me.

Mi tía Isabela turned to Señora Rosario and began explaining everything. She told her to explain it all to me in Spanish. For a moment, Señora Rosario looked as if she was going to disobey her. My aunt widened her eyes, and Señora Rosario turned to me.

"Señora Dallas and Señor Baker think it's going to take you too long to learn English here while you spend so much time helping with housework. Señora Dallas wants you to learn faster and get to school."

I nodded. That didn't sound so bad. No more housework.

"Señora Dallas and Señor Baker think it will be better for you if you are somewhere where no one speaks Spanish so you will have to learn English quickly."

"Where?" I asked. "*Dónde*?" Were they talking about me living in his house again?

"Señora Dallas owns many properties. She has a house in Indio that you and Señor Baker will use. It's not that far away from here."

"Only me and Señor Baker?" I turned to him. He was smiling at me gleefully. I felt my heart begin to thump. I shook my head.

"Don't you dare shake your head!" *mi tía* Isabela screamed at me. "Tell her if she doesn't do what I tell her to do, I will contact her grandmother and let her grandmother know how disrespectful and disobedient she is." She smiled, folded her arms under her breasts, and stood straighter. "Tell her I will stop sending her grandmother money to help her survive."

Señora Rosario told me, and I looked up with surprise. Aunt Isabela was sending money to my grandmother?

"That's right, Delia. I am sending her money now," she told me in English. "She's an old, old lady. She can't work hard enough to keep her house and herself alive. Without my help, she'll be out in the street. Tell her what I said, and ask her if she would like that."

Mrs. Rosario translated.

"Well?" my aunt demanded, bringing her hands to her hips and stepping closer to me. "Are you going to do what I want you to do or not? Yes or no? I have no more time to waste. Tell her!"

Señora Rosario told me.

The tears broke free from the corners of my eyes. I couldn't imagine *mi abuela* Anabela left to live on the street. Her friends wouldn't permit it, but I also knew she was too proud to accept charity. I lowered my head and nodded.

"Good. Get her miserable things together," my aunt told Señora Rosario. "Mr. Baker has wasted enough time. Bring her back in two weeks speaking English well enough to get by, or I'll see to it that you're deported along with her," my aunt threatened him.

Señor Baker laughed, but whatever she had told him brought a little fear to his face, especially into his eyes.

"Don't worry. I know I'll be successful," he said. "We'll be successful," he told me in Spanish.

"Go on. Get her started!" my aunt ordered.

Señora Rosario returned to my room with me to make sure I hurriedly gathered my things. I put everything back into my little suitcase while she stood there looking very sorry. My tears flowed even more freely.

"I don't want to go with Señor Baker," I told her. "I don't like him."

She bit down on her lower lip as if she was stopping herself from saying something she would regret and then shook her head.

"I'm sorry," she told me. "Do the best you can. It's what we all do. Come along."

I followed her to the front of the house, where Señor Baker waited in his car. He was all smiles, eager to help me with my suitcase. Then he opened the car door for me.

"*Adentro.* Get in," he said.

I got into his car, and he closed the door and got in behind the wheel.

"I'll start your lessons by identifying every part of the inside of the car," he told me, and then, as he touched something, he pronounced the English word for it. He asked me to repeat what he said and then touched the part again without speaking and asked me to identify it in English.

Despite my nervousness and fear, I was able to do it easily.

"See how easy it can be when we work like this?" he said loudly enough for Señora Rosario to hear. He nodded and smiled at her, but she just stared at us. "That was so simple. You liked that, didn't you?" he asked me.

"*Sí.*"

"Yes."

"Yes."

"Okay," he said, starting the engine. "We'll have a little tour of the desert. We'll stop and get groceries, and I'll teach you words all along the way. It will be good. You'll see. I've gotten you out of slave labor here, too," he said loudly, and nodded at the house and Señora Rosario, who continued to stand there on the steps watching us. She grimaced and shook her head slightly.

"The housework you will have with me will be nothing in comparison with what they made you do here," he said, leaning over to whisper, "and you won't have to put up with that spoiled brat, Sophia. I'm the only spoiled brat in your life now." He laughed.

"Now, here's another good idea," he said. "I'll teach

you a song that will teach you numbers in English. Ready? It starts like this: *One hundred bottles of beer on the wall, one hundred bottles of beer. If one of the bottles should happen to fall, ninety-nine bottles of beer on the wall.* See? Sing along. Come on," he said as he drove away from the house.

I looked back at Señora Rosario and saw her shake her head again and turn to go back inside. Despite what Señor Baker said and how I had been treated, I was not happy about leaving with him. We continued down the long driveway, past the beautiful flowers and hedges, the statues and fountains.

"Sing what I sing," he ordered.

I did.

"Louder. Be happy, energetic. You're off to begin a new life. *Ninety-seven bottles of beer on the wall . . .*"

The gate opened for us, and I looked back one more time as Señor Baker continued to sing and forced me to sing along with him.

Now I don't even have a phantom family, I thought.

Why should I care what awaited me when we reached zero bottles of beer on the wall?

7

Newlyweds

As he had promised, along the way, we stopped at a supermarket at the center of a big shopping mall. Señor Baker explained that we had to get basic necessities and enough food to keep us for at least a week or so. He said my aunt told him that all of the kitchen utensils were there, dishes and glassware, too. A vacuum cleaner, pails and mops, brooms and rags for cleaning were in the pantry. As she had said, it was a house she usually rented out. From the way Señor Baker spoke, it sounded as if *mi tía* Isabela owned many properties. Señor Baker told me *mi tía* Isabela's husband had been very smart about his real estate investments.

"You should be very grateful," he said. "Your aunt is making a big investment in you. She's paying me a lot of money to teach you English quickly."

He looked at me to see if I appreciated what *mi tía* was doing for me, but it didn't feel as if she was helping me. It felt more as if she was looking for a way to get rid of me.

"Your aunt is paying for everything we need and buy, so choose whatever you like to eat," he said. When we entered the supermarket, he said, "Go on. Get anything you want, just like a kid turned loose in a candy store."

He gave me a cart to push and fill up. I had never seen a supermarket as big as this one. There were so many choices of every food imaginable. I *was* like a child turned loose in a candy store. How did anyone know what to choose? Pictures on boxes told me what many things were, but many were difficult to understand.

Señor Baker followed along and explained things, translating them for me and telling me something about everything. I had to admit it was very educational. He actually paused to tell someone I was his student.

"Nothing like hands-on, day-to-day life to help someone learn a language fast," he explained to a woman who seemed to know him. "Right, Delia?" he asked me. He repeated what he had said in Spanish quickly, and I nodded. It did sound right.

Maybe what he was doing would be good, I thought hopefully. Maybe he wasn't as terrible a man as I imagined he might be. He was a teacher, and when I thought of a teacher, I thought of Señora Cuevas. Like her, surely, he had to have some pride in his students and his accomplishments. If I learned English well and quickly, he would be successful, and I had no doubt that *mi tía* Isabela was paying him well and might even give him some sort of bonus.

I felt myself relax and became more and more interested in the choices of cereals, rices, beans, and breads. The sight of the meat and fish counters was overwhelming. There was so much. This was truly what I was told to expect in America.

"Are you a good cook?" he asked me.

I explained how I had learned many dishes from *mi abuela* Anabela. When I described some, he made sure we had everything we needed to prepare them. Every item I chose he identified in English and had me repeat. As we moved about the supermarket, he would nod at people and things, saying the English words. "That woman is wearing a blue hat," he would say, or "That man is here with his son." Whatever he said, he had me repeat and then explained and had me repeat again.

"You see," he said, holding out his arms, "this way, the world is our classroom. Now, do you understand why I wanted to take you out of your aunt's home and away from all of that distracting housework?"

I had to admit I did understand, although I still felt very nervous and uncomfortable about it.

Before we reached the cashier to get ourselves checked out, he made me go through the entire cart of food, calling each item by its English name, correcting my pronunciation.

When the food we bought was checked out, he reviewed the numbers on the bill, and when we rolled the cart out of the supermarket, he stopped, turned to me, and asked in English, "Where do you want to go now?"

"Where?" The question seemed so obvious I thought I was misunderstanding him. "*Dónde?*"

"No, no, only in English. Where?" he asked again.

I shrugged.

To the car, I thought. Where else?

I said so, and he smiled. "That's it. Think in English. Say to the car," he commanded, and I did.

In fact, everything we did, every move we made, he described in English and had me repeat.

"We are loading the groceries into the car's trunk. This is a trunk. I am opening the car door for you. This is where the passenger sits. The passenger. Repeat it all," he told me, and I did. I was beginning to feel like a big parrot. He corrected my pronunciation and made me repeat the words until he was satisfied.

Even after he started the car and drove out of the parking lot, he continued identifying and describing as much as possible along the way, each time having me repeat the words, and then, if we saw another similar thing, he would point to it and ask me to identify it in English. From the way he was reacting, I thought I was doing very well.

At one point, he began to review what he called idioms, expressions that were common.

"Every morning when you wake up, you say?"

"Good morning."

"And?"

"How are you today?"

"What kind of a day is it?"

"It's a sunny day."

On and on we went, driving and talking. He would recite, and I would repeat. Then he surprised me by asking me to tell him what I was thinking, using as many English words as I could. I didn't know what to say, but I managed, "The car is long."

"You don't mean the car. You mean the ride in the car," he corrected. "It's not that long," he added. "Well, maybe because of all these lights and the traffic. Too many cars," he said, pointing to the automobiles in front of us.

Finally, we turned down a side road and passed some

smaller houses, and then we turned onto another road and stopped in front of a tan stucco house not much bigger than *mi casa* back in Mexico. This had a thin light blue gate around it, and there was a nice lawn, but there wasn't much land. A rim of low mountains loomed behind it. It reminded me of places in Mexico. It was truly as if I had closed my eyes for a while, opened them, and found myself back home. The terrain was that similar. It gave me pangs of sadness and homesickness. How I missed Abuela Anabela.

Señor Baker had to get out to open the gate to the short, narrow driveway. There was no garage, just a carport. He identified it in English and again narrated every little thing we did and what we saw and touched. There was a side entrance to the house from the carport. He took out the keys and opened it, reciting the words for *key, door, open, unlock.* As with everything else, he made me repeat and corrected my pronunciation.

The door opened right into the small kitchen. There was a preparation table and a small sink beside it at the center. The appliances looked old and used, and the floor was covered in a dull, light brown, scuffed linoleum. We brought in the groceries and set them on the table. As he took things out of the bags, I had to identify them in English again. If I missed one, he put it back into the bag. He went on to another item and returned to the one I missed until I recalled it and pronounced it adequately. He said until I did, he wouldn't take it out, and if I didn't, he would never take it out. I thought he was being silly, but he looked very serious, so I concentrated hard until I got it right.

Once everything was put away, he went through the kitchen, identifying everything in English and having me repeat the words. He also made me put some words together, such as "I am putting the dishes in the sink." Then he would ask me, "Where did you put the dishes?" and I would reply. My confidence grew. Maybe this was a very good idea, I continued to tell myself.

We walked through the living room. The gray rug looked tired and worn and in need of a good vacuuming. The furniture didn't look much better. The arms of chairs and the sofa were scratched, and the pillows looked as if they needed a good airing. Gazing about at the coffee-colored walls, I saw there were no pictures anywhere, but there were nails where pictures had been hung.

As in the kitchen, he reviewed the English words for everything in the living room and again put them into sentences and questions. "Where will you sit?" "Sofa." "What's on the floor by the sofa?" "A rug." He looked very pleased with how I was doing.

"Your aunt is going to be amazed," he told me, and explained what he meant by *amazed*. "It's good to know a few words that mean almost the same thing," he explained. "We call those words synonyms. Words that mean the opposite are antonyms. Let's try it. What's a word for the opposite of warm?"

I told him, "Cold."

"Great!" he said. It was more like a game now. I smiled. I'm going to be all right, I thought. This will be fine.

He tried the television set. It received only a few local stations. The pictures came in cloudy and powdery, which upset him.

"No damn cable hookup," he muttered, and then turned to me and explained what that meant.

I told him we had a much smaller television set with

even worse reception in Mexico, but there were places we went to watch television, and one place had a satellite receiver.

"At least we have an old video player here," he said, pointing to something under the set, and again explained what that meant. Of course, I had heard of it and seen them.

"I'm going to pick up some movies for you to watch repeatedly, because you could learn a lot more English that way," he said. He said he knew someone who learned Spanish that way.

"He watched one movie three hundred times if he watched it once," he said.

That was how I had learned most of the English I knew. This would be more fun than just reading an English textbook.

We continued through the small house, pausing at the one bathroom. Although it was bigger than the one I shared back at *mi tía* Isabela's estate, it didn't look all that much nicer. There was no shower stall, just a tub and a shower with a plastic curtain. The bathroom did have a large window, however, which made it brighter but also clearly showed the stains in the floors, walls, sink, and toilet.

"You'll have to do some cleaning here," he said. He described the words *wash, rinse, scrub, polish,* and *mop.* I didn't think it would take much work, because it was nowhere as large a bathroom as Sophia's.

I told him that, and I told him what a mess her bathroom and her suite were.

"I know," he said. "She's as spoiled a brat as you could find anywhere in the world. I heard what she did to you in her shower, but don't worry. I can tell already. You're much smarter than she is," he said.

His compliment made me blush.

"Such a sweet, innocent face," he said, touching my cheek. "You're a fresh breeze, believe me. I love innocence," he added. "It's pure."

He looked at me more intensely now, and my heart seemed to trip over itself. Then he quickly smiled again and continued our tour of the house.

We inspected the two bedrooms, one with a king-size bed and one with two double beds. He checked the closets in the room and the one in the hallway.

"Damn. Your aunt forgot about some other basic things," he said.

I shook my head, not understanding, and he explained that *mi tía* Isabela had sent us up here without telling him that we needed towels, washcloths, sheets, pillows, and pillow cases. At the supermarket, we had bought what I would need to start cleaning the small house.

"Now I'll have to return to the shopping center," he told me. "We'll bring in our suitcases first. You unpack your things and start cleaning up the house. Start with the kitchen, because we're going to have our first dinner here."

He looked around and nodded.

"The place will work for us. We'll be fine here," he told me, his voice insistent. Then he suddenly smiled the smile of someone who had just had a lightbulb go on in his head.

"This is called setting up a home. Newlyweds do it," he told me. "You and I are like newlyweds. That will help you learn faster, and it will be more fun pretending to be newlyweds."

The word threw me. I knew *wedding*, but *new wedding*? How could there be a wedding here? I asked him.

"No, we're not having a wedding here. It's like we already had the wedding," he explained. "That's it. We'll be like a bride and groom. Everything will be easier to explain that way."

Again, I shook my head. How could we be like a bride and groom? And why would that make it easier?

"Don't worry," he said when I asked, and then he went into a brief explanation of the word *worry*. "Your aunt is worried you won't learn English well enough to attend school and you will be a big problem for her. We'll show her she has nothing to worry about, right?"

He stepped up to me, put his hands on my upper arms, and held me while he smiled.

"Right, Señora Baker?" he asked.

I pulled my head back. Señora Baker? Why was he calling me Señora Baker?

"We're newlyweds, remember? That means you are Señora Baker, and I'm your husband."

He kissed me on the forehead, then turned to leave and paused in the doorway.

"Put your suitcase in the bigger bedroom," he said in Spanish, and then he said it again in English and had me repeat the words *suitcase, bigger,* and *bedroom.* "No need to use two bedrooms. Our work will take all day and all night. We'll be inseparable for these few weeks." He explained it in Spanish, and then he stopped smiling and added that in a few days, he would stop listening to my questions if I didn't try to use the English words first.

"It will be as if I don't hear you," he said. "If the house caught on fire and you didn't say *fire,* I would not hear you, and we'd burn up with it," he told me.

Again, I thought that was silly and just meant to scare me, but he had no humor in his face when he said it or right afterward. In fact, his eyes burned with seriousness.

"I'm not going to fail here," he told me in Spanish. "Which means you'll do whatever I tell you to do and learn quickly, or else. *Entiende*? Well? *Entiende*?"

"*Sí*," I said. His mood changed so quickly I was afraid to say anything else. There was much here I did not understand.

"Not *sí*, damn it. Yes, yes. Say yes."

"Yes," I repeated.

"Get your things into the drawers in the bedroom," he ordered. "*Comprende*? You know what that means?"

"Yes."

"Good. Let's get organized. C'mon." He beckoned.

I followed him, took my suitcase, and watched him back out.

"Get started!" he shouted at me. "Clean the kitchen, and start on our first dinner as newlyweds." He laughed as he turned the car around and headed away to buy whatever else we needed.

I clung to my suitcase.

The world around me looked desolate. I thought I had reached the bottom of the pit of loneliness at my aunt's house, but my descent into hell apparently went deeper yet. I had the urge to start down the road in the direction opposite where he had gone, but where would that take me?

Back in Mexico, my grandmother was full of hope for my new future. It comforted her to know I was in the United States and exposed to so much more opportunity. Surely, if she saw me now, standing in the carport of this small, very simple house, confused and lost, her fragile heart would collapse inside her chest, and I'd be going to another funeral, only I would be standing there at her grave and wondering if I could have prevented her death by simply swallowing my fear and muddling my way through this hard time. I had to find the same grit and strength in myself that she had. As she often told me, "*No hay dolor de que el alma no puede levantarse en tres días.* There is no sorrow the soul can't rise from in three days."

Maybe, once I did learn English well enough, my aunt wouldn't be as ashamed of me, and she would give me a place in the family, and I would give my grandmother the happiness she needed to take with her to her final rest. She would die with a smile on her face instead of a grim expression of defeat.

I owed her that much.

Pulling myself up with new determination, I went into the house and put my things away. Then I started cleaning the kitchen, finding the pots and pans, and beginning the dinner, silently reviewing every English word Señor Baker had just taught me about the kitchen. Losing myself in the preparation of food reminded me of *mi abuela* Anabela losing herself in food preparation to prepare for the crowd of mourners.

Work was truly the raft upon which we floated in this sea of sadness. It kept us from drowning. It was all we had to cling to, and it kept us from thinking about our dire situations. No wonder my people were out there in the fields, churning away at their chores, looking almost grateful there was at least that.

I smiled to myself, recalling another one of *mi abuela* Anabela's *dichos* when we had to work hard: "*La pereza viaja tan lentamente que la pobreza no tarda en alcanzarla.* Laziness travels so slowly that poverty soon catches up."

Back in my small village, we were always one step ahead of poverty.

A little more than an hour later, I heard Señor Baker drive into the carport. He was whistling as he entered the house, his arms full of some of what he had purchased.

"There is more to bring in, Señora Baker," he said. "Look in the back of the car. In what?"

"The trunk," I said.

"Good. Go on."

I wiped my hands on a dish towel and went out to see. There was a blanket in a plastic wrap and two pillows. He waited for me in the short hallway and directed me into the larger bedroom.

"Make the bed," he said. "I'll put everything else away."

"Why are we having only one bed?" I asked. "Aren't you staying here, too?"

He smiled. "Of course. Even in your sleep, you will be learning."

"In my sleep? How can I learn in my sleep?"

"Don't worry about it," he said sharply. "Just do what I tell you. Your aunt has put me in charge, hasn't she? Show respect."

I felt my face brighten. His outburst of anger surprised and frightened me. I turned away quickly and went to make the bed. When I returned to the kitchen, he was looking at the food preparations and smiling.

"This all looks and smells delicious, Señora Baker," he told me, and then he went about the kitchen making me identify everything in English. He was happy about my retention. "This is working," he said, sounding surprised at his own idea. "This is really going to impress Isabela. Just continue with the dinner preparations, but repeat what I tell you," he ordered. I did as he asked.

He translated every move we made and everything we touched in the kitchen and at the table. He made me recite repeatedly until he was satisfied with my pronunciations.

"Every day, I will test you on the things I have taught you the day and the night before," he said. "When I think you are ready, I will ask you not to speak in *español,* only in *inglés,* understand? If you make a mistake, you will have to pay for it."

"Pay for it? I have no money."

He laughed. "There are other ways to pay for things, Delia. Everyone knows that. Especially women," he added, and laughed.

I was afraid to ask him any more questions about it.

"Look what I bought you, Señora Baker," he said after we had eaten our dinner and I was cleaning up the kitchen. He showed me a video. "It's one of my own movies, from my own collection. There are many good words to learn in English, words you will have to know when you are out there in the world meeting boys and men. If you don't understand these words, you will be at a big disadvantage, and you don't want to be at any disadvantage when it comes to young men, Delia."

I stared at the video box. There was a picture of a man wearing the skimpiest pair of underwear and a woman with her back to him leaning against him. She was obviously naked. I did not understand the title, *Bubbles, Bangles, and Bedsheets,* even after he translated each word.

"You'll figure it out after a while," he told me. "Finish up here, and we'll watch our movie."

It all made me very nervous, especially his calling me

Señora Baker. My fingers trembled around the dishes, and I dropped one. It shattered on the floor, sending shards everywhere. He came rushing back.

"What's going on? Damn it," he said. "We can't break things here. Your aunt will not be pleased."

I started to cry. Were these dishes expensive?

"Get it all cleaned up," he said. "And you'd better not break another thing," he warned. When he spoke, I smelled whiskey on his breath.

I hurried to get the broom. He kept calling to me from the living room, telling me he was getting tired of waiting for me. He wanted to start his movie. I moved slowly, hesitant, my instincts telling me that I was falling deeper and deeper into some sort of danger. Finally, I had nothing more to do and had to go to the living room.

"It's about time. Do you people always work so slowly?" he asked me. "Everything's left for *mañana, mañana.* Well, there is no more *mañana.* You understand?" Before I could answer, he smiled and said, "Of course, there are some things you should do slowly." His smile confused me. "Sit," he said, patting the place beside him on the sofa. I saw he had a bottle of whiskey on the table and a glass with some in it.

I sat, and he turned on the television and then the video player. His movie began, and almost immediately, a man and a woman undressed each other. He sipped his whiskey and began to translate what they were saying to each other, but it didn't make sense to me. Clothes were "peeled off." She wanted him to "raise her temperature." He wanted her to "pump him up."

Soon they weren't talking. They were just moaning and groaning, and what they were doing shocked and embarrassed me. He stopped the video and told me he was rewinding it to teach me the words again. This was why a video was good for learning language.

"You can go over and over it until you learn the words perfectly," he said, but he spent more time on the sections where they were doing nothing but moaning and groaning.

"You ever do that?" he asked me. He finished his whiskey and poured himself some more.

I shook my head, my eyes wide. He laughed.

"Nothing's wrong with doing that," he said. "It's how we get to know each other better."

The man in the movie was soon with another woman, doing the same things and saying the same things. I became more and more uncomfortable. I saw that Señor Baker was getting more and more agitated. His face reddened, and beads of sweat appeared on his forehead. If he was so uncomfortable watching this with me, too, why didn't he stop it?

"I know you like watching this," he told me instead. He sneered. "All girls your age love watching these movies."

I hadn't seen many movies, but none of them was anything like this.

"No," I told him. "I don't like it."

"Sure you do. You're just being coy," he said, and went into a long explanation about the word *coy*. He said it was a natural part of being a woman. Women pretended they didn't want the same things a man wanted, but they do, he insisted. "It's all right. You can be coy," he said.

I shook my head. Now that I understood what it meant, I wanted him to know I wasn't being coy, but he wouldn't believe me.

Suddenly, he grew angry and shut off the television.

"It's time you took your bath," he told me. "I want you to take a bath every night. I like my girls to be clean and smell sweet, fresh, and innocent. Go on," he urged.

He jumped from one mood to another the way a little girl would jump from one square to another in a game of hopscotch. I hurried away from him. I took out my nightgown and my slippers and went to the bathroom with my things. I heard him turn on the television set again and start watching something else.

I locked the bathroom door and ran my bath. He had bought some bath oils and soaps and new towels and washcloths. While the water flowed into the tub, I sat on the toilet seat and wondered what would happen to me next and what I should do. I had learned a lot of new words, stuffed many new things into my head, but I was so frightened and confused now that everything was jumbled. I would probably not do well on any test he gave me, and then what would he do? What did he mean by saying I would pay for things without money?

When the tub was filled enough, I got undressed and stepped into the water. I was barely in it a minute before I heard him try the door.

"Why did you lock the door?" he screamed. He rattled it hard. "You never lock a door in this house. I lock the doors in this house! Open this door now," he demanded.

"I am in the bathtub," I cried.

He was quiet a moment.

"You unlock this door as soon as you're out!" he shouted. "Don't dry yourself completely first. First, open this door. Understand?"

"*Sí,*" I said, holding my breath.

"Not *sí,* yes. Yes!" he screamed.

"Yes."

"From this moment on, every time you use a Spanish word instead of the English word I taught you, you will be penalized," he declared.

I listened hard and thought he had left, but suddenly, he pounded the door with his fist once.

"Just wash yourself and get out!" he screamed.

I unplugged the bathtub and reached for one of the towels. As quickly as I could, I dried myself enough to put on my nightgown.

He started to pound on the door again, so I unlocked it. He stood there looking in at me.

"I thought I told you not to dry yourself completely," he said.

"I had to so I could put on my nightgown."

"I wanted you to wait," he said. "You don't listen well. You're going to be here a lot longer than necessary, because you don't listen," he warned me, waving his forefinger in my face. He paused and looked at me. His eyes were glassy, his mouth twisted like someone who had just had a stroke. "Clean up after yourself in here, and get to the bedroom," he said. Then he left, mumbling to himself.

I let out a breath that was locked in my chest and began to wipe off the tub. I brushed my teeth, folded the wet towel, and left the bathroom. I could hear the television still going. He didn't come out of the living room. Perhaps he was going to sleep in there after all, I thought, and went to the bedroom. I got down on my knees and said my prayers. My heart was still thumping. I was eager to get to sleep and end this strange and difficult day, but moments after I had gotten into the bed, he came to the doorway and flipped on the lights.

"No, no, no," he said. "We have work to do yet, Delia. You don't go to sleep so fast."

"What work?"

"Work. Get up!" he commanded. "Now!"

I lowered the blanket, sat up, got my feet into my slippers, and stood up. What work was left to do? He entered the bedroom and stood before me.

"All right. At the end of every day, we test you on what you've learned that day. Let's begin with the parts of the car I taught you before we left your aunt's home. In English. What did I describe? Go on."

I recited every word he had told me, visualizing it all and amazing even myself. Perhaps the fear made my memory stronger and keener. I saw the surprise in his face.

"Very good," he said, and then began a very fast list of Spanish words, requiring me to translate. If I hesitated, he screamed the word in my face. I started to cry, and he demanded I stop.

"You made five mistakes in the last minute," he said. "You must be penalized."

"Penalized?"

"Remember? You must pay. Turn around," he ordered. "Go on. Turn around, bend over, and put your hands on the bed. Do it, or I'll add to the punishment."

I felt blood drain down to my feet.

His breath was all whiskey now, too, and I had seen what whiskey could do to a man.

I wasn't forgetting that my parents were killed by an *hombre borracho,* either. I turned and did what he said. As soon as I did, I felt him lifting my nightgown to my waist. For a moment, he did nothing else. I thought that would be it, and then he slapped me on my rear so hard and sharply that I fell forward, and tears immediately came into my eyes. Before I could cry out, he slapped me again and again. He did it five times.

"Five for five mistakes," he said, his hand on my lower back, his weight on me holding me down. I was crying openly now, sobbing and moaning. "You should say thank you. Thank you, not *gracias*. Go on."

"Thank you," I muttered between sobs.

"Right, good."

He lifted his hand off my lower back, but I was afraid to turn around. I heard him walk around the bed. He sat and began to undress, mumbling to himself. He had drunk too much, I thought. He was actually wobbling.

Slowly, I slid back and off the bed.

"Go to sleep," I heard him order. "I'm better in the morning. In the morning, Señora Baker." He laughed.

I raised myself and peered over the bed at him. He was on his back, stark naked. Cautiously, so as not to wake him, I edged toward the bedroom doorway. I was actually crawling on all fours toward the door, praying and crawling. I couldn't keep my sobbing and gasping subdued. The stinging pain wasn't as terrible as the terror raging through my body. I was nearly to the door and about to stand up, when I saw him walk to it and slam it closed. He looked down at me.

"That's not a very ladylike way to behave, Señora Baker," he said, smiling. He reached down and grasped my hair, pulling me up. "Get back into bed," he told me, and shoved me toward it.

Then he went to his pants, took off his belt, and brought it to the bed.

"Lie down," he ordered. "On your back."

I gazed at the belt in his hand and at his face. Was he

going to beat me? I started to shake my head when he raised his hand, and I cowered.

"In the bed!" he screamed.

I did what he said, and then he got into the bed, wrapped the belt around his thigh and around mine, and buckled it. He ran his hand down my shoulder, over my arm, and around and over my breasts. He lingered there, and then he went down to my stomach before lying back himself.

"Good night, Señora Baker," he said. "Well? What do you say? Say it!"

"Good night," I said through my gasps.

He closed his eyes and mumbled to himself. I stared into the darkness. The tight belt made it impossible for me to turn away or even think about getting up again. I didn't want him to wake up. I tried even not to breathe too loudly, but what would happen to me in the morning?

8

Rescue

My eyelids grew heavier and heavier, but I was too frightened to let myself fall asleep. Soon, I heard Señor Baker snoring. I was happy he had passed out, but all I could think about was what would happen to me the moment he woke. Gathering my courage, I moved in tiny increments until I was just about sitting up. Then I felt for the belt buckle. Twice he stopped snoring, and I froze, but he didn't open his eyes.

Our sheer curtained windows did little to keep out the moonlight that streamed through like a giant flashlight. It helped me see what I was doing, but if he opened his eyes, he would see what I was doing, too, I thought. *Please keep him asleep,* I prayed.

My fingers trembled around the buckle, but I worked as carefully as I could until I managed to loosen the belt. I paused to see if he had felt it, if it had woken him. He grunted and moved, but he continued to snore. His lips were puffed out with the air he exhaled. I could still smell the whiskey on his breath, now combining with the sweat from his body. The odor nauseated me, and I had to keep swallowing to stop myself from gagging. Even a subdued gasp might wake him.

With as much care as *mi abuela* Anabela would take bandaging my small scrapes and cuts, I peeled the belt off my leg and carefully and slowly moved my leg away from his. He snorted again, and I paused and waited until his breathing was regular. Continuing to inch myself away, I finally slipped softly off the bed. I stood and waited to be sure he hadn't heard or woken, and then I moved with the silent grace of a ghost, scooping up my clothing and my shoes and tiptoeing out of the bedroom.

I dressed in the dark in the living room as quickly as I could, all the while listening keenly for any sounds of his awakening. In this deep silence, even the creaking in the floor seemed loud enough to alert him. I had no idea where I would go or what I would do. I knew only that I had to get away.

When I opened the side door, it creaked so loudly I was sure it would wake him. I hesitated, listened, heard nothing, and then stepped out and closed the door behind me softly. The moonlight was now my friend. It lit the road and showed me the way. No longer tiptoeing or trying to be quiet, I shot out of the carport and started to run down the road. I had no idea whether I should go left or right. I just ran to my left, crying and praying as I charged forward. I ran and ran until my side felt as if a giant hand had grabbed me and was squeezing. The pain reached my chest, and I stopped, gasping.

When I gathered enough breath and strength to continue, I walked on. I saw houses now on both sides of the road. Their windows were lit. It wasn't terribly late yet. I was sure people in their homes were still watching television or just talking together. I thought about stopping at one and asking for help, but what if they didn't speak or understand enough Spanish? Did I know enough English to get them to understand? Would the sight of me frighten them so they would slam the door in my face? What would I ask them to do for me, anyway? Send me back to Mexico? Maybe they would call the police, and the police would do that. I was not a citizen here. From what I understood, that could mean I would be deported unless my aunt stepped in to stop it, and why would she now?

I wanted to return home, of course, but I was also concerned about how *mi abuela* Anabela would react if I was sent back by police. She might blame herself for my being in this situation. The rosy future I was supposed to begin would be gone and with it her hopes for me. She was happy she was doing what my parents had wanted, providing a better life for me. This was far from being a better life.

What should I do? What should I want?

For a few moments, I stood there submerged in so much indecision, confusion, and fear, I felt as if I had gone close to the edge of the world. One more step forward, and I would fall off and sink forever into the darkness below.

Suddenly, I was awash in light. I turned and saw a car approaching very quickly. The driver slowed down as he drew closer to me.

It's surely Señor Baker, I thought. He woke up, saw I had left the house, and has come after me. It will even be worse for me now.

I started to run. The driver sounded his horn, and I

ran harder and faster until my legs weakened and I fell forward, catching myself with the palms of my hands but tumbling over twice and actually falling into a ditch. The car stopped. I moaned with the stinging pain in my palms and knees. As I struggled to stand, I saw the silhouette of the driver approaching. When he loomed over me, I screamed.

"Easy, easy," Edward said, reaching toward me. "It's okay. *Bueno, bueno.*"

He took my hand, but I didn't move. I stared at him in the moonlight. He seemed to have come out of nowhere. Had Señor Baker called my aunt, and had she sent Edward to get me and bring me back to him? Could he have gotten here so quickly? Whom could I trust?

"C'mon." He beckoned. "Come into my car. C'mon. I've come to help you. You'll be all right."

I stepped out of the ditch and slowly followed him to the car. He opened the door for me. I looked at him, still very confused and afraid.

"No quiero volver a Señor Baker," I told him. I'd rather die than return.

"No Señor Baker," he said. "No." He smiled and nodded. "It's okay," he said again. *"Bueno, bueno."*

I got into the car. He closed the door and hurried around to the driver's side. After he got in, he put on the lights inside the car and turned my hands to look at my palms. He shook his head, looked at my knees, and said, "We'll get you cleaned up." He made gestures with his hands to explain. I said nothing. I was still feeling too numb and frightened.

He reached down between us on the seat and picked up a sheet of paper.

"Casto wrote this *en español,*" he told me, moving

his hand over the paper, and then he began reading. His pronunciation was good enough for me to understand every word.

"I found out my mother had sent you off to live with Mr. Baker for a few weeks in one of our rented houses," he began. "I was very upset to learn this, and she and I had a bad argument. I told her I was upset with her for not telling me and my sister the truth about you, too. She claimed she was preparing to do that but first wanted to make you presentable.

"I told her it was a terrible way to treat you, and she shouldn't have sent you off with Mr. Baker. I know Mr. Baker. It was a very bad idea."

He paused and in English said, "I'm not surprised to see you running away." He saw I wasn't sure what he meant, so he pointed to me and said, "You." He made his fingers look like someone running and nodded. "*Bueno,*" he said.

"Señor Baker *no es bueno,*" he added, and I nodded. He pointed to the road in front of us. "*A mi casa,*" he said, put the paper down, and drove on.

He was taking me back. What would my aunt say? What would she do? She would be furious. Would she stop helping my grandmother?

"Don't worry," he said. He pointed to himself. "I *inglés* to you, and you *español* to me. *Comprende?*"

"*Sí,*" I said. "Yes. You make me speak English, and me make you speak Spanish."

"Right, right. Perfect. *Perfecto.*"

Soon after we drove onto a busy highway, he pulled into a shopping center and told me to wait in the car while he went into the big drugstore. Minutes later, he returned with a bottle of disinfectant and some Band-Aids.

He had tissues in his car. He poured the disinfectant on the tissues and started on the scrapes on my knees. Through gesture and facial expressions, he warned me it would hurt, sting, but he made such an exaggerated grimace I laughed, even though it did hurt. He carefully put on the bandages, too, and then he cleaned off my palms and put bandages on those scrapes as well.

"Okay?"

"*Gracias,*" I said. "Thank you."

"You're welcome."

"*De nada.*"

"Right, *de nada.* See? We are good teachers. *Bueno* teachers."

"*Profesores,*" I told him.

"Great. I'm a professor already."

He laughed and drove on. He tried to get me to relax and feel better, but all I could think of was what would happen now, what terrible new fate awaited at my aunt's home. He surprised me again by pulling into a restaurant parking lot and telling me to wait in the car. I started to explain that I wasn't hungry, but he waved me off and went into the restaurant. A good five minutes later, he came out with a young girl at his side. She was in a waitress uniform.

"This is Elena Jimenez," he told me. "You talk with her. *Habla* with Elena, okay?"

The girl got into the car on his side, and he got into the rear. She had short black hair and was very pretty. She must be his girlfriend, I thought.

"*Hola,*" she said.

"*Hola.*"

She explained that she was a good friend of Edward's from school, and he had asked her to speak with me and learn exactly what had just happened to me. She said Edward had gone to look for me when he found out where I was.

"When he got to the house, he found you were gone. When he saw Señor Baker, he was very, very worried about you and went looking for you. He knows something terrible happened." She looked back at him. "He won't tell me why he thinks that, but he thinks it. What happened?"

I looked back at him, too, and he nodded, pointing to Elena.

"Tell her."

"He doesn't understand Spanish that well," she continued. "So you don't have to worry if there is something you would rather a boy not hear."

I didn't say anything.

She leaned over and looked at my hands and my knees all bandaged.

"Damn, girl," she said. "You've been through a little hell, I see."

I nodded.

"Did Mr. Baker do this to you?"

"No. I fell, running."

"Why were you running? Tell me what happened," she said. I was still hesitant. It was embarrassing to tell it.

"Edward's a great guy. I like him as a friend. I'm not his girlfriend," she continued. "I know a lot of girls who would like to be his girlfriend, but he doesn't have one. He likes you or cares about you. That's pretty obvious, although he hasn't told me why yet," she said, and looked back at him again. She said something to him quickly, and he laughed.

"He has to know exactly what happened to you, otherwise he won't be able to help you, Delia. So," she said, "as I understand it, you went off to study speaking English with Mr. Baker. You were in some house with him? Just with him?"

I nodded.

"And you were supposed to live with him?"

"*Sí*."

"I'd have run away, too," she said. "I know something about him. He's not a regular teacher anymore. He had to resign two years ago under a cloud of suspicion. I'm surprised Edward's mother hired him to tutor Edward's sister, in fact."

I asked her what she meant by a cloud of suspicion.

"*Nube de la sospecha*? Some young girls said he had done things, touched them in places he shouldn't. The school didn't make a big deal of it. They tried to keep it quiet. He supposedly resigned for health reasons, but most people knew the truth."

She turned around and said something to Edward, who leaned forward to say, "Baker *no bueno*. He's a sicko."

"So?" Elena asked again. "What just happened to you? It's better that you tell everything."

I looked back at Edward, and then I began. When I told her he was calling me Señora Baker as soon as we entered the rental house, her eyes widened.

"He said we would be newlyweds."

"He said that?"

"He made me watch a bad movie."

She wanted to know what I meant, and I told her about some of it.

Edward kept asking her what I was saying, now impatient with waiting.

"Wait," she told him. "And then what?" she asked, I quickly got to how Señor Baker had spanked me for making mistakes in English.

"On your bare ass?"

"*Sí,* yes."

"What?" Edward cried. "C'mon, Elena, what is she saying?"

"Go on," she said, ignoring him and looking even more interested.

It really embarrassed me to continue, but I did. I told her about his nudity and about his drinking and then fastening me to him with his belt. As I spoke in Spanish, she translated for Edward in English, and he kept mumbling, "The son of a bitch. The bastard."

"So, he fell asleep before he could do anything more to you?" Elena asked pointedly. "If he did anything more, you should tell us, Delia."

"He fell asleep, yes. That was when I ran away."

"And then Edward went there to get you, discovered him, and went looking for you."

She repeated more to Edward, and he spoke.

"He said he found you running in the road, and he's sorry he caused you to fall."

"I thought it was Señor Baker coming after me."

"I don't blame you for being terrified. Jeez, Edward, are you going to take her to the police?" she asked him. "You should go to the police," she told me.

I couldn't help but be afraid of that. What if Señor Baker told them lies about me? What if they didn't believe me? Would they put me in jail? And what would happen to my grandmother if she learned such a terrible thing? Would everyone in my village find out and believe bad things about me?

"No, I can't do that," Edward told her. "They'd come to the house and create real noise. They'd want to know why my mother sent her off, everything. No police," Edward said, looking at me.

"Big deal, Edward. So they ask your mother questions? They should. I don't understand why your mother hired an illegal Mexican immigrant girl who can't speak English well and then decided to pay for private tutoring. Who tutors their help around here, especially illegal help?"

"I didn't say she was illegal, exactly."

"Well, is she or isn't she?"

"It's complicated," he said.

I was able to pick up only a few words of this, but I could tell he wasn't telling Elena everything, and she knew it and wasn't happy about it.

"Well, what are you going to do with her?" she asked, pointing to me.

"I'll figure it out," he said. "Don't worry. I'll get my mother to do the right thing now, or else. *Mi madre* will be *bueno* with you. Don't worry," he told me.

"I don't know, Edward. He's such a creep." She looked at me. "Señor Baker *es una serpiente en la hierba.*"

"*Sí,* yes," I said, "a snake in the grass."

She smiled. "She can learn English pretty fast, Edward. Besides, she can be put in that transition class at the public school, the ESL class, can't she?" She turned to me to explain what she had said.

If there was such a class at the school, why didn't my aunt just send me to it?

"Damn right," he said. "I forgot about that. Thanks, Elena. You've been a great help. I owe you one."

"You owe me more than one," she said, smiling at

him. *"Buena suerte, Delia,"* she said, wishing me luck, and got out of the car.

Edward and she spoke for a few moments before he got into the car again.

"She's nice. Elena *bueno.*"

"Yes, very nice," I said.

He drove out of the restaurant parking lot and headed for my aunt's estate. The tension and the questions reeling in my head exhausted me. I was looking forward even to my stark, nothing room and ugly bed. All I wanted to do now was sleep and forget, but I couldn't help trembling as we drove onto the estate and up to the house.

"C'mon," he said, getting out of the car.

I followed slowly, my legs still wobbly.

The house was very quiet when we entered. I had been holding my breath, expecting to see my aunt standing there fuming, imagining that Señor Baker had called her and told her all sorts of lies about me by now, but there was no one, not even Señora Rosario.

"What you need now is a good night's sleep," Edward said, and pressed his hands together, tilting his head on them.

"Sí, sueño," I said.

"C'mon."

However, instead of leading me through the house to the entrance at the rear and out to the other building, he directed me to the stairway. I stood there confused.

"It's all right. *Bueno,*" he said, urging me to follow him up the stairs.

I did, and he led me down the hallway, past Sophia's room. He paused at a door.

"Mi room . . . *mi* . . ."

"Dormitorio."

"*Sí, dormitorio.*"

I thought he meant for me to go into his room, but he continued walking to another door and opened it to show me another bedroom.

"Guest *dormitorio,*" he said. He struggled to explain. "Visitor . . . extra . . ."

I nodded.

"*Para una huésped.*"

"Right, whatever," he said, smiling, and stepped back for me to enter.

It wasn't quite as big as Sophia's bedroom, but it was very big, and it had a king-size bed with a beautiful dark cherry-wood headboard and four posts. The comforter was burgundy, and there were pillows as big as the ones Sophia had. At the moment, nothing looked more inviting to me than this bed.

In such a bed, there can be only good dreams, I thought, recalling something my grandmother once told me.

Edward showed me the bathroom. There was a brand-new toothbrush and other toiletries for guests in the cabinet. The bathroom was tiled and had a very big tub and shower stall. I reminded myself that this was the room I had dreamed would be mine. I had followed a twisted, painful path to get to it, but here I was. But how long would I be here? As I looked around at the comfort and luxury, I thought about my aunt finding me here and exploding into another rage. Edward saw the concern in my face.

"Don't worry," he said. "It's all okay. I'll make sure," he said, pointing to himself. "You *sueño.*" Then he thought for a moment and raised his hand. "Wait. I'll be back," he said, and hurried out of the room.

I didn't move. Less than a minute later, he returned

and handed me a pair of what I was sure were his pajamas.

"Okay?" he asked.

"Yes, *gracias*."

He started away again. I stood there, still timid and afraid, expecting to see my aunt appear at any moment and begin yelling at us both. Surely, Señor Baker had called her by now, I told myself.

"*Sueño, sueño*," Edward said standing in the doorway. "*Buenas noches.*"

"*Buenas noches. Gracias,*" I called to him as he started to close the door.

He smiled at me and closed the door. I remained standing there, still expecting something terrible to happen. Surely, this was too good to be true. I had gone from a nightmare to a beautiful dream. The silence convinced me I was all right for now. I went into the bathroom, cleaned myself as best I could with my painful scrapes, and then got undressed and put on his pajamas. They were too big, of course. When I looked in the full-length mirror, I had to laugh at the sight of myself.

I got into the big bed. The comforter, the mattress, and the fluffy big pillows all felt so wonderful. This had to be what it would be like if I could sleep on a cloud, I thought. However, despite all Edward had said and done for me, I still felt quite anxious and listened hard for any sound of footsteps or shouting, but the house remained quiet.

My head was spinning because of all that had happened so quickly. I had never been on a real roller coaster, but I couldn't imagine it being any more dramatic and frightening than the roller coaster of emotions I had just ridden.

I turned off the lights with the switch beside me and in moments sensed myself sinking into sleep. It felt as if I were sinking deeper and deeper into the large, soft mattress, but I didn't care if I disappeared. I never welcomed sleep as much as I did at this moment, and disappearing didn't seem all that terrible to me at the moment.

In the morning, I woke to the sound of loud arguing in the hallway. Although I didn't understand what they were saying, I clearly heard my aunt and Edward. Edward said something that caused my aunt to be quiet. Then I heard Sophia. Edward was shouting at her as well.

Moments later, there was a knock on the door. I was so frightened I almost couldn't find my voice, but I managed, "*Sí?*" and then quickly said, "Yes?"

Edward stepped into the room. He was dressed for school. I glanced at the clock and saw how late I had slept.

"*Todo bien,*" he said. "You stay *aquí,*" he added gesturing at the bedroom. "*Aquí. Comprende?*"

"Yes. I am here."

"Exactly," he said, smiling. "Now you are here. You will go to school. School, *comprende?*"

"*Escuela.*"

"Right, *escuela.* You will go. *Mi madre* will . . . how do you say it . . . make it happen . . . do it . . ."

I nodded.

"I've got to go. Don't worry," he said. "*Todo bien.* Damn, I have to learn more Spanish quickly. You teach me *español* every day."

"Okay," I said, smiling. "And you teach me English, yes?"

"Yes, but you'll learn it quickly in the classroom. *Gracias. Hasta la vista,*" he said, and backed out, closing the door.

It was quiet again, but then I suddenly heard a lot of talking and coming and going just outside the bedroom door. Shortly afterward, it was opened again, and Señora Rosario came marching in, her arms full of clothing. She looked upset and just dropped the clothes on the bed.

"Sophia is giving you these clothes. She doesn't wear any of it anymore. Don't ask me any questions. I do not know why she's giving you these clothes. I know she's not your size, so I brought you this needle and thread and these safety pins, too," she said, dropping them next to the clothes. "When you've found something you can wear and you're dressed, go down to have some breakfast. That's all I've been told. I don't know why you're in here now or what else is going on. This is a crazy house," she added, and marched back out, closing the door sharply.

I rose slowly and started to look over the clothes. She was right, of course, most of it was either too small or way too big for me, but I found a skirt I could wear and a blouse that didn't swim around me as much as the others with a little creative pinning. I would have to ask that someone go get my own clothes, I thought.

Just as I stepped out of the bathroom to go downstairs, the door opened again, and my aunt stepped into the room. She closed the door behind her and glared at me. Then she smiled.

"Señor Baker called and told me what happened, how you tried to seduce him so he would tell me nice things about you. It doesn't surprise me that you won over Edward so quickly, Delia," she said in perfect Spanish. "Like most men, he is easily impressed. What's that stupid proverb, *dichos* your grandmother, your father's mother, would quote at me all the time? It's not the fault of the mouse but the one who offers him the cheese? Of course, her precious son could do no wrong. It was girls like me who were offering the cheese.

"If anyone knows how untrue that is, it's your mother. Or I should say, it was your mother. She's been dead to me so long I forget she just died."

"Why was she dead to you?" I dared ask. It wasn't that I had suddenly become brave; it was my raging curiosity. How could anyone turn against her own family so much?

She smiled at me again and moved across the room to the window. With her back to me, she asked, "Your mother has never told you why?"

"No, Tía Isabela."

She spun around.

"Tía Isabela," she wailed, her grimace deepening. "You should be calling me Madre, not Tía."

The look on my face made her laugh.

"Don't worry. You're not really my daughter, Delia. But," she said, returning to that burning face of anger, "you should be."

I shook my head. None of this made any sense.

"Why should I be?"

"Your father should have been with me, not your mother," she replied. "I found him first. He was my boyfriend first, don't you know?"

I shook my head.

"That was before I got smart, before I realized what a hole I was living in and where I could go if I made an effort. Your parents, their parents, the whole lot of them, were content to wallow in their poverty, in their hand-to-mouth existence, blaming everything bad on the devil and giving every extra peso to the church. The church, the church, the church . . . cooking for the church, working to rebuild and repaint the church, cleaning the church.

"Your father was always upset with me because I complained so much about the way we all lived, and he didn't like my looking at any other men. He would go to complain to your mother, and she was smart. She was his shoulder on which to rest his poor, troubled head. I knew what she was doing. She didn't fool me.

" 'Oh,' she cried, 'I didn't mean to hurt you, Isabela. I didn't mean to steal your lover. It just happened.' "

She laughed.

"It just happened? Like a bolt of lightning hit them both? One day, he couldn't live without me, couldn't breathe if I didn't love him, and the next day, he was in love with your mother? And they accused me of being the flirt, the loose one? Oh, yes, your mother, my sister, was always the good girl, and I was always the bad, but she was the one who slept with your father before they were married, not me. I didn't give it away that easily, no matter what people said or thought.

"Don't look so shocked, Delia. Your mother was far from the sainted woman she pretended to be. She wanted the same things I did, but she was more hypocritical about it. I saw no reason to be a phony.

"Yes, I enjoyed twisting young men around my finger, leading them along, giving them hope, but I was not stupid, Delia. I don't know if you are or have been, but let me tell you one thing, once you give away your mystery, you are forever at their mercy.

"Forget all this talk about equality of the sexes. Men still lord it over women, even here where they are supposed to be so liberated, and these women, like dumb *burros,* put up with it. Believe me, I made my husband beg and give me everything before he enjoyed himself with me.

"In her own way, your mother was just as conniving. I know you don't want to believe it, but she was. After she and your father came to me and confessed their love for each other, I laughed in their faces and went off to find and marry a man who would take me so far away and so high above them they wouldn't be able to see the soles of my feet."

She paused and studied me.

"You remind me more of myself than you do your mother, even though your mother was as sneaky as could be."

I started to shake my head. "It's not true," I said. "That was not my mother. She was not sneaky and conniving."

"Believe what you want," she said, waving the air as if my words were like flies to chase off. "I certainly would have given your father more children. Maybe I was lucky, after all. It doesn't matter to me anymore."

She focused on me again.

"Just know that I know you inside and out. All right," she said. "What's done is done. You won over Edward quickly."

"He knows I'm not lying. He knows Señor Baker is lying."

"I don't care. I don't know what happened between you and Mr. Baker, and I don't want to know. I'll see to it that you are admitted to the public school. I certainly won't pay for you to be in the private school, no matter what Edward wants.

"You can stay in this room for now," she continued. "I guess I'll have to admit who you are if my son insists on blabbing it all over the community. I'll provide you with your basic necessities, but you'll look after yourself, and you'll still help with the housework. You'll have to earn your keep. That's as far as I'll give in," she said.

She started for the door and turned.

"I'll make the arrangements for you to attend school. The first time you embarrass me, I'll send you back. You have to remain here under my guardianship before you can be considered a citizen, and if I don't perform that role, you will be sent back on a donkey wearing rags."

She smiled.

"We'll soon know whether you belong here with us or back there with . . . them. Don't expect me to speak to you in Spanish unless I find it absolutely unavoidable," she concluded. "If you want to ask me anything, do it in English. Learn the words. I was willing to spend the money for private lessons. You couldn't handle Mr. Baker, fine. Now you're on your own.

"Sink or swim," she said, and walked out.

Maybe you're not as high above us as you think you are, Tía Isabela, I thought. *Maybe you sank a long time ago and drowned in your own unhappiness, and all your riches can't save you.*

Maybe you brought me here to satisfy yourself that you were so much better, and maybe for now, I give you that feeling and help you believe it, but I swear on my dead parents' souls, you will come begging me for forgiveness someday.

You will cry in church for yourself, and you will beg for mercy.

You will beg to come back to your family.

I know this is true as I know the sun will rise tomorrow.

And then I thought, *Perhaps this is why, perhaps this is the reason I was brought here.*

9

School

Although my aunt wanted as little to do with me as possible, she had to accompany me to the public school to enroll me. She made me sit up front with Señor Garman while she sat in the rear as usual. This would be the first time she openly revealed that she was declaring herself my legal guardian. She had some official-looking documents with official government stamps her attorney had provided.

There was no doubt she wanted to get this over with quicker than a dentist appointment. As soon as we entered the school, I practically had to run to keep up with her. She had said nothing to me the whole time except for "Don't you dare embarrass me by doing something stupid at school, something you might do in Mexico. This is not Mexico." She told me this just before we left the house and had Señora Rosario translate it. It wasn't necessary. From the face she wore and the way she waved her forefinger at me, I understood what she was saying. How many threats would she whip at me before saying one nice thing? And what did she think went on in Mexico? Not everyone was the young girl she had been.

We went directly to the main office. I could see that the administrators and the secretaries knew who she was or, rather, how rich she was. They jumped to attention when we entered, and they were very accommodating. To me, it seemed they were treating her as if she were royalty. In America, the rich are coronated, I thought, but maybe it was the same everywhere. The wealthy people were always treated with more respect in and around my village.

"I'm in a hurry," she told them, and a secretary brought us quickly to the guidance counselor's office.

The guidance counselor, Mr. Diaz, a tall, dark-haired man with a gentle smile, spoke to me in Spanish. I saw immediately that my aunt was annoyed.

"I wish you wouldn't do that," she told him. "If everyone speaks Spanish to her, she won't learn English."

"Oh, she'll learn, Mrs. Dallas. I promise you. We have a wonderful ESL teacher here."

He explained in Spanish that my aunt thought I might be lazy about learning to speak English well if he continued to speak to me in Spanish. I wanted to warn him that she understood Spanish. Because she had such airs about her and did not use a word of Spanish, he assumed she didn't. I saw her bristle.

"She might very well be lazy," she told him sharply in Spanish. "I don't know much about her. She lived in Mexico all her life, where the main word for everything is *mañana,* and she has just arrived after the death of my sister and brother-in-law. I haven't had all that much time with her, but I'm sure her schooling was nothing compared to what it is here."

She didn't mention that she had come from my village, too.

He stiffened quickly, looking as if she had just slapped his face.

"Oh, yes, of course," he said, fumbling with his papers. "I'll take a personal interest in her and keep in constant touch with you."

"Do whatever you have to do," my aunt told him, speaking in English again. "I'm not asking for any special favors, and I don't intend to treat a girl this age like some sort of baby. I won't nursemaid her. She'll sink or swim on her own, and she knows it."

"Of course, of course," he said, still shuffling papers to keep from looking at those furious eyes.

He walked out of the office with her and spoke to her for a while in the hallway. When he returned, he looked brow-beaten and happy she was gone.

"I'll take you to your classroom and your teacher now," he said.

I rose with trepidation. The school was bigger than any I had seen, and there were so many students in the hallways and classrooms. Surely, I thought, I will get lost here.

"Your aunt is quite a woman," Señor Diaz told me as we walked out of his office. I saw from the way his eyes twinkled that he wasn't giving her a compliment. "We'd better not disappoint her, eh, Delia?"

I nodded. I was afraid to utter a word in Spanish or in English.

He brought me to a classroom to be with ten other

boys and girls who had recently come from Mexico. The teacher, Señorita Holt, reminded me a little of Señora Cuevas. She was far prettier, with shoulder-length auburn hair, and she was much younger than Señora Cuevas. However, I saw immediately that she was just as serious and had little patience for inattentiveness or disruption.

As part of the day's lesson, I was introduced in English to each student. Señorita Holt had provided each student with a sheet of questions in English we were to ask to learn about one another. While we were in this classroom, Señorita Holt insisted we speak only English. If we didn't know a word, we were to ask and then use it. I found out quickly that the other students ranged from ages twelve to seventeen, the oldest being a boy named Ignacio Davila, whose father now owned his own gardening business.

I learned Ignacio's father had come to America to work and eventually developed his own company. Afterward, he sent for his wife and four children. Ignacio was the oldest. I was placed next to him in the classroom. I thought Ignacio was a sullen, unhappy boy, not very interested in learning how to speak English well. Except for attending the ESL class, he had little to do with the school, because he had to work in his father's business most of he time.

All but one of the other students' parents worked as gardeners or maids. The one whose didn't was the daughter of a man who sang and played guitar with a group of mariachis in a big Mexican restaurant. She was twelve, and her name was Amata, but the others simply called her Mata. She had black hair down to her wing bones and had a face like a small doll's face, with diminutive features and ebony button eyes, lighting her smile with innocence and happiness. Her tiny voice and little hands made you feel like hugging her.

Señorita Holt broke us into three work groups to practice what we were learning in the textbook and on the tapes she had us play, all of us listening on earphones. Before the class ended, we watched a television program in which important English words were spelled and sounded out. With the words I had known before coming to the United States and the words I did pick up from my lessons with Señor Baker, I managed to do well enough to get a compliment from my teacher my first day.

After she had enrolled me in the public school, my aunt had given me money to take a bus, which would drop me off almost a mile and a half from the estate. She provided me with the address, but she didn't take the time to explain any directions. Anyone would think she was hoping I would not find my way back.

Ignacio, who had said little to me in the classroom, rode the same bus. He would ride it much farther. At the bus stop where we boarded, he asked me why I had come to live with my aunt. He had heard of my village in Mexico and knew it was populated by farmers and small tradesmen with almost no tourism, but he had never been there. When he learned what had happened to my parents, he became less indifferent.

"I know who your aunt is," he said. "We don't have her property to service, but we have one nearby. She's very rich. Why doesn't she have someone take you to school and pick you up? If you miss the bus, you sometimes have to wait an hour for the next one. And when you get off at the closest station, you'll have a good long walk."

"I like to walk," I told him.

"Wait until it's very hot. You won't be happy. Your aunt knows that."

How was I to explain my aunt?

"It's the way she wants it," I said. "It's not so bad. I have never been on such a long bus with such comfortable seats and air conditioning."

The truth was, I had never been on a bus at all.

He shrugged. "My father promised me that next year, I could get a car. I have to save at least half the cost from working myself. I had my grandfather's truck in Mexico," he told me. "I drove it when I was only ten."

"I never drove," I told him. "We had only a truck, and my father rarely used it for anything other than going to work and back. You will be very fortunate to have your own car."

"It's not for sure. It's hard to save money here," he said.

I was happy he was talking to me. He had very beautiful black eyes, a shade of ebony I had not seen. Sometimes they had a green glint. His hair was as short as a soldier's. He saw I noticed and explained that his father insisted his employees look clean and respectable. He would never permit drinking alcoholic beverages on the job, not even a bottle of beer. A man he knew who worked for someone else was drunk on the job and nearly cut off his foot. Now he had a very bad limp and hardly worked.

"He sends very little back to his family in Mexico. He's illegal, undocumented, you know. He doesn't have any insurance and is afraid to complain about anything, or he'll get sent back, and he won't even be able to get them the little he does."

"That's very sad."

"Yes. Sometimes he has nothing and begs on the streets. My father says he's an embarrassment to our people. You know men don't beg like that in Mexico. They'll try to sell anything first, trinkets, souvenirs, anything," he said, sounding bitter, as if this man embarrassed all of the Mexican men living here.

"*Sí*," I said, afraid even to suggest I disagreed.

"My father has five other men working for him," he said proudly. "And they all have a legal right to work here. He won't hire any undocumented Mexicans, and he pays all his taxes, including payroll taxes. I wish he didn't sometimes. I'd make more and get my car for sure."

"Why is it hard to save money?"

"There's so much to buy and so much to do," he said. "Too many temptations. There's even a movie theater that shows films in Spanish. Lucky for me, my father makes me work all the time, but on Sunday, when I go to the mall, I have to keep my hands in my pockets."

I laughed.

"I do!" he emphasized. "My friends call me a miser, but I don't care. I want my car."

"I hope you get it," I said. "I feel confident that you will."

He liked that.

"You know how to go from the bus station to your aunt's *hacienda*?"

"I think so, but I'm not sure," I said.

He explained very carefully.

"If I had my car," he said, "I'd drive you home every day."

That brought a smile to my face, but my smile seemed to frighten him. He turned away quickly.

A shy boy from Mexico, I thought. He's the first I've met. It brought a laugh inside me.

When the bus pulled up to my station, he followed me down the aisle and repeated the directions until I was nearly out the door. I thanked him and stepped off the bus. He looked out the window at me, and I waved, but he didn't wave back. He turned to look forward quickly, as if he was afraid someone would notice a girl was waving to him. I watched the bus go off and started for my aunt's *hacienda*.

Actually, speaking with Ignacio and spending my school day with other students recently from Mexico helped me feel better about being here.

"When you're with your own people, people who share your traditions, your language, and even your memories, you are not far from home," my grandmother had told me the night before I left for America, "no matter how long it would take you to get back." I thought she was telling me all this to keep me from being afraid, but now I thought she was right.

As if it was meant to happen on my walk just to emphasize what my grandmother had said, music from Mexico could be heard coming from a radio two men were listening to as they painted a garage. I knew the song, and for a moment, I just stood there with a half-smile on my face, listening, too. If I closed my eyes, I could easily imagine I was standing back in our village square. Everyone was dressed in their nicest clothes and feeling happy, some because they were drinking tequila. In the coolness of the early evening, with the dancing and the food, everyone seemed younger. It was all so simple and yet so magical. Would I ever feel that magic here?

"Delia, Delia," I heard, and turned to see Edward in

a red convertible sports car. It had only two seats. How many cars did he have? The car he had driven when he came looking for me was a sedan. "C'mon, get in. I'll drive you home," he shouted.

I approached the car, still hesitant.

"Get in," he said. He beckoned, and I opened the car door and slipped into the seat. "I was afraid I had missed you," he told me. I shook my head, not understanding. He pointed to his head. "I thought you no *aquí,* too late."

"Oh. Yes."

He smiled. "Between my sign language and broken Spanish and your broken English, we'll do just fine," he said, and started away. "Did you like *escuela*?"

"Yes. I like *mi profesora.*"

"Great," he said, smiling. "Learn English quickly so you can tell me more, *más* about you," he said, pointing. "*Yo*?"

"Yes, you. *Yo*? You sound like Rocky," he said, laughing. "Yo!"

I laughed, too, although I wasn't sure exactly what I was laughing at, maybe just how happy and pleasant he was. Through his gestures, his little Spanish, and the English I understood, he apologized for not being able to take me to school every morning. His private school was in the opposite direction, and there was not enough time to go to both.

"But I can get you to the bus station," he said.

As we drove up the driveway to the house, we could see another sports car parked in front. It was blue and just as new and beautiful. However, when we drew closer, I saw it had a very bad dent on the right front fender. Edward grimaced.

"Sophia's boyfriend is here," he said. "Bradley Whit-field. He takes her home when I don't, which is most of the time." He looked at me, pointed to the car, and added, "My sister's boyfriend. Boyfriend."

He embraced himself and pursed his lips, closing his eyes and shaking.

I laughed and said, "*Muchacho amante.* Lover boy."

"Right. *Muchacho amante.* Good. That's what I'll call him."

When we entered the house, we heard their laughter. They were in the living room.

"Don't tell me you picked her up at public school," Sophia cried as we approached.

"What I do and don't do is none of your damn busi-ness, Sophia," Edward told her. "I told you that last night, and I meant it."

Sophia laughed. "I wonder why you're getting so lovey-dovey with her. What do you think's the reason, Bradley?" she asked the boy sitting beside her.

He had long blond hair, strikingly blue eyes, and a firm, strong mouth. I thought he was at least as tall as Edward and more athletic-looking because of his broader shoulders. His light blue sports jacket was folded beside him on the arm of the sofa, and his white shirt was opened at the collar, showing his thick gold necklace. His light hair and blue eyes were emphasized by the contrast with his dark complexion. My first thought was, Why would someone as movie-star good-looking as he is have anything to do with Sophia?

"She's your cousin," Bradley said. He looked at me and in perfect Spanish said, "*Sí? Usted es su prima?*" he asked me.

"Stop showing off, Bradley," she snapped at him.

"*Sí,*" I said and added, "*Pero no es mi culpa,*" which meant *but it isn't my fault.*

He roared with laughter.

"What did she say, Bradley?" She pushed him hard, and he cried out in feigned pain.

Edward had a big smile on his face, even though he didn't fully understand what I had said.

"She said it isn't what?" he asked Bradley.

"Her fault."

Edward laughed as hard as Bradley.

Sophia's face reddened. "She's supposed to report to Mrs. Rosario immediately on getting home, Edward. Remember? Mother said she can stay in the guest room, but she still has to do her house chores. Mrs. Rosario!" she screamed. "Delia is ready to wash the toilets."

"Shut up, Sophia," Edward told her.

"She's wearing my throwaway clothes," she told Bradley. He looked at me again.

"Really? Throwaway? They don't look so bad. Maybe because they're on her."

"Go home, Bradley. You make me sick," she told him, and stood up.

He laughed, but looked a little frightened. "Take it easy. We're just having fun."

"I don't think it's fun."

Señora Rosario appeared in the hallway. Sophia practically leaped at her.

"She's back, Mrs. Rosario. Don't you have things for her to do?"

Señora Rosario looked at her and then turned to me. "*Venga,* Delia."

"I think she should change her clothes first, Mrs. Rosario," Edward told her.

She nodded and told me to come to the kitchen after I changed. The bathrooms did have to be cleaned, and afterward, I would help with dinner preparations. I would not, I found out, eat with the help anymore. I would eat with Edward and Sophia and my aunt when she was home for dinner. Edward had managed to get my aunt to give in on some things but not others. All of that still puzzled me, but, as Abuela Anabela often said, "*Hay que tomar lo bueno con lo malo.*" You have to take the good with the bad. I was just not sure if eating with my cousins and my aunt was good.

I hurried to the stairway.

"Nice meeting you," Bradley called after me.

"You're such a jerk, Bradley," Sophia said.

Edward followed me upstairs and went into his own room. I changed and went to work under the new arrangements: chores to do every day, eat with my so-called family, and then off to study English until I was too tired to keep my eyes open. True to his word, Edward did drive me to the bus station every morning. Most of the time, Sophia's boyfriend, Bradley, picked her up in the morning, but some mornings, he didn't or couldn't. On those mornings, Sophia had to go to school with Edward, who couldn't use his sports car then. She hated it and made me sit in the back, while she talked incessantly on her cell phone, to ignore me more than anything, I thought. Edward was always criticizing her, and she was always saying nasty, even dirty, things to him.

I soon realized that although someone who heard them might think they were just being a brother and a sister, Edward and Sophia really didn't like or trust each other. Their arguments weren't simply brother-sister tiffs. Sophia complained to her mother about Edward more than Edward complained to her about Sophia. Moving between them was like crossing the border of two countries poised to go to war but each afraid to begin. I could see they kept secrets from each other and were in no way as close as a brother and sister should be.

However, it didn't surprise me that they had secrets. This was a house full of secrets and distrust. The servants didn't like the people they were working for and were very suspicious and anxious, never expecting compliments and always expecting criticism. It was like moving about while lightning streaked through the air around you, whether you were inside or outside the house. You were always afraid of being burned or singed or stung by either a dirty look or a nasty word. Fortunately for me, my aunt was very absorbed in her social activities and her romances.

I soon realized that whoever my aunt's male companion was one week or even one day would never be seen again the next. She put people on and off the way she changed clothes. Nothing made her happy long. Sophia appeared to be a clone of her mother, very spoiled, very self-centered, and very disrespectful of any she considered beneath her. I was definitely included in that group.

During the week, I had taken some of the other clothing she had Señora Rosario dump on my bed, and I had cut and sewn and pinned all the garments until they fit better. I could see she was disappointed and even annoyed that I had tailored them so well. Edward told me most of it no longer fit her because she had gained so much weight. When I cleaned her suite, I saw where she had hidden candy. She must have forgotten about some of it, because it was old and attracted ants.

I was soon learning English fast enough to get the

gist of most of their conversations at dinner, although I was far from competent enough to participate comfortably. Most of the arguments Sophia had with her mother were over her weight or letters the school sent about her, complaining about her behavior in class. Edward enjoyed teasing Sophia about it, too, and later in the week, he picked up on the comment her boyfriend, Bradley, had made about the clothes I wore. He mentioned it at dinner.

"Bradley wasn't kidding. Your clothes never looked that good on you, Sophia. It was very nice of you to give them to her."

Her eyes flared. She cocked her pupils on him like two pistols and seemed ready to dump one curse after another on his head but held back. Instead, she turned a furious glance at me and cut me with her smile. Surely, she was plotting some vengeance. Why she disliked me so much, I did not know, but I avoided even her shadow, asked her nothing, and avoided looking at her at the dinner table. Now I understood what Señora Rosario had meant about staying out of Sophia's way.

Edward, on the other hand, seemed to enjoy using me like salt on a wound.

Rather than stop her children from arguing and being nasty to each other, my aunt seemed pleased. She yelled at them only when they raised their voices and annoyed her. When I asked Señora Rosario about it, she smirked and said, "Señora Dallas believes it's better to be a lion than a rabbit."

"*Por qúe*?"

"Why?" She shrugged. "She thinks we're at war, and in war, it is better to be a lion."

"Who's at war?"

"*Todos nosotros,*" she replied.

"All of us? But why?"

"When you find out, let me know," she said, and walked away.

Life was so much simpler in Mexico, I thought. It gave me a lot to consider. Despite my workload and my schooling, I had plenty of time to think about all of it, especially on my walks.

Twice during the week, Edward, because of other commitments, was unable to pick me up at the bus station or on my way back. Actually, I didn't mind the walk so much. It was still not terribly hot in Palm Springs, and I did enjoy looking at the homes and observing people. There was an elderly man who always waved hello to me as he pruned the bushes and flowers in his front yard. Not everyone here was so wealthy that he or she had servants.

I wrote four letters to my grandmother that first week, not telling her one terrible thing. I was afraid she might see through my exaggerations but made everything sound as wonderful as I could, anyway. Señora Rosario made sure my letters were mailed out. I had yet to receive one back but looked forward to it every day.

Ignacio often asked about her and any news from Mexico. I could see he was homesick, too, despite all of the opportunities and better money to be made here. He lost more and more of his shyness as time passed, and we spent more time talking on the bus and sometimes at lunch at school. I don't know if it was because of me or because he had simply decided he had to speak English better, but I could see he was trying harder and working harder at improving. We began to practice more on the bus as well.

English was not easy to learn, but whenever I got a little discouraged, I thought of my aunt when she was my age back in Mexico, determined to lift herself out of poverty and the hard life. I had to give the devil her due. Despite how mean I thought she was, I couldn't help but admire her for her achievements. I would never want to be like her, but I wouldn't mind being as rich as she was. Who wouldn't?

It occurred to me that I was very much like Cinderella now. I lived in a wealthy world, but I was treated like a poor servant. I was surrounded with expensive things—art, furniture, beautiful cars—and I was on an estate that rivaled those of presidents, kings, and queens. However, I still cleaned toilets and wore hand-me-downs.

Unlike Cinderella, I had no one with a magic wand to turn me into a princess, even just until midnight. I had no glass slipper. My cousin Edward was the only one I thought was really kind to me. Sometimes I felt he enjoyed how his kindness to me annoyed his sister and his mother. I knew he didn't approve of the way either of them lived and treated people, especially servants. It didn't take me long to realize that not only was I in a house without any sign of religion or faith in anything other than what money could buy, but I was in a house without any sign of love.

When I stepped onto the bus each morning, I wondered what would happen if I just sat and never stepped off. Would I end up in Mexico? Mata told me her father said Mexico was really only a few hours away. Of course, to get back to my village would take days by car or bus, and, of course, I had to have the proper papers. However, not a morning or an afternoon passed without my daydreaming about it. I was that homesick.

I was doing just that one afternoon after I had stepped off the bus and said good-bye to Ignacio, who had gotten up enough nerve to wave back when I waved. I started along as usual, taking my time, not all that anxious to get back to my aunt's *hacienda* and start my chores. It was another magnificent day, when the birds seemed to want to sing more than usual. It caused me to remember my grandmother telling me the birds were jealous of my mother's voice. How I longed to hear her again. Perhaps she was singing to me through the beautiful birds that followed me from branch to branch on trees along the street. I waved to the old gentleman, who waved back.

When I rounded the corner, I heard a car horn and stepped to the side, but the car didn't pass me. I assumed it was Edward catching up to me as he occasionally did now, but it wasn't Edward. It was Sophia's boyfriend, Bradley Whitfield.

"*Hola, señorita. Venga. Quiere un paseo?*"

A ride? Where was Sophia?

"*Venga,*" he repeated. "Don't be afraid, come on," he said when I still hesitated. "I won't bite you." He laughed at my shyness.

I got into his sports car, and he drove off.

"*Dónde está Sophia?*"

"*Con sus amigas que fuman el pote, yo estoy seguro.*"

He was sure she was smoking pot with her girlfriends? Why would he tell me?

He laughed at the look of shock on my face.

If he knew where Sophia was, why was he driving down this street? I asked him.

"To see if you were walking along," he told me, and smiled.

Then he turned left when he should have gone straight.

"Me? Why?"

"Why not?" he replied.

"*Dónde vamos*?" I asked him.

"Where are we going?" He thought a moment, then smiled and said, "Just for a ride. Let the wind blow through your hair in your chariot, m'lady." He laughed.

And for a moment, only a moment, I wondered if Cinderella had found her prince.

10

Bradley

I asked Bradley where he had learned to speak Spanish so well, and he told me he had been brought up by his nanny, Maria De Santas, who always spoke to him in Spanish.

"I knew how to speak Spanish before I knew how to speak English."

"Why were you brought up by a nanny? Where was your mother?"

"She left us when I was only six months old," he told me.

"Left you? I don't understand."

"Me, neither," he said. He paused and then added, "She ran off with the manager of my father's auto-parts plant."

"Where did they go?"

He looked at me as if I was asking a stupid question.

"Somewhere in Florida, I think. My father knew because of the legal stuff that followed, but he doesn't like to talk about it."

How could a mother leave her own child? Were all of the women in America as selfish as *mi tía* Isabela? Why wasn't family as important here as it was in Mexico?

"I don't think about it anymore," he continued, now sounding more angry. "To me, it's the same as if she died. My father finally remarried, and I have a young sister, Gayle. She's six. Maria is still with us, so Gayle is speaking Spanish well, too. It doesn't hurt to know how to speak Spanish around here, with all you Mexicans," he added.

"It doesn't hurt to know how to speak English, either," I told him, and he laughed. Then he looked at me in the strangest way. It was as if he was looking at me really for the first time.

"You're a very pretty girl, Delia, but I bet you know how pretty you are, right?"

"No," I said, blushing. I wanted to tell him about the evil eye and why doting on myself was not good. Besides, he was supposed to be Sophia's boyfriend and shouldn't be saying such things to other girls. "Don't you think Sophia's pretty?" I asked.

"She's all right," he said quickly. "She needs to lose weight, but I'll never be the one to tell her. She'd have me assassinated."

Talking about her with him made me nervous, even though I was the one who had brought up her name. Maybe it was my way of getting him to remember who his girlfriend was so he would stop paying so much attention to me, although I couldn't help but be flattered by such a handsome boy.

"I should go now to my aunt's *hacienda*," I said. "I have work."

"Don't worry. You would never be home by now

walking, anyway," he told me, and turned down a side street. "My father is fixing up some houses here for resale on this street," he said. "He has his hands in a lot of things. Matter of fact, here's one." He made a sharp turn into a driveway. It was a house no bigger than the one *mi tía* Isabela sent me to live in with Señor Baker. "Let's see how well the work is going." He shut off the engine and got out of the car. "C'mon," he urged.

I looked at the house. There was no one working around it and no other vehicle in the driveway. Behind us, the street was very quiet. There was no one outside any of the homes, and I had yet to see another car drive along.

"I have to get back home," I insisted. "Please."

"We'll just be a few minutes. You'll still get home faster than you would have walking, I promise," he told me.

He looked as if he wouldn't get back into the car unless I followed him to look at the house, so I got out.

"This one should be nearly done," he told me. He led me around to a rear door. Under a mat, he found a key. Why were we going in through the back way?

The door opened on a small kitchen. I could see some tools on a table and some sawdust on the floor where a cabinet had been trimmed to fit a new dishwasher. At least he was telling me the truth about the restoration, I thought, and relaxed a little. He walked about, inspecting some of the work.

"My father's made me his refurbishing assistant. I'm responsible for what goes on here. Eventually, I'll take over most of his businesses, you know. He wants me to go to college to major in business education, but I'm not sure it's necessary. We buy these houses for nothing, put in some money, and sell them at great prices."

I followed him into the living room, where I saw work had been done around a fireplace and a new wood floor had been laid. He studied a window frame and shook his head.

"They could do better than this," he said. "These gaps are unnecessary. Come here and look at what I mean."

I stepped up and saw where he was pointing.

"See what I mean? Shoddy craftsmanship. Just because it's an inexpensive house doesn't mean we'll tolerate that. My reputation is always at stake. You understand what I'm saying?"

"Yes."

He smiled at me the way he had in the car. It was as if his eyes could undress me. It made me nervous.

"Man, you are a very pretty girl, Delia. I've never seen such beautiful eyes. Do you have a lot of boyfriends back in Mexico?"

"No," I said. "I had no boyfriend."

"What, are they all stupid? I thought girls like you were gobbled up."

He ran his hand softly down my hair and my cheek, and then he leaned in and kissed me. I knew he was going to do it, but rather than back away quickly, I felt myself grow numb, frozen, helpless. He took that to mean I had wanted him to kiss me, wanted him to do more. He pulled me to him and kissed me harder, then kissed my cheek and my neck, his arms around me so tightly I couldn't push him back.

I was so shocked I didn't know what to say or do.

"I've been thinking about you ever since you walked into the house with Edward that afternoon," he said. "Twice I drove the streets hoping to catch you walking home before Edward did."

Why? I thought. What about Sophia? He kissed me again before I could ask anything, and this time, he accompanied his kiss with his hands moving over my shoulders and down over my breasts, before he embraced me around the waist and started to lower me to the floor.

Finally, I found the strength to resist.

"No, please," I said. "Stop."

"Don't you like me?" he asked.

"Yes," I said, "but . . ."

"That's all that matters. Forget *but*," he insisted, pulling me down harder until I sat on the floor.

Before I could say another word, he leaned over me, kissing my face, moving his lips down over my chin to my neck, as his hands now went under my blouse. He lifted it against my meager resistance and then had his lips quickly between my breasts, working his fingers over the bra clasp until it was undone and he had moved the bra away so that his lips could find my nipples and then move over and under my bosom. I was both shocked and frightened at how quickly the surge of excitement flowed down to my thighs and circled my stomach with a warmth that seemed to weaken me further. He was completely over me now, and we were sprawled on the floor.

When he put his hands on my thighs and started to lift away my skirt, I pushed hard on his chest.

"Easy," he said, putting his hand over mine and holding it there against his chest. "Easy. I know what Mr. Baker did to you. Sophia told me. This is different. This will be different. I promise you."

He leaned in to kiss me again, and I pulled back.

"No," I cried, shaking my head. The mention of Señor Baker shocked me into greater resistance.

"Take it easy," Bradley said softly.

I twisted and squirmed, burning my shoulder against the wood floor, but my resistance didn't discourage him as I had hoped. Bradley pressed down harder on me.

"Hey, don't be a tease. You like me. You want me. Just relax," he said.

"No," I said. "I don't want this now. Please."

"Come on, stop the innocent act. I know girls your age have been with plenty of guys in Mexico. That's why you have so many children so young."

"No, it's not true. Let me go."

I pushed his face away, and anger flashed like lightning through his eyes.

"What is this? Why did you get into my car so fast, huh? Don't play around, Delia."

"I'm not playing. Please," I said, continuing to push at him, but he was too strong. It was like pushing a wall.

He stared down at me, gazing at my exposed breasts, and then he smiled.

"Keep pushing," he said. "I like it."

He had his hands under my skirt and was tugging my panties down. I seized his hair and pulled his face and his lips off my breasts. He grimaced and cried out, bringing his hands to my wrists, and we struggled for a few moments.

"I'm going to tell Sophia you tried to seduce me," he warned when he pulled my hands away from his hair. "And she's going to tell your aunt. I'm going to tell them you saw me driving by and waved me over and got into my car and that you asked me to take you for a ride and tried to seduce me. Think your aunt will believe that of you?" he asked me, smiling wryly. "Sophia told me what Mr. Baker had said about you."

I felt my resistance weaken. I shook my head. "No, it was lies."

"How will she feel about a little tramp from Mexico coming to live in her house and embarrass her? Huh? I'll tell you how she'll feel, awful and very angry, especially after I tell my stepmother, who gossips in the same social circles. Your aunt will have you deported, sent back in chains, and everyone in your village will hear the story."

"Please!" I cried. "Don't do that."

"Relax. I'm not saying I'll do that for sure," he said. His hands returned to my panties. "Why should I do that? I like you."

I started to sob softly. He was moving quickly now, and I didn't know what else to do. "Please," I begged him.

"I like that, too. Keep saying that. Please. Go on, say it again. Please."

I shook my head madly when I felt him pushing into me.

"Please," he continued to mimic. "Please."

I closed my eyes. The pain and the disgrace flowed through me in equal waves. I felt myself rise out of my body to stop myself from thinking about what was happening to me. However, some time during his passion and his assault, I heard a voice inside me say, *This didn't happen to Cinderella.*

When he was finished, he lay there still sprawled over me, breathing hard.

"You really were a virgin," he muttered, and rolled over to pull up his pants.

I was still too much in shock to speak or even to cry.

"You can use the bathroom," he told me, gesturing in its direction. "There are towels there for the workers and such. Go on," he ordered. "We've got to get going, or you will be very late after all."

He walked out of the room. Slowly, I fixed my clothing and got up. When I went into the bathroom, I saw how inflamed my face was. It was streaked with tears I hadn't felt. I cleaned myself as best I could and then sat on the toilet seat and tried to regain my composure. He knocked on the door and told me to come out to the car quickly.

"Move it. I'm leaving in a minute, whether you're there or not."

I didn't want to go with him, but I was in a daze. He talked incessantly all the way back to my aunt's estate, his voice calm and happy, as if we really were boyfriend and girlfriend and nothing terrible had occurred. It made it all seem that much more unreal to me. Maybe it didn't happen, I told myself, but my sore shoulder and the scrapes I had on my rear and lower back reminded me it had.

When he pulled up to the *hacienda,* he sat back, smiling.

"I wouldn't make up any stories about this afternoon," he warned. "It will be your word against mine, Delia, and this will be the second time you were in trouble with a man since you arrived. No one will believe you. Besides, you probably enjoyed it. If you're honest with yourself, you'll admit it."

I shook my head and opened the car door. "You're no prince," I said.

"Huh?"

"You're a disgrace to your nanny," I told him. "You have sinned against everyone who loves you."

His smile seemed to freeze on his face. Then he pointed his right forefinger at me. "You'd better keep your mouth shut, Delia. I'm warning you."

"I don't have to tell anyone," I said. "God has seen what you have done."

I got out and closed the car door. He pulled away quickly and sped down the driveway. Then I brushed down my clothes and started up the stairs. When I looked at the doorway, I saw it was open, and Sophia was standing there glaring out at me.

"You bitch," she said. "Mr. Baker was right about you!" she shouted, turned, and went back inside.

My heart bobbed like a yo-yo in my chest. Feeling like a trapped animal, I followed her into the house and hurried up the stairs to my room to get out of my soiled clothes and start my chores. Now I understood what Cinderella felt when the clock struck twelve and she fell back into her state of despair. Only, unlike her, I had no one coming in search of me.

Later, as I did my chores, I thought about the irony. Those who had seen me leave my village in the limousine were certain I was on my way to some sort of promised land. They thought I was being comforted and compensated for my great grief. They thought some sort of mercy had been thrown over me. They didn't know that the evil eye was not finished with me yet.

I vowed to keep my laughter, my smiles, my happiness, should it ever come, locked deep inside me. I would not tempt the *ojo malvado* again. I did my best work that afternoon, never scrubbing as hard or cleaning as completely. The work kept me from crying. Señora Rosario was impressed enough to give me a compliment, but I didn't say thank you. I would not even accept compliments anymore. Everything frightened me now. Good only led me to more bad.

Later, after I had changed to go to dinner, Edward came to my bedroom, knocked, and entered.

"Bradley Whitfield took you home today?" he asked me.

I looked away when I answered so he wouldn't see my face.

"Yes."

"Watch out for him," he warned. "He's a smooth talker."

"Smooth?" I shook my head.

"Yeah, that means he's sly, er . . . tricky . . . dishonest."

"*Sí,*" I said, now understanding.

"But I bet you knew that anyway," he added. "See you at dinner," he said.

I waited for him to leave, and then I finally began to cry.

Before I went down to dinner, I showered and saw the burns and scrapes on my body from my struggle with Bradley. Some of them stung badly and took my breath away when the water hit them. I sucked in my tears, dried myself gently, and dressed for dinner.

The moment I took my seat in the dining room, my aunt was on me. She leaned toward me, her eyes dark and cold with accusations.

"Sophia tells me you had Bradley Whitfield drive you home. How did you get him to do that?"

I turned away from her, my whole body shaking.

"Well?" she asked. "You understand what I'm asking. Don't pretend not to understand," she snapped.

I turned back to her. She was pressing her lips together and glaring hatefully at me.

"I did nothing, Tía Isabela," I said. "I was walking from

the bus, and he came with his car and told me to get in."

"Told you?" Sophia asked, smirking. "I doubt that he told you."

"Why do you doubt it, Sophia? It doesn't surprise me," Edward said. "You think you're the only girl he's with these days? Don't flatter yourself."

"Shut up, Edward. At least he's with a girl."

Edward's face reddened. Then he relaxed and smiled. "Why don't you tell Mother why you didn't go home with Bradley and why he was alone in the first place?"

"What does that mean?" Tía Isabela asked.

"Let Sophia tell you."

"Sophia?"

"Go on, Sophia. Tell Mother why you weren't with Bradley today," Edward taunted.

"It's nothing. I was with some of my girlfriends, that's all. I don't need to have Bradley around me all day long, but I don't need someone else chasing after him, either, someone who lives here," she added, pointedly looking at me. "Especially my long-lost, sweet, innocent, poor, and helpless cousin, who turns out to be not so helpless after all."

I understood most of what she was saying.

"No," I said, shaking my head and looking at my aunt. "It's not so, not . . . true."

"Of course, it isn't. How could Delia chase after him?" Edward asked. "She's not in our school. When would she have seen him?"

"She saw him here."

"That was just the one time."

"Boys need to see a girl like her only once to know what she's like."

"That's crap, and you know it!" Edward screamed at her.

"You don't know where or how this girl was brought up, Edward," Tía Isabela said, sitting back and nodding at me. "I do. Sophia's not all wrong."

"She's way more than all wrong, Mother, and so are you."

"That's enough! I won't have it. I won't have sexual promiscuity in my house."

"Unless it's your own," Edward muttered, and Tía Isabela slammed her hand on the table so hard all the dishes and glasses jumped.

"Get out of my sight!" she screamed at him, and pointed to the door.

"I think I'm entitled to have my dinner," Edward said calmly, and continued to eat.

Tía Isabela looked as if she would soon be having smoke pour out of her ears. I was shifting my eyes from one to the other so quickly I thought I'd get dizzy. How could Edward be so defiant? Was it because of what Señora Rosario had said, that he had inherited the property and wealth, too?

Tía Isabela stared a moment, nodded to herself, and then rose, keeping her eyes down.

"I will not remain, then," she said, and marched out of the dining room.

"Good work, Edward," Sophia told him. "You drove our mother away from her own dinner defending this tramp from Mexico."

He didn't reply.

"I don't understand why you defend Delia so much," she continued. "Have you already done it with her? Is that it? She makes it easy for you? Have you finally lost your virginity?"

Without any warning or indication that he was even listening to his sister, Edward lifted his glass and heaved the contents, grape juice, across the table at her. It splattered over her face and clothes. She screamed, leaped to her feet, and rushed out of the dining room, crying.

Edward continued eating as if nothing at all had happened. He glanced at me.

"Go on," he said. "Finish your dinner. Around here, you need your strength."

I had no appetite. My insides felt tied up in knots, but I was afraid of not eating. For the moment, at least, everyone seemed crazy here.

"I have a lot of homework and a term paper to do," Edward told me when he was finished. "Don't worry. I'll drive you to the bus tomorrow."

I watched him leave, and then I helped Inez clear the table and clean up the kitchen before I went up to my room. Not eager to practice any English, I sat at the desk and tried to write a new letter to *mi abuela* Anabela, but every attempt was filled with so much self-pity, practically begging her to take me back, I tore it up.

It was difficult to fall asleep, even difficult to say my prayers. I felt God was not pleased with me now. I had not fought hard enough to stop Bradley Whitfield, and in the beginning, I was too flattered and welcomed his compliments and attention too much. I envisioned Father Martinez shaking his head at me. In my imagination, I saw myself in our village church, but my prayers and singing echoed off the walls and ceiling and never made it up to God's ear.

I moved like someone in a daze the following morning. Bradley did not come by to pick up Sophia. I understood enough of her conversation with Tía Isabela at breakfast to understand that she and Bradley had had a bad argument over the telephone during the night. She didn't want to get into the car with Edward, either, but her mother wouldn't assign Señor Garman to drive her and certainly wouldn't drive her herself. Pouting like a four-year-old, she sat in the rear and said nothing the entire time it took to bring me to the bus.

"Don't worry," Edward said before I got out. "I'll be waiting here at the station for you this time."

I nodded and closed the door. Sophia had her head down and wouldn't look my way when they drove off. There was a small crowd waiting for the bus. Some students from the school were there and some adults on their way to their respective jobs. I did not know any of the other students, because I was still only in the ESL classroom. None of them paid much attention to me, anyway. I was the last to get on the bus when it finally came, but Ignacio was saving a seat for me. He smiled as I approached.

"Good morning, Delia," he said in English. "How are you today?"

"Fine," I said, and sat without saying more.

"You don't look fine," he said, in Spanish this time.

"I'm fine," I said sharply. I didn't look at him.

He looked back at the station as if the answer to why I was the way I was remained back there. I felt his gaze on me.

"*Problemas con su familia?*"

Problems with my family? I thought, and nearly laughed.

"They are not my family," I said. "My family is in

Mexico. I want to go home," I told him. "I wish I had money to help you buy your car so you could drive me back."

He smiled. "If that's what you want, I would do it," he said. "I promise someday, maybe."

I nodded and thanked him.

Everything was more difficult for me all day. I couldn't shake off the feeling that I was soiled inside and out. It depressed me and made me inattentive in class, which annoyed Señorita Holt. I stumbled over words and sentences I had long since mastered. At the lunch break, she asked me if I were feeling ill. I was afraid she might have the school call my aunt to tell her I was sick, so I said no. I told her I had a bellyache the night before and couldn't sleep well. Lying was not something that had ever come easily to me. I was too quick to shift my eyes.

Señorita Holt didn't speak. She stared at me in silence.

"I cannot help you solve your problem if you do not tell me what that problem is," she said.

I was silent. How could I tell her?

"Okay, go have your lunch, Delia," she told me, and turned away.

Now I felt even more guilty and unworthy. I barely ate my lunch. Although he didn't say much to me, I felt Ignacio's eyes watching me. I was even mean and disinterested in little Mata, who wanted to be friendlier with me. When I returned to class, I tried harder to be attentive and do better in my work, but I was still not doing as well as I should, and Señorita Holt let me know it with her frequent expressions of dissatisfaction, turning now to annoyance and disappointment as she openly criticized me. I was practically in tears when the bell for the end of the day finally sounded. I hurried out before she could call me aside again for a lecture or interrogation.

Ignacio was right behind me as I left the school building. At the moment, I didn't want to talk to him, either. I was sure he would be asking me more questions, too. I just wanted to get back to the *hacienda* and lose myself in the housework. Maybe if I worked very hard and got myself very tired, I would sleep better that night.

On the way to the bus station, however, Ignacio caught up with me.

"You didn't do so well today," he said. "I know Señorita Holt thinks you're the best student in her class."

"No, I'm not the best."

"I think you're the best," he insisted. "Just listening to you, I learn a lot."

I shook my head. Why now, why was everyone trying to give me compliments? The evil eye didn't just have eyes; it had ears. As if to prove it, the *ojo malvado* ordered its vengeance to continue.

I heard him call my name.

Both Ignacio and I stopped to look at Bradley in his sports car. He had pulled up to the curb.

"Get in," he ordered.

I shook my head.

"Who's that?" Ignacio asked.

"You caused trouble between me and Sophia!" Bradley shouted. "My father heard about it through my stepmother already. Get in," he demanded again.

I still hesitated. I felt Ignacio move up beside me protectively.

"Go away," he told Bradley.

"You keep out of this, José, or I'll sic the INS on you."

"My name is not José and I'm not afraid of the INS. I am legally here."

"Yeah, right. Delia, either you get in, or I'm driving over to speak with your aunt right now. Well?"

"What does he say? Who is this boy?" Ignacio asked me. I shook my head.

"It's all right," I said.

"I don't think so," Ignacio replied quickly, and glared at Bradley.

I took a deep breath, lowered my head, and went to his car.

"Now you're being smart," Bradley said.

I got in and almost didn't get the door closed before he shot off, throwing me back in the seat. I turned and looked at Ignacio, who was standing there looking confused, angry, and troubled.

See, Delia, I told myself, anyone you touch gets wounded.

11

One Grief Cures Another

"Okay, what exactly did you tell Sophia, huh? No lies, either, because I can easily find out the truth. Speak!" he shouted.

"She saw you drive me to the house and called me names. All I told them was that you told me to get into your car, and I did not ask you to give me a ride."

"Edward wasn't too friendly today. Are you sure that's all you told them?"

"Yes, that's all," I said.

He relaxed and nodded. "Okay, then, Sophia's lying. She said you said I wanted to be your boyfriend, which doesn't surprise me." He smiled. "Your aunt's not too happy with you, huh? There's a lot of trouble between her and Edward because of you. Isn't that true?"

"Yes," I admitted.

He smiled. "Well, we can't have that, can we? Maybe I'll fix things up for you," he said. "I can do that, you know. I'll tell them we just went for a harmless little ride, and you were very polite and sweet. I'll tell them nothing happened. It's what I told Sophia. She wouldn't believe me, but what she believes doesn't matter as much as what your aunt believes, and she'll believe me. Would you like me to do that, help you out?"

I looked at him to see if he was really sincere.

"I'm not lying to you. It's not a good situation for me, either, to have Edward angry at me," he continued. "I'd like to hear you say, 'Please help me.' "

I was silent. I could feel his anger.

"Do you or don't you want me to help you with your aunt, Delia? I don't have to do anything."

He smiled at my continued silence, but I was afraid to do anything, say anything anymore.

"Okay, I'll just go to your aunt and cry and complain about how you tried to get me to be your lover," he threatened. "I'll get my father to come along, and your aunt will have no choice but to send you back in disgrace. Maybe it will be in the newspapers, too. Hell, you made a lot of trouble for me. I should be very angry."

I started to cry.

"Lucky for you, however, I'm not so angry," he added. "You just do what I ask, and we'll get along fine, and everything will go back to the way it was."

"What do you ask?"

He smiled. "Nothing much, no big deal. Not for you," he said, and slowed down to pull up beside another car in which two boys sat smoking. The driver leaned out of his window as soon as we stopped.

"Hey, Bradley."

"This is Jack and our friend Reuben," Bradley said. "Say hello."

I stared out at them.

"Yeah, hi, Maria," the driver said.

"Her name's Delia, not Maria, Jack."

"Oh, yeah, right. Delia. What's the deal, Delia?" he asked, and they laughed.

"These are good friends of mine," Bradley said. "Say hi. Be nice."

"Hi," I said, and looked away quickly.

"I'd like you to do a little more than that, Delia," Bradley said. "It's what I ask in return for helping you."

"What?" I glanced at them and then back at him. "What do you mean, a little more?"

"All you have to do is go for a ride with them, and things will be just fine between us. I'll fix everything with your aunt," Bradley said. "Go on. Get into the backseat of their car," he ordered.

I shook my head. The terror that shot through me sizzled like a bolt of lightning.

He leaned toward me. "I'm not kidding about this. I'll drive over to your aunt's house right now, and I'll tell her a story that will make her eyes bulge out. She might even have you arrested or something. You'll be in jail with other undocumented Mexicans. They keep the men and women in jail together sometimes, too. They'll ship you back in a cage."

"C'mon for a ride with us, Delia," Jack said. "We're nicer than Bradley."

"Well?" Bradley said.

I opened the car door slowly. The boy named Reuben opened his door at the same time and came around to open the rear door of their car for me. I gazed into it and then back at Bradley, who was waving me on. I looked at Reuben, whose smile reminded me of a coyote pulling back its lips to reveal its teeth, and then I turned and ran as hard as I could down the street, back toward the school. I didn't look behind me, but I heard Bradley curse and then the squeal of tires as he made a sharp U-turn and sped after me. He passed me, waited for some traffic to go by, and turned around again to pull up to the curb and get out of his car to face me.

I stopped running, holding my hand against my side, gasping for breath.

"You're embarrassing me, Delia," he said. "I promised those guys you'd go for a ride with them."

He started toward me. My eyes were so clouded with tears I could barely see. Before he reached me, I heard him cry out and looked up to see Ignacio spinning him around. Both boys were about the same height. Bradley looked broader in the shoulders, but Ignacio had strength more subtle and deep, because when Bradley pushed back on him, Ignacio seized his wrist and turned his arm so easily and hard, Bradley fell to one knee.

"Stop, or I'll break your arm," Ignacio told him, and pulled him toward his car before releasing him.

Bradley looked up at him and then at me. "You'll be sorry, you bitch!" he cried, pointing at me.

Ignacio stepped toward him, and Bradley practically leaped into his car. He cursed at Ignacio and then drove off, nearly running me down.

As soon as he was gone, Ignacio came to me. "Are you all right? What did he do to you?" he asked. "Who is he?"

I shook my head and started to cry again. Ignacio put

his arm around my shoulders and led me back to the sidewalk. Some other drivers looked our way as they passed, and some of the students heading toward the bus station who had seen everything stood watching us.

Ignacio led me to a bench in a small park and sat me down. He stood waiting for me to catch my breath and stop crying.

"So, who is he?" he asked.

"He is my cousin Sophia's boyfriend," I told him. "His name is Bradley Whitfield."

"If he is your cousin's boyfriend, why is he after you? What did he say to make you get into his car, and why were you running away from him?"

"He wanted me to get into another car with other boys."

"What?"

"He wanted me to go for a ride with them."

Ignacio gazed off in the direction Bradley had fled. He looked as if he would tear off after them in a rage.

"Just because you are Mexican, he thinks he can take advantage of you."

I looked away. I was far too ashamed and embarrassed to tell him the rest of it.

"Yes," I said. "I think you are right."

"Such things have happened to other Mexican girls I know, some much younger than you, but because their parents might not be here legally, they don't do much about it," he told me.

"He's very angry, I'm sure. I'm afraid of what will happen now if he goes and tells my aunt stories."

"You must tell your aunt everything first. Tell her how he offered you to his friends."

"She won't believe me," I said.

"Why not?"

"It's complicated . . . my family history. She doesn't want to believe me," I added.

"What do you mean by your family history?" he asked, suspicious.

"No one brought shame on our family name."

"Then what do you mean by family history?"

"She and my grandparents never got along. My grandfather disowned her when she married Señor Dallas. He was much older. She ran off and married him. My parents, my grandmother, none have had much to do with her or she with us until now."

"Then why does she want you here? Why did she send for you and pay for you to come?"

"I don't know," I said.

He shook his head with confusion. "You should speak with my mother and father. They will know what to do. Come to my house."

"I can't. I have to go home to do my work, or she will get even more angry."

"You will come to my house on Saturday, then. I'll get my father to let me use the truck and pick you up. We are celebrating my sister Rosalind's birthday. She will be seven years old. We'll have a wonderful fiesta."

"I'll try," I said, wiping the tears from my face.

"Good. C'mon, I'll walk you to the station. We have not missed the bus yet, but we must walk quickly, okay?"

I nodded.

He took my hand, and we started down the sidewalk. I was very nervous, anticipating Bradley returning with his friends, perhaps, but they didn't come, and we got to the station a few minutes before the bus arrived. When the bus reached my station, Ignacio wanted to get out and walk me to my aunt's *hacienda*.

"It's all right," I said, seeing Edward waiting in his car. "That's my cousin Edward. He is nice to me. I'm okay now."

Ignacio looked out suspiciously. "Are you sure?"

"Yes, I'm sure."

"Remember Saturday," he said.

"Thank you, Ignacio." I leaned over after I stood up and kissed him on the cheek.

Then I hurried out of the bus and to Edward waiting in his car.

Edward didn't start the car and drive off when I got in. Instead, he looked hard at me and glanced back at the bus.

"Who is that boy you kissed?" he asked me.

I was surprised that he had seen me kiss Ignacio.

Before I could respond, he added, "You made a boyfriend quickly."

"No, he's not my boyfriend."

"Then why did you kiss him?" Edward asked. His eyes now resembled his mother's, dark, suspicious. They made me feel guilty of something bad, even though I wasn't.

"He helped me," I said.

"Helped you? How?"

Before I could answer, my tears came pouring down my cheeks. His looks of accusation and suspicion evaporated.

"What happened, Delia? You look terrible, now that I think about it," he said. "You look *enferma*. Are you sick?"

I nodded. *Sick* seemed to be the right way to describe me and all that had happened.

"Bradley *vino a mi escuela,*" I said.

"He came to your school? When?"

"Today."

"Today? Why? *Por qué?*"

How was I to explain this in my elementary English to someone who knew very little Spanish?

"He take me to other boys."

"For what?"

I stared at him. There was no need for any words in any language to get the answer across to him. His eyes widened.

"That bastard," he said.

He started the car. Then he stared ahead a moment and turned off the engine. My heart had started thumping even before he turned back to me, his eyes now showing more than anger. They looked fearful.

"Bradley," he said. "Yesterday. Did he take you right home? Did you go straight to *mi hacienda?*" he asked, gesturing ahead.

I knew what he meant but hesitated, pretending not to understand, so I could think about what I should say.

"He didn't, did he?" he answered for me. "Where did he take you?" he asked. "What did he do?"

I started to cry.

Edward's eyes widened. He nodded and sat back, staring. Without saying another word, he started the engine again and drove. He didn't say another word or ask any more questions until we arrived at the *hacienda.*

"Don't worry," he told me. "He won't bother you anymore. Bradley, *no más.*"

I said nothing. He did not get out with me. Instead,

as soon as I was out, he drove off again. I watched his car speed down the driveway and turn the corner so sharply the tires screamed. A sense of dread came over me. It was as if heavy clouds had moved over the sun. It was still a nearly perfect sky, but I felt shadows pouring down over and around me nevertheless, shadows that followed me into the house.

My sadness and anxiety were driven away the moment my eyes spotted the letter from *mi abuela* Anabela waiting for me on the marble table just inside the entryway. I recognized her handwriting immediately and practically lunged forward to seize the envelope. I hurried upstairs to read it in the privacy of my room.

I placed the envelope on my bed and gazed down at it as if it were some very precious jewel to be admired and not touched. The stamp, the paper, and her handwriting sent me flying back over miles and time to my little village.

Once again, I was walking to school with my girlfriends, waving to store owners opening shops and *cantinas,* seeing the farm workers seated in the backs of trucks heading out to the fields, some of the younger men calling out to us and making us giggle. The village made its own music, music we heard just listening to the sounds of our people as they woke and dressed and ate breakfast to prepare for their day. Back home, my grandmother was preparing her tortillas and listening to the radio.

In the distance, I could see the sun spread its light like butter on bread across the mountains, exciting the birds. On mornings like this, life opened around us like the blossoms of beautiful flowers. As children, we trusted the future, looked forward to fiestas and holidays and the pending excitement of our own maturing.

Our dolls would give way to real babies, our make-believe weddings would evolve into real weddings, with our families celebrating, our mothers crying with both joy and sadness over losing their little girls, and all of our fantasies would settle like light rain and glisten into modest ambitions. It all seemed so simple and true. We weren't even aware of how poor we were and how unhappy we should be. Was it all one great lie?

I sat on the bed and opened the envelope. Before I read the letter, I brought the empty envelope to my nostrils and smelled it to see if I could catch some wonderful aroma I associated with our small *casa, mi abuela*'s cooking, or simply the scent of wildflowers behind the house, anything that would bring me home for an instant. There was nothing. I sighed and began to read.

> *My dearest Delia. You must forgive my spelling and grammar.*
>
> *I have read your letters with such happiness in my heart. To learn about the wonderful* hacienda *you are in, the warm way your cousins have welcomed you, and to think your aunt had already thought of a private tutor to help you with English . . . how wonderful.*
>
> *I read and reread each of your letters every night. Everyone asks about you, of course, and now I have things to tell them, to read to them. I can see how impressed they are. I know when you return, you will already be a real lady, educated and even more beautiful than when you left.*
>
> *You must not worry about me. I am fine. I have some new* mole *customers, and occasionally, I bake something for Señor Lopez, who insists on paying me. So I am fine.*

I know you are busy with your new life, but whenever you can, write to me. Having your letters is the next-best thing to having you here.

I am in church daily praying for you, and Father Martinez has written special prayers for you as well.

I am sure that your parents would be proud of you and what you accomplish in your new life.

Remember you are loved.

Abuela Anabela

My heart felt so heavy under my breast that I was certain it would simply explode with sadness and I would die on this bed. No one here would shed all that many tears for me, if anyone shed any. Since I had come, I had brought only trouble. It didn't matter whose fault it was. None of it would have happened had I not come.

But it was Tía Isabela who had brought me here. I was still confused about why she wanted me. She didn't need another house servant, and when she looked at me, all I did was remind her of her unhappy days back in Mexico. There had to be a good part of her, something inside her that was strong enough to overcome her anger and her hate. Surely, there was a part of her that wanted her family back, and perhaps that was why I was brought here.

I must have patience, I thought. I must have faith, even in this house that had no faith in anything. I knelt beside my bed, and with *mi abuela*'s letter in my hand, I prayed for everyone, even Sophia, who I believed was burning up inside herself. Her selfishness, jealousies, and spite would eat away at her until she was torn apart.

Rising slowly, I took deep breaths and neatly folded my grandmother's letter to put it back into the envelope. I slipped it under my pillow. I would read it again before I went to sleep, and I would read it every night until I received another letter from her. It would be my way of remaining close to her.

I changed clothes and went to do my chores. When I was cleaning one of the downstairs powder rooms, I heard a scream and then the sound of many footsteps in the hallway. I stepped out to see Señor Garman hurrying past the kitchen on his way to the front entrance. Señora Rosario and Inez came hurrying down the hallway as well. Slowly, I walked out and saw *mi tía* Isabela rushing down the stairway.

"What's happening?" I asked Inez.

"Señor Edward was in a car accident," she told me. "An ambulance is taking him to the hospital."

"Hospital?"

My blood chilled, and my heart began to pound.

"The car's out front, Mrs. Dallas," Señor Garman told her, and held the door open.

I watched Tía Isabela run out the front entrance. Señor Herrera came up behind us, and Señora Rosario explained why there was such commotion. He shook his head and returned to the kitchen.

"Where's Sophia?" I asked, looking back up the stairway. "Isn't she home yet?"

"Forget Miss Sophia, just finish your work," Señora Rosario told me. "There's nothing for us to do but that."

My hands were trembling so badly I didn't think I could do anything, but I returned to the powder room and washed the tile floor. Hours passed, and we heard nothing. Sophia didn't return home, either. I showered and changed my clothes for dinner as usual and then went down to the kitchen, where Señor Herrera, Inez, and Señora Rosario were all sitting around the table talking. Nothing was being prepared.

"What's happening?" I asked, my voice so thin and low it betrayed my fear of hearing the answer.

"Señor Garman called to tell us Señor Edward was seriously injured and is still unconscious," Señora Rosario said.

"He may die," Inez added.

Neither of them contradicted her.

"Señora Dallas won't be home for dinner. You can get yourself something to eat," Señora Rosario said. She was looking at me but really looking through me at the tragedy unfolding.

"I'm not hungry," I said. "Thank you."

"None of us is hungry," Inez said.

"What should we do?" I asked.

"We can do nothing but wait," Señora Rosario replied.

I thought about sitting with them but chose instead to return to my room, where I could say a prayer for Edward. Then I lay on my bed, looking up at the ceiling and listening to the sounds around me, the clock ticking, the murmur of the voices below, and the *thump, thump, thump* of my own troubled heart. Close to two hours later, I heard someone running up the stairway. My heart stopped and started. I sat up when my bedroom door was thrown open.

Sophia stood there, glaring in at me.

"What did you tell Edward this time?" she demanded, her hands on her hips. Her hair was wild, and her eyes were blazing as her nostrils flared.

"How is he?" I asked, instead of answering her.

"What did you tell Edward?" she screamed at me.

I heard more footsteps in the hallway. Señora Rosario came up beside her.

"What's going on?" she asked me.

I shook my head.

"Ask her what she told my brother," Sophia ordered. "Go on, ask her. Do it!" she screamed at her when Señora Rosario hesitated with confusion.

Then she spoke in Spanish. "What did you tell her brother?"

"I know what she wants. I understand. First tell me how he is now," I insisted.

She asked Sophia, who rattled it off quickly. From the look on Señora Rosario's face, I knew it was very bad.

"He was driving much too fast and went off the road and hit a stone wall. The airbag exploded in his face, and it seems right now that it has seriously affected his eyesight."

"His eyesight?" I touched my face under my eyes, and Sophia brightened with even more fury.

"That's right, you idiot. Edward is blind!" she screamed. "Blind!"

"They don't know yet if he will be blind long, Señorita Sophia," Señora Rosario told her.

"I heard the doctor, not you. He sounded very pessimistic about it. Well?" she shouted at me. She turned to Señora Rosario. "You translate so she has no excuse, Mrs. Rosario. Translate everything word for word."

She turned back to me.

"What did you say to him? Tell me everything. Whatever you said to him sent him after Bradley. They had a bad argument, and Bradley ran away from him, drove off quickly. Edward went after him, and that was when he got into the accident. Bradley said you made up lies and told them to Edward. What did you tell Edward?"

I understood most of it, but Señora Rosario did translate for her.

"I made up no lies," I said firmly. "No lies. I don't care if you believe me or not."

Sophia deflated a bit and stepped closer to me. "Okay, then, what did you tell him?"

I looked at Señora Rosario.

"Señorita, this is . . ."

"Make her tell me. My mother is very upset."

Señora Rosario looked at me. "Do you wish to tell her?"

I nodded. "Edward was waiting for me at the bus station," I began. "When I got into his car, he saw I was very upset and knew something bad had just happened."

"What?" Sophia asked. "Tell me, or I swear . . ."

"Bradley came for me at school," I said. I was speaking rapidly in Spanish now, and Señora Rosario was translating without comment as quickly as she could. "He said if I didn't get into his car, he would come here and tell your mother stories about me, and she would have me arrested and sent back to Mexico in disgrace."

Sophia smirked, but her skeptical expression was weakening. "Go on, talk," she ordered.

"I got into his car, and he brought me to another car, where there were two boys."

"What two boys?"

"A boy named Jack and another named Reuben," I said, and the skepticism left her face completely.

"Jack Sawyer and Reuben Bennet?"

"I do not know their family names."

"And?" she asked.

"He wanted me to get into the car with them and go

for a ride with them, but it would be more than a ride. They, too, would do bad things to me."

Señora Rosario's eyes widened as she translated. I was too nervous to use any of the English words I had learned.

"What did you do?"

"I got out of his car and ran down the street, back toward the school. Bradley came after me, but my friend Ignacio Davila, a boy in my ESL class, chased him away."

Sophia looked pensive now. She was silent for a moment. Señora Rosario was looking at me and shaking her head.

"And you told all that to Edward?" Sophia asked.

"*Sí*, and what Bradley did to me the day before. I had to tell him," I added.

"Did to you the day before? I thought you said he just drove you home. That's all you told my mother at the dinner table."

"I was ashamed," I said.

"Well, where did you go with him?"

"He took me to where his father is rebuilding a house. There was no one else there working, but he said he wanted to look at what was done."

"He took you to that house?" Her mouth opened and closed. "That's where he tried . . . and what happened after you got there?"

"He forced himself on me," I said.

Señora Rosario didn't translate. She just stared at me, and then she asked, "*Él le violó?*"

"Yes, I was raped," I said, crying.

"What did she say? What did she just say?"

Reluctantly, Señora Rosario translated.

"That bastard, liar. I knew it."

Sophia shook her head, looked at Señora Rosario. Then, mumbling to herself, she walked quickly out of my bedroom, slamming the door behind her. It was like a firecracker.

Señora Rosario looked after her and then turned back to me. She still wore a look of amazement and shock.

"I am sorry to say it, but maybe you should return to Mexico, Delia," she said. "Maybe that would be the best thing for you now."

"Don't be sorry. There is nothing I want more, Señora," I told her. I looked toward my pillow, under which was Abuela Anabela's letter. "Nothing."

12

Hospital Visit

My grandmother had a saying whenever tragedy struck someone again and again. *Un clavo saca otro clavo.* One nail removes another—one grief cures another. I didn't understand it then, but now I thought I did, because after learning what had happened to Edward, I soon put aside grieving over the terrible thing that had happened to me. This sorrow, this tragedy, diminished my own. It did not cure it, but it caused me to put it aside, to stop thinking about poor me and think about poor Edward shut up in this darkness, his beautiful, promising young life perhaps cut off at the knees, as my father might say.

I thought now it was certain that Tía Isabela would send me back to Mexico. I waited in my bedroom, anticipating her arrival any moment. Sometime after midnight, I heard the voices of some people talking below, and then I heard footsteps outside my door. I was sitting on my bed, my hands in my lap, my head down, when she opened the door and entered. There was no longer any pretext, any airs of superiority, in her demeanor. She looked tired but, more important, like someone brought down to walk the earth with us mere mortals. Tragedy had sent her reeling back to her origins. As if to underline all of this, she spoke Spanish as if she had never learned how to speak English.

"You have heard what happened to Edward?"

"Yes. I am so sorry. How is he? Is it true that he is blind?"

"He has retina damage to both eyes caused by the airbag. He will need eye surgery, and the doctor doesn't guarantee anything. They never do," she said dryly. "Both retinas were torn badly."

"I am so sorry."

"Yes, well, instead of worrying about himself, he insists on my bringing you to see him first thing tomorrow morning, so you will not go to school," she said.

"Me?"

Her eyes grew smaller as she stared at me. "Yes, you. He wouldn't tell me why he was chasing after Bradley like that, driving so recklessly, and Sophia has locked herself away in her room. Some people are blessed with children. I am cursed with them."

I shook my head. I wanted to say it wasn't possible to be cursed with children, but I recalled how my mother had described her father's feelings about Isabela. Surely, he had felt cursed, too. He was very bitter, and when she had left them and he had considered her dead, he justified it by saying, "*Cuando el perro se muere, se va la rabia.*" When the dog dies, the rabies are gone.

It would be too cruel to remind her of all that, I thought, even though it was on the tip of my tongue to say, *As ye sow, so shall ye reap.*

"Be ready to go right after breakfast," she told me, turned, and left.

I never thought I would do it, but at that moment, I pitied her and felt sorrier for her than I did for myself. I prayed for Edward and even prayed for Tía Isabela that night. The emotional fatigue of the day and the evening was enough to send me reeling into a dark pit of sleep, with horrid images flashing through nightmares strung together in a bracelet of misfortune and terror. I awoke with a start, feeling as if I had just come up from a pool of ink, gasping. My head felt like one large rock on my neck.

Not having had anything for dinner the night before, I managed some appetite, even though my stomach had turned into a hive of bees. Sophia did not come down for breakfast as usual, and Inez, who had taken back the responsibility of bringing her breakfast to her room, reported that Sophia was still sleeping when she knocked on the door. She didn't want anything, and she would not get out of bed. Tía Isabela went up to speak to her but returned shaking her head.

"That girl seizes on any excuse not to go to school," she muttered to Señora Rosario. "I have no time for her today." She turned to me and told me to be outside in five minutes.

Her Rolls-Royce was brought around, and Señor Garman, glaring at me with disapproval, opened the door for her. I expected I would be told to get in the front passenger seat, but he continued to hold the door open, so I got in after Tía Isabela. I glanced at her and thought she was never underdressed, no matter what the occasion. Even going to the hospital to visit her injured son, she was dressed as if she were going to a grand fiesta.

She wore expensive-looking rings on all of her fingers and a white-gold necklace with diamonds that had matching diamond teardrop earrings. With her fashionable hat and her olive-green dress and shoes, she looked like royalty. I could only be in awe of that air of superiority about her. Once again, she seemed untouchable and far above ordinary people and things in this world. Now that she had regained her strength, even family tragedy dared not disturb her. What were her dreams like? Was she so strong that even nightmares dared not enter her sleep?

There was so much about *mi tía* Isabela that I despised but so much I envied. Was that wrong?

She looked out the window and fiddled with her jeweled purse as we drove along. I didn't want to stare at her, but I kept glancing her way, anticipating her saying something to me. She didn't speak, however, until we arrived at the hospital.

"Just follow me, and wipe off that depressing poor-Mexican-girl look," she said as Señor Garman opened the door for her.

How could she hate what made us both Mexican so much?

She shot off, clearly making me think she wanted me to walk behind her and not side by side. I did just that, but I kept my eyes down and my face turned away from people.

In the elevator, she patted the back of her head and took a deep breath that she didn't release until the elevator opened on Edward's floor. It was as if she were going underwater. Again, I wondered if there was something to learn from how she handled hardships.

She had Edward in a private room with a private-duty nurse. As we drew closer to it, I grew even more nervous, and when we entered the room and I saw Edward's head with bandages over his eyes, I gasped and bit down on my lower lip. His cheeks were bruised, as were his nose and his chin. It looked as if the skin had been peeled off in places.

His nurse, who was sitting near the bed and thumbing through a magazine, nearly leaped to her feet when Tía Isabela entered. Edward sensed she was there. After all, who else could cause a nurse to jump like that?

"Mother?"

"Yes, Edward, I'm here," she said. "How is he doing?" she asked the nurse.

"His vitals are good. He's gotten some sleep," she said.

"Was the doctor in this morning?"

"No, Mrs. Dallas, not yet. I believe he's to be here within the hour."

"Did you bring Delia?" Edward asked the moment they stopped talking.

"She's right here, Edward."

"I want to be alone with her," he said.

"What is the reason for all this intrigue, Edward? It's . . ."

"None of your business, Mother," he finished for her.

She stiffened, glanced at the nurse and then at me.

"Fine. Let's leave them," she told the nurse, and they left the room.

"Delia, come closer," Edward said.

I stepped up to his bed. He reached up, and I took his hand.

"I am sorry for you," I said, and he started to smile and then cried out in pain.

"It hurts to laugh," he said. "You don't mean you're sorry for me. You're sorry for what happened to me."

"Yes."

"I wanted you to come here right away," he said. "Don't let anyone blame you. Do you understand? This is not your fault. I already know you well enough to know you'll blame yourself."

I said nothing. He was right. In my heart, I thought it was my fault. If I had not come to live with him and his sister and mother, he would not be in this hospital bed, and he would not need a serious operation on his eyes.

"You must not return to Mexico," he continued, as if he had the power to read my thoughts. "Don't let my mother send you back."

"How can I stop her?"

"You can stop her. My mother respects only strength. She pushes until someone pushes back. You understand?"

I did understand, but I couldn't imagine pushing back on Tía Isabela.

"I need you to help me get better. Okay?"

I was still holding his hand. "Yes, but how?"

"You'll see. I was afraid you were already sent back. That's why I wanted you brought here right away. Do you understand what I'm saying, Delia?"

"Yes, I do," I said.

"Good. *Muy bueno.* Now I will have plenty of time for you to teach me how to speak Spanish."

I smiled and was still holding his hand when Tía Isabela returned with the doctor.

"You'll have to end this tête-à-tête, Edward. Dr. Morris is here."

Edward released my hand. "Delia is going to help me with my recuperation," he told her. "We've just settled on it. She'll read to me."

"She can't read English, Edward."

"She'll manage. I want to learn more Spanish, anyway."

"We'll discuss this later, Edward. Now is not the time. Let's not jump too far ahead," Tía Isabela said.

"That's what I want," he said sharply.

The doctor put his hand on Tía Isabela's arm to get her to stop any possible argument or unpleasantness. She glared at me, spun on her heels, and retreated to a corner of the room.

"Go wait in the visitors' lounge," she told me in Spanish.

Edward plowed through his pain to smile. "Haven't heard you speak Spanish in some time, Mother," he said.

"Go," she told me, and I left the room. I had no idea where the lounge was, but I stopped another nurse in the hall and asked, "Where I wait?"

"The lounge? Oh, go through that door, and turn right," she said, pointing down the opposite end of the hallway.

"*Gracias*. Thank you," I said, and walked down the hallway.

In the corridor, standing by the door, was a boy about Edward's age, wearing a pair of jeans, a tight black T-shirt, and a royal-blue sports jacket. His light brown hair was very thick and, although not as long as Edward's hair, was nearly down to the base of his neck and over his ears. He had it brushed away from his indigo-blue eyes. I thought he had a very gentle, almost angelic smile.

"Hi," he said. "You're Delia, right?"

"*Sí*, yes."

"I'm a friend of Edward's, Edward's *amigo*. Jesse Butler." He extended his hand. It was as smooth as mine, with thin fingers. On his pinkie was a black onyx ring with a tiny diamond at the center. "*Cómo está* Edward?"

I shook my head and started to explain in Spanish.

"Whoa, sorry. I just know a little Spanish, *un poco español*."

"His eyes," I said, moving my hands over my head to explain the bandages. "Bruises," I added, and ran my fingers over my cheeks, nose, and chin.

He looked through the window in the door and nodded.

"The doctor's in there. Doctor?"

"Yes," I said, "and *mi tía* Isabela."

"Oh, right. Okay, I'll just wait with you," he said, and nodded at the lounge.

We went into the lounge. I thought it was very nice that a friend of Edward's had come right away to see him. He had not mentioned Jesse to me, but he had told me very little about his life, his friends, or even what interested him most to do.

There were only a few other people in the visitors' lounge, but one of them was a woman with a little girl who looked no more than three or four. She spoke Spanish to the girl, who focused her beautiful ebony eyes on me and smiled when I smiled. I began to speak to her in Spanish, too, and her mother asked me who I had here. I explained that my cousin was in a car accident, and she told me her sister's husband had fallen from a scaffold while painting an office building's window frames. Her sister was in with her husband now, and she was watching their little girl. I asked her if she spoke any English, and she said very little. However, she and her sister and her sister's husband were not from Mexico. They were from Costa Rica.

When I asked her how long she had been in the United States, she grew very nervous and mumbled an answer. As if to make things sound okay, however, she told me her sister's little girl, Drina, had been born here. Jesse, who said he spoke little Spanish, listened keenly to our conversation.

He leaned over to whisper in my ear. "I think she's illegal," he said. "Maybe the parents are, too."

I told him Drina was born in America.

"She's an anchor baby," Jesse said.

I shook my head. "Don't understand."

"Baby born *aquí*?"

"*Sí.*"

"Illegal parents are anchored to the U.S. because the baby was born here. You know the word *anchor*?"

I shook my head.

"Tied down, like a boat is tied," he explained, gesturing with his hands.

"Oh," I said. "They stay because of the *niña*."

"That's it."

Drina's *tía* saw we were talking about them and grew even more nervous. She got up and walked Drina out and down the hallway.

Moments later, my aunt came into the lounge. "You

can go see Edward again," she told me, and looked at Jesse.

"Hello, Mrs. Dallas. I'm sorry to hear about Edward's accident."

"Yes. Me, too, Jesse," she said dryly. "You can go see him, but don't stay more than fifteen minutes. Bring her down to the cafeteria, please," she told him, nodding at me. "I'm going to get myself a cup of coffee and something. I haven't eaten much today, as you might imagine."

"I will," Jesse said.

He walked out with me, and we entered the floor and went to Edward's room.

"Hey, stupid," Jesse said as we entered.

"What are you doing here?"

"I figured I'd use you as an excuse to avoid Kasofsky's pop quiz. What do you think I'm doing here?"

Edward reached out, and Jesse took his hand. They held on to each other firmly.

"You look like hell."

"You should know what hell looks like."

Jesse laughed.

"Is Delia with you?"

"Right next to me. So, what happened?"

"I told you what I suspected about that bastard Whitfield."

"Yes."

"Well, it was true. She told me so," Edward said, and Jesse turned my way. From the look on his face and the few words I had picked up, I understood completely. A wave of shame washed through me and reddened my cheeks.

"You went after him?"

"Damn right."

"What would you have done if you caught him, Edward? That's like those dogs who go chasing and barking after trucks. What if they caught up with the truck? What then?"

He looked at me, but I shook my head. He was speaking too quickly and saying things I didn't understand.

"I would have found a way to smash in his face."

"Looks like you found a way to smash your own instead," Jesse said.

Edward was quiet.

I noticed they were still holding hands.

"Make sure she's all right," Edward finally said, nodding in my direction. "No telling what my mother might do because of this, and it's definitely not Delia's fault."

"I'll check up on her," Jesse promised.

"Good."

"I guess I'll have to come around more often, anyway. You're not exactly rushing out and around again."

"Thanks."

"What are they going to do?"

"Operate day after tomorrow on my eyes."

Jesse's face filled with concern; his eyes looked as if they were flooding with tears.

"Don't worry," Edward said, as if he could sense Jesse's feelings through his hand. "My mother won't permit the operation to be a failure."

Jesse laughed. "I gotta take her down to the cafeteria to meet your mother now. I'll come by later tonight."

"Right."

Jesse glanced at me, and then he leaned over and kissed Edward on the cheek. The sight of two young men being so affectionate with each other stunned me for a moment. Jesse smiled at me.

"Describe the look on her face," Edward told him.

"A cross between being electrocuted and finding a pot of gold."

Edward laughed and then moaned with the pain. "Hey, Delia," he said, reaching toward me.

I moved quickly to take his hand.

"You hang in there until I get home, okay? Everything will be all right. How do you say everything will be all right in Spanish?"

"*Todo será bien,*" I said, and he repeated it and laughed.

"Ow. It hurts too much to laugh. Get out of here so I can feel sorry for myself," he told Jesse.

"Right. See you later."

"*Hasta la vista,* you mean."

"*Sí,*" Jesse said. He touched his hand, nodded to me, and we walked out.

He glanced at me with a soft smile as we went to the elevator. "Edward and I like each other very much," he said when the elevator door closed and we were the only ones in the elevator. "You understand?"

"Yes," I said.

"You okay about it?" he asked. "Okay?"

"Yes."

"It's our secret. *Secreto,*" he said. "Okay?"

"Yes," I said. I was still a little too shocked to say much more.

I followed him out and down the corridor to the cafeteria, where *mi tía* Isabela was sitting at a table by herself, looking out at the hospital employees, doctors, and nurses with a condescending expression, as if she were in charge of everything and wasn't entirely pleased.

"Oh, Jesse," she said as soon as we approached. "Do me a big favor, will you?"

"Absolutely, Mrs. Dallas."

"Take Delia to her school. I have a beauty-parlor appointment I must get to. My stylist is worse than a doctor when it comes to schedules."

"No problem. I'll be glad to take her," Jesse said.

"Good. Thanks. Go with him, and don't get into any trouble today," she told me in Spanish.

"I don't get into trouble," I said, recalling Edward's advice to push back. I wanted to say more, but I pressed my lips together to trap the fiery words that were threatening to burst out. She seemed to sense it. I thought there was almost a smile of appreciation on her face, as if she were seeing something about herself in me. Maybe Edward was right, or maybe I was hoping and dreaming too much, I thought, and quickly left with Jesse.

Although it wasn't a sports car, he had a very expensive-looking automobile. He saw how I was looking at it and told me it was a Mercedes.

"It was my older brother's car, but he went to college, and I inherited it," he explained. "My older brother's . . . now mine."

I nodded. "I understand."

"You've picked up a lot of English already."

"I knew some English before I came. *Poco*. Then I learned more quickly, and now I have a good teacher."

"You'll learn English quicker than Americans learn Spanish, I'm sure," he said. He continued, speaking very slowly, almost as if he were talking in his sleep. "Edward and I have known each other for some time, but we became close friends only about a year ago. You understand?"

"Yes."

"No one really knows how close we are," he said. "Most think it or suspect, but no one knows for sure."

I nodded. "*Secreto,*" I told him, and he smiled.

"Yes, for now, that's better. His mother," he said, shaking his head and widening his eyes.

I laughed. He didn't have to say any more about it. I could easily imagine Tía Isabela's face if she had seen them kiss like that.

"You're a smart girl, Delia, and very pretty. I hope things get better for you here."

"*Gracias.*"

After he pulled up to the school, I thanked him for the ride. As I started out, he reached for my arm.

"Edward was always trying to get back early to take you home from the bus, right? Home from the bus?"

"*Sí.*"

"I'll take you home from the bus," he said. "Wait for me if I'm not there right away. Understand?"

"Yes, thank you," I said.

"Have a good day," he told me, and I got out of his car. I watched him drive away, and then I headed in and hurried to my classroom.

Señorita Holt paused in the middle of whatever she was telling the other students when I stepped in.

"Why are you late?" she demanded. "In English. Reply in English."

I looked at the others, who were all staring at me. Ignacio looked very concerned.

"My cousin Edward," I began, "banged his car into a tree and is in hospital with bandages . . ." I gestured around my head. "Bad with his eyes."

"Not bad with his eyes. Say it properly," she ordered.

I thought. Everyone was so still they looked as if they were all holding their breath for me.

"Hurt his eyes. Now he's blind."

There was an audible gasp from some of the other students.

"Maybe not forever," I added, proud of myself for remembering the English word *forever*.

"Very well. Take your seat. We're practicing how to order food in restaurants right now. It was chapter seven. Did you read chapter seven last night?"

"No, Señorita Holt. My cousin . . ."

"Where are your books and workbooks?"

"I was at the hospital, and . . ."

"Never mind. Enough time has been wasted. Just sit down and do as well as you can. Who was next?" she asked, and Marta raised her hand eagerly.

Ignacio followed me with his eyes to my seat. He was afraid to speak, but he slid his chair and desk closer so I could use his book with him. I glanced at Señorita Holt to see if she would be upset, but she said nothing. It was hard to concentrate on the work, but I did my best, and I thought I did well with her questions, even though I hadn't read the chapter.

Later, when we broke for lunch, I told Ignacio all that had happened. I did not talk about Edward and Jesse's relationship, of course.

"I am sorry about your cousin's accident," Ignacio said. "Are you still able to come to the fiesta at my home on Saturday?"

"I do not know. I have not yet asked my aunt," I said. "It's not a good time for me to talk about going to a party."

"No," he said, his face darkening with disappointment.

"But let's wait to see," I added, bringing some brightness back into his eyes.

"It will be like going home for you," he promised. "You'll see."

I must have done even better in the afternoon in class, because Señorita Holt pulled me aside at the end of the day to tell me she was happy with my rapid progress and hoped I would not let anything slow me down.

"I am hoping to get you into regular classes sooner than anyone would expect," she said.

I thanked her and hurried out to make the bus. Ignacio was saving me a seat. When I excitedly told him what Señorita Holt had said, he didn't look happy for me.

"You'll be a *gringa* before you know it," he said. "And forget me."

"I'll never be a *gringa*," I said, smiling. Then I stopped smiling and said, "I am who I am forever, and I would never forget you."

He liked that and talked mostly about the upcoming fiesta at his house to celebrate his sister's birthday. He told me about the relatives who lived near enough to attend and all of the different foods and pastries that were being prepared. He added that he played a little guitar and would be performing.

"I'm not very good," he said, "but I'll do it for my sister and my mother."

When we arrived at the bus station, I saw Jesse was already parked and waiting. I quickly explained who he was, so Ignacio would not think I had found a boyfriend. However, he still looked suspicious. His proud Latin way wouldn't permit him to watch me walk to Jesse's car and get in. I saw how he kept his face forward and didn't even glance in my direction.

"Hi," Jesse said, opening his door and going around to open the door for me. "*Cómo está?*"

"*Bien,*" I said, and got in.

"Your cousin Sophia?" he said when he got in again.

"Yes?"

"She turned up at school this afternoon . . . came to *escuela.*"

"Oh?"

"To go after Bradley. There was some to-do."

"To-do?"

"Argument, fight . . . big mess. She's telling everyone you were raped."

I just stared at him.

"You know that word?"

"Yes. *Violado.*"

He nodded. "Like violated. Right. That's what she's telling people," he said. He started the car and drove toward my aunt's *hacienda.*

She was telling everyone I was raped? My aunt still did not know what had actually happened to me. What would she say or do now?

"If there's one person you don't want on your tail, it's Sophia Dallas," Jesse said, smiling. He looked away and then back at me. "You all right, Delia?"

I found that for the moment, I was unable to speak. My throat felt as if it had closed up.

I didn't have to wait long to find out what this would all mean for me. As soon as Jesse let me out at the house and I started up the stairway to the entrance, the door opened.

My aunt Isabela stood there looking out at me.

"It doesn't take you long to go from one to another, does it?" she asked me, gazing toward Jesse's disappearing car.

I stood looking up at her, confused.

"But you told him to take me to school."

"Yes, but not to take you home. Never mind. Follow me to my office," she said. "We have a lot to discuss, you and I."

She turned away, leaving the door open for me.

I looked back toward the gates and thought, *Just run, Delia, run.*

Cross back over.

Go home.

Just as Señora Rosario suggested.

Surprisingly, however, a part of me rose along my spine, as if the sleeping pride of my Latino ancestors had woken and stood now in full parade dress.

With my head high, I entered my aunt's home and followed the sound of her footsteps down the long marble corridor to what I knew would be a different sort of battlefield.

Edward's words echoed in my mind: "My mother respects only strength. She pushes until someone pushes back. You understand?"

I understood.

But was that enough?

13

In Confidence

I hadn't yet been in Tía Isabela's office. It was, I imagined, originally her husband's office. The walls were paneled in dark wood, and there was a slate floor with a rich-looking ruby oval rug under and around the desk. Covering the wall on one side of the office was a bookcase from floor to ceiling, each shelf filled with volumes of reference books and novels. On the wall behind the desk was a large portrait of Tía Isabela and her husband, dressed formally and standing in front of the fireplace in the living room. It looked like a portrait of royalty. All they needed were crowns and scepters.

In the picture, Tía Isabela looked much younger and resembled my mother much more. I felt sure now that she had had a plastic surgeon work on her face, changing her nose, especially, not that she wasn't very attractive before that was done.

She stood behind the large dark cherry-wood desk,

folded her arms under her breasts, and nodded at the dark brown leather chair in front of the desk.

"Sit," she said, and I hurried to the chair.

She glanced up at the portrait as if she needed guidance from her husband. It made me wonder how she had managed to conduct business affairs all these years after his death. As far as I knew, she never had formal higher education. She married when she was a waitress in a hotel and hadn't even finished high school. I was sure she had known nothing about business. My mother said money went through her fingers like sand.

Had her husband taught her all she needed to know, or did she have very good people working for her? Despite the manner in which she had treated me when I arrived, and still treated me, I couldn't help but be interested in her. It was difficult to imagine her coming from the same small village, learning her basics in the same small school, walking the streets I walked, and being part of the simple fiestas and activities in our small village to get where she was now. From where or what had she gotten her ambition? Was it merely rooted in hatred for all that she was and had, or did someone inspire her?

Once again, she turned a scrutinizing, suspicious face at me, her eyes small. Her look made me terribly self-conscious. I was afraid to move a finger or take too deep a breath. Her gaze was like a hot, glaring light in a police station turned on a suspected criminal.

I think because she was so upset about Edward and so impatient with my understanding of English, she again spoke in *español*.

"Why didn't you tell me what Bradley Whitfield had done to you? Why did you let me believe he had only brought you home? I have to hear about this from a friend whose daughter brought the story home from school? Thanks to Sophia, of course. My big-mouth daughter. How dare you keep this from me? Well?" she snapped before I could utter a sound.

"I was ashamed," I said.

"Ashamed?" She laughed and pulled the desk chair out abruptly. After she sat, she shook her head. "If he forced himself on you, why should you be the one who is ashamed?"

"I was too innocent to realize what he had intended. I did not . . ."

"Resist enough?" she asked, that wry smile still on her lips.

"Yes."

"Maybe you didn't want to resist," she said.

I shook my head.

"Maybe you were hoping he would do just what he did. Maybe you led him on and encouraged him, just like you encouraged Señor Baker."

"Oh, no, Tía Isabela. I did nothing to encourage anyone, especially not Señor Baker."

"Right, you did nothing," she said, nodding. "Not only do you look like your mother now, but you sound just like her. No woman is ever that innocent, Delia," she said. "Not even your mother."

"I am. I was."

"Oh, please. I am sure you knew what Bradley Whitfield wanted the moment you got into his car. For a woman, it's instinctive. You can almost smell their hunger."

"No, Tía Isabela. I am not lying to you. I suspected nothing. He was Sophia's boyfriend, so I didn't imagine . . ."

"Right. How often have you been with boys like that in Mexico? How often have you not resisted enough?"

"Never, Tía Isabela."

"So, you claim you're as pure as the driven snow, is that it?" she asked.

"I do not understand."

"You and your mother, the holy angels." She sat back, her smile still sharp, cold. "Everyone knows you Latinos have hotter blood than the rest of us."

"Us? Are you not Latino, too?"

"Never mind me," she snapped. "I'm not the one who has brought shame on this house." She leaned forward. "And I assure you, I don't want this sort of performance going on in my home."

"Performance?"

"This innocent act. You do it so well, just like your mother, and now you drove Edward to go off like some knight fighting for your honor, only he injured himself very badly. There is a very, very good chance he'll never regain his full vision."

I felt the tears coming, my throat tightening. "I did not ask him to do that."

"Oh, stop it. We all know how young girls ask boys to do things for them and to them. They don't have to actually say anything. Your face, your eyes, your wounded look is enough to tear up their hearts. Edward has always been particularly vulnerable to that sort of thing. I think that's why he hasn't had a girlfriend for any significant period of time. He loses his heart too easily and flits about. I've tried to give him some advice, guide him, warn him, but he's like . . ."

"Like you were when you were younger," I dared suggest.

She stared a moment, and then she smiled again, but this looked like a smile of appreciation more than sarcasm.

"Yes, exactly. That's why I knew he could get himself into trouble if he wasn't careful." She stared again, this time silently. I could see she was deciding what to say next, whether or not to tell me something. It made me uneasy. I squirmed in the chair. Her silences were like needles.

"What did you think of Jesse?"

"Jesse? Edward's friend?"

"You know another Jesse?"

"No, Tía Isabela. I thought he was very nice, kind. He was very worried about Edward."

"Very. How did they behave together?"

"Behave?" I couldn't stop my face from reddening with the memory of how Jesse had kissed Edward.

I saw she was considering me harder.

"Maybe you have been too cloistered in that hovel they called a home. Tell me, were you taught to look away if you saw two people doing something unclean, forbidden, sinful? Well?"

"Yes," I said.

She looked away and stared out the window. Then she glanced up at the portrait again, looking as if she were hearing her husband's voice.

"I should send you right back," she finally said. She said it like a thought aloud.

"I will understand," I said, a little too quickly.

She turned back to me with a look of surprise. "You would, wouldn't you? You'd understand, and you would accept your pathetic fate. You'd even go to church and give thanks."

"Yes," I said. "I would."

She slapped the desk and leaned forward. "Damn you. Don't you see how that would be a defeat, a retreat? Have you no spunk at all? Isn't any of my blood flowing through your simple brain? Where is your ambition, your hope for yourself? Don't you see the opportunity for yourself here? You can't be that stupid."

"I am not stupid."

"No. Your teacher thinks you're rather bright, actually. I've already been told." She sat back again. "Well, I'm not sending you back," she said after a moment. "First, Edward would be very upset, and I don't want to do anything to hurt his potential recuperation. If you have any feelings, you would think of that, too."

"I do. I want to stay to help him."

"Help him," she muttered. She looked out the window again, thought for a few moments, and then turned back to me. "All right, I'm going to let you stay, and I'm going to do more to help you fit in here. I'm going to get you a better wardrobe and not just those hand-me-downs from Sophia. I'm going to arrange for your safe delivery to your school and return. No more buses and accepting rides from boys. You won't have to do any more household duties.

"The whole community knows now that you're my niece, so there's no point in pretending anything else, but that means you have even more responsibility to protect my good name and my reputation. If you behave, help, I'll see to it that you're well provided for, especially if you are capable of attending college. In short, I'll make you into a *norteamericana.* And I will continue to send something to your grandmother periodically to keep her from starving or dying in the muddy street."

Before I could even think to say thank you, she added something more.

"But I want you to do something for me."

"What, Tía Isabela? What can I possibly do for you?"

"Not for me so much as for Edward, I suppose," she said.

"Edward?"

"I want you to tell me if his friendship with this Jesse is more than just a friendship. I'm worried about him."

I was stunned for a moment. "You mean you want me to spy on Edward?"

"And you can spy on Sophia, too. Let me know if she does anything wrong. We might as well make full use of your goody-goody innocence."

I didn't know what to say. I was surprised about Edward and Jesse, but to betray them, betray Edward, and then to be a tattletale on Sophia, too? Didn't she hate me enough already?

"I would not like to be . . ."

"Don't pretend any discomfort about it, Delia. I saw the expression on your face when I asked you about Edward and Jesse before. You either saw something or sensed it, too. Well?"

"They are friends. They . . ."

"I have spoken my piece," she said, standing. "You know what I want, and you know I am going to reward you. Just be like you really are, like everyone else, like both your mother and me, selfish, and you'll be just fine. I've got other things to do," she added, and started out of the office. At the door, she paused. "This weekend, we'll go shopping for your clothes."

"This weekend?"

"Yes, this weekend. Must I repeat everything?"

"I was . . . invited to a fiesta, a birthday party my friend Ignacio's family is having for his sister. I would like to attend Saturday night," I said

"Why?" she asked, stepping back toward me. "Why do you want to continue to have anything to do with riffraff? Don't you want to mix with people from higher-class homes, wealth?"

"They are my people," I said. "They are not riffraff."

She stared.

I had the sense that I could be more demanding now that she had been so revealing and had demanded such a thing from me.

"I want to go," I said firmly.

"So, go," she said, waving her hand. "Wallow in the poor, immigrant swamps. Maybe I can't do anything for you, after all. Maybe you are your mother's daughter."

She left, her words ringing in my ears.

"There's nothing I want more, Tía Isabela," I said softly in her wake, "than to be my mother's daughter."

Of course, she didn't hear me. She never would, I thought.

What a surprise this private talk with her had been for me. It left my head spinning, because what she had said was filled with both threats and promises. She looked down on me, and yet she reluctantly expressed admiration for my intelligence. Was I part of what she hated, or was I somehow her personal project, someone she wanted to save? Should I hate her or admire her?

Practically in a daze, I made my way through the house and up to my room. I started to change my clothes to go down to help with dinner preparations, when I re-

membered Tía Isabela had declared that I would have no
more chores. Never before in my life had I gone a day
without helping in the house in some way. This, too, left
me confused. Now I would be one of those waited upon
and looked after? I sat on my bed, actually lost for a few
moments. What should I be doing?

My door was abruptly opened, and Sophia came in.
She closed it behind her and stood there for a moment
staring at me.

"How was my brother?" she asked, speaking each
word slowly and loudly, as if I were deaf. "I'm told you
speak better English, or at least enough to understand
most things," she added when I didn't respond quickly
enough.

"A little better," I said.

"What? He was a little better, or you speak English a
little better?"

"He is hurt," I said.

"I know he's hurt, stupid. Jeez."

She walked over to the vanity table and fidgeted with
my hair brush.

"I want to know about Bradley," she said, turning.
"Did you let him know you liked him? Is that what happened?"

I shook my head. "I don't like him," I said.

"He's a creep," she told me. She drew closer, until
she was right in front of me. "Did he pin you down or
what?"

"Pin?"

"Jeez. Did he jump on you, push you to the floor,
what? I want to know the details."

I shook my head. "I don't understand. Jump?"

"Oh, my God. You don't know enough English yet.

How am I supposed to talk with you, huh?" She thought a moment and then said, "Okay, you know what *pretend* means?"

"Yes, pretend, make-believe."

"Good. Pretend I'm Bradley, okay?" she said, and then she lunged at me, seizing my upper arms, and pushed me down. Before I could resist, she lay over me. I didn't know what to do. She was heavy, and she was pushing hard on my arms. "Was this how it happened?"

I shook my head and then nodded quickly.

"Yes or no? Forget it," she said, turning over on her back beside me. She stared up at the ceiling. I was afraid to move a muscle. Then she turned and braced herself on her elbow. "You want to know something?"

"Know? Yes."

"I never did it with Bradley. Everyone thinks I did, but I didn't. Not that he didn't try. I wasn't ready to let him, and then you go and do it with him."

"No," I said. "I did not let him."

"I don't know whether to believe you or not, but I accused him of it anyway. You weren't a virgin, right? You did it before, right?"

"No."

She thought a moment, still remaining beside me, propped on her elbow. "But did you like it? I mean, after you couldn't stop him, was it still . . ."

"No," I said, shaking my head vigorously. "I did not like it, like him. No."

"I don't know whether to believe you or not. You know," she said, her eyes beady, mean, "in some places in the Middle East, if you're raped, your own family could have you killed or something. You may not understand every word I'm saying, but you get it," she added, and stood up. She glanced at me angrily and walked about the room again.

"Bradley's going around telling my friends that he went with you because I frustrated him. He called me names, a tease. I can't stand him now. We should have him arrested. My mother should have him arrested. You will go to the police, and then you'll go to court, and he'll go to jail," she said. "You go tell my mother to do that. That will shut him up."

"Police?" I shook my head.

"You've got to!" she screamed at me. "Or you're a liar!"

"I'm not a liar."

"Then you'll do it. It's settled," she said, and went to the door. "We'll inform my mother at dinner. I'll do the talking. I'll tell her you asked me to do the talking." She pointed her finger at me. "You just nod when I nod, understand? Nod."

I started to shake my head, but she walked out.

Later, still trembling from the things Sophia did and said, I went down to the dining room. I felt very strange, just going in to sit without doing a thing in the kitchen, but both Señora Rosario and Inez behaved as if it had always been this way.

"Are you coming with me to the hospital to see Edward after dinner, Sophia?" Tía Isabela asked her.

"I hate hospitals," she replied. "I'll go after the operation. Maybe."

Tía Isabela glanced at me, but she didn't ask me to go with her.

"Garman will be taking Delia to school every morning," she told Sophia, "and picking her up at the end of the day from now on."

"How am I getting to school? Edward can't drive me, and I wouldn't be seen breathing the same air Bradley Whitfield breathes."

"For the time being, I'll have Casto take you in the station wagon," Tía Isabela said.

"Some Mexican worker taking me to school, and in that old beat-up car we use for deliveries and junk?"

"If you had worked at getting your driver's license, Sophia, you'd be able to drive yourself."

"Well, why don't you let Casto drive her in the station wagon and let Garman take me? They could speak Spanish together. It would be easier for her."

"I want Garman looking after her," Tía Isabela said. "With him around, neither Bradley nor any of his idiot friends will so much as look her way."

"But . . ."

"That's final."

"I won't go to school. I'll stay home."

"You'll go, or I'll take away every other privilege you have. Don't test me," Tía Isabela warned her.

Sophia glared at me, looked at her food, and then folded her hands and took a breath. "Okay, Mother, but what are you going to do about Delia's situation?"

"What situation?"

"Her rape, Mother. She came to my room just before we came down to dinner, and she asked me to ask you to go to the police."

"What?" Tía Isabela turned to me.

"Didn't you ask me to ask her?" Sophia asked me before Tía Isabela could speak. She nodded to signal that I should nod, but before I could, Tía Isabela spun on Sophia.

"I'm not going to drag this family and this name

through some ugly courtroom drama. Are you mad? You want to see us in the newspapers? You want to see me shunned by everyone?"

"He shouldn't be able to get away with it!" Sophia cried. "She wants you to do it."

Tía Isabela turned to me and asked in Spanish if I had gone to Sophia to ask for such a thing. I looked at Sophia. She was nodding to prompt me. I did the best I could to get out of the situation diplomatically. I simply told Tía Isabela that we had spoken of it, but I said nothing about asking her.

"It's out of the question," Tía Isabela told Sophia. "You'll have to get your revenge some other way, Sophia."

Sophia mumbled and sulked throughout the rest of the dinner. As soon as she finished, she rose and marched out of the room.

Tía Isabela turned to me. "Edward will be operated on tomorrow morning," she said. I wondered why she hadn't told Sophia. "I have the best eye surgeon in the area."

"I will pray for him," I said. "I would go to the church with you and pray, Tía Isabela."

"Go to the church with me? Let's not overdo it, Delia. You've got yourself into a good thing here. You don't have to do any more than what I asked you to do."

She rose, and so did I.

"Saturday morning, I'll take you to my boutique, and we'll get you some of the clothing I promised. You'll have something nice to wear to that . . . fiesta," she said, as if it were something disgusting. "I'm sure you'll be the nicest dressed."

She looked toward the doorway and then to me.

"I want to know if that daughter of mine is into any drugs, even marijuana. You let me know instantly," she said, and walked out of the dining room.

Inez came in immediately and started to clear the table. Out of habit, I joined in, but Señora Rosario came to the doorway and stopped me.

"You don't do that anymore," she said. "Enjoy her generosity while you can. Believe me," she added, "it won't last long."

Why was it I didn't feel that I was the recipient of any generosity?

Maybe another of my grandmother's expressions had the answer. I suggested it to Señora Rosario.

"*No es el que puede dar pero el que quiere dar.* It's not the one who can give but the one who wants to."

Señora Rosario laughed.

How strange, I thought, but this was the first time she had laughed at anything I had said or done.

Even Inez was smiling.

I left for my room to study my ESL workbook assignments and to pray for Edward's recovery.

The moment I entered my room, Sophia came in behind me and closed the door.

"You didn't help very much with my mother," she said. "You didn't nod," she added to be sure I understood. "That's all right. I'll come up with a way to have Bradley pay. You want him to suffer, don't you? At least you want that, right? Understand? Make Bradley suffer. You know suffer?"

"Yes, but God will make him suffer," I said.

"I know that, but there's no reason we can't help God, is there? He'll appreciate it. Look," she said, smil-

ing, "I'm sorry I was mean to you when you arrived.
You're my cousin . . . what's *cousin* in Spanish?"

"*Prima.*"

"Right. You're my *prima*. We have to look out for
each other, help each other, okay? *Sí*?"

"Yes," I said.

"Good. We'll pal around. You can go out with me
Saturday night."

"Saturday night?"

"Right. There's a party. Bradley will be there, and . . ."

"No, I'm to go to a fiesta Saturday."

"What? A fiesta? Where?"

"*Mi amigo* Ignacio . . . *el cumpleaños de su hermana.*"

"What? What's that? In English," she ordered.

"His sister, a birthday."

"Ignacio? Wasn't he the one who beat up Bradley?"

"Yes," I said.

"He likes you, huh?" she asked, smiling. "You know?"
She pressed her lips into a kiss.

I felt myself blush. "*Quizás,* maybe."

"Right, maybe. I'm sure he wants to be your boyfriend."

"*Quizás.*"

"*Quizás, quizás*. I'm sure he does, or else he wouldn't
invite you to a fiesta." She thought a moment. "Does he
know what happened to you, everything? Does he know
everything?"

"No, not everything."

"What, then, just what Bradley tried to do with you
with the other boys?"

"*Sí.*"

"But he was very mad, very angry when he heard
about that, right?"

"Angry, yes. He looked like . . . like *él le mataría*."

"What? English. Tell me in English."

"Kill . . . kill him if he found him."

"Good," she said. "Let me know where your fiesta is going to be. *Dónde* fiesta, okay?"

"*Por qué* . . . why?"

"Leave it up to me. I'm on your side, remember? I'm your *prima*." She smiled. "Here," she said, taking off her beautiful gold and diamond bracelet. She took my wrist and started to put it on me. "You need to look good now. You're my *prima*." She fastened it. "See? Beautiful, right?"

"Yes, but it is yours."

"Not anymore. Now it's yours," she said. "Remember. *Dónde* fiesta?" she added, smiled, and left.

I stared at the beautiful bracelet. I knew enough about jewelry to know it was worth *mucho dinero*. What it cost could keep my grandmother with enough food and necessities for a year, maybe even two. I stared at it, thinking about all the work, all the *mole* she would have to make to equal its value. In an instant, with almost no thought at all, Sophia had given it to me. She had no appreciation of what this much money meant back in Mexico, which was part of her heritage as well as it was mine, even though *mi tía* Isabela had kept her from thinking so. It wasn't just national boundaries that had kept us apart. I was crossing much more when I crossed into America and came to this house and this family.

Whenever I had complained about not seeing my other cousins very much in Mexico, my grandmother would smile and tell me what her grandmother had told her, *Más vale amigos cercanos que parientes lejanos*. It is better to have close friends than distant relatives.

As I continued to stare at the bracelet, fascinated with its beauty and value, I wondered in my heart if she had been right. Perhaps I should have kept my relatives distant.

Of course, I had no choice.

I went to the window and looked out on the beautiful property, now bathed in a silvery moonlight that made it all seem more like a setting in a dream, and I thought to myself, how simple, how easy it would have been for me not to be here.

If only my father had taken a little longer that morning and started out a little later. If only my mother would have needed to do one more thing before leaving the house. If only another vehicle had slowed them down or my father had to stop on the way because of something he had forgotten. If only the drunken driver had gone a little slower.

What were my parents talking about just before it had happened? Were they talking about my party, my birthday, about how quickly time had gone by and how grown-up I was? Were they happy about it or sad? Were they thinking about my future, planning to do more and more for me? Were they as hopeful as ever, their imaginations running freely? Were they laughing? Did my mother lean over to kiss him?

Did they shout for me that terrible moment when they knew what was coming?

I could hear them now. I could hear their voices.

To what place had they crossed over? Wherever it was, were they thinking as hard about me as I was about them?

I looked at the time. My grandmother was asleep by now back in Mexico. Knowing her, she probably had said good night to my empty bed.

"*Buenas noches,* Abuela Anabela," I whispered.

And then I knelt and prayed for Edward and, as I was sure *mi abuela* Anabela would have wanted, prayed for Tía Isabela and for Sophia and for Abuela Anabela, of course, before I prayed for myself.

I went to sleep with the bracelet still on my wrist, feeling guilty about taking it but also feeling some security because of its value.

For now, I realized, if I left tomorrow, fled back to Mexico, I would return with something more than my name.

What I had lost in the exchange and what more I might still lose was the toll I had paid for crossing boundaries that truly might have been forbidden.

14

A Warning

I could see that Señor Garman was not happy waiting for me outside by the car when I came out to go to school. He leaned back against the Rolls-Royce with his arms folded, his hands on his elbows, and glared at me as I approached. The morning sunlight, unhampered by a single cloud, danced over the polished metal around him. He had taken Tía Isabela to the hospital to await the outcome of Edward's operation and returned.

Everyone in the house now knew what was happening, knew that this was the morning of Edward's critical eye operation. Sophia was raging with fury that her mother had not told her the night before. When she asked if I knew, I nodded, which made her even angrier.

"So now I'm to be a bodyguard to a Mexican teenager," Señor Garman muttered. "How did you manage to convince Mrs. Dallas?" he asked me. I wasn't completely sure what he was saying, so I didn't answer. He grunted and opened the door for me.

A few days ago, I was walking quite a distance to take a public bus to school, and now I was being driven by a chauffeur in a car that might be worth all of the cars together back home in my village. I sat rigidly and waited for him to get in and start away. Before we did, I saw Casto Flores drive up in the dull light brown station wagon. The right rear fender had a deep dent in it, and it looked as if it needed a good washing.

Sophia came out and looked at the Rolls and then the station wagon before marching down the steps in a huff to get in. She looked as if she were holding her nose. I saw that it amused Señor Garman.

"You're in this, and the princess is in that. Let me know your secret," he told me.

My secret, I thought, is to win the trust of my cousins and then reveal their secrets.

The sight of a golden Rolls-Royce with a chauffeur bringing a poor Mexican girl to the public school not only raised eyebrows, but stopped conversations and all activity in the parking lot and at the front of the school. I was almost too embarrassed to get out when Señor Garman came around to open the door for me. I clung to my workbooks and kept my eyes down. He asked what time I came out of the building at the end of the school day, and I told him so quickly he had to have me repeat it. Then I hurried to the nearest entrance, walking, I was sure, as would a Japanese geisha. I heard some catcalls and laughter but ignored everything.

The news of my luxurious transportation to school

preceded me with electric speed, however, and I over-heard students asking one another who I was. Before, I was nothing more than a passing shadow, another Mexican teenager not worth noticing. No one had even asked my name or given me more than a passing glance. I felt invisible. Now, I was thrust into the center of attention.

The windows of the ESL class looked out over the parking lot, so all of the other students who had already arrived had seen me brought to school in my aunt's Rolls-Royce. Ignacio's face was awash in questions, and Señorita Holt gave me the strangest look. It was almost as if I had somehow been deceiving her. I took my seat quickly, and she brought the class to order. Despite the work we were all told to do, I could feel the eyes of curiosity around me.

It wasn't until our lunch break that I could speak with any of them, but it was only Ignacio who had any idea whatsoever why I would be delivered to school in such a manner. He thought it might have something to do with Edward's accident, however. I told him it was my aunt's way of protecting me and herself from more embarrassment. I told him more about Edward's injuries.

"It's nice that he wanted to protect you from those boys. I worry for my little sister, worry that something similar could happen to her someday. That's why it's best we stay with our own people."

I calmed him and pleased him when I told him my aunt had given me permission to go to his family's fiesta for his sister Rosalind's birthday.

"I will come to your aunt's *hacienda* at three o'clock on Saturday to bring you there," he said. Suddenly, he noticed the bracelet Sophia had given me. "Where did you get such a valuable piece of jewelry?"

"My cousin Sophia gave it to me," I told him. "She wants to be my friend now."

His lips folded into a half-smile of skepticism. I remembered what Sophia wanted to know.

"Where is your home exactly?"

He gave me his address and quickly added, "I must tell you about *mi abuela* who lives with us. She is originally from San Cristóbal de las Casas and still holds on to some beliefs you might find strange. She forgets where she is now. She might ask you what animal is your spiritual double."

"What is that?"

"Funny belief," he said, "the belief that the animal shares your destiny."

"If any animal shares my destiny, I feel sorry for that animal."

He laughed. "Tell her your double is a margay. She likes that."

"A margay? It is like a spotted cat. Do I remind you of a cat?"

He laughed. "She favors cats and is especially fond of the margay. Do you know about San Cristóbal? It's in the state of Chiapas, and the tribes all speak languages derived from the Mayan."

"I'm ashamed to say I don't know anything about them or as much of Mexican history as I should."

"Don't be. I wouldn't know it if it weren't for my grandmother. But don't let anyone here make you feel ashamed. Just listen to the *gringos* when they talk about their own past," he continued. "They know just as little about their own history. They are richer, more powerful than we are, but they are not better."

"I never said they were, Ignacio."

He nodded, and I thought it was this chip on his shoulder, this underlying anger, that had made him reluctant about learning English.

"Perhaps we can help them," I said, smiling, "by giving them some of our rich culture. We are older."

Finally, he laughed.

"I look forward to the fiesta very much. I miss the ones I so enjoyed at home," I told him.

His eyes sparkled with delight, and we returned to class. At the end of the day, Señor Garman was there with the Rolls-Royce. He was standing the same way, eyeing everything and everyone as the school population emerged. Ignacio, who had walked me out, gazed at him suspiciously.

"He does look like a bodyguard," he said. "I thought your aunt was not sympathetic with your problems here. Why is she now so concerned about protecting you? Were there other threats?"

"No, no. She wants to protect herself," I said.

He tilted his head with confusion. "Herself?"

"Her good name."

"Oh. Yes, I understand." He thought a moment and then said, "I hope she won't be upset to see me drive up in my father's old truck."

"She won't be upset; she'll cover her eyes," I told him, and he laughed again. "I'll see you tomorrow."

I hurried to the car.

"How is Edward, Señor Garman? The operation on his eyes. It was good?"

"No one tells me nothing," he said, opening the door.

I got in quickly. Ignacio was still standing there looking our way. He lowered his head and walked off just before Señor Garman drove away. Behind us, I could see some of the students chattering about me and laughing.

I did pity my spiritual animal double.

Sophia was already home when I arrived. She was sitting in the living room across from Tía Isabela, who was sipping a glass of white wine. I spotted another letter from Grandmother Anabela left for me on the entryway table and quickly scooped it up. Then I stepped into the living room.

"How is Edward?" I asked.

"I'm emotionally exhausted from all this," *mi tía* Isabela said instead of answering. "I just this moment sat to have a glass of wine and relax."

I stood there, waiting. She looked at Sophia, who smirked and fidgeted with her skirt.

"You told me to sit, and you would tell me what's happening as soon as Delia arrived, Mother. I'm sitting, and she's here, too, now, so talk already."

"Do you ever realize how unpleasant you can be, Sophia? Do you ever, ever think about the impression you make on other people?"

"Oh, please, not another stupid lecture."

"No, there's no point. You're right. You can sit on the sofa, too, Delia," she told me, and I went to it and sat next to Sophia.

"Edward's surgeon is not optimistic about Edward's right eye. He is hopeful that the left will have a near-full recuperation."

"What is optimistic?" I asked.

"It doesn't look good for the eye to get better," *mi tía* Isabela explained.

"What does that mean? He's going to wear one of those patches like a pirate or something?" Sophia asked quickly.

"I have no idea yet, Sophia. Whatever has to be done will be done," Tía Isabela said, and then paused, looking closely at me. "Isn't that your bracelet Delia's wearing?"

"Yes, it is," Sophia said, sounding as pleasant as could be. "I decided to give it to her as a belated welcoming present, especially after the terrible things that have happened to her."

"Really? That bracelet was one of your special birthday gifts last year, Sophia. Have you any idea what it cost?"

"Well, it's still in the family, Mother," she said. "Isn't it? She's your sister's daughter."

Tía Isabela glared at her.

"What?" Sophia said, unable to stand the scrutiny.

"You're up to something no good, Sophia. The last time you were kind to anyone was when you were still in the cradle."

"Very funny, Mother. Are we through here? I have some homework to do."

"Yes, we're through," Tía Isabela said, and Sophia stood up.

"Only one more thing."

"What?"

"Your brother will be coming home the day after to-morrow. He doesn't have to remain in the hospital recuperating. When he's home, I don't want you aggravating him, teasing him, doing anything that will create tension for him, understand?"

"I wouldn't do that, Mother. I think it's terrible what's happened to him."

"I'm sure you do."

"I do!" she cried. Her face started to crumple in preparation for tears.

"Just go do your homework, Sophia. I'm too exhausted to put up with your dramatics," Tía Isabela said, and sipped her wine.

Sophia glanced at me with tear-filled eyes and rushed out of the living room to the stairway. Maybe deep down, she did love her brother, I thought. I felt like crying for her and the way Tía Isabela was treating her. How could she ever be good if whenever she tried to be good, it was doubted?

I started to stand.

"Don't go yet," Tía Isabela said, and I sat back. "What did she ask you to do for her before she gave you that bracelet? What is she paying you to do?"

"Nothing," I said. She hadn't asked me to do anything for her.

"I don't like it. It smells rotten. Don't trust her," she said.

How could a mother have such a low opinion of her own daughter? Usually, mothers were notorious for avoiding their children's weaknesses and faults.

"Remember," she added, finishing her glass of wine in a gulp and rising, "I warned you."

She turned and left me sitting there, wondering if somehow I had, as Grandmother Anabela would say, gone from the pot to the fire. After a moment, I rose and went upstairs to my room, too. I wanted to read my new letter from Abuela Anabela right away, but I wasn't there a minute before Sophia came in, closing the door softly behind her. I put the letter in with my ESL workbook and turned to her.

"Did you hear that?" she asked me, wiping her eyes with a tissue. "Did you hear what's happened to my brother, to Edward? He's going to lose an eye!" She held her hand over her right eye for emphasis.

"Yes, it is very sad," I said.

"It's more than just sad. It's horrible," she said, flinging her tissue to the floor. She paced in front of me. "And it's all Bradley Whitfield's fault, all of it. I hate him. I hate the air he breathes," she said, and turned quickly to me. "Don't you? Don't you just hate him now?"

"I do not want to see him ever," I admitted. It was the closest I could come to saying I hated him.

"You're being too kind," she said, with the thrust of an accusation. "You're not going to go preach this forgiveness junk, now, are you? I know you're way more religious than I am, but you can't do that. You just can't, not with my brother in the hospital and losing an eye. An eye!"

"I have heard that to be forgiving is good, but I have also been told *perdonar a una persona mala es de permitirlo a ser malo.*"

"What the hell does that mean, Delia? You know I barely can say *buenas noches.*"

"It means to forgive an evil person is to let him be evil."

She smiled. "Yes, exactly. That's more like it. We can't forgive him. I agree. We don't let Bradley be evil. Exactly. I knew you were okay." She stared at the floor a moment, pressing her lips together so hard her bloated cheeks looked as if they would explode. "What about the fiesta for Ignacio's sister? Where is it?" she asked, looking up quickly at me.

I told her the address.

"That's like Little Tijuana. Good. Go."

"Why did you want to know?"

"Never mind. Don't worry. I'm going to look after you better now and make sure no one takes advantage of you ever again," she said. "I promise." She smiled and suddenly hugged me. "Poor Edward," she said. She knuckled another tear away, smiled again, and said, "I'll talk to you later." She hurried out as if she had forgotten something important.

I shook my head in amused confusion. Sophia had hugged me and said she cared about me, but was Tía Isabela right about her? Never trust her? Why was everything so complicated here? It was as if I had walked onto a stage. Everyone was playing a part, and you couldn't tell who anyone really was. It reminded me of how simple my life had been back in Mexico. Even more eagerly, I went to Abuela Anabela's letter. This one was shorter, her writing harder to read.

My dearest Delia,

You must be doing wonderful things there, and as I had hoped, you surely must have won your aunt Isabela's heart. Today, I received another money order from her attorney in California. I have put it with the other one, and when I can, I will go to the bank or perhaps have Señor Cortez do it for me. You know how he loves having a responsibility.

You must not worry about me. I am glad you are learning English quickly. Your mother and father would be so proud and happy.

Señora Cuevas asked after you and was so pleased to hear your good news.

I send you all my love.

Abuela Anabela

How quickly I read all her words. It was more painful to have this brief contact with her than no contact at all, I thought, for all it did was make me long to hear her voice, see her face, and have her hold me in her arms that much more. My chest ached, and my tears flowed. At least, my aunt was telling the truth. She was sending money to Abuela Anabela. My coming here had done some good after all.

I read and reread the letter five times before finally folding it up and putting it with the other one, stroking them both gently, as if I were stroking my grandmother's arm and seeing her smile. I even closed my eyes and felt her kiss me on the forehead. I could hear her whisper her love for me. Homesickness was like a knife in my heart.

It took me a while to settle down enough to be able to do my assignments in my ESL workbooks. I was far ahead of most everyone in the class now. The last thing Señorita Holt had said to me before I left for the day was that I had what she called a propensity for learning languages. She complimented me on my grasp of pronunciation, too. She was thrifty when it came to spending compliments on her students, so to hear one so flattering was encouraging. It was the true highlight of my otherwise most difficult day.

At dinner, Tía Isabela asked both Sophia and me if we wanted to accompany her to the hospital to visit Edward. Sophia claimed she had too much homework and tests to study for. Tía Isabela swung her eyes to me and smiled, as if to say, *Have you ever heard a bigger lie?* I simply said I would go.

Once again, the two of us sat in the rear of the Rolls-Royce. This time, however, Tía Isabela talked to me in *español* all the way to the hospital—so Señor Garman could not eavesdrop, I thought.

"Sophia likes to think she is a strong, independent

young woman, but she's very weak when it comes to doing substantial or important things. She can't face adversity, trouble, and she has a very low tolerance for pain and discomfort. She hates any responsibility. It's all her father's fault. He spoiled her rotten until the day he died," she said.

"When did he die?" I asked. I was almost afraid to speak, afraid she would stop talking to me if I dared ask a question.

"A little more than ten years ago. She was five, and Edward was seven. I admit that he spent more time with the two of them than I did, but I had to spend my time learning how to be a *norteamericana*. I had to educate myself to be socially sophisticated, intelligent about art and clothes and food. I didn't have as much time for Edward and Sophia as my husband did. Anyway, children were more important to him."

How could children not be more important to their mother? I wanted to ask but dared not.

"He was more like a grandfather than a father because of his illness."

"What was his illness?"

"He was a heavy smoker all his life and had what is called emphysema, and by the time he realized he had it, it had caused severe damage to his lungs. He was the most depressing sight to see, walking around with a portable oxygen tank strapped to his body, those ugly things in his nose. It got so he couldn't walk up the stairs. He had to sleep in a guest room downstairs, not that I wanted him in my bedroom wheezing and gasping all night. Toward the end, Edward would push him about in a wheelchair. He aged years in weeks.

"And do you want to know something stupid? He

still smoked until the day he died. Tell that to your Mexican friends who start smoking even as early as six. Don't deny it. I know I did it, and so did my girlfriends when I lived there, but it was always a dirty habit to me, making your teeth yellow."

"It's not only Mexican children who do that," I told her, but she ignored me and ranted and raved about Sophia, who had grown up seeing her father degenerate and still went off sneaking cigarettes or worse.

"Up until now, I haven't caught her, and she hasn't been caught with marijuana, but I know she uses it. The best thing you can do for her is help me catch her with it. The moment you see one of those joints or whatever they call them, you come get me, understand? You owe me, and this is how you will repay me," she declared.

"She's too smart for her own good. No one has a more deceitful, deceptive, and conniving child than I have. She's bound to do something serious to embarrass this family. We must prevent it. We must protect our family name, Delia," she said, implying now that I was part of the family that had to be protected. "If you understand anything I'm saying, you should understand that.

"I warned her many times. I told her I would send her away to a behavior camp where she would be locked up if she was caught doing any of those drugs or worse, and I will, too. Secretly, of course. I can't have her be-smirch my reputation in this community.

"Are you listening to me?" she suddenly asked, loudly and forcefully.

"Yes, Tía Isabela."

"You'd better, because I'll send you off as quickly as I send her. You could end up in some federal detention center," she warned. "Oh, I feel like I'm keeping my finger in the dike," she moaned. "If he knew he wasn't going to live long, why did he spoil them so much and leave me with this mess?"

She wasn't asking me. Was she asking God? Did she ever pray? Why were there no crosses or religious icons anywhere in the house? I knew Señor Dallas was not a Catholic, but didn't he have any religion? Dare I ask that now?

She stared out the window for a few moments and then turned to look at me, shaking her head. "I can't believe she just up and gave you that bracelet. The only thing Sophia gives freely is grief."

I put my hand over the bracelet. Perhaps I should not wear it when I was with Tía Isabela, I thought. It brought only anger and unhappiness out of her.

"Why is it I feel like I'm waiting for the second shoe to drop?" she muttered.

Once again, I found myself feeling sorrier for her than I was feeling for myself.

When we arrived at the hospital, she walked more slowly, allowing me to stay alongside her. The hospital staff who saw us greeted her and wished her good luck with Edward. She still had him in a private room with a private nurse, but when we started down the corridor, we saw the private nurse at the nurses' station laughing and talking with the other nurses.

"I'm glad I'm paying her so much money to watch over Edward," Tía Isabela said angrily.

As soon as Edward's nurse saw her, she shot toward us.

"His friend Jesse is with him," she told us. She acted like someone being caught goofing off. "Being they're young men, I thought they'd like to have some time to chatter. He's still a little out of it," she added, "but the nausea is gone."

Tía Isabela didn't respond. She glanced at me, nodded as if we shared a deep secret, and headed to Edward's room. I walked in beside her.

Jesse was sitting next to the bed and holding Edward's hand. The moment we entered, however, he let his hand go and rose.

"Hello, Mrs. Dallas," he said.

Tía Isabela stared without speaking. I knew what she was thinking—two young men holding hands.

Jesse continued, nervously rattling on. "He's not nauseous anymore, but he's still a little uncomfortable . . . chilled. I've been helping him sip liquids. That's what his nurse wanted. He's not in any pain, but . . ."

"Hello, Mother," Edward said.

"Edward."

"Who's with you?"

"Just Delia," she said. "Sophia was concerned about her schoolwork."

"Good. Avoiding me might make her a better student," Edward said. Jesse laughed. "*Hola,* Delia," Edward continued, smiling. "*Cómo está?*"

"*Bien,* Edward, and you?"

"I'm peachy keen, right, Jesse?"

Jesse didn't reply.

"I hear from Jesse that you have made arrangements for Delia's going and coming from school. Garman's taking her and picking her up?"

"Yes, Edward."

"That's very considerate of you, Mother. How's Sophia taking it? I imagine she has to ride the bus."

"Don't be ludicrous, Edward. Casto is seeing to her transportation to and from school."

"Casto? And she hasn't thrown a tantrum?"

"I didn't say that," Tía Isabela said. Edward smiled.

"I would like to spend a few minutes alone with my son," Tía Isabela said, "to discuss his operation."

"Oh, right," Jesse said, standing quickly again.

"Why alone?"

"I'd like it that way, Edward."

"Uh-oh, I hear something ominous in your tone of voice, Mother."

Tía Isabela looked at Jesse, who moved quickly toward the door.

"I'll just go for a soda," Jesse said. "Delia, would you like a soda, too?"

"What's the word for soda, Delia?" Edward asked me.

"Edward, do you mind if we get to more serious matters? I have things to do," Tía Isabela said.

"Soda?" Edward insisted.

"Soda," I said, and he laughed.

Jesse raised his eyebrows and looked at Tía Isabela.

"I don't mind their staying to hear the news, Mother," Edward said. "Really. In fact, I think I'd like them to stay, if you don't mind."

"Very well, if you insist." She moved closer to his bed. "Mostly, your operation went well, Edward, but Dr. Fryman is not optimistic about the recovery of your right eye."

"Shouldn't that be ophthalmistic or something?" Edward asked.

"This is not a joke, Edward. Your behavior, your recklessness, has caused you severe injury. I hope you've learned something from it. First, it wasn't your place to go rushing off like some vigilante to punish Bradley Whitfield."

"Why, would you have done something about it, Mother? Did what he did to Delia bother you enough?"

"I'm afraid I wasn't given as much information as you were, and if I was given that information, I certainly wouldn't have rushed off like some lunatic. There are ways to do things and ways not to do things, but unfortunately, that's not the issue at the moment."

"It's exactly the issue. It will always be or should always be the issue. Delia's family now, our family. She's living in our home. She deserves our protection. All I was trying to do was make sure she had that."

"Oh, please. Don't be ridiculous and dramatic, Edward. You have set yourself back considerably with your education, your future, your . . ."

"Your reputation," Edward finished for her.

Tía Isabela pulled her shoulders back. "I'm not here to argue with you, Edward. We have to concentrate now on doing what we can to help you. I'm making arrangements for some home tutoring. You won't be attending school for some time."

"I don't need home tutoring. Jesse will bring me the work every day and help me keep up."

"That's hardly—"

"It's what I'd like, Mother. And I expect Delia will be tutoring me in Spanish now. *El español,* Delia, *sí*?"

"*Sí,*" I said, smiling.

"Impressed, Mother? Jesse's learned some Spanish for me. We both decided we should have a working familiarity with the language. I never understood why you prevented it in the first place."

"That's enough nonsense," Tía Isabela said. "I'm going now to talk to your doctors and nurses and see about the plans for your release from the hospital, what arrangements, medications, and other things Dr. Fryman will be leaving with his instructions. I expect you'll be coming home the day after tomorrow."

"Whatever," Edward said.

The moment she walked out, Edward reached out and called for me, and I took his hand.

"Tell me how school went for you today," he said. "*Cómo estaba la escuela hoy*? How's that, Jesse?"

"Impressive."

"I bet your *amigos* were surprised to see you brought there in a Rolls-Royce, huh, Delia?"

"*Sí,*" I said. "But Sophia was the most surprised," I added, and both he and Jesse laughed.

"That's a beautiful bracelet you have, Delia," Jesse said. Because I was still holding Edward's hand, my wrist and bracelet were quite obvious.

"What bracelet?" Edward asked. He felt for it. "Where did you get that?"

"Sophia gave it to me," I said.

He pulled his fingers away as if the bracelet had become too hot to touch.

"Sophia gave you something? That? I don't believe it. *No creo,*" Edward said.

"She did," I said.

He turned toward Jesse. "You'd better keep your eye on things, Jess. When my sister starts giving things away, something's not kosher."

"Will do," Jesse said. "Don't worry."

Nevertheless, Edward suddenly looked more uncomfortable.

"Some nausea?" Jesse asked.

"Yeah, a little. I'm not sure if it's an aftereffect of the anesthesia or my mother's visiting me."

"I'll go tell the nurse," Jesse said, and hurried out.

Edward held on to my hand again. "Be careful, Delia," he whispered. "You know what is careful?"

"*Sí,* Edward."

"Good," he said. "Good." His fingers weakened, and he turned away. "You'd better go," he said. "I'm feeling sick, and it might not be pleasant."

"Okay," I said. "I'm sorry. Really, I am."

"I know. It's all right."

I left just as his private nurse came rushing back into the room.

Edward didn't realize it, I'm sure, but I had meant that I was sorry for everything.

Jesse was standing in the hallway, leaning against the wall, his eyes gazing at the floor.

"Jeez," he said when I approached. "He's losing an eye. I know we should be grateful he wasn't killed, but I know he's just putting on a brave front, trying to look *fuerte,* strong."

He looked as if he would break out in tears. I gazed down the hallway at my aunt, who was still talking to a doctor. She would not appreciate a young man being so emotional, I thought, especially with all of her suspicions. I put my hand on his arm.

"We will help him," I said. "Do not worry."

He smiled. "Yes. We will. It's good that you're here, Delia."

I laughed to myself, thinking he might be the only one who truly believed that.

15

Spy

"Don't tell me," Tía Isabela said later when we were in the Rolls-Royce and being driven home, "that Jesse wants to be just pals with my son. I've always been suspicious of that Jesse Butler. He practically haunts our house and Edward. His family hasn't been here that long. I have a feeling they moved from Orange County because of something dark in their family closet, something maybe related to him. He just looks . . . looks like the type.

"Of course," she continued, "I want to believe the best about my son. Your children are a big reflection on you. You get blamed for everything they say and do. But I know peer pressure is usually stronger than parental pressure. You're always judged by the friends you keep. Don't forget that. It's especially true in the circles I'm in. Everyone is eager to cast the first stone, and believe me, no one is without sin."

She looked at me and nodded.

"You'd better learn that fast, Delia. You'd better grow a tough shell like I did. Yes, I did," she said, nodding and looking forward again. "I don't let people judge me. No one is better than I am, and I let them all know it, too. Why, the first time one of my so-called girlfriends laughed at my being born in some nothing village in Mexico, I jumped down her throat so fast she gagged on the words. That's the way they are around here." She turned back to me. "Everyone just loves tearing someone else down. They're just jealous, all of them. Why, if any of these wonderful friends of mine got wind of something more going on between my son and Jesse Butler . . ."

She paused and kept herself facing forward, looking as if she was in very deep thought.

How could she keep them as friends if they were so eager to find a way to hurt her? Was she so desperate for friends, even with all she had?

She turned to me so suddenly it was as if she could hear my thoughts, but she was thinking about something else, something terrifying, in fact.

"Edward likes you, Delia. That's obvious. He likes you, I hope, in a manly way, too. Don't pretend you don't understand what I'm saying, either," she added quickly when I started to shake my head. "I never saw him get so emotional about anyone else. Why, he certainly wouldn't run off to protect his sister like that, and despite what's happened to him, he still believes he was right to do it. He has feelings for you, deep feelings.

"Stop shaking your head. You know as well as I do that first cousins can be more than cousins. In Mexico, it's legal to marry your cousin. I see the way you look at him as well. The fact that he's your cousin doesn't stop that. You think he's handsome, attractive."

"He's handsome, yes, but . . ."

"I know that look on a young girl's face when she sees a good-looking young man. Believe me, I know."

I shook my head more emphatically now.

"You don't have to worry, Delia. I'm not angry about it, and I'm not asking you to do anything, actually, but since he obviously is drawn to you, I would like you to test the water for me."

"I do not understand, Tía Isabela. Really. Test the water? What does that mean?"

She leaned closer, eyeing Señor Garman even though she was still cloaking her words in Spanish.

"I want you to tempt him sexually to see if he has any interest in girls at all."

What was she suggesting?

"I don't know what you mean, Tía Isabela."

"Stop it! You know exactly what I mean. I'm sure you spent half your time back in that mud hut of a village teasing boys. Don't play the innocent. I told you that before."

"I did not tease boys. I do not play at being innocent, but what you are asking . . ."

"You'll do it, and you'll do it right away," she said, making a plan in her head rapidly. "While his eyes are still bandaged. I'll be there watching."

"I am not pretending. I really don't know what you want me to do, Tía Isabela."

"Don't you worry about it. I'll tell you exactly what I want you to do. If I have to, I'll draw you a picture."

I was shaking my head again, but she wasn't looking at me. She was talking and keeping herself faced forward.

"My husband would turn over in his grave if he

thought there was even a suspicion like this about his son. He would take it far more personally than I would. The man personified testosterone. He had loose eyes. A female didn't cross in front of him without him following the movement in her legs and hips, no matter what they looked like. I was competing with every woman he could see, smell, touch. And my genes aren't particularly neutral when it comes to men and sex," she continued. "Edward couldn't have been bred any better if his parents had been Antony and Cleopatra. I'm confident that he wouldn't be with such a boy as Jesse Butler if he wasn't simply misguided, confused, maybe. He's not outgoing with women or showing interest in them because he's just unusually shy. That's all. Eventually, he'll get over it," she said, now sounding like someone desperately trying to convince herself more than anyone else.

She glared at me.

"I won't stand for it being anything else, but I have to know in order to . . . do something. Do you understand? I'm sorry it's come to this, to where I have to use you, but my children have grown too secretive. I'm not stupid. I know they hide things from me."

I didn't know what to say. I know I was still looking at her as if I thought she had gone mad. It only made her angrier.

"I have a friend whose daughter is a lesbian. Everyone knows, but she pretends her daughter is just away, far away. She doesn't mention her ever, but she looks . . . guilty about it. I won't ever let anyone make me feel that guilty, that inferior. You'll do just as I tell you," she said, turning to me more fiercely. "Don't cross me, Delia. I can make much trouble for you and your grandmother. I have friends in Mexico, high up in the government. You hear me? How do you think I got you here so quickly? I can pull strings, for good or for bad just as easily, and I won't hesitate to pull them."

Tears came to my eyes and choked my throat. I could barely breathe in this car filled with such rage and such threats. I nodded.

"Good," she said. "Do what I ask, and you will be rewarded. Don't do it, and you'll regret the day you were born . . . almost," she said in a near whisper, "as much as I did."

My eyes nearly exploded. "Why?" I asked. "Why would you regret the day I was born?"

She was silent.

I thought she wasn't going to answer, and then she turned to me again, this time more slowly, more deliberately, her eyes sharper, and said, "Someday, when you fall in love, if you ever do, you'll understand."

She said nothing more. We rode the rest of the way in a funereal silence, like the bereaved heading toward the realization of a grave.

Two days later, on Thursday, Edward was brought home while both Sophia and I were in school. Tía Isabela's words and threats haunted me every night, but I was looking forward to seeing him. Jesse arrived to visit with him before either of us did and was in Edward's room with him when I got home. As soon as I entered the house, my aunt greeted me at the door and told me so.

"They're up there with the door locked," she said, looking toward the stairway. "I was upstairs and heard the lock click. Why would two boys want to be in a room with the door locked? That Jesse wanted it locked, I'm sure, but don't worry. I'm sure Edward will tell him to let you in."

She took my arm and drew me closer to her, whispering now, even though there was no one nearby. Her eyes were so wide and full of fire I really did think she had gone mad.

"Observe every move between them, and try to listen to whatever they say. You've learned enough English to make sense of most things. I'll be in my office reviewing some papers sent over by my business manager. Come see me as soon as Jesse Butler leaves or if you see or hear anything serious."

"What about Sophia?"

"She's out doing something no good. This morning, she told Casto not to come for her. She said one of her girlfriends would be bringing her home. That reminds me. I'd like to know exactly where she goes after school and what she does. See if she will tell you," she ordered, and went to her office.

I felt as if I were spinning in my shoes. First, I was practically a persona non grata here, treated more like a leper than a relative, and then suddenly, I wasn't sure why, I became my aunt's secret confidante, her extended eyes and ears, peering deeply into the lives of my cousins, into the hearts and souls of her children.

I went upstairs as she had ordered, but I was hesitant about knocking on Edward's locked door. I felt as if I were intruding. I imagined he would much rather spend his time with his friend and hear about all he had missed at school, but I did finally knock. Jesse opened the door just a little to peer out. When he saw me, he smiled with relief and opened it wide.

"It's Delia!" he cried.

"Alone?"

Jesse looked past me down the hallway. "It appears so, Edward."

"Good. Let her in, and lock the door again," Edward told him.

Why did they have to lock the door, anyway? Jesse gestured for me to enter.

"Hey, Delia," Edward called to me as soon as he heard the door close behind me and Jesse lock it again.

"How are you feeling?" I asked.

He was in his bed, propped up against two very large pillows. His eyes were still bandaged, and although his facial burns and scrapes weren't as red, they were still far from healed. He was wearing a pair of light blue pajamas, the top almost completely unbuttoned. I didn't know he had a bad bruise on his chest until I saw it now.

"*Cómo está,* you mean," Edward said. "We've been studying Spanish. Show her, Jesse."

"I brought him this CD set of lessons in Spanish. We've both been listening to it and practicing." He showed the disc to me, and I read what was written in Spanish on the cover. It was ten elementary lessons for the basic, necessary expressions. I handed it back to him.

"But now we have the real thing here, Edward. We don't need this," Jesse told him.

"*Sí, correcto,*" Edward said, and laughed. There was something unusual about the way both of them were behaving, I thought, and then I got a whiff of Jesse's breath.

I quickly looked around and realized they were drinking tequila. The bottle and the two glasses were on Edward's side table.

"You are drinking tequila?" I asked, pointing at the bottle.

"Discovered?" Edward said.

"We've hardly made an attempt to prevent it," Jesse told him, and they both laughed. It seemed nothing anyone would say or do would not make them laugh. No wonder they had locked the bedroom door.

"Should you be drinking tequila, Edward? The doctor said it's good for you?"

"Dr. Butler said so. Right, Doc?"

"*Correcto,*" Jesse said, and they both laughed again.

"Right now, it feels good, Delia," Edward said, smiling. "Just trying to take the edge off. How do you think you say that in Spanish, Jess?"

"No idea. You understand what he said?" Jesse asked me. "What he wants to know?"

I shook my head.

"The tequila, it helps make him . . . it helps relax him," he said. "He needs to relax, and so do I."

"You?" I asked Jesse. Edward laughed, so I turned to him. "I do not understand, Edward."

"It's simple, Delia. He's afraid of my mother," Edward said. "Terrified of her, actually."

I looked at Jesse. He had reason to be afraid of her, I thought.

"How do you say that, Delia?" Edward asked. "*Cómo se dice en español,* he's afraid of my mother?"

"*Él está asustado de su madre.*"

"Yeah, right. *Asustado.* We'll be speaking Spanish in no time, Jess."

"You will, probably. You've got the tutor living here, with you night and day," Jesse said. He sounded a little jealous.

"Exactly."

Jesse looked at his watch. "I've got to get going, Edward. My uncle Joe is coming over for dinner tonight and bringing his newest possible long-term relationship."

"Where did he find this one?" Edward asked.

"She just walked into his travel agency, and he booked her a trip she never forgot. He was her personal guide, if you know what I mean."

They laughed again.

"I'll sneak the tequila out," Jesse said, and put it into his bookbag. Then he paused and reached for Edward's hand. "See you," he said.

"When?" Edward asked.

"I don't know."

"Cut school, and spend the afternoon with me tomorrow," Edward told him.

"What? I don't know if your mother will appreciate that."

"She won't be around, I'm sure. Just do it. I'm feeling much better."

Jesse looked at me. Edward sensed it.

"She's all right. She's not going to go blab to my mother. Don't worry. Just get your rear end over here."

"I'll try."

"Try hard," Edward said, still holding on to his hand.

Jesse glanced at me again. I pretended interest in Edward's books and turned away. I didn't want to see them do anything else, anyway. I thought they kissed, and then Jesse walked past me.

"See you, Delia," he said, and unlocked the door. Just as he stepped out, we heard Sophia in the hallway.

"You moving in already, Jesse?" she asked him as she stepped up.

"I don't think I could live under the same roof with you, Sophia."

"I wonder why not," she said, laughing at him. She saw me standing in the doorway and pushed past him to enter. Jesse looked back, shook his head, and continued down the hallway.

"Hello, idiot," Sophia said to her brother.

"I wonder who that is," Edward said. He pretended to sniff the air. "Smells like my rotten sister."

"Funny, funny. I brought you something," she told him, and went to the bed to reach for his hand. Then she dipped into her purse and pulled out what looked like two joints. "Don't light up until I tell you," she warned, and looked back at me. "You keep your mouth shut, Delia. It's good for him. It will take away discomfort."

Edward stuffed the joints under his pillow.

"You look like hell, Edward," Sophia told him.

I closed the door softly but didn't approach them.

"Thanks," Edward said. "Actually, with my eyes bandaged, you never looked better."

"Ha ha. You'll probably have scars."

"Thanks again, Sophia. You know how to make someone feel good."

"I'm just telling you the truth. You're always lecturing me about facing the truth."

"Right. Forget it."

"Bradley's laughing at you," she told him, and glanced at me. "He's not a bit sorry about what happened."

Edward was silent, but his face hardened.

"He's going around school telling everyone you were just plain stupid believing what a Mexican girl told you. He's making up other stories about you, too."

"What other stories?"

"Telling everyone you have a thing for Delia, that she told him you were sleeping with her and you were simply jealous."

"That bastard."

"Exactly. And what has mother done about all this? Zip. She hasn't even complained to the Whitfields."

"Don't worry. I'm down now, but I'm not through with him," Edward said. "When I get back on my feet . . ."

"Good," Sophia said.

Edward smirked. "What bothers you more, Sophia, what happened to me or what he did with Delia?"

"Both bother me the same," she said.

"At least she's honest," Edward said to me.

I wasn't sure if I understood it all, but I could see Sophia was pleased.

"If you need me to do anything for you, let me know," she told him.

"Is that really you being nice and considerate?" Edward asked her, and she laughed.

"See, Delia?" Sophia said to me. "I can't be nice to my brother, either, without being doubted. You're the only friend I have in this house now."

Edward stopped smiling. "What are you up to, Sophia? How come you gave her your bracelet? You never took it off from the moment you were given it, and you flashed it so much you could have worked for the jewelry store."

"I'm trying to change my selfish ways, Edward. I had a wake-up call," she told him.

Wake-up call? I wondered. How does that change you?

He just laughed. "I'll believe it when I see it, and that will be a while," he told her.

"Whatever," she said. She started out. "I have to get to my homework."

"Huh? You worried about homework? You really are on some drug."

"Very funny. I'll see you later," she told him, and paused next to me to whisper. "Come into my room later. I have exactly the dress you'll want to wear to the fiesta. You just have to take it in a bit like you did with my other things. This isn't old, either. It will just look better on you than it does on me, and I don't wear it. Understand?"

"Yes," I said, "but Tía Isabela is taking me to buy clothes this weekend."

"What? My mother is taking you to buy new clothes?" I nodded.

"I can't remember the last time she went shopping with me. What's got into her?" she wondered aloud. She looked very suspicious for a moment, suspicious enough to set my heart in a pitter-patter, especially when she looked a little harder and longer at me. Then she shrugged it off. "She's probably just feeling guilty about it all," she decided. "Still, I have a dress she would certainly not buy for you. It cost eight hundred dollars."

"One dress?"

"Yes," she said, laughing. "One dress, and I have a dozen that cost more," she added, and left the room.

While we were talking, Edward slipped down in his bed and had his eyes closed. I stared at him a moment and then walked out, too, closing the door softly behind me. I stood in the hallway, thinking. Sophia had gone into her room and closed her door. The *hacienda* was quiet. Below, Tía Isabela was waiting for me to make my spy's report. I couldn't avoid it. What would I do? What would I say?

If I told her what Sophia had given Edward and where he had put it, they would know immediately that I was the one who had told her. And if I told her about the tequila, they would know that I had told her about that as well. I was terrified, because I didn't believe myself capable of lying to her. She would know immediately that I was holding something back.

I remembered once when my mother and my grandmother were talking about a neighbor of ours, Señora Delgardo, who they both thought drank too much tequila during the day. They pondered whether or not to tell her husband.

"He must know himself," my grandmother decided. "How could he not know?"

"But if he does, why does she still drink so much?" my mother asked. "Why does he permit it?"

"He knows but says nothing, maybe."

"Why not?"

"Maybe he knows that yelling at her would only make her drink more. *Debe saber más verdades que dice,*" she said, which meant more truths should be known than said. "She knows her own truth. She has to say it to herself."

It might be the same with Edward and Sophia, I thought. My aunt yelling at them and punishing them after I turned them in might only drive them to do it more, but could I convince her of that? Dare I even suggest it?

Slowly, I descended and walked to her office. She was sorting through some papers at her desk when I stepped through the open doorway. She sat back and looked at me.

"Well?"

"Jesse has left, and Sophia has returned and is now in her room," I began.

"I don't need you to tell me that. What did you see, observe? What were they doing?"

"They were practicing Spanish," I said. It was the truth. I was comfortable saying it.

"What?"

"Jesse brought Edward a disc, a CD of lessons in speaking Spanish."

She stared at me, incredulous. "What else?"

"They asked me some questions, some words to translate, and then Sophia came when Jesse had to leave because of an uncle coming to dinner at his home."

I was still standing on the truth. I didn't wobble, but she looked quite dissatisfied.

"What happened then?"

"Sophia told Edward that Bradley was not sorry for what had happened. She said he was making up stories about Edward and me, telling people I said such things to him."

"Why did she tell him that? The fool. She'll just get him more agitated. What else?"

Even though hearing this annoyed her, she seemed pleased with that information.

"You are right. It upset Edward."

"Exactly. And then what? Come on. I don't have all day. What else did Sophia say? What did she tell you?"

"She is giving me one of her expensive dresses for my friend's fiesta on Saturday."

"I told you I was taking you to buy you clothes Saturday."

"I told her. She was upset about it."

"Oh, she was, was she?" She smiled and nodded.

"Good. Maybe it will seep into her thick head that if she acts decently toward me, I could be very nice to her."

That would be like buying your love, I wanted to say, but I pressed my lips shut.

"Then what?"

"She left to do her homework, and I saw Edward was falling asleep, so I left," I said. I was still speaking the truth. I had just not spoken all of it. Finally, I dared to add, "If you yell at Sophia because of what I told you, she will know I told you, and she will not trust me near her. I will not be able to tell you anything else."

I could see her consider and then nod.

"Don't worry. That's not enough yet for me to reveal our confidence." She smiled coldly. "You're smarter than you pretend to be, Delia."

I started to protest, but she put up her hand.

"Don't bother denying it, Delia. I know you better than you think. It's all right. I'm not upset about it. In fact, I admire you for it."

I nearly dropped my jaw. She was giving me a compliment?

"A little deception goes a long way," she told me. "It's never good to reveal everything. Sophia, who has lived a protected, soft life, doesn't know how to be subtle, shrewd. She's too obvious, because she's not in any danger, and she couldn't care less about pleasing me. Or anyone else, for that matter.

"You and I grew up in a different world. Even at a very young age, we had to live by our wits. Just don't try to fool me, Delia. I'm an expert when it comes to deception.

"Now, then, tonight, after everyone has gone to bed, I will come for you. We will go to Edward's room.

He won't know I'm there. You will enter and pretend you've come to see how he is and if he needs anything. Before we go, I will tell you what to do.

"That's all for now," she said, waving me off and turning back to her papers.

I started to turn away.

"Oh. Don't worry about what you're to wear when you go into his room. I'll be bringing you one of my sheer nightgowns. That's all you'll wear," she added, and looked down at her papers.

All I'll wear?

My heart stopped and started, and then I fled from her office.

16

"The Ojo Malvado Lives Not Only in Mexico"

Right after dinner, Sophia called me into her room to give me the party dress.

"Try it on," she told me. I was hesitant, but she kept insisting. "It's a Valentino. I forgot. This one was more than a thousand dollars."

"A thousand dollars!"

I held the stretch jersey knit in my hands, actually terrified about wearing something that cost as much as some people made in a year back in my village.

"Go on," she urged. "You'll be the hit of the fiesta."

Slowly, I took off my skirt and blouse.

"You have a great body, Delia," she said. "No wonder Bradley went crazy. I've just got to lose some weight," she muttered, gazing at herself in the mirror.

The dress had a mock turtleneck with three-quarter-length sleeves. There was white lace at an empire waist, with a straight skirt. It was a beautiful shade of yellow, but it was much shorter than I had expected, barely reaching two inches above my knees. There was too much material around my torso. But she acted as if it was nearly a perfect fit.

"You have the right-size boobs for the top, Delia. Just take it in a little here," she said, squeezing the material together behind me to make it fit snugly around my waist.

I held the material where she had held it and turned to look at the dress in the mirror, especially the back of the dress.

"*Cómo me inclino?*"

"What? In English," she said, grimacing.

"How . . ." I imitated bending over, and she laughed.

"Oh. You bend over very carefully," she said.

I shook my head. I couldn't imagine my mother or my grandmother, not to mention my father, permitting me to go to a party in such a dress.

"Stop worrying about it. You want to be in style, don't you? With my bracelet and some earrings I'm going to loan you, you'll look fantastic." She rolled her eyes. "Beautiful, beautiful," she chanted.

"I don't know," I said. "How do you say . . . it's not for me."

Her face hardened. "I'm just trying to help you, to be a good cousin. You want to fit in here, don't you? You want people to like you, admire you, don't you? Nobody appreciates anything I do for them," she whined, and turned away, embracing herself.

"I am sorry. I appreciate your gift," I said. I looked

at myself again. Even though it was too big in places, it hugged at my hips. It looked as if it had never been worn, and she looked as if she had her heart set on my accepting. "It is very beautiful, Sophia. Thank you."

"Then you'll wear it? Yes?" she said.

I nodded, and she smiled.

"I knew you would like it. I wore it only twice, but both times, I received many compliments."

I took the dress off while she searched through her jewelry and then handed me a pair of earrings. They looked as expensive as the bracelet.

"Those are real diamonds," she said. "Diamonds."

"Oh, I must not take them."

"Don't worry about it. All of our jewelry is insured. If you need any help with your makeup, let me know," she said. To be sure I understood, she showed me her vanity table and all the makeup she had. I had never seen so much in one person's possession. She could open a store.

She pointed to my feet and then to the dress.

"Make sure my mother buys you shoes that match the dress," she said. "I'd give you a pair of mine, but we really have different shoe sizes. My feet are like a cow's feet compared to yours." She showed me a pair of her shoes and then put her feet next to mine. They did look much bigger.

I nodded to show I understood. She was sad for a moment and then smiled again.

"All the boys will drool over you. The boys . . ." She widened her eyes and ran her tongue over her lips. She looked so silly I had to laugh, and she did, too. Then she hugged me.

My aunt is wrong, I thought. She just needs a friend,

someone to trust and someone to trust her. We will be cousins after all. I thanked her again for everything she was giving me.

"You will have a good time," she said.

I took the dress to my room and thought about how I would take it in to make it fit. I wished there was a way to get the hem longer. I was so involved in the work I didn't hear Tía Isabela come into my room. I hadn't realized how much time had gone by, either.

"That's the dress she gave you for your fiesta?" she finally asked.

I spun around. "Oh, I didn't hear you, Tía Isabela. Yes, this is the dress," I said, wondering how long she had been standing there watching.

She stepped over and took the dress out of my hands.

"Do you know how expensive this dress is?"

"*Sí.*"

She tossed it back to me. "Her new generosity is driving me crazy." She thought a moment and nodded. "All right, if you're going to wear it, we'll need to get you a pair of matching shoes Saturday," she said. "I'm taking you to my favorite department store, where everyone knows me. We'll get special attention, and in a few hours, we'll have a very nice start for your own wardrobe."

Now it was her generosity that was worrying me.

"It's time," she said. I hadn't seen her put the nightgown down when she first came into my room. Now she reached for it and handed it to me. "Edward's awake, listening to that CD of Spanish lessons. It's perfect timing. Get undressed and into the nightgown," she ordered.

I looked at the flimsy garment. "I am still not sure of what I am to do, Tía Isabela."

"Don't worry. I'm going to show you exactly," she said. "Get undressed."

My fingers were trembling over the buttons and on the zipper of my skirt. She wanted me to take off my shoes and socks as well and put on a pair of slippers. While I was undressing and putting on the nightgown, she went to my door and locked it.

"Okay," she said. "We're going to practice this."

"Practice?"

"I'm going to pretend I am Edward."

"You?"

She went to my bed and set herself the way Edward was in his, with the pillows behind her.

"We'll enter the room," she began. "I'll remain just inside the doorway, but you go right to him and tell him you are there to see how he is. I'm sure he'll be very happy about it. Then you sit here," she said, patting the space beside her on the bed. "Go on, do it. Do it!" she repeated when I hesitated.

I moved to the bed and sat beside her.

"Turn yourself more toward me, toward Edward," she directed, and I did so. "Now, you reach for his hand. Go on. Reach for his hand."

I did.

"Good. Tell him you never had a chance to thank him for what he tried to do. Tell him you really appreciated his concern for you. Go on, say it. I'll help you with any English words."

I did as she asked, and she corrected my English and had me repeat it.

"While you speak, you are holding his hand as you are doing now with mine, only take your other hand and gently stroke his hand and his arm. Go on. No, stroke, don't pat," she instructed, and demonstrated until I did it as she wanted. "Okay. Now, I want you to tell him you like him very much, and you wish you could do something for him that would make him happy. Let me hear you say it."

I said it, but she didn't like the way I was saying it.

"You sound too frightened. Say it like you mean it. Stop behaving like a child," she snapped. "We're going to do this right."

I said it again, and she made me do it three more times, until she was happy with the way I sounded.

"He'll be a little confused, maybe, so take his hand and gently press it to your breast. Go on, do it. Gently. Hold his hand there. He'll realize you're basically naked. I want you to move his hand slowly over your breast, over your nipple. Go on. Do it!"

I did, but I felt very strange and frightened by the way she looked at me. She really was pretending to be Edward and reacting as she hoped he might. I felt as if I had wandered into someone else's mad dream.

"Good. He'll either smile and say something nice to you, or he'll be silent, stunned, and, as they say, turned on. You know that expression?"

"Yes."

"I thought so. Drop your hand and his into your lap, but hold on to his hand. Slowly, everything has to be done slowly. It's more erotic that way. Good. Move his hand between your legs, and press yourself toward him."

I started to shake my head.

"Go on. It's nothing."

"If I do this, he will hate me, Tía Isabela. He will think terrible things about me."

"Or he'll smile and let you get yourself and him turned on. He'd have to be made of stone not to react to this."

I felt tears coming but swallowed them back. She was looking at me very intently.

"I want you to do one more thing, Delia. I want you to lean over and kiss him on the lips, softly. Remember, everything is gently, softly. Then start to rise. If he holds on to your hand, stop and let him touch you again. If he lets go, it's all right, but ask him if he would like you to come back to see him tomorrow night. Go on, do it all," she said.

She let go of my hand, and I asked the question. My voice was shaky, but she thought that sounded good, sounded as if I was aroused myself.

"Good, now, let's start again," she told me.

"Start again?"

"I want this to go perfectly right. Step back to the door. Go on."

I went through it all again, with her correcting me, guiding me. She wasn't happy with how I was performing. As strange as it sounds, rehearsing like this reminded me of rehearsing for a school skit. Maybe, if I could pretend I was someone else, I could get through it, I thought. After the third rehearsal, she said I was ready, but she seized my shoulder, squeezing so hard it hurt.

"I know you're not happy about my asking you to do this, Delia, but it will help me to understand Edward more. You're doing this for me and, in a way, for him. It's not so terrible. You're not going to sleep with him. I wouldn't want you to do that, even if he wants to do it, understand? That would make me very unhappy, unhappy enough to hurt you," she said, taking on that cold, threatening tone again. Her fingers tightened.

"What I really hope is that you'll stir up his interest in other girls, and maybe, after he recuperates, he won't be so involved with that Jesse Butler," she added, speaking more to herself than to me.

After another moment, she released her grip on my shoulder. I wanted to rub it, it hurt that much, but I took a deep breath instead.

"Okay, let's go."

She went to the doorway and stood there looking at me. My legs wouldn't lift me off the bed.

"If you don't do this . . ."

I moved quickly to her side, and we stepped into the hallway. She indicated that we should be very quiet as we walked down to Edward's room. At the doorway, she smiled at me.

"Remember, I'm depending on you to do this right. Everything should be done slowly, gently. Understand?"

I nodded, and she opened the door. Edward was sitting up in his bed, and the CD was going just as she had described. She put her hand on my shoulder and pressed to move me forward and into the room, while she remained just inside the doorway. Although he was listening to the CD, Edward heard me entering and quickly turned it off.

"Who's there?"

"It's Delia," I said.

He smiled. "Hey, just in time. Listen to this. *Qué hora es*? What time is it? *Dónde está el baño, por favor*? Where is the bathroom, please? *Cuánto cuesta?* How much does this cost? How's my pronunciation?"

"Very good," I said. I looked back at Tía Isabela. She urged me forward.

"You mean, *muy bueno*."

"*Sí*," I said. I glanced back at Tía Isabela and then moved to Edward's bed. I took a deep breath and sat just where I had sat during our rehearsal. I could see that it surprised Edward immediately. "I have come to see how you are, Edward."

"You mean . . ."

"Yes, *cómo está usted?*"

"*Bien, gracias.*"

I could feel Tía Isabela's eyes on the back of my neck. I reached for Edward's hand. He smiled.

"I never thanked you for what you tried to do for me," I said. "I really appreciated your concern for me."

I couldn't help it. I knew I sounded as if I were either reading it off a piece of paper or reciting something I had memorized. His face looked surprised, confused, and he tilted his head just a little as I started to stroke his hand and his arm the way Tía Isabela had demonstrated.

"I like you very much, and I wish I could do something for you that would make you happy," I added.

"Oh, you don't have to . . ."

I brought his hand to my breast. My heart was pounding. Surely, he felt it, I thought. He didn't speak. I could feel Tía Isabela behind me. I didn't turn, but I sensed she had inched closer to watch. I closed my eyes and moved Edward's hand over my breast.

He didn't pull away, but he didn't speak, and his lips stretched into a grimace of confusion. Then I brought my hand and his to my lap.

"Delia," he said. "You don't have to . . ."

I knew she was watching, waiting, so I moved his hand along with mine down my thigh. It was then that he pulled back and cried, "Stop! What are you doing? Why have you come here like this?"

I looked back at her, but she had no instructions. She just stared at us.

"I wanted to thank you," I managed.

"Not like this. This isn't you," he said. "I hope it isn't you," he added, now sounding not quite so sure. "You didn't . . . you didn't lie to me about Bradley Whitfield, did you? Delia!" he cried when I didn't answer. His shout made me wince.

I stood up quickly. When I looked back, Tía Isabela was no longer there.

"I'm sorry," I told him. "I'm sorry."

"Me, too," he said. "You'd better leave. Please."

"I'm sorry," I said again, and ran out, the tears streaming out of my eyes.

When I stepped into the hallway, I didn't see Tía Isabela there, either, but standing in her doorway was Sophia, and she was smiling.

"What's going on?" she asked. "Why are you practically naked in Edward's room, and why are you crying?" She fumbled for the little Spanish she knew.

I shook my head and hurried into my own room, closing the door quickly. I sat on my bed, stunned and confused. Why had my aunt forced me to do this, and why had she left me there? *Edward thinks I was lying about Bradley now. He has lost all respect for me.*

I flicked the tears off my cheeks and tried to breathe. My chest felt as if it had turned to stone. A few minutes later, when the door was opening, I expected to see my aunt, but it was Sophia instead. She stood there smiling and looking in at me.

"What did you do to poor Edward?" she asked. "I went in to see what was happening, and he was red in the face and wouldn't speak. You didn't try to seduce him, did you? You know what that means?"

It was close enough to the Spanish for me to understand her question. I shook my head.

"Look how you're dressed—or undressed, I should say." She indicated the sheer nightgown. "You tried something," she said, laughing. "Good for you, only I could have told you it was a waste of time. Stick with your Mexican boyfriend. You're better off."

She stepped back, laughed, and closed the door, leaving me trembling so much I was actually shivering. I sat there anticipating my aunt, but she never came. After a while, I crawled under the covers and buried my face in my pillow. I fell asleep without even saying my prayers.

Tía Isabela did not join me for breakfast the next morning. As usual, Sophia took her breakfast in her room, but before I left to go to school with Señor Garman, Señora Rosario told me that my aunt had left instructions for me to expect her to take me shopping after school instead of during the day Saturday. She had something else she had to do on Saturday. The way Señora Rosario said it made it sound as if my aunt was going off on a date herself, maybe for the whole weekend.

Still dazed from what had happened the night before, I went out to the Rolls and quickly got in. Señor Garman was even quieter than usual and said nothing the whole trip. He grunted a good-bye at the school, and I hurried into the building.

I knew I was behaving strangely throughout the morning. I didn't pay attention in class, and I answered Ignacio's questions quickly and mostly with single words. All I wanted was to go somewhere and be alone.

I was feeling ashamed of myself. Ignacio was very worried about me. He kept asking me questions about what was happening at the *hacienda*.

"Is there more trouble? How is your cousin? Were the police there? Are they questioning you?"

He fired one question after another at me, hoping I would answer one. I just shook my head.

"You're still coming to the fiesta, aren't you?" he finally asked.

"Yes, I am."

"Good. But you're not feeling well?"

"I'm just very tired today," I said. Assuring him that I was still going to the fiesta seemed to satisfy him.

Señorita Holt, on the other hand, did not hide how cross she was with me when I missed questions, didn't hear things she had said, or failed to follow her instructions.

"Next week," she warned me at the end of the day, "you had better come to class better prepared and alert. I do not like wasting my time."

I apologized and left, not remembering until I was nearly out of the building that my aunt was coming to take me shopping. I wondered, of course, what she would say about last night in Edward's room.

The Rolls was there when I stepped out of the building. I hurried to it, and Señor Garman opened the door. I stood there for a moment. My aunt was not in the car.

"*Dónde está mi tía* Isabela?"

"How should I know? She just told me where to deliver you. Someone is there at the store waiting with instructions. I have her name. I'm to deliver you to the right department at the store," he said. "Get in."

So my aunt wouldn't be taking me shopping. Sophia

had nothing to be jealous about after all. Rather than *mi tía* Isabela presenting me with loving gifts from a loving aunt, she was treating me like someone who was to be paid off for carrying out orders. It made me feel even cheaper and more ashamed of myself.

I could feel the eyes of salespeople and customers on me as Señor Garman marched me into the store and to the young women's department. A short woman with dark brown hair greeted us and introduced herself as Mrs. Lester. She was very businesslike and had all of the garments for me to try on set aside. There were a half-dozen dresses, another half-dozen skirts and blouses, and, amazingly, the pair of shoes I needed to match the dress Sophia had given me. Apparently, the dress had been bought here and was on some record they kept at the store.

Mrs. Lester complemented everything with the proper accessories. There were three different purses and some costume jewelry, stockings, even a stylish red hat. Señor Garman stood off to the side, waiting, but he glanced my way every time I emerged from the dressing room and Mrs. Lester studied and adjusted the clothing. An assistant was called to carry the boxes and bags out to the Rolls. Señor Garman stood there gazing at it all in the trunk.

"You hit the jackpot here, Delia," he said. It was the first time I had heard him say my name. "You must have done something to please your aunt."

I said nothing. I was still quite shocked myself at how much I had been given. I did not see the bill, but I did see some of the price tags and estimated it was well into the thousands of dollars. Señor Garman's remark stirred up my guilt and embarrassment again. How could I face

Edward? What would I say to him, and what would he say to me?

When we arrived at the house, I carried in as much as I could, and then Señor Garman sent for Inez to carry in the rest. Her eyes bulged. She followed me up to my room, her arms full, and then went down to get what was left. I knew her brain was twisting and turning with all sorts of questions. After all, one day I was working beside her, cleaning grease off pots and pans, and almost the next day, this. She asked nothing, however. Before she left, she simply turned to me and said, "*Usted es muy afortunada,* Delia."

I looked away.

I didn't feel very lucky. The truth was, I was so conflicted inside that my stomach twisted like a rubber band. At the moment, it seemed everything Abuela Anabela had wished for me was coming true. I had the beautiful room and now the beautiful clothing. I was being treated like a princess, taken to school in a most expensive automobile driven by a chauffeur. I did not have to do housework, and I had been accepted as a member of the family.

Perhaps there was a way for me to apologize to Edward and win back his affection and respect. I did not know how to explain what I had done without angering my aunt, of course, but another apology might help. With that in mind, I left my room and went to his. As if he were able to see through the closed door, Jesse opened it before I knocked and stepped out, closing the door behind him. I saw from the look on his face that Edward had told him everything that had happened the night before.

"I want to speak with Edward," I said.

He shook his head. "Edward asked me to tell you to leave him be for now. He is not very happy. *No está felíz.*"

My lips trembled. "I am sorry for what happened," I said.

"He is sad, Delia. He thinks he might have hurt himself for a lie."

"No. It is not so."

"Just leave it be for now," he said, holding his hand up.

I wiped a tear back before it could emerge and shook my head.

Jesse grimaced. "Why did you do it? *Por qué?*"

I stared at him. How could I begin to explain? What could I tell him? My aunt thought he and Edward were lovers? I was there to test Edward's sexuality? Not only would it not make things better, but it could cause an explosion in this *hacienda,* and in the end, everyone would hate me.

"I think we both know why you did it, Delia. Disgusting," he said. "*Disgusto.*"

He turned toward the door and then turned back to hand me something before he went into Edward's room.

It was the CD of Spanish lessons.

I started to protest, but he closed the door in my face. I stood there looking down at the floor until I heard footsteps on the stairway and turned to see Sophia. She smiled immediately and hurried to me.

"What's that?" she asked, nodding at the disc. "A present for Edward?"

I shook my head as the tears began streaming down my cheeks, and then I fled to my room.

She followed. I had thrown myself on my bed and lay there facedown.

"What's your problem now?" she asked. "What's wrong?"

I didn't answer, but I could hear her moving about. She opened some of my boxes and looked at what had been bought for me.

"Wow. And you got the shoes, too! My mother was very generous."

I turned and looked at her sifting through the skirts and blouses.

"Some of this she recently bought for me. In fact," she continued, inspecting everything, checking labels, "wait a minute. It's all what she bought for me! What the hell?"

She glared angrily at me. I had no idea what would make her so angry so quickly.

"Of course, you'll look a helluva lot better in all this than I will."

"I do not understand," I said.

"My mother bought you the same clothes I have," she said. "Same, same, you know the meaning of *same*?"

"Yes."

"Well, these clothes . . . same," she said, pointing to herself. "She bought them in the same store. Did she take you to Mrs. Lester?"

"Mrs. Lester, yes," I said, wiping my cheeks. "But she did not take me. Señor Garman . . ."

"Where the hell is my mother?" she cried. "She's just being bitchy. I know what she's going to say, too, if I complain. She'll say, what am I upset about? After all, I gave you my necklace and dress."

She stood there with her weight on one foot, her arms folded under her breasts, fuming. I still did not understand all of what was happening. She looked at me strangely, and then as quickly as her anger had filled her face, it left, and she smiled.

"It's all right. It doesn't matter. Don't worry about anything. I'll fix everything. After all, we're cousins, right? Cousins?"

"*Primas, sí.*"

"Yes, *primas.*" She smiled, and then she went over to Edward's CD, looked at it, and turned to me. "I'll use this and learn some Spanish. Then maybe we can get even closer, be closer, understand?"

Before I could reply, she took the CD and left my room.

Something was telling me that getting closer to Sophia was like ignoring the rattle of a rattlesnake.

I could see Señora Porres waving her finger at me.

"Foolish girl," she was saying. "The *ojo malvado* lives not only in Mexico."

The evil eye had followed me.

17

Interrupted Fiesta

"Well, guess what?" Sophia said, coming back to my room just before we were to go down to dinner.

I had showered and changed and was reading the last chapters of my ESL workbook. I had finished nearly all of the exercises and completed all of the homework Señorita Holt had assigned. I worked just to keep my mind off what was happening.

"What?"

"My mother sent word that she won't be home for dinner and probably won't be home until Sunday. I'm sure she's with that Travis. He's ten years younger than she is! It's all right for her to act like a fool, but not us."

"Tía Isabela *no está aquí*?"

"No, she's not home. Speak English. I took the disc to learn Spanish, but you have to give me a few months."

"What about Edward?"

"What about him?"

"Aunt Isabela is not worried?"

"He's got his private nurse, Jesse," she said. "What do we care? We'll have breakfast together tomorrow, and then we'll go out on the lounges and get some sun. Later, I'll help you get ready for your fiesta, help you with your hair, the makeup, everything. Come on, let's get something to eat. I'm starving. I'll diet tomorrow or next week."

She reached into one of my boxes and took out the red hat. I watched her put it on and adjust it in front of the mirror.

"This looks good. I don't have one like this, come to think of it. Mind if I borrow it? Borrow? You know *borrow*?"

"*Sí*," I said.

She kept the hat on her head and went to the door. "Come on, already," she said, and I put my workbook aside to follow her out.

Edward's bedroom door was still shut. How I wished I could find the words to explain why I had done what I had done so that he wouldn't be so angry at me. Nothing bothered me as much as losing his respect.

"Don't worry about them," Sophia said, seeing where my gaze had gone. "They're having a private dinner, I'm sure," she muttered as we went by. "Good riddance."

When we entered the dining room, she took her mother's chair. Señora Rosario made a face when she came in from the kitchen and saw her sitting there.

"What are you growling at, Mrs. Rosario? I'm in charge when my mother's away," Sophia announced. "In fact, I've decided that we'll have some white wine with our dinner tonight. My mother's and my favorite is in the wine cooler. Bring us a bottle and two wineglasses."

"Your mother did not say such a thing to me," Señora Rosario responded. "And you know she would not like you wearing a hat at the dinner table."

Sophia threw her a look full of darts and jumped up, went into the kitchen, and returned with a bottle of white wine and the two wineglasses. She struggled a bit getting the cork out but then smiled at me and poured us each a full glass. Señora Rosario gave me a disapproving look, but I wasn't about to throw Sophia into one of her tantrums.

"To cousins," Sophia said, lifting her glass and nodding for me to lift mine.

Señora Rosario returned to the kitchen.

"Come on, don't be afraid. You're a member of this family, not a servant," Sophia said when I hesitated. "To cousins."

I lifted my glass, we clinked, and then we drank. I sipped mine, but she seemed to gulp hers.

"It's good, right? *Bueno*?"

"*Sí, bueno.*"

She drank some more and poured more into her glass and into mine, even though I had drunk very little. When Inez brought out our dinner, which was a delicious chicken in some sort of lemon sauce, Sophia attacked her food as if she had not eaten for a week. Tía Isabela was always criticizing her for eating too fast. She was finished before I had eaten less than half of mine. She drank two more glasses of the wine and urged me to finish mine so she could empty the bottle.

"This is fun, isn't it?" she asked. "With my brother and his *amigo* locked away, we have no one to tell us what to do and not to do."

She glared at Señora Rosario when she came in to check on things.

"What's for dessert?"

"There is chocolate cake," she replied.

"I want vanilla ice cream on mine, and so does my cousin."

Señora Rosario asked me if I did, and I told her to give me a small piece and just a little ice cream. I knew that if I didn't eat it, too, Sophia would be upset, and the wine was making her more irritable and nasty to both Señora Rosario and Inez. It was better just to go along with everything and then go to my room, finish my schoolwork so I would have nothing to worry over during the weekend, and then go to bed. However, Sophia had other plans for us.

She finished the last drop of her wine, insisted I finish mine, and devoured the dessert almost before I had one bite of my cake swallowed.

"You want more?" she asked me. "*Más?*"

"No, *gracias.*"

She sat back to watch me eat.

"How come you're not fat like so many of the Mexican girls I know?" she asked. Then, to answer her own question, "You were very poor in Mexico, right? Poor?" she asked, pointing to me.

I shook my head. "I was not rich, but I was not . . . *no tenía hambre.*"

"Huh? In English, I told you!"

"Not no food." The wine loosened my tongue. I leaned toward her. "You are not right. Most girls in Mexico are not fat. Girls are fatter here," I said, and she twisted her mouth and looked away.

She thought a moment and then turned back, smiling again. "Maybe that's because the food's better here," she said.

"No."

She looked at me sharply. "What?" she asked, ready to laugh. "You think the food is better in Mexico?"

"My grandmother is a better cook," I said, nodding toward the kitchen.

That struck her as funny, very funny. She laughed so hard and long that Inez came back in to see what was happening. I shrugged, and she returned to the kitchen. Sophia stopped laughing suddenly and stared at me.

"Your grandmother," she said. "That's not my mother's mother, right?"

For a long moment, I did not reply. How could she ask such a question? Did my aunt Isabela not tell her children anything about her own parents, at least that they were both dead and gone?

I shook my head.

"I didn't think so," Sophia said. "C'mon," she told me, rising. "Let's go up to my room. I have something to show you."

Just as I stood, Jesse came down the stairs and headed for the kitchen with the tray of dishes and glasses from his and Edward's dinner. He glanced at me with scorn and continued walking.

"Well, look who's here," Sophia said. "Edward's nurse. Is that what you want to be when you grow up, Jesse, a nurse, maybe a wet nurse?"

"I am grown-up," he replied. "But you have plenty of time to decide what you want to be, since you have a long way to go to grow up."

"Very funny. Isn't he hilarious?" she asked me.

Jesse kept walking.

"C'mon," she said, and walked quickly toward the stairway. For a moment, she had to seize hold of the banister, because she was so dizzy. She regained her balance and climbed the steps as quickly as she could. I followed slowly.

"Will you catch up?" she screamed back at me. Everything she was doing now was exaggerated, whether it was talking too loudly or making a face. I felt what the little wine I had drunk was doing to me and could see clearly how so much more of it was affecting her.

She stopped at Edward's doorway to wait for me.

"We have to see how my brother's doing," she said with a wry smile.

I started to shake my head, but she seized the doorknob and opened the door. I could hear Jesse coming up the stairs quickly behind me. I paused, because Sophia stepped back instead of forward.

"Jesus," she said.

I walked slowly toward her and got to the door just as Jesse came up the stairs. Sophia nodded, urging me to look into Edward's room.

He was facedown on his bed, totally naked.

Jesse charged up to the doorway.

"You two are sick," Sophia said.

"I'm just giving him a rubdown, stupid. He's sore from being bedridden."

"Right. C'mon, Delia, before I throw up."

"Jesse?" Edward called. "What's going on?"

"Nothing," Jesse replied. He mumbled some curse, entered the room, and closed the door. We heard him lock it.

"If my mother saw that, she'd have a heart attack,"

Sophia told me. "So, if you want to kill her, tell her." She headed for her room.

I stood there looking after her. Could she possibly know that her mother wanted me to do exactly that, report anything I had seen to her?

"Will you come on?" she cried from her doorway. "You move like an old lady."

I was tempted to go to my own room and lock the door, too, but I followed her. She flopped onto her bed.

"Shut the door!" she ordered, and gestured.

I closed it and stood there. She closed her eyes, and I thought for a moment that she was just going to fall asleep. I wished she would, but her eyes snapped open, and she sat up quickly.

"Come here," she said, and nodded at the chair beside her night table. Then she pulled her legs back and sprawled on her stomach, reaching for a pillow at the same time. She folded her arms and positioned herself to rest her head on the pillow and look at me in the chair. I walked slowly to it and sat. For a few moments, she just stared at me. It made me uncomfortable. What did she want?

"You know enough English to tell me what Mr. Baker did to you at the rented house?"

"No," I said, shaking my head. "Too much to tell."

"Did you do it with him, too? Did he make you?"

I shook my head. She looked disappointed.

"He never tried anything with me," she said, sounding unhappy about it. "He was a lousy teacher. He had bad breath. My mother hired him just to torment me."

She stared at me again, making me feel very uncomfortable.

"What about in Mexico?" she asked.

"In Mexico?"

"You did it with boys there?"

"No."

"Bradley was the first?"

I didn't answer, which was an answer for her.

"Oh, I get it. You people in Mexico don't believe in birth control, right? No stopping birth," she added when I grimaced with a bit of confusion. "You have lots of babies. Where are your sisters, your brothers?"

"No sisters, no brothers."

"Just you?" She pushed herself up to a sitting position. "Why? Your father had birth control?"

"No more babies," I said. I didn't know the details about it, but I understood there was a reason my mother couldn't have another child. We just didn't talk about it.

"Probably decided not to have one and used something," Sophia thought aloud. "If it wasn't for my father, my mother wouldn't have had Edward or me," she added. "My father wanted children, not my mother, understand?"

"*Sí,* I understand."

She studied me again and smiled.

"You know, you might be pregnant. Maybe there is a baby in you," she said. "Bradley's baby."

I started to shake my head.

"Did you get your period . . . bleeding?"

"No, not time for it," I said.

"So? You don't know," she said, satisfied.

The thought had passed through my mind, but I had chased it off so quickly it had been forgotten until now.

"Don't worry. If you're pregnant, I'm sure my mother will have it taken care of . . . abortion. Unless you're so religious you won't do it."

I didn't answer. I wouldn't let myself think about it.

She smiled. "My mother would make you. She would be too embarrassed to have a pregnant teenage girl in the house. You have to be more careful, now that you're going to have a boyfriend."

She reached down to the bottom drawer in her night table and pulled it open to pluck out a small case. She smiled at me.

"Know what this is?"

I shook my head.

She opened it and took out a dome-shaped rubber disc.

"It's called a diaphragm. My mother got it for me. Do you know what this does?"

I knew, but I had never seen one. Tía Isabela had bought it for her? It was like sending her out to be promiscuous, I thought, or at least accepting it. The widening of my eyes made her laugh.

"Don't look so surprised. She just came to me one day and said, 'I know you're not going to be careful, Sophia, so I want you to be protected.' She was right about that," she added, and laughed again. Then she grew serious. "You need one of these. My mother should get one for you, too. I'll show you how it works."

She showed me the spermicidal jelly she smeared in and around it and began to describe how she inserted it. I imagined she had not studied or mastered anything at school with as much enthusiasm.

"I haven't used it yet. The first time was supposed to be with you-know-who, but he wasn't as interested in me as he was in you." Thinking about Bradley brought the rage back into her face. She put her diaphragm away, slamming the drawer closed, and fell back on her bed.

"I've got a headache," she said. "I ate too much." She leaned on her elbow and looked at me. "Don't you eat too much ever?"

"*Sí,*" I said. "When *mi abuela* Anabela makes her chocolate *mole* chicken. She makes the best guacamole and the best burritos. I work with her in the kitchen. She has taught me many things her mother taught her."

It looked as if hearing about my good family memories made her angry, so I stopped.

"You obviously miss her. Why did you leave her if you miss her so much?"

"She wanted me to come here. She is ninety years old and was afraid for me."

"If she was afraid for you, she shouldn't have sent you here," Sophia said, lying back again. "Look at what's happened to you so far. I bet you haven't told her anything. I bet if she knew, she would just die."

I did not reply. She closed her eyes and mumbled something under her breath. I sat there thinking and looking at her, waiting for her to say something else, but she didn't. When I stood up, I saw she had fallen asleep. Quietly, I went to the door, opened it, looked back at her, and left to go to my own bedroom and think about all she had said. She had thrown my mind into a whirlpool of terrible thoughts.

Could I be pregnant? Would Tía Isabela send me back to Mexico like that, and would that break Abuela Anabela's heart? What should I do about seeing Edward naked on the bed? Should I tell Tía Isabela? Would Sophia tell her, and then would she know I had seen it, too, and not said anything?

I was in such turmoil I didn't think I would fall asleep, but somehow I did. I woke during the night and thought someone was in my room, standing by my door. It turned out to be just a shadow, but it put another shiver in my heart. I had a nightmare about it in which the ghost of Señor Dallas came to see me. He was very upset about both of his children but especially Sophia. He wanted me to help her, but he also warned me to be wary of her.

She did not come to breakfast as she had said she would. In fact, I did not see her until nearly one o'clock. Apparently, Jesse had stayed the night with Edward. In the morning after breakfast, he took Edward for a walk. I was afraid to speak to either of them and just watched them from a window in the living room as they strolled about the grounds. Edward still had his eyes bandaged. Jesse held Edward's arm and guided him. They looked inseparable but also a little sad to me.

After I had some lunch, I went to my room to think about my preparations for the fiesta. Sophia came in, apologizing for not getting up earlier.

"I had a terrible headache this morning," she said, rubbing her forehead to illustrate. "I didn't think I'd ever get up. Did you take in the dress I gave you? Is it ready? The dress, the dress," she repeated when I didn't respond quickly enough.

"*Sí, bueno.*"

"Good. I can't wait to see it on you. What time is Ignacio coming for you?"

"He comes at three."

"Three! There's not much time. Come on to my room. I'll work on your hair at my vanity table, and we'll experiment with some makeup, eye shadow, and lipstick. You can take a shower in my room first, if you want. Well?" she said when I didn't move.

I started to get up.

"Don't forget the dress," she said, "and the shoes and the earrings."

I gathered it all and followed her to her room, not without trepidation. This would be the first fiesta I had gone to outside my little village in Mexico. I wondered if the people there would be so much different from my people back home that I would feel as if I was with strangers, like a foreigner. Wearing Sophia's beautiful and expensive dress, putting on makeup, and wearing expensive jewels would perhaps make me look alien, too different. And yet I had nothing good enough from my own wardrobe.

I did not like the way Sophia wanted my makeup, but if I made the smallest complaint or questioned anything, she went into a rage, telling me I was ungrateful and that she was just trying to help me look beautiful.

"You have to look American beautiful," she said, "not Mexican. You're my cousin."

I had no idea what that meant, but I put on the eye shadow, lashes, rouge, and thick red lipstick. We brushed out my hair and had it lie differently from any style I had worn before. Afterward, she was dissatisfied with the way the dress fit me and made me wear one of her older bras, something she said raised my breasts and made my cleavage deeper. It was nearly three by the time we were finished. She said that because I looked so beautiful, she wanted to lend me a shawl for the night hours, when it would be cooler.

Then she and I went downstairs to wait for Ignacio. He called from the box at the gate, and Señora Flores pressed the button to open it for him. She came out to tell us Ignacio had arrived to pick me up. He was right on time. Sophia went with me to the front entrance, and we watched him drive up in his father's pickup truck. There were still some pieces of lawn machinery in the back. Sophia laughed at the sight of it, but when Ignacio stepped out, dressed in his traditional fiesta outfit, she stopped laughing. He did look very handsome.

He wore a gold-embroidered black jacket with gold running down the sides of his pants, a white shirt with a red sash, shiny black boots, and an embroidered sombrero. His shoulders looked fuller and wider.

"He's good-looking," Sophia said. "Go have a good time." She pushed me out, closing the door quickly as if she didn't want him to see her.

I hurried out to greet him. I could see that the makeup, my changed hairstyle, and the expensive dress took him by surprise. He quickly smiled.

"*Muy bonita,*" he said, nodding at me.

"*Gracias. Y usted, muy hermoso,* Ignacio."

He gazed at the front door. "*Su tía*? I should say hello, no?"

"She's not home. *No está aquí,*" I said.

He nodded, looking a little relieved, and then moved quickly to the truck and opened the door for me. I glanced back at the house and thought I saw Jesse looking out of Edward's bedroom window. The curtain closed quickly.

"I cleaned the seat," Ignacio said, thinking that was why I was hesitating.

"*Gracias,*" I said, smiled, and got in quickly.

"To live in such a big house," he said, looking at my aunt's *hacienda* and shaking his head. "I'd get lost, I'm sure," he said in Spanish.

I nodded.

I am lost in there, I thought, but I said nothing more

about it. I was thinking about the fiesta now. I had not been here long, but all that had happened left me so insecure that I wasn't confident about anything I was doing. I so longed for the warmth of family, for the love that Ignacio enjoyed. I wanted to be a part of this, because I knew it would be like going home. I only hoped that I would be accepted.

We went off the main highway onto a side road and then to his parents' home. It was not hard to see that a fiesta was about to take place. The outside was decorated with streamers of red, green, and white, the colors of the Mexican flag, and balloons were tied to every place possible on the front of the small but well-kept house. Because his father owned a gardening and landscape company, there were especially pretty, well-trimmed hedges, bougainvillea along the walls and fences, a rich green lawn, and a yard filled with grapefruit, orange, and lemon trees.

Both sides of the street were already lined with the cars of their guests. Families were parking and walking to the front entrance when we pulled into the driveway. Everyone was dressed in traditional Mexican style, except me, of course. I was afraid to get out of the truck now that I saw the women and the young girls approaching the house. There were women in white cotton and lace *campesinas,* or peasant farmer dresses, dresses with embroidered flowers, and simple white shifts with loose tops we called *huipiles.* Everything looking hand-made. Both women and men wore sombreros. Most of the men wore pleated shirts with red or green scarfs and dark pants or red and green sashes.

I realized that the simple clothes Abuela Anabela had packed in my old suitcase would have been more appropriate. Dressed as I was, I was sure I looked like a Mexican girl trying to put on airs. What was I thinking? Why did I let Sophia send me off like this? Was it more important to please her or to please Ignacio's family and friends, people with whom I shared so much more? I wished this was my aunt's home instead of the palace in which she lived and where we were all in different ways trapped.

"C'mon," Ignacio urged.

"I feel foolish," I said. "I am not dressed correctly."

"Nonsense. You look beautiful," he insisted. I sensed that if I had worn a sack, he would have said the same thing.

He stepped out of the truck, came around to open the door for me, and held out his hand. Reluctantly now, I took it and joined him. We entered the house, but the fiesta was set up in the backyard with the tables decorated. At the center of the yard, hanging from the branch of a tree, was a large, multicolored *piñata* shaped like a *burro*. Before the fiesta ended, all of the children would be blindfolded one at a time, spun around two or three times, and given a stick with which to strike the *piñata*. When it finally broke, the children would scramble for the toys that fell out.

Before I had even met any of Ignacio's family, just the sight of these people prepared to enjoy the birthday fiesta and the music coming from five mariachis who played guitars, trumpets, and the accordion immediately made me feel at home. Ignacio told me the lead guitarist was none other than Mata's father. They were playing and singing "*Las Mañanitas,*" a folk song traditionally sung on a birthday. No matter how many times I had heard it before, it had never sounded so beautiful.

Ignacio's father, who was only an inch or so taller than he was but wider in the shoulders, stood at the entrance to the yard, handing out small clay pots to the men and women to wear around their necks. Into them was poured tequila. I could see Ignacio got his strong, manly good looks from his father, who had a full, coal-black mustache and striking black eyes, with firm lips and high cheekbones. His eyes narrowed when he saw us. The women who had already gathered looked our way as well. I was sure that I was the one attracting the attention, because I was the only one who didn't look as if I belonged.

Ignacio introduced me to his father.

"Welcome," he told me, and asked me the name of my village. He said he knew it and had even been there once when he was a young boy traveling with his father. He said he thought we had one of the prettiest and best-kept squares he had seen. Talking about it brought tears to my eyes.

As we headed toward Ignacio's mother and the other women, he whispered, "Don't forget, when I introduce you to my grandmother, if she asks you what is your spiritual double . . ."

"I remember. A margay."

"*Sí*," he said, smiling.

Like any mother, whether Mexican or not, I'm sure, Ignacio's mother was very interested in the girl who interested her son. Her gaze on me was intense. She was a pretty woman with brown eyes that had specks of green in them. Ignacio had told her why I had come to America, so she was very sympathetic, but underlying that sympathy was a stream of concern. I was, in her eyes, a young woman without family just when I needed guidance the most. Would I go astray? Had I already?

We talked a little about how I was adjusting to life here, and then she had to tend to the fiesta.

It was then that Ignacio introduced me to his grandmother, who reminded me of Señora Porres, because her eyes, eyes that had surely seen so many sad and tragic things, were filled with trepidation. It was as if she saw ghosts hovering in every corner. Since I was the only real stranger, she looked for signs of trouble in me and finally did ask what animal shared my fate. I glanced at Ignacio and told her the margay. It seemed to relieve her a little, but I could feel her eyes following me constantly.

We went to a table Ignacio said was reserved for us and his friends, who were not there yet. Every table already had traditional garnishes at the center. They included red and green salsas, a mixture of chopped onions and cilantro, and lime wedges. There were juices made from mangos and tangerines. Ignacio gave me a glass of the traditional *horchata,* a milky rice drink flavored with cinnamon.

Ignacio's sister Rosalind had ten of her friends at her long table. All of them were dressed in traditional costumes. Ignacio's mother had prepared a kids' *sangria* for them consisting of cranberry juice, oranges and lemons mixed with 7UP. His uncle Thomas, a tall, thin man who could easily be a circus clown, organized their games and had them play Benito Juarez, which was a form of Simon Says, and then had them pin the tail on the *burro.* He did a great job of entertaining them.

Toward evening, the adults did most of the dancing. I offered to help with the food, but Ignacio's mother told me they were fine, and I should just enjoy the party with him and his other friends, who had finally arrived. Three of them were boys his age who spoke English well enough to be mainstreamed in classes at our school: Luis, Manuel, and the shortest but hardest-looking one, Vicente. Despite Ignacio's warning them that his father would be displeased, they managed to get some tequila and mix it into the sodas.

As with our fiestas back in Mexico, all of the women who attended brought something wonderful to eat. There were foods I had never had, such as a grilled *jalapeño*-flavored *masa* cake filled with *queso añejo,* an aged, salty, cow's milk cheese, and *sierra* fish marinated with avocados, onions, cilantro, and lime juice. Abuela Anabela often made the shredded chicken stewed with onions, garlic, *chiles,* and fermented maguey cactus juice, as well as the tequila *carnitas,* a meaty stew made with pork confit cooked with *chiles,* onions, tequila, and beer. There were, of course, fresh tortillas in the clay gourds.

The food, the music, the games, and the dancing went on and on. Despite how I was dressed and how I felt, I was enjoying the company, the conversations all in Spanish, the sight of the excited children around the *piñata,* and the wonderful air of family love and comradery that filled the fiesta. I was truly, if only for a few hours, back home.

My only concern was how much tequila Ignacio's friends from school were consuming. They were all showing off, I thought, and Ignacio was getting more and more annoyed. His father was shooting chastizing glances our way, too.

And then, right before the children were to start beating the *piñata,* I was shocked to see my cousin Sophia and three of her girlfriends come strutting into the fiesta. She went directly to Ignacio and introduced herself and her friends, Trudy, Delores, and Alisha. They all looked as if they were dressed for a rock concert, with dark makeup and lipstick, leather pants, and armfuls of silver bracelets. Trudy had a ring in her nose.

"We just dropped by to check on my cousin," she said loudly enough for anyone to hear. "My mother is very worried that she is all right."

"Of course," Ignacio said, not knowing what else to say or do. "You are all welcome."

"Looks like a great party," Sophia said. Her girlfriends smiled at Ignacio's friends.

"Would you like something to eat?"

"Anything to drink?" Sophia asked. She sauntered over to our table and seized one of the boy's glasses. He laughed when she sipped from it and widened her eyes.

I could feel Ignacio's father's eyes on us.

"Why did you come here?" I asked her.

"We're really worried about you, Delia," she said, swinging her eyes toward Ignacio. "You know, she's been through hell. I heard how you protected her, but we can't help but worry."

"She's safe here," he said firmly.

"We're so grateful for that," Sophia told him. She stepped very close to him. His friends were all smiling licentiously. This and the tequila they had drunk made them laugh at everything Sophia said and did. Soon they were all around her and her friends. She directed herself more toward Ignacio's friends, who spoke and understood English better.

"You know what happened to my cousin, right?" she asked them.

They all shook their heads.

"Sophia," I said. "*No más.*"

"Oh, stop. She's afraid because she's not yet a legal citizen, but I don't think it's right that she was raped and no one will do anything about it," she added without hesitation.

Ignacio looked at me sharply. "What does she say? You never said this," he told me.

"Sophia, please, no."

"She's so ashamed. Imagine if it happened to your sisters," she told them.

"Who did this to her?" Ignacio's friend Vicente asked her, and she told them.

"He brags about how he got away with it. Ignacio saved her from even more damage," she added.

They turned to him and asked him in Spanish if he had known. He shook his head and looked at me with some annoyance now.

"She never told me that," he said.

"She's just too embarrassed," Sophia continued.

"Where is this Bradley Whitfield?" Vicente asked her.

"Oh, I know exactly where he is right this moment, in fact," she told him. "He's going to abuse another young, innocent girl. She might be Mexican, too. I'm not sure."

They looked at Ignacio.

"You going to let Delia be dishonored this way?" Luis asked him.

Ignacio looked toward his father and then at me and his friends.

"No," he said.

Sophia smiled. "Well, finally," she said, "someone who really cares. C'mon. He's not far. He's having a private party in the very house in which he raped Delia. Let's go there and surprise him."

I shook my head at Ignacio.

"Let's go," Vicente said. "Time for some justice, Mexican-style."

Ignacio hesitated.

"You should be the one telling us to go," Manuel said.

"*Sí*, what's wrong with your courage?" Vicente asked him, and Ignacio reddened.

"I am not afraid. I nearly beat him once before."

"And now there is even more reason," Luis said. They all agreed.

Sophia beamed.

"Wait," Ignacio said. He pulled away from my hand and crossed to the table where his mother and some of her friends were sitting. "We'll be right back," I heard him tell her. "We have a little errand to do."

"What errand?" she asked.

"Just an errand," he said.

She looked at me and then at her mother, who was nodding as if she had heard someone whisper in her ear, telling her something she had known her whole life.

Ignacio and his friends followed Sophia and her girl-friends out of the yard and around the side of the house. I ran after them all, hoping to turn them back. Sophia's friends stopped me and told me to get into their car.

"Ignacio!" I shouted, but he was already in his friend's car. They shot away from the curb.

"Well, all right," Sophia said, exploding with excitement. "Finally, some real action."

So, this was why she had insisted on knowing where the fiesta was being held. She had planned this all along, I thought, every part of it.

Everything was happening so quickly. I felt helpless.

Moments later, the caravan of vigilantes was heading into the night.

18

Scene of the Crime

Seeing the house in which Bradley had forced himself on me immediately made me cringe. All the way over, Sophia and her girlfriends were giggling and talking excitedly about what they anticipated happening. It was as if they were going to a show. This was to be their entertainment. Sophia's girlfriends congratulated her on how well she had orchestrated it all and how clever she had been to get the Mexican boys angry enough to do something so quickly.

I sat there listening to them and to Sophia bragging about how easy it was to get Ignacio and his friends riled. I realized exactly how Sophia had manipulated me, too. Her gifts, her acts of kindness, and her feigned concern for my welfare were all part of her plan, and here I had thought we were finally becoming close, becoming good friends, if not like sisters. I could almost hear Señora Porres telling my grandmother, "*Solamente*

hay amigos fieles: la esposa vieja, el perro, y el dinero."
There are only three true friends: an old wife, a dog, and money. She would turn to me and say, "Believe in nothing else. Trust nothing else."

She would say, if she were sitting beside me now, "See? Am I not right?"

Someday I might be someone's old wife, but right now, I had no dog, and I had no money. I had no true friends. She was right.

The house was dark except for one dimly lit window, the light flickering. The girls pulled their car up right behind Ignacio and his friends' car. Sophia turned to her girlfriends and me and told us the light inside the house came from a candle or two.

"Jana Lawler is in there with him," her girlfriend Trudy said. "He barely takes a breath between victims."

"Is she Mexican?" I asked, remembering she had said that at the fiesta.

"No," Sophia said, smirking. "Hardly."

"But you told Ignacio . . ."

"Figures Jana would fall for his line," Sophia continued, ignoring me. "He's like a spider luring you into his web with all his romantic gimmicks. Candlelight, some wine, some soft music, and all his phony promises. Jana is the perfect little fly."

"You should know," Alisha said.

"Ha ha. Thanks."

"Hey, don't knock it if you haven't tried it, I say," Delores quipped, and they laughed.

Although Sophia had intended to make Bradley seem deceitful and disgusting, her girlfriends talked and looked at the house with fascination. The way they were acting, I thought each really wished she were the one who had been invited into what Sophia described as Bradley's web.

The second Ignacio and his friends stepped out of their car, Sophia leaned out of the window.

"Go around the back. That door is unlocked," she told them in a loud whisper. They started for it.

"This is not good," I said.

Sophia spun around to face me. "What are you talking about, not good? You were raped, stupid, or is it *stupido*?"

She laughed, and the others joined her.

"My cousin Delia is very religious. She believes in forgiveness," Sophia said. "She knows nothing about birth control, either. I'm trying to teach her."

"Did Bradley use anything with her?" Delores asked.

"She doesn't like talking about it, but I doubt it," Sophia told them. "He depended on me for that sort of thing. She's so . . . naive."

They all looked at me as if I were from another planet, and then their attention returned quickly to the house and the boys.

Ignacio and his friends moved up the driveway and around the side of the house like shadows cut loose in the moonlight, hovering close together, a monster with four heads.

"Bradley is about to get the shock of his life," Sophia said. "I hope they rearrange his face."

No one spoke. Suddenly, Trudy realized the seriousness of what was about to occur.

"Maybe this wasn't such a good idea. That short Mexican boy looked like he could kill someone, Sophia," she said.

Sophia looked at her and then at the house.

"Trudy's right, Sophia. These Mexican boys carry switchblades and stuff. Maybe we should follow them in and make sure they don't go too far," said Delores, who was sitting next to me.

"I'm not going in there," Sophia said. "Don't be stupid. That would be exactly the wrong thing for us to do."

"Why?" Delores asked.

"Why? Right now, we can't be blamed for anything that happens. We'll say we followed them because we were afraid they might do something, understand? But we became afraid and stopped following them."

No one spoke.

A part of me wanted me to get out and run up to the house, shouting warnings and screaming at Ignacio to stop before he got himself and his friends into big trouble, but I was too frightened to move.

"Bradley's father is a pretty important man around here," Delores said. Her words hung in the air like a threat.

"We haven't done anything," Sophia reminded them. "We can't make boys that age do what we want, can we, especially Mexican boys? Maybe they're all illegal or something, too. You going to get between them and their revenge?"

"Yes, but what if there really was no need for revenge?" Alisha asked her.

"What do you mean?"

"Except for your brother, you, and your mother, no one knows what Bradley supposedly did to her," Alisha said. "And your mother didn't go to the police."

"So?"

"Why wouldn't she?"

"Ask her when you get the chance," Sophia said.

"Are you absolutely sure that Bradley raped her? You said she won't talk about it."

They all looked at me.

"Go on, tell them what he did to you, Delia. You can't be bashful anymore. It's too late. Talk."

I shook my head.

"Alisha's right, Sophia. What if she is lying?" Trudy asked.

"Shut up, Trudy. You're just making everyone crazy."

"Did your mother take her to a doctor, at least?" Delores asked. "And have her examined? They can tell if you've been raped."

"No. I told you my mother didn't do and isn't doing anything about it. That's why Edward got so angry and why we're here. Which reminds me . . . what about my brother? Forget about Delia for a moment. What about what happened to him? He lost an eye, Delores, and you know who's responsible. What if that happened to your brother, huh?"

"All right, all right. We're just asking, Sophia. Don't burst a blood vessel."

"Then shut up," Sophia said. She glared at me. "You could at least speak up for yourself, Delia."

"I do not want Ignacio to get into trouble," I said. "It is not right."

No one spoke. We all looked at the house and waited. Suddenly, we heard the sound of something being smashed against a wall. I flinched, and so did Delores.

"What was that?" she muttered.

There was shouting and a girl's scream. The shouting got louder, and there were more loud bangs. Moments later, we were all stunned to see Bradley Whitfield come flying through the front window naked. He hit the floor of the front deck of the house, shards of glass raining down after him. All was quiet a moment. Then came another shrill scream.

"Let's get the hell out of here!" Delores cried.

Trudy started the car.

"Wow," Sophia said. "I can't believe it. Did you see that?"

Trudy shot away from the curb and sped down the street, nearly missing the turn. The wheels screamed, and we were all thrown to one side.

"Slow down!" Delores shouted.

Trudy did, and then we made another turn and headed into the busier street.

"I'm freaking out," Trudy said. "He came through the window! Right through the window. Did you see how it shattered, too?"

"I didn't see him get up," Delores said. "I looked back after we pulled away, but I didn't see him."

"Forget about it," Sophia said excitedly. "Remember, we didn't see anything. We followed the Mexican boys for a while and then lost them because we got frightened and they drove too fast. We never saw anything, because we weren't there, got it?"

"What about your cousin?" Delores asked, nodding at me.

Sophia turned to me and leaned over the front seat. "You understand, Delia? You don't say anything about this. *Silencio* or whatever," she said, gesturing to show her lips being zipped shut. "You weren't here."

"Jeez, don't you know how to say anything in Spanish?" Alisha said, and turned to me. "*No diga nada, Delia, entiende?*"

"You're such a big shot, Alisha," Sophia said. "Honor student."

"Delia, *entiende*?"

I looked away. I didn't need the translation.

"She understands," Alisha said.

"I don't have to speak Spanish to make sure she does. Don't worry," Sophia said. "Let's go to the Roadhouse. This has all made me hungry. I need a brownie sundae right away."

"Really?" Trudy asked her.

"Yes, just go, go," Sophia said.

"He came crashing through that window just like in the movies or something," Delores said.

"Shut up about it, already," Sophia said. "The more you talk about it, the more chance you'll screw up and we'll be accused of something."

"She's right," Alisha said. "Let's not talk about it, especially at the Roadhouse. Someone might overhear."

"He got what he deserved," Sophia added. "End of story."

"Can you imagine the look on Jana's face, though?" Trudy asked.

They all laughed.

"Especially if they were right in the middle of it," Delores said. "This might ruin her love life for some time," she added, and they laughed harder.

I looked out the window. How could they laugh? How quickly my wonderful night had turned sour. What happened to the fiesta? What happened to my visit home?

We pulled into the parking lot of the restaurant. I did not want to get out and go in, but they insisted.

"Remember, we stick together," Sophia told me. "If any one of us gets into trouble, you get into trouble, get it, *mi prima*?" she said, poking me in the chest with her right forefinger. "C'mon. I'm hungry."

I followed them in. The excitement did seem to stimulate their appetites. They all ordered sundaes. I didn't want anything, but they made me order some coffee.

"And don't look so glum," Sophia warned.

"She means don't look *triste*," Alisha said.

Don't look sad?

My aunt had forced me to do something so provocative with my cousin Edward that he no longer liked me and even thought I was deceitful and promiscuous. He now believed that he might have lost his eye defending someone who didn't deserve it, which made him feel worse and made me feel absolutely horrible.

My cousin Sophia had tricked me, lied to me, used me to get revenge on her old boyfriend and might very well have gotten a very nice young man and his family into trouble. At the very least, they surely would not want me around them anymore.

Who knew what had happened to the girl they called Jana?

All of these things were directly or indirectly caused by my arrival, and I was not to look sad?

"You'd better keep her locked up for a while," Trudy told Sophia, eyeing me. "I don't like the way she's acting."

"Don't worry about it. She knows if she does anything stupid and gets us into trouble, my mother would make life so miserable for her she would wish she were dead," Sophia said.

I stared at the cup of coffee and said nothing. As if they had already forgotten about what had just happened, they started to talk about an upcoming Sweet Sixteen party a girl named Ashley Piper was having in one of the big hotels. They went on and on about their clothes and the boys they hoped to see there.

They devoured their ice cream sundaes, Sophia eating all of hers first and then dipping her spoon into everyone else's. When they were finished and had paid the bill, we got back into Trudy's car. Delores suggested we drive by the house to see if there were any police or anything, but Sophia told her that would be very stupid.

"Besides," she added, "what house? I have no idea what you're talking about, Delores."

Everyone but me laughed nervously. Sophia decided she and I should go home. The plan they set was that if anyone heard anything, she was to call the others right away. Trudy made a turn and headed for my aunt's *hacienda*.

"Okay, here's the story we'll use right now," Sophia said when we drove onto the property. "We went to the Mexican house to rescue Delia from what we knew would be a boring party. We spoke to the boys, who were already angry about what Bradley had done. As far as we know, Delia told them everything. We saw them take off in their car, followed them for a while, lost them, and went for ice cream. The waitress will verify it. We don't know anything else, got it?"

"You're so wicked, Sophia," Trudy said, and they all laughed.

"Not as wicked as Bradley Whitfield," Sophia said. "Or maybe just not as stupid."

That brought more laughter. I was happy to get out of the car and head into the house.

"Just go to your room," Sophia ordered after grabbing my arm at the door. "Don't stop to talk to Jesse if he's here, and especially not Edward. I'll let you know what's going on later if I hear anything tonight."

I said nothing. I was too numb and tired. I hurried in and up the stairs to my room, where I sat staring out the window into the night. My window looked out onto the front of the *hacienda*. I saw the lit driveway, the lights on the gates, and some headlights of automobiles passing along the street that ran in front of my aunt's property. It had become partly cloudy, but there were still stars and some moonlight to warm the dark sky.

I couldn't stop myself from trembling, even after I was alone in my room. I didn't know how long I sat there. I did fall asleep for a few moments, because when I opened my eyes, I was confused at first. It was late, and except for the sound of my own deep breathing, I heard nothing.

Just before I was about to rise to prepare for bed, I saw a pair of headlights turn toward the main gate. I watched and then heard a phone ringing. It rang a few times before it stopped, and the gate swung open for the automobile to start up the driveway. Without knowing who it was, I felt my heart begin to race. As the car drew closer to the house, I knew why.

It was a police car.

Doors opened and closed, and I heard footsteps in the hallway. I went to my door and opened it slightly to listen. The front door opened, and I heard the murmur of people talking below. I recognized Señor Garman's gruff voice. I heard him speak with Jesse, who had apparently spent another night with Edward while Tía Isabela was away and had gone downstairs to see what was happening.

Sophia surprised me. I was looking in the opposite direction and did not hear her approach my door. She pushed it open and shoved me back, closing it quickly behind her. She was in her nightgown and a robe.

"Why are you still dressed?" she asked, her face twisting in pain. "You look like you just got home. Quickly," she said, turning me around. "Take off those clothes, and put on a nightgown. Hurry!"

I rushed to do what she said while she stood guard at the slightly opened door, listening.

"Someone's coming up here," she told me as I slipped into my bathrobe and then my slippers. "You didn't even wash off your makeup, you fool!"

She grabbed a washcloth and roughly scrubbed at my face.

There was a knock at my door. We both froze.

"Who the hell is it?" she cried.

"Jesse. You'd better come downstairs with Delia right now," he said. "The Palm Springs police are here."

"Why?"

"Just come downstairs, Sophia. Bring her. This is very serious."

She went to the door and opened it to face him. "Why are the police here?"

"They want to speak with Delia," he said. "And you."

"Why?" she demanded, putting her hands on her hips.

Jesse looked past her at me. "It's what they want."

"I don't care what they want. My mother's not home. Tell them to come back when my mother's home."

"Don't be stupid, Sophia. You'd better come downstairs right now."

"Why? Why is it so important to talk to them now? It's late. We were both about to go to sleep."

"Sophia . . ."

"Tell them that, Jesse."

"They won't go away, Sophia."

"Why not?"

Jesse looked at me. "Because Bradley Whitfield *está muerto.*"

My heart had already stopped, and the blood had drained from my face. It felt as if the air had been baked around me. For a moment, I couldn't breathe.

"What the hell does that mean?"

"It means he's dead," Jesse said.

Sophia stepped back as if he had spit at her. She looked at me and then at him. "That's impossible. How could he be dead?"

"How could he be? Apparently, someone threw him through a window, and the glass severed an artery. He bled to death before the ambulance arrived."

"Bled to death?"

"The girl he was with, Jana Lawler, was too hysterical to get to a phone in time."

"He's really dead?"

"Yes."

"Well . . ."

Sophia looked at me. I was sobbing softly, my tears seeming to pop out of my cheeks instead of my eyes.

"Well . . . why did the police come here?"

"Jana said four Mexican boys burst in on her and Bradley. She knew one of them. They went to the boy's home and found out Delia was there and you came with some of your friends. You all left with the boy and his friends. That's what they know. That's what the police just told us. Satisfied? I'll tell them you're coming right down," he added, and left us.

"Damn," Sophia said. She backed herself into the chair at the vanity table.

I leaned against the bedpost to keep myself from falling.

"That Jana is such a moron. Why couldn't she get to a phone if she saw he was bleeding so badly?" Sophia muttered. Then she looked at me quickly and stood up. "Stop crying like that. You can't fall apart now, Delia. You have to stick with our story, understand? You remember our story? Don't say anything else. Make believe you don't understand anything. I'll tell them we won't talk until my mother gets home, understand? Don't tell them too much.

"Delia!" she said, grabbing my arms and shaking me hard. "Are you listening to me?"

I nodded, but her words were like marbles rolling around in a can.

"You'd better, or you'll be in very big trouble, very big. You're not even an American citizen yet. You'll go to jail, a terrible jail just for Mexicans," she said.

Could that be so?

"All right. C'mon," she said, taking my hand. "I'll be right there with you. Just look at me before you answer anything. Let me do most of the talking. I'll keep holding your hand. If I squeeze it, don't answer. I hope you understand, Delia, for your sake more than mine," she said, her eyes riveted on me and full of threats.

We started down the stairs. As we descended, I saw the two policemen waiting with Señor Garman at the entryway. Jesse had gone back to Edward to tell him what was happening. Señor Garman was in a pair of old pants and an undershirt. He glared at us with such anger I was afraid to get too close to him. Sophia took my hand as soon as we stepped off the stairway.

"What's going on?" she asked with remarkable aggressiveness toward the police. "My mother is away, and she wouldn't want us talking to police without first talking to a lawyer, I'm sure."

"Why, do you think we're here to arrest you for something?" the taller of the two policemen asked her sharply.

"No," she said, but she hesitated to step forward.

The shorter policeman, a younger, better-looking man with a quiet smile, nodded at me. "*Usted es* Delia?" he asked me.

"*Sí,*" I said. Having him speak to me in Spanish relaxed me a little, but Sophia was shocked.

"I don't understand Spanish, so . . ."

"He wasn't speaking to you. This girl is recently here, correct?"

"This girl is my cousin," Sophia said.

We heard Jesse and Edward coming down the stairway behind us.

"Oh, crap," Sophia muttered. "My brother."

"What's happening here, Mr. Garman?" Edward asked, halfway down the stairs.

"A young man has been killed," he said. "The police are here to question your sister and Delia." He turned to the policemen. "Mr. Dallas was in a bad car accident, and . . ."

"Yes, we know about that accident," the taller policeman said.

"What exactly do my sister and Delia have to do with this?" Edward asked. Jesse brought him right up to us.

"That's what we're here to find out," the taller policeman said. He turned to Sophia. "You and your cousin and some of your friends went to the home of Ignacio Davila tonight, is that correct?"

"My cousin went there with Ignacio to celebrate his sister's birthday, yes, and then I went there with my friends to be sure she was doing all right," Sophia said, tightening her grip on my hand.

The younger policeman asked me if I knew where Ignacio was now.

"No," I said.

"What did he ask her? I don't like her answering questions without an adult here. She doesn't know anything. She's not here that long. Her mother and father were killed in Mexico, for God sakes. She's not over the tragedy," Sophia rattled off.

"Do you know why those boys went after Bradley Whitfield?" the younger policeman asked her.

She lowered her head. "We don't like talking about it," Sophia said. "We're ashamed of what's happened."

"Sophia," Edward said, "stop it. Tell them whatever you know right now."

"I am, Edward," she snapped back at him, and then she turned to the policeman. "We believe Bradley Whitfield took unfair advantage of my cousin."

"Unfair advantage? What exactly does that mean?" the taller policeman asked.

"Figure it out," Sophia told him.

The younger policeman asked me if it was true. I looked down and said yes.

"How come no one reported such an incident?" the taller policeman asked. He looked toward Edward.

Everyone was silent for a moment, and then Sophia spoke.

"How come your nose is so long?" she shot back at him.

"Oh, you're really a smart-ass," he said.

"She is that," Edward said. "What do you want to know now, officer? My mother isn't at home, and we're all underage, but we'll try to help."

"Do any of you know the whereabouts of this Ignacio Davila?"

"We don't. Sophia, if you know, tell them."

"I don't know. We don't know. Yes, we were at the party, and they were very upset about what Bradley had done to a Mexican girl, especially one so innocent and pure and religious. We heard them say it was time for Mexican justice."

"They said that?" the taller policeman asked.

"That's what we heard them say."

The younger policeman asked me in Spanish if I had heard those words. I had, so I told him. I wanted to tell him more, but Sophia's grip on my hand was so firm she was stopping the flow of blood.

"Give me the names of the girls who were with you," the taller policeman told Sophia. She rattled them off. "They were all present when those words were spoken?"

"Yes, they were," Sophia said, sounding more pleasant.

"And then what happened?" the taller policeman asked.

"They rushed out of the party, and I told my girlfriends we should follow them to see what they would do, but they drove so fast, we gave up and went to the Roadhouse. You can check. The waitress's name was Christina."

"How did the Mexican boys know where to find Bradley Whitfield?" the younger policeman asked her.

Sophia let go of my hand and put her arm around my shoulders, drawing me closer to her. "They knew where he violated my cousin," she told them. "Delia is in an ESL class with Ignacio," she added, which was as much as saying I had revealed it all.

The policemen were quiet.

"Is there anything else, officer?" Edward asked.

"Not for now," the taller policeman said. "If anyone knows the whereabouts of Ignacio Davila and his friends and does not tell us, he or she could be charged with obstruction of justice. Keep that in mind."

They thanked Señor Garman and left. The moment they did, Sophia tugged my hand and started for the stairway.

"Sophia," Edward called to her.

"What do you want?"

"Bradley Whitfield is dead."

"So?"

"If you had anything to do with it . . ."

"What are you, deaf as well as blind right now, Edward? You heard everything."

"Delia," he called to me, "is that the truth? *La verdad*?"

Before I could respond, Sophia tugged me back and stepped between me and Edward and Jesse.

"We're both very upset, Edward, especially Delia. You can't see her face, but she's devastated. Just leave us alone," she told him, and continued to tug me toward the stairway.

"That was good," she whispered as we ascended. "I'll go call the girls. We'll be just fine. Just as long as we stick together, understand?"

I wanted to let go of her hand. She wasn't handing me a life line, I thought. She was dragging me down into darker places along with her and her friends. She made me sit beside her in her room while she called each of them and described what had occurred with the police and what she had told them. From the way she spoke, they all sounded absolutely terrified and shocked by the news of Bradley's death. She ended each conversation the same way: "If you don't do and say exactly what we planned, you could get yourself and all of us into very serious trouble. We could be accessories to murder or something!"

What did she mean, *could be*? I thought. That was exactly what they were, and by being cooperative and going along with it all, I was no different.

How far I had fallen from the morning I stood with my parents at the altar to celebrate my *quinceañera*.

How much farther away would I fall?

Had I crossed too far to the dark side ever to return?

19

No More Lies

Wherever Tía Isabela had gone for the weekend, she was close enough to hear about the events immediately in the morning. She called Sophia, and Sophia came into my room to wake me and to tell me that her mother was rushing home.

"I never heard my mother so upset. She can be worse than the police," she warned. "So be very careful about what you tell her."

And then, as if we were participants in some big, national, exciting event, she told me that Bradley's death was on the front page of the newspaper and on television news already. She was very excited about it.

"Of course, because we're underage, our names aren't mentioned," she added, as if that were something bad.

The little sleep I had gotten the night before did nothing to alleviate my numbness and shock. I still felt as if I were floating in some limbo, caught in another sticky nightmare. Sophia's words were stunning. I stared at her in amazement. If there was any sign of real worry and real remorse, it was well hidden beneath the electricity in her eyes and the enthusiasm in her voice. Why wasn't she as terrified as I was? How could she still see this as something exciting, something fun, even after it resulted in Bradley's death?

"She won't be here for an hour or so, so let's both get up and have our breakfast and act as if nothing is wrong. *Nada,* get it?"

"Nothing? How can we pretend there is nothing wrong?"

"Well, you know what I mean." She grimaced. "Don't start that. Don't start acting guilty. You didn't do anything, anyway. You certainly didn't throw him out the window, and we didn't tell them to go kill him, did we? It's not our fault they went too far. You can feel sorry for him and his family if you want, but you can't blame yourself or us, understand?"

I didn't respond. I just closed my eyes and turned my head. She really believed she had done nothing wrong. I wondered if people who lied a lot to others were good at lying to themselves.

"Don't just lie there moping. Get dressed," she ordered. "I'm starving this morning. Just stick close to me, and you'll be all right. Delia! Are you listening to me?"

"Sí," I said. "I'm getting up."

I sat up in bed to satisfy her, and she left.

No matter how long I remained in the shower or how much soap I used, I couldn't wash off the layers and layers of guilt I felt. There must have been something more I could have done to stop Ignacio and his friends. I should have shouted, pleaded, run after them.

Of course, she was right. I shouldn't feel so terrible for Bradley Whitfield. Look at what he had done to me and what sort of young man he was. But I couldn't just forget all of the sorrow his death would cause in his family. He should have been punished, but this was too much. I wondered just how much Ignacio actually had to do with it, too. When he and his friends faced judgment, would they use me as their justification? How I wished Father Martinez was close by, so I could confess to him and hear his words of advice and comfort.

And what if somehow my grandmother Anabela heard about this? What if Tía Isabela was so angry she wrote or called to tell her? It brought tears to my eyes just thinking about her hearing such things. All of her hope, all of her prayers, would have seemed to have gone to waste.

Sophia was dressed and waiting impatiently for me when I came out of the bathroom.

"Hurry up," she said. "Get dressed. You're taking too long. I want us to be eating and looking totally relaxed when my mother comes home." She checked her watch. "Move it."

I dressed quickly and followed her out. Jesse was just leaving the house when we descended the stairway. He paused at the door.

"Edward and I know you're lying about all of this, Sophia," he said, looking up at us. "This time, not even your mother will be able to help you," he added, and walked out.

"That's what you think, Mr. Nurse. Good riddance!" she shouted after him.

Everyone in the house and on the grounds apparently had heard about the terrible events. I could see it immediately in the faces of Señora Rosario and Inez. Both were looking at me as if I were a different person entirely, as if I had shed my skin like some snake and was now truly who I was. I was dying inside to tell them everything, to explain so they would understand, but Sophia was practically attached to me this morning.

I watched her eat everything ravenously, even with all of the tension and turmoil, and I thought to myself that where most people had feelings, emotions, nerves, she must be made of steel. Despite what Bradley had done, was he not once her boyfriend? Didn't she describe to me how she had wanted to be intimate with him? She had feelings for him once. How could she not shed a tear, or did she do so in private so she could keep up this tough appearance in front of me? For her sake, I hoped so. I hoped she had at least a small piece of heart and was capable of caring for someone else besides herself. Otherwise, she would grow up to be as lonely and as bitter as her mother.

Tía Isabela came charging into the house so fiercely I thought she was going to find and beat on us both. I cringed at the sound of her voice, hearing her shout, "Where are they?" the moment she entered. We heard Señora Rosario talking to her in a low murmur, and then we heard her slam something and start for the dining room. Her footsteps were like nails being driven into my very soul.

She seemed to explode in the doorway. Maybe it was because of my own fear, but she loomed larger than ever, her eyes as hot and as bright as molten lava. She was in a pair of tight-fitting red leather pants, a white blouse, and a red leather jacket. With her face flushed, she looked as if she had been formed out of blood. For a long moment, she just stood there gaping at us, and then she focused on Sophia. I lowered my gaze to the table and held my breath.

"You went to the Mexican fiesta? You followed her there?" she demanded.

Sophia shrugged to make it seem like nothing, but I could see that even her cold, confident heart was finally cringing. Mine was as tight as a fist in my chest.

"We just thought we should check on her, Mother. She's still a little stupid when it comes to boys."

"She's stupid when it comes to boys? Her?" She pointed to me as though she wanted to be certain Sophia was talking about the same girl.

"Well, I just thought since she . . . I mean, look what happened to her with Mr. Baker, and then Bradley took advantage of her so quickly, and . . ."

"You idiot. When it comes to men, she's twice as sly and as conniving as you'll ever be. She's my sister's daughter!"

"Well, I didn't even know she was your sister's daughter until after she was here," Sophia fired back. "How would I know anything about your sister, anyway? Why are you so full of secrets about your own family?" she added, turning to the offensive.

Tía Isabela nibbled on her lower lip a moment and then stepped forward to the table. She put her hands on the back of her chair and glared first at me and then at Sophia.

"You're not going to change the subject on me like you do so often, Sophia. This is very serious. I want to know exactly what your part was in all this. I have Web Rudin coming here to see you and Delia and me in an hour, but before you speak to our attorney, I want to know every detail about your involvement in all this."

She stood up straight and folded her arms under her breasts.

"Well? Go on," she commanded. "And there had better not be a single lie in your story, or believe me, I'll toss you to the wolves."

Sophia started to cry. Her ability to turn her tears on and off like a faucet was astonishing.

"No one loves me in this family since Daddy died," she said through her tears.

"Oh, please."

"Right away, you assume everything is my fault!" Sophia moaned.

Tía Isabela smirked. "That's because it usually is, Sophia. And don't try to play me like you play your teachers and your friends. Unlike most mothers, I never doted on my children, and I never made excuses for their weaknesses and failings."

"Well, maybe you should have," Sophia replied. "Maybe then we wouldn't be in so much trouble."

"Don't you dare try to find a way to blame any of this on me," Tía Isabela told her. "Now, exactly what happened? I want to know what you did. Don't skip a single detail."

"All right, I'll tell you," Sophia said, as if she was going to make her mother sorry she demanded it. She wiped away her artificial tears and took a deep, exaggerated breath. "First, I helped her get ready," she said, nodding at me. "I showed her how to do her makeup, and I loaned her a pair of earrings and helped her with her hair. She wears it so plainly, and . . ."

"I'm not talking about any of that!"

"Well, you just said don't leave out a detail."

Tía Isabela sighed. "And then?"

"Ignacio, her Mexican boyfriend, drove up in his filthy old pickup truck. It was so gross I was hoping it wasn't as dirty inside as it was outside. After all, she was wearing an expensive dress. He was wearing this costume like a mariachi or something. I didn't think he liked the way she was dressed, and I thought she might not enjoy herself, because those Mexicans would make her feel out of place or something."

"Oh, so all of a sudden, you were worried about how she would be accepted by Mexicans? You were that concerned about her happiness?"

"Well, she's my cousin. You told us she was going to be part of the family, Mother. You said . . ."

"Just go on with the story," Tía Isabela said.

"Later, I met up with Alisha, Delores, and Trudy. We were going to go to a movie, but I told them about Delia and the way Ignacio looked at her. They thought it would be a good idea to drop in on the fiesta to see if she was having a bad time. They thought if she was, we'd take her with us."

"They thought? It's always someone else who comes up with these ideas."

"It was my idea, too. I wanted her to spend time with American girls. If she is going to live here and be part of our family . . ."

"And?"

"And I was glad we went, because when we got there, I could see she was sort of by herself. I could see the Mexicans were looking at her funny, like she was some kind of a traitor or something for not dressing in those costumes. They probably never heard of Valentino. Most of them looked like they dyed some rags and wrapped . . ."

"Sophia! Get to what I want to hear," Tía Isabela shouted.

"I'm telling you like it happened. Isn't that what you want? You said to be exact."

"Go on," Tía Isabela said, now looking exhausted.

"Well, almost immediately, her boyfriend Ignacio pulled me aside and asked me if it was true what Bradley Whitfield had done to her. She had apparently told him everything, every nitty-gritty dirty detail about her rape."

I spun around. I was able to follow most of what she was saying well enough and had no doubt about what she had just said. I started to shake my head, but her eyes burned through mine to singe my brain with another warning.

"What could I do, Mother? I had to say yes. I don't know or remember even if you knew it, but it was Ignacio who beat Bradley away when he came after her to get her to do it with his friends, right, Delia? Didn't Ignacio help you before? Well?"

Tía Isabela looked at me to see what I would say. I nodded. She had thrown a tidbit of truth into the pool of lies. I couldn't deny it.

Tía Isabela turned back to her. "Then what?"

"The next thing I knew, he was off to the side whispering with three of his friends and with her. I think she told them where Bradley had raped her. She must have, in fact. They started to leave the party, cursing Bradley and threatening Mexican justice."

"Mexican justice?"

"Something like that. I stopped Ignacio and said, 'You'd better not do anything to Bradley Whitfield. His father's pretty important around here.' I guess I shouldn't have said that. It made him angrier, all of them angrier. He pushed me aside, mumbling about how terrible we treat Mexicans now, and continued out.

"Alisha said we had better follow them to see what they were up to. I told Delia she had to come with us, that this was happening because she had told them too much. We all got into Trudy's car and tried to follow the Mexican boys."

"What do you mean, tried?"

"They went so fast we couldn't keep up. Delia was crying, sorry for what she had done. We were all getting frightened by now, so we went to the Roadhouse to calm down. We came home right afterward. Next thing I knew, Jesse was banging on Delia's door late at night. I was in her room with her, trying to get her calm enough to go to sleep. She was crying and mumbling all sorts of things in Spanish I couldn't understand."

"Jesse came to get you?"

"Yes, he's been here the whole time, Mother, practically locked up in Edward's room."

She looked at me and then back at Sophia. "And that's all of it?"

"No. Jesse insisted we go down to speak to the police. They were pretty nasty. I told them you wouldn't want us to talk to them without a lawyer, and they ridiculed me, treating me as if I was the one who threw Bradley through the window. I did tell them how we had gone to the Roadhouse and even gave them the name of the waitress who waited on us. You can go and check on that yourself if you don't believe me."

Tía Isabela stared a moment and then relaxed and slipped into her chair.

"Inez!" she shouted.

It was pretty obvious to me that Inez had her ear to the door and had been listening to everything. She was there in a second.

"Yes, Mrs. Dallas?"

"Get me a cup of fresh coffee and a glass of ice-cold water."

"Yes, Mrs. Dallas."

"How was your weekend, Mother?" Sophia asked her, as if this was just another morning. She finished her cranberry and orange muffin in a single bite. "Where did you go, anyway? Were you with Travis again?"

"Don't worry about my weekend, Sophia. I told you not to change the subject."

"Well, I told you everything! What else do you want?"

"Do you or Delia have any knowledge of the where-abouts of these Mexican boys?"

"How would we? That was the first time I had ever met any of them. I'm not in the habit of hanging around with Mexican boys, Mother."

"I can't believe this," Tía Isabela said after a deep sigh. "I'm already a nervous wreck. Tomorrow, we take Edward to his doctor to see how his eyes are healing."

"What are you nervous about? You said he's losing the use of one, didn't you?"

"We don't know to what extent yet, but most likely, yes," she said.

Inez appeared with a glass of ice water for her. "In a minute, the coffee," she said, and left.

Tía Isabela drank her water, thought a moment, and then turned to me.

"*Ella está diciendo la verdad?*" she asked me.

"You never speak Spanish, Mother," Sophia said immediately. "What are you asking her?"

"*La verdad?*" Tía Isabela asked me, ignoring her.

I knew if I said no, that it wasn't the truth, Sophia would hate me and try to hurt me in some way. I saw what she was capable of doing, and I feared her almost as much as I feared my aunt, but I remembered that Grandmother Anabela used to say, "*Es más fácil de atrapar a un mentiroso que a un cojo.*" It's easier to catch a liar than a cripple.

Besides, I had little faith in the loyalty of Sophia and her friends. One would betray the other if she was in any danger, I thought, and eventually, Tía Isabela would know what was true and what wasn't. Up until now, I had traveled with them into the dark side, but it was time to go back, or at least try to go back. Tía Isabela was no Father Martinez, and I expected no forgiveness nor wanted any from her, but I would no longer bathe in the same water or breathe the same air as my cousin Sophia. To do so would stain the memory of my parents and move them closer to that third death.

"*No lo dije a Ignacio. Estaba ella.*"

Tía Isabela nodded, smiling coldly.

"What did she say? Huh? What did she say?"

"She said she didn't tell Ignacio about Bradley raping her and where he was; you did."

"What? She's lying. She's afraid she'll get into trouble and be deported or something."

Inez returned with a cup of fresh coffee for Tía

Isabela. No one spoke until she left. Tía Isabela sipped some coffee first, thinking. Then she nodded to herself.

"Actually, it's more believable that she would tell him," she said. "It's better for us. And for her," she added, looking at me. "People will sympathize and understand. She was violated. It's natural for her to turn to Mexicans for help. You tell everyone that you told him about Bradley, not Sophia, Delia. *Entiende*?"

I understood. I just couldn't believe that she would rather I lie. My silence annoyed her.

"I'm getting my lawyer to defend you, all of you. I'm paying for all of this, and it's going to cost a lot of money. I'm not about to have this family dragged into something so ugly. You will do as I say. *Entiende*?" she shouted at me.

She brought her coffee cup down so hard that it shattered the saucer. I felt myself leap inside my own body.

I nodded quickly.

Inez and Señora Rosario came rushing in to see what had broken.

"Not now!" she shouted at them. They stopped, looked at me, and returned to the kitchen. My aunt sat there drumming her fingers on the table as she thought. Then she turned back to me.

"Until I say otherwise, you are not to leave the house. *No salga de la casa*. Not even for school. I don't want to take the chance of your saying something by accident, *entiende*?"

Again, I nodded quickly. She looked at Sophia and pointed her right forefinger at her.

"This time, you've gone too far, Sophia. After this is over, if you just look the wrong way, I'll have you skinned alive. Now, get ready to meet with Mr. Rudin in my office. Both of you. And be sure your stories coincide. Inez!" she screamed and stood up.

Inez hurried back into the dining room.

"Clean all of this up," she ordered, pointing to the shattered saucer. Then she turned and left us.

Sophia sat there steaming while Inez worked. The moment Inez carried away the broken pieces of saucer, Sophia turned to me.

"Traitor," she said. "You'll be sorry." She got up and walked out of the dining room.

I looked after her and thought, I'm sorry already.

A little more than a half-hour later, we were both called to Tía Isabela's office to meet with my aunt's attorney, Web Rudin. He was a robust man, not quite five-feet-ten, with dark brown hair and dark brown eyes. His ears stuck out a little too far, but he had a rich, smooth complexion, with soft facial features and eyelashes that would make any woman envious. He sat across from Tía Isabela at her desk, close enough to write on a long yellow pad he had set there.

"You know Sophia, Web. This is my niece, Delia, who recently came from Mexico." She turned to me. "Mr. Rudin is the attorney who prepared the papers I needed to bring you here."

I looked at him, but he still didn't smile.

"She had a little working knowledge of English but has learned a lot since she's been here," Tía Isabela added. "She's a bright girl."

Finally, he started to smile at us and then stopped, as if he had nearly done something very wrong. He glanced at Tía Isabela, and she nodded at the leather sofa. We both sat, Sophia glaring at me once more in warning.

"Go on, Web," she continued. "Tell them what you told me."

He put his pen down and pressed his palms together. "Three of the Mexican boys have been found and are in custody. The fourth is still a fugitive."

"Which one?" Sophia asked.

Mr. Rudin glanced at his pad. "Ignacio Davila. Has he tried to make contact with either of you?"

"No," Sophia said. She looked at me.

I shook my head.

"I'll have to have a clear understanding of the extent of your involvement in all of this," Mr. Rudin went on. "I have a general idea of what these boys told the police. Let me hear it all from you two."

"It will be faster if Sophia speaks for them," Tía Isabela said, smiling. "You can ask Delia questions after that. I'll help her if there is anything she doesn't understand."

"Sure," he said, and sat poised.

Without the smallest change in her story, Sophia retold everything as she had told Tía Isabela. Then, as an afterthought, she added that she and her friends had been very worried about what the Mexican boy Vicente would do. "He looked like he could kill his own mother," she said, and glanced at Tía Isabela, who stared without expression. "That's why we tried to follow them."

"So, you're saying you didn't urge them on, you didn't tell them exactly where to go or what to do when they got there?" Mr. Rudin asked.

"No, sir," Sophia said, with eyes that would melt the heart of the sternest judge.

"You weren't there? You didn't witness any of it?"

"Oh, no, Mr. Rudin. We went to the Roadhouse, as I said. I'm sure the police have checked on that."

Mr. Rudin wrote something and then turned to me and asked me to describe the previous event when Ignacio had come to my defense. Apparently, Tía Isabela had already told him something about it. I did the best I could with Tía Isabela helping whenever I stumbled over an English word or expression.

"Well," he concluded, "if what they're telling me is true, I think we can keep the girls out of this, Isabela. Make sure no one speaks to anyone, of course. It all goes through me from now on. Call me as soon as any police or investigator contacts you. Both girls know that if they are approached at school, they should call you immediately."

"They do now, Web," she said firmly. She didn't tell him that I wasn't going to school for a while, that she was keeping me almost a prisoner here.

"Very sad thing," he said, finally expressing some emotion about it all. He closed his pad. "Bradley was the apple of Rod's eye, the one bright and hopeful thing he had. He was very proud of him. It's going to be hard for him to face all of this."

"Children unfortunately often turn out to be disappointing," Tía Isabela said.

I raised my eyebrows.

Surely, her father had uttered the same words about her many years ago in a different place, in a different country, in a different world.

She stared at me a moment, as if she knew exactly what I was thinking.

And then we were excused.

Sophia said nothing to me. She simply gave me a

hateful look and went to her room to call her girlfriends
and report, I was sure.

Later, Tía Isabela came to my room.

"You did well," she said. "For the time being, while
you're not going to school, you'll return to household
duties. I've already spoken about it with Mrs. Rosario. I
will not have you simply lying around."

I didn't say anything. Of course, I would rather be
in school, but I wasn't afraid of work. In fact, I was
grateful for anything that would keep me from thinking
about all that had happened.

"I hope we'll get this all cleared up, but if things
don't go right and it gets any more serious, I'll have to
inform your grandmother. I'm not sure I shouldn't do
that now, in fact."

I pressed my lips together to keep from bursting into
tears. She looked satisfied with how she had made me
cringe, nodded, and left, closing the door behind her.
I sat there staring in silence, feeling like someone who
was waiting for the second shoe to drop.

It came a little while later, when Sophia appeared to
give me some updated news about Ignacio and his family.

"I just spoke with Alisha. They haven't caught him
yet, but the police are looking for him everywhere because of how important Bradley's father is in this town.
His father is going to make things hard for Ignacio's
father, too, Alisha says. They all might as well just pack
up and go back to Mexico. Maybe his whole family will
be deported."

"That's not right," I said.

"You almost got me into big trouble with my mother.
I told you not to contradict me. You know what that
means? I told you we stick with my story."

"I do not like to lie."

"Oh, no, not you, not Señorita Perfecto. Give me back my bracelet," she demanded. "You don't deserve it. C'mon, give it back."

I took it off, and she seized it out of my hand.

"I'm taking my dress back, too," she said, going to my closet. She ripped it off the hanger, looked down at the shoes Tía Isabela had bought to match it, and grabbed them, too. "I have a real friend it will fit now, thanks to what you did to it. I think she's your shoe size as well. You'll never wear it again, anyway. You're nothing more than a servant again, *prima* or no *prima*."

I said nothing. Actually, it felt good to have her take back her things. It was like a cleansing. She mistook my failure to look upset to mean I felt superior to her.

"You think you're so smart. We'll see. I'm not finished with you yet," she said, and left.

Soon after, Señora Rosario sent Inez to tell me to come down to help with the kitchen duties. I worked on the downstairs bathrooms as well and then helped rearrange the pantry and wash the floors. We were to do a general dusting of everything as well. Sophia walked past me as I worked, smiling gleefully.

When I was finished with the household chores, I went up to shower and change. I was not sure if I would be permitted to have dinner with my aunt and Sophia. Edward, who had remained in his room all day, would probably have his meal there, too, and wait for his bandages to come off the next day. I had not seen Jesse all day and wondered what Edward was doing to pass the time.

I didn't need to wonder long.

He was thinking about me.

I came out of the bathroom and went to my dresser to take a pair of panties out of the drawer. I was just slipping them on when I realized I wasn't alone.

Standing just inside the doorway, dressed in his robe and pajamas, was Edward.

I gasped. I was naked, but he still had bandages over his eyes.

"What do you want, Edward?" I asked when I gathered my wits. Even though he couldn't see me, I quickly slipped my bathrobe on again.

"I want the truth," he said. "*La verdad.*"

20

An Opportunity Arises

For a moment, I simply stood there looking at him. What truth did he want?

"Sophia is my sister, and when it comes down to it, I will love her as I should love a sister, but I know she has never been the one to accept blame for anything she does. Do you understand what I'm saying, Delia? Sophia always lies and lies until it's no longer possible, until she is forced to tell the truth, and even then, you have to check and be sure.

"Don't pretend you don't know what I'm talking about, Delia. You know enough English to understand what I want," he added, and waited.

I was still unsure about what I should and shouldn't say. I could see that my continual silence was annoying him. He stepped toward me.

"My mother told me what Sophia told her about this entire incident. She said you admitted to stirring up the trouble, and she's busy trying to protect you. You know what that means, stirring up the trouble?" he asked, gesturing to imitate someone stirring a soup or a stew.

Why had she told him that? Why must everyone lie to everyone in this house?

"I did not do this," I said. "This stirring."

He nodded. "Okay. I'm listening. Tell me what you did do, then. How did this all happen?"

"I went to the birthday fiesta with Ignacio, his sister's birthday."

"I know that. I know that," he said, impatient. "What happened, damn it? Talk!"

His anger frightened me. I stumbled for the words. "Sophia . . . her friends came *luego* . . . later."

"And they riled up the Mexican boys, didn't they? Sophia's friends are just like her. Well?"

"*Sí.* Sophia told Ignacio what Bradley did."

"And she told him where Bradley was, right? She would be the only one who would know where he was at that moment. Well? Did she tell him?"

"Yes, Edward."

"I thought so. She hasn't been innocent since the moment she was born, and even that is questionable," he said.

"I don't understand."

"Forget it. I just wanted to know what really happened."

"*Sí,* this happened, but *su madre,* your mother, does not want this to be said this way. She told the lawyer different, and I must do and say as she says."

He nodded and felt his way to a chair, lowering himself carefully.

"Tell me what really happened after that, Delia. *Qué sucedió*? After the Mexican boys left the fiesta?"

"Sophia and her friends wanted to . . . how do you say, follow, go behind Ignacio and his friends."

"And she told my mother you lost them because they were going so fast. My mother should have known that was a lie. Since Sophia knew where Bradley was, it wouldn't matter if they had gone so fast ahead of them, right? Which means you were all there when they attacked Bradley? You saw what happened to him, didn't you?"

"*No adentro . . . no en la casa.*"

"You didn't go inside the house, but you saw what happened to Bradley?"

"*Sí,* yes. The window . . . he came out. Fell . . ."

"And then what?"

"Sophia's friend drove away quickly. I didn't know . . . *no sabía . . .*"

"You didn't know how badly Bradley was hurt?"

"*Sí.*"

"Why did you go with them?" he asked angrily, and then shook his head. "That's a stupid question. What else could you do?"

He put his elbows on his knees and lowered his head to his hands.

"I don't know what to believe about anyone anymore," he said. He raised his head slowly. "Why did you come to my room nearly naked?" He pointed his finger in my direction. "You are not as innocent as you pretend to be, right? Well?" he demanded. "*La verdad.* You've been with other boys in Mexico, right? You knew what you were doing when you came into my room. You weren't so innocent in my room. Does that mean you weren't so innocent with Bradley? Well?"

I was shaking my head, but he couldn't see, of course.

"I did not want to be in your room. I . . ."

"Then why did you do it? *Por qué*? Huh? Why? I liked you, Delia. I thought very highly of you, and I felt sorry for you when Mr. Baker took you away and treated you that way. Why would you come into my room and do something like that? Is that how you got boys to like you back in Mexico? Is it?" he practically shouted. He looked as if the effort gave him pain.

"No."

"You grew up fast, huh? You might as well tell me the truth. It doesn't matter now. C'mon," he said, taunting me. "Tell me some of your Mexican stories about you and your boyfriends. Go on, tell me."

"No, Edward. There are no such stories."

"Right. You just decided to come into my room and offer yourself to me."

"No, I did not want to do this."

"So, how did you come to do it?"

"*Su madre*," I began.

"My mother?" He stopped smiling. "What about my mother?"

My lips fell shut, but I realized I had already opened the door. The truth was like a balloon I was trying to flatten; it just kept popping up here and there. His face seemed to brighten as he thought.

"Are you saying my mother sent you into my room like that?" He grimaced. "But why would she do that?"

"*Para ver* . . . to see."

"To see? You're saying she was there at the time?

Mi madre estaba . . . in the room? Tell me!" he nearly shouted, now standing again.

He was angrier than before. I thought I would burst into sobs and not be able to speak. My throat was tight, but I said, "*Sí.*"

He was quiet. He nodded softly. "*Por qué,* Delia? Tell me why she was there."

"To see if you would like . . ."

"Like what? What?" he demanded, stepping toward me.

"*Chicas,*" I said.

"*Chicas* . . . girls?"

"*Sí,* girls."

He paused. And then he did something I did not expect. He smiled.

"What? She watched to see if I liked girls? She was testing me with you? Is that what she said? Is that what you're telling me? She sent you into my room like that as a kind of test . . . like an exam?"

"*Sí,*" I said, nodding, even though he couldn't see me nodding. "A test, yes."

He was silent. Then he shook his head.

"That doesn't make sense. Why would my mother . . . she's always known who I am," he muttered, thinking aloud. Once again, he thought I was lying. I had gone too far to stop now.

"With Jesse, she worries," I said, trying to explain more. "She told me this. She asked me to help her."

"Help her? How?"

"To tell her what I see, what I hear."

"To spy on me? No," he said, shaking his head. "My mother and I have had that conversation. We talked about it. Nothing should have surprised her. My mother did not need to watch a test."

I started to cry. "I do not lie, Edward."

He was silent, thinking again. "Maybe not," he said, and smiled as another thought came to him. "Yes, maybe not. I believe she would do that, send you into my room almost naked. But not to run a test."

"I do not understand, Edward. I'm sorry."

"It's simple," he said. "My mother and my sister are the same . . . you know, same, similar? What's a good Spanish word for sneaky, deceitful, sly like foxes . . . what? *Cómo se dice* sly *en español*?"

"*Furtivo,*" I said. But I was still very confused. "But *por qué*?"

"*Furtivo,*" he said, nodding. "My mother did not want me to trust you, Delia. My mother did not want me to be your . . . to be *su primo* or *su amigo*. I took your side too strongly against Mr. Baker and her, matter of fact. I was the one who insisted she let you stay in this room, be a member of the family, stop being a servant. I told her I would tell what happened if she didn't do what I said. She did it, but she doesn't like being told what to do."

He paused to think again.

"However, she's never been this ruthless," he said. "There's something else, something I don't know, some reason she feels the way she does about you and wants me to feel the same way. Neither Sophia nor I know much, if anything, about our family. You know that. I didn't even know about you.

"What is it? What happened years ago in Mexico? Do you know why my mother does not want to remember her family, why she does not like her own family? *Por qué mi madre no le gusta su familia*? *Sabe*?"

"*Sí,*" I said.

"Why?"

"*Mi abuelo,* my grandfather, was angry when she married *su padre.* He said she was *muerta* . . . dead to him."

"Yeah, I kinda knew about that, but there must be more. Why wasn't she closer to your mother, to her own sister, after their father died?"

"She wanted *mi padre* to be her *marido.*"

"Huh? *Marido?*"

"Her husband."

"Oh." He smiled. "I see. He fell in love with her sister instead, and she blames your mother?"

"*Sí.*"

"So she hated her sister and, by proxy, you."

"I do not understand this word *proxy.*"

"She couldn't take revenge on your mother. Your mother was already dead. She's taking her revenge on you. That's good old Mom. Now this makes sense to me."

He laughed. His laugh actually frightened me.

"Why do you laugh?"

"Don't worry about it," he continued, now moving toward the door. "I'll take care of it."

He paused at the door, fumbling for the knob. I started toward him to help him, but he found it and turned back to me. He reached out.

"Delia."

"*Sí,*" I said, and I took his hand. He held it firmly and smiled.

"I am happy I did not make a mistake fighting for you, Delia. Thank you for having the courage to tell me the truth."

He brought my hand to his lips and kissed it, and

then he opened the door and left me standing there, not sure if I should be happy or even more terrified. It would not be much longer before I would learn which one I should be.

In the morning, Sophia went off eagerly to school. Before she left, she caught me in the hallway and told me how exciting it was going to be for her. I thought I was making a mistake with the English.

"Exciting?" I shook my head.

"Yes, *stupido*. Everyone is going to want to know what happened. All of a sudden, everyone is going to want to be my best friend. Alisha and I have already discussed how we are going to behave and what we will say and won't say. Too bad you don't go to my school. You'd be *número uno*."

I didn't know what to say. Why would I be *número uno*? I just looked at her in confusion, and she laughed and went sauntering off. A little while later, I saw Tía Isabela taking Edward to see the doctor and have his bandages removed. She didn't look angry, and she didn't speak to me at all. I went about my work. I could see Señora Rosario and Inez were still upset about me. They were not as friendly and kept their distance all morning. When the mail was brought into the house, I hurried to see if I had received another letter from Abuela Anabela, but there was none. I had hoped for one. Even a short note in her handwriting would have brought me some comfort.

Later in the afternoon, Edward and Tía Isabela returned. I was dusting in the library. Señora Rosario told me to take out every single book, to dust it and dust around it. There were so many books I would be there for hours, I thought, but I did not complain. I heard Señora Rosario greet Tía Isabela and Edward at the front door. They spoke too softly for me to hear any words. My heart was pounding because I was worrying about Edward's eyes. What if they were both too damaged? No matter how much he believed in me or cared about me, he wouldn't be able to help hating me. If I hadn't come . . .

The sound of Tía Isabela's footsteps on the travertine tile stopped my thoughts and brought a trembling to my fingers. I dropped the book I was dusting. When I looked up, she was standing there looking in on me. She turned and closed the library doors. For a moment, she just stood there gazing at me with the oddest smile on her face. It was not one of her cold, sharp smiles that sent shivers down my spine. She looked as if I had done something that pleased her. It reminded me of the rare smile Señora Cuevas would flash on me or any other student who had done something that delighted her. I waited, my own smile of confusion rising into my face.

"How are Edward's eyes?" I asked. There was no time to struggle with English, and she and I had been speaking Spanish to each other off and on now.

"It's what the doctor predicted," she told me. "One eye is about ninety-five percent restored, but the other is too damaged. I'm sure he'll tell you about it in more detail during one of your very private tête-à-têtes."

"Our what?"

"Your secret talks," she said, still holding that smile. She peeled off her hat and undid her hair, shaking her head to let it fall freely. Then she sat on the settee and folded her hands in her lap. "I should have known not to trust you," she said. "I should have expected it, but you are good. You did such a convincing performance when you first arrived."

"I do not understand. What performance?"

"Your little show of innocence, of weakness. I should have picked up on you when you flashed that defiance that first day, but you quickly slipped back behind that mask, far enough behind so that I would trust you, eh?"

I shook my head. "I do not understand, Tía Isabela. What mask?"

"It's okay. I have no one to blame but myself. I should have remembered one of my father's sayings: '*La confianza también mata.*' Trust also kills, right, Delia? I haven't believed in anyone but myself since I left Mexico, and then I go and believe in you, the one person I should have distrusted from the beginning."

"I have done nothing, Tía Isabela."

She laughed. "I would have said the same thing. You're too much like me, Delia." Her face turned hard, her eyes cold. "It's of no use to pretend otherwise." She smiled again. "We are cut from the same cloth, you see."

"I am not like you," I said firmly. I could feel my spine harden. "I have lost my mother and my father, and I am far from my home and the people I have known and loved all my life, but you are far more lonely than I will ever be, because you do not have the comfort of your memories."

Her smile froze and then dissipated. The cold, angry face I had seen that first day returned. "How dare you pity me. You own nothing, not even the clothes on your back. You breathe this air only because I permit it. You'd be groveling in the dust and the grime of that poverty right this moment, if it wasn't for my generosity. You're too stupid to know what side your bread is buttered on."

"What is it you want?" I asked, tired of her rage.

"You go and you betray me, try to drive a wedge between my son and me, and you want to know what I want?"

"I did not try to drive a wedge between you. He came to me and asked for the truth, and I could not lie to him anymore."

"Oh, you couldn't lie anymore? You poor thing, troubled by the weight of your deceptions." Her face hardened again. "When I rewarded you for them, you accepted it all, didn't you? The clothes, the acceptance as a member of the family so you would be waited on just like the rest of us, so you would enjoy all of this," she said, gesturing at the house. "You ate at my table. You were driven to and from school in a Rolls. You took Sophia's gifts. You were starting to accumulate quite a little fortune for an immigrant barely here long enough to grow warts, but warts you've grown, right on the tip of that pretty little nose, warts only I can see, but they are there nevertheless.

"Okay," she said, pulling herself up straighter on the settee, "you've won a little battle and caused a rift between my son and myself, but it will pass, and eventually he will be too consumed by his own needs and wants to devote so much time to you.

"To ensure all that, I've decided to reward you for your little betrayal. I may not have my attorney do any more than absolutely necessary to defend you. You might be held accountable for your part in this horrible event, you and your Mexican boyfriend. We'll see. After all," she said, "those Mexican boys would not have attacked Bradley Whitfield if it were not for you, anyway. He's dead because of you, and Edward is half-blind because of you."

She stood up.

"Keep dusting," she said. "You're used to filth, and you'll be visiting it again, I'm sure."

She turned and walked to the doorway, paused after opening it, and looked back at me.

"You're wrong. I do have the comfort of my memories, the comfort of knowing I have buried them long ago." She smiled. "They have passed on through the third death."

"And how will your children treat the memories of you when you die, Tía Isabela?" I replied quickly. "How long will it take for you to pass through the third death?"

Her eyes widened. She flashed her clenched teeth and then walked out, closing the door behind her, the silence that followed crashing down like a curtain made of iron.

I did finish my dusting in the library. It took me hours, but while I worked, I did not cry. When I was finished, I went upstairs slowly. The door to Edward's room was open wide enough for me to look in as I was passing. I saw him sitting on his bed beside Jesse, who had his arm around his shoulders. They were talking softly, and Edward was looking down, looking as if the weight of the reality of what had happened to him was settling on him. I walked on quickly.

The door to Sophia's room was open even wider. I could hear her laughter. She was talking to one of her girlfriends on the telephone.

"I just love the way they all trailed after us, pleading for a tidbit of information," I heard her say.

I went into my room and closed the door. For a long moment, I just stood there looking at everything. This was a wonderful room, a beautiful room, a room in a palace, a dream room for any of my girlfriends back in Mexico. There were many who would do much more to be here. There were many who would think me a fool to have put any of it at risk.

I walked to the windows and looked out onto the large, lavish property. How many times had I been told that the good and the pure of heart might not be rewarded on this earth, but they shouldn't be sad, for their rewards would be much greater in the life to come? Was it true, or was it just a rationalization, a way to keep the poor and the underprivileged from rebelling, from becoming thieves? Why were the poor and the pure of heart given any life of hardship? How much should they be tested?

Was that what was happening to me? Was I not only Cinderella but Job, whose every earthly blessing was taken away to prove his faith and devotion? How many times had Father Martinez told that story in church? Maybe someday he would tell my story to deliver the same message.

I stood for a while longer and watched the April sun sinking behind the San Bernardino Mountains to the west. Not having been here before, I wasn't sure what the weather should be like, but I had heard people say that it was much hotter much faster this year. It seemed to be true everywhere, so I imagined it was warmer back in Mexico as well. I thought of the children swimming in the river, floating on old inner tubes, and remembered when I did it, too.

Despite the air conditioning, I had worked up a sweat working in the library. I went to shower and change for dinner. I had no idea what it would be like eating at the table with Tía Isabela, Sophia, and Edward now, but I did not know what else I should do. Of course, I wondered if Tía Isabela would send me back into the kitchen to eat with the servants the moment I appeared.

Not only didn't she do that, but she acted as if nothing at all was wrong or changed. Jesse was eating with us this evening, too, and it seemed he had cheered up Edward. I felt I was really in a dream now. No one talked about Edward's eyes. No one mentioned the events that had led to Bradley Whitfield's death, not even Sophia, who babbled on instead about an upcoming school party. She and Tía Isabela talked about clothes.

Was I going mad? Had I imagined everything that had happened? Was I really there? When the dinner ended and I started to rise to help clear the table, Tía Isabela told me to stop.

"You don't need to do that," she said. "Go upstairs and work on your schoolwork. I've decided you can and should return to your class tomorrow."

She didn't smile when she said it, but she didn't sound angry at all. I looked at her and at Edward and Sophia, but I saw nothing but agreement. Jesse looked pleased and told me he expected I would be mainstreamed very soon. They were all congratulating me on my further mastering of English. Even Sophia chimed in with, "It's easier to talk to her now."

I looked at Tía Isabela. Where was that anger, that hate? Why did she suddenly act so forgiving? Despite all of this, I felt like the male black widow spider, tempted by the female to join her in making a new family of spiders and then stung to death. There was a new web of deceit being spun around me. What had she promised Edward, I wondered, that he was so trusting of her sweet tone and generosity toward me?

After dinner, Sophia rushed off, supposedly to do her homework. Edward was occupied with Jesse, who had brought him schoolwork, too. Tía Isabela went to her office. I had started for the stairway to go up to my room when I heard Inez call to me. She had stepped out of the kitchen and was in the hallway. Surprised, I hurried to her. She looked about for a moment and then pulled me back into the kitchen. There was no one else there.

"Casto wants to talk to you," she said, practically in a whisper. "He's waiting outside the door."

"Casto?"

"Sí."

I went through the rear entrance. For a moment, I saw no one, and then Casto stepped out of the shadows.

"Someone has come to see you," he said.

"Who?"

"Ignacio Davila."

"Ignacio! Where is he?" I asked.

"He's behind the pool house, waiting. You must not be seen with him," he warned, and then disappeared into the same darkness from which he had emerged.

I hurried across the lawn toward the pool and the pool house, watching for anyone as I walked. When I got to the pool house, I paused, checked again, and went around to the rear. At first, I didn't see him, and then his silhouette was clear at the corner. He called to me.

"Ignacio, where have you been?"

"A friend of my father's has kept me safe," he said.

"I am sorry you are in so much trouble. It's all my fault."

"No, no. It is not your fault. You were the victim."

"What happened? Why did you hurt him so badly?"

"It wasn't meant to be that way. He put up a big fight,

and Vicente put his head down like a bull and charged at him just when he backed up in front of the window. I thought Vicente would go through the window, too, but he didn't. We didn't wait around after that. The girl was screaming."

"You didn't know how badly he was hurt?"

"We ran off. No one stopped to look. Later, when we heard, we separated. My father was very angry at me. I think he would have turned me into the police if it wasn't for my mother. He got his friend to hide me, and I learned the others were caught. I was afraid for you, but I couldn't come here."

"Why did you come here now? Is it not as dangerous?"

"Yes, but I wanted to say good-bye, Delia. I can't stay here any longer. No one will believe it was not meant to be that terrible. I'll be sent to prison. My father believes this, too."

"Where are you going?"

"Back to Mexico. My father has given me the money I was saving for a car, and I'm using it to pay a coyote to take me across."

"Back to Mexico?"

"*Sí*, Delia. I have come to tell you I am not unhappy I met you and . . ."

"I must go with you," I said quickly.

"What?"

"Back to Mexico. If you can cross over, you must take me back, too."

"No, no, it is not a crossing for you to make. I must be smuggled through Tucson. From there, I will cross through the desert with my coyote to Sasabe, Mexico.

It's miles and miles of walking, and with this unexpected heat . . ."

"I will go," I said.

"It's too dangerous."

"You are going. You are taking this chance."

"Yes, but I have no choice. Even my family wants me to go back."

"I have no choice, either," I said.

"How can you have no choice? You are Señora Dallas's niece. Look where you live."

"She is not fighting for me, defending me. She will let the police believe I sent you to do this thing. She wants to see me in trouble."

"Why?"

"It's a long story, Ignacio. I do not wish to stay here any longer, and they won't let me just return to my grandmother. Not now, not with all of this going on."

"I don't have the money to pay for you, Delia."

"What if you did?"

"Delia, it is very dangerous. It's not only the hardship of crossing the desert, so many miles, there are other dangers to face."

"I want to go home, Ignacio."

"I did not mean to come here to get you to go," he said, shaking his head.

"No, but you have come, and we must believe a higher power made you come."

"Where will you get this money?"

"Remember that bracelet?" I asked.

"*Sí*. Where is it?" he asked, looking at my naked wrist.

"Don't worry. I will bring it. Surely, it's enough."

"Yes, it might be enough," he said. "I can't promise you. My father's friend is making this arrangement. He might not do it if you are with me."

"Tell him he'd better, or else," I said. There was enough light for me to see him smile.

"Since when did you become so tough, Delia Yebarra?"

"Since I came to America, to a harder life," I said, and he laughed.

"Harder life? What harder life? This is the promised land."

"The promise was not made to me," I said, and he smiled again.

"Okay. Here is what you must do, and I warn you, if you are late, I won't be able to wait for you."

"I won't be late," I said.

He told me how far I should take the bus.

"When you get off, you will walk to Sixth Street. You will go to the first corner and turn right. When you get to the third house on the left, you will see a broken chain-link fence. Go through the opening in the fence, and go to the house behind that house. I will be there. We will not wait for nightfall. We are going in a van to Tucson and then in a car with the coyote. The driver of the van has been paid. He will want more when he knows you've come, but I have that much more. It's the coyote in Tucson who will take us through the Buenos Aires wildlife reserve. He will have to agree to take your bracelet. I'm sure he will."

"Okay. *Gracias,* Ignacio."

"But how will you get to the bus? Your aunt has you driven back and forth to school, right?"

"I'll find a way. You wait for me. I'll be there," I said.

"If you don't come, I'll understand. I would like you to come. I would like you to be with me, Delia, but the good part of me wishes you would not," he said.

He leaned forward to kiss me, and then he slipped back into the shadows. Like a shadow, he disappeared in the thicker darkness.

Maybe I'm still in a dream, I thought, but if I am, I do not want to wake up until I am standing in my family's front door and looking at my wonderful Grandmother Anabela.

21

Dangerous Journey

I did not come to be a thief in the night, I told myself as I walked over the grounds and back to the main house, planning to steal back the bracelet Sophia had given me and taken away. I did not come to cause my cousin to become blind in one eye or another young man to die. The trouble I had found was begun years ago in Mexico, when my aunt sought revenge and defied her father. My father had dared to choose my mother over her, and she would hate every part of her past, hate as far back as she could go, rejecting her heritage, her language, and her people. I was running away not only to return to the only family I had left, but I was running away from her words, her terrible words comparing me to her. If I remained here, I was afraid I would become as spoiled as Sophia and maybe more like my aunt than I had ever dreamed I could be.

Everyone was busy with his or her own things when

I returned. I went up to my room to see if there was anything I should take along with me tomorrow. When I looked at my old clothes, I decided tomorrow I would wear the dress I was wearing when I had first arrived. I chose the best shoes for walking on the desert floor, and then I listened carefully at my doorway, waiting to hear Sophia leave her room. She often went downstairs to get a soda or some cookies before she went to sleep. This night, however, she wasn't coming out.

Without the bracelet, I would not be able to get back to Mexico, I thought. What would I do? It was getting later and later. She could go to sleep, and I might not be able to get to the bracelet in the morning. An idea came to me, and I looked at myself in the vanity mirror. Was I capable of being the person Tía Isabela accused me of being? Did I have enough of her in me after all? Could I do unto them as they had done unto me?

I sucked in my breath and tightened myself like a gladiator going to battle. You can do this, Delia Yebarra, I told myself. You can do this. Then I stared at myself until I was able to bring tears to my eyes, turned, and walked out of my room. I crossed the hallway and knocked softly on Sophia's door.

"What?" she shouted.

I opened the door slowly, my head down, and entered.

"What do you want?" she snapped.

I lifted my head, wiped a tear from my cheek, and made my lips tremble.

"What is it now?" she asked, annoyed. She was on her bed, her phone receiver in her hand. "I was about to call someone, so make it quick," she ordered. "Well?"

"I am sorry, Sophia," I said.

"Sorry? About what?" she asked suspiciously.

"About not being your friend when you were being a friend to me. I am sorry I did not tell the story as you wanted it to be told," I said.

She stared at me. I lowered my head, and she hung up the receiver.

"I'm glad you realize it. I told you it would be better for all of us," she said.

I nodded. "Yes, I see. I am in so much trouble."

"Oh, you're not in so much trouble," she said, waving her hand. "You heard Web, our lawyer."

"No, I will go to school tomorrow, and my classmates will know everything, and they will think I am no longer wanted in this house. More rumors will spread, and everything will get very, very bad."

"That's nuts," she said. She sat up.

"I will do anything to be your friend again," I said. "Please."

"I should be angry at you forever," she replied. She looked at me and thought a moment. Then she nodded and smiled. "Maybe it would be better if we took you with us this weekend. I'd like you to tell some people what Bradley did to you."

"Yes," I said. "We should tell."

"I'm glad you finally realize that, too. All right. I'll let you hang out with us again."

"Thank you, Sophia."

"Just remember not to say anything stupid."

"Yes, *sí*."

"I'm going to call someone now," she said. "You can go back to your room."

"Would you . . . maybe . . . so my classmates don't

think you don't like me . . . let me wear the bracelet tomorrow?"

She stared. I lowered my eyes, but I could see her smile.

"You are getting smarter," she said. "Okay, but now you're just borrowing it until I feel you deserve it."

"Thank you, Sophia."

She got up, went to her jewelry box on the vanity table, and plucked it out. The way she looked at it, I thought she would change her mind, but she extended her hand, and I hurried to take it. She didn't let go. She held on to it.

"You'd better behave," she said.

"*Sí*. We will be friends."

"Maybe," she said, and let go.

"*Gracias,* Sophia."

"Don't speak Spanish whenever you can say the English words. That's an order," she told me.

"Yes, thank you."

I flashed a smile and turned away.

"Be careful about what you tell anyone from now on," she warned when I reached the door.

"Yes, I will be careful."

She smirked at me, and I left her room, closing the door softly behind me.

Then I let out the trapped breath I was holding.

I can be Tía Isabela, I thought. I should have been happy about it, because I had the bracelet, but I couldn't help being disappointed in myself as well. I could play with the devil, too. I comforted myself by repeating something I had read and heard my father say. *Engañar al engañador no es una deshonra.* To deceive the deceiver is not a dishonor. Liars deserve to be lied to, I thought, and returned to my room, far too excited even to imagine falling asleep.

Sophia was back to having breakfast in her room the following morning. Inez hurried to deliver it. Edward joined me at the table. He was nervous about returning to school, too nervous to notice my nervousness. He was going to wear a patch over his bad eye for a while, and he still had the evidence of abrasions on his face, especially his chin, so he anticipated having to tell his story repeatedly. I wished him luck, and he smiled and told me not to worry.

"After this bad time passes, I'll make sure you're happier here, Delia," he said.

He does not know his own mother, I thought. She would not let this bad time pass so easily. Her threats still hovered over my head. Nevertheless, I thanked him. Jesse came for him, and they left before I did. I met Señor Garman at the Rolls and told him I had to remain in school an extra hour to make up for time missed. I could see he wasn't happy about it, but he said nothing.

When I arrived, I saw the school was still electric with chatter about Ignacio and his friends. I could feel all eyes following me through the corridor, and as soon as I entered the classroom, my fellow students, especially Mata, whose father had been playing at the fiesta, looked surprised to see me return. Señorita Holt did her best to keep us concentrating on the work. She said nothing, nor did she ask me anything about the events. To keep anyone from suspecting anything, I worked very hard.

During the lunch hour, many students left the school building to buy a sandwich or a hamburger at one of the nearby fast-food restaurants. It was more fun than eating in a school cafeteria, and when they were away from the building, they could smoke. This would give me an excuse to leave the school as well. I tried to be as unnoticeable as possible leaving the building. Some students saw me, however, and threw questions at me, even sarcastic remarks. I pretended not to understand, and they grew bored and went their own way. When I felt I was no longer the center of anyone's attention, I walked quickly in the opposite direction and waited for the next bus at the bus stop down the street.

I was close enough to the school to hear the bells ringing to alert the students that lunch hour was nearly over. The bus was taking forever, and I was afraid that Señorita Holt would immediately report that I was missing. Before the final bell rang, however, the bus appeared. Because of the hour, there were few passengers riding, but I went all the way to the rear of the bus and practically disappeared behind the next-to-last seat, hovering closely to the window and watching all the stops carefully. It took more than an hour to get to the stop Ignacio had described. I practically leaped across seats to get off.

It was another day of unusual heat. Temperatures were hovering a good ten to fifteen degrees above what was normal for this time of year. The walk I had to make seemed very long to me because of that. I tried moving as quickly as I could, terrified that Ignacio would leave before I had arrived. I wasn't sure if he had realized how long the bus ride would take and how long the walking would be.

Suddenly, I was troubled by the possibility that he had given me the wrong directions and the wrong time deliberately, just so I would be unable to go with him. When I didn't see the fence he had described, I began to panic. I broke into a run and then finally saw it ahead. Relieved that at least this much was true, I slowed and walked the remaining way to the opening he had described. I saw the small house behind the one on the street, too. I looked about to be sure no one was watching me, and then I slipped through the fence opening and walked quickly toward the house. Just before I reached it, Ignacio stepped out from the rear.

He did not look happy to see me.

"I was hoping you would not come," he said. "I have never made such a journey, but I have heard many terrible stories, Delia. I have been told that this man, this coyote, will leave us if we do not keep up or either you or I get hurt. There are drug smugglers and bandits, and with this heat"—he looked up as if the high temperature was falling around us like rain drops—"it means we will have to travel nights, maybe as much as three days, depending on what we have to avoid and what route the coyote takes."

"I am not afraid, Ignacio."

"Then there are snakes and scorpions."

"I am not afraid," I said more firmly.

He nodded.

I extended my arm. "Here is the bracelet."

He shook his head. "This is all happening because I have done a terrible thing, me and my temper," he muttered. "Come inside. I am not even confident that the driver that my father's friend is sending will show up. He might have gotten frightened. If he is caught transporting me, he could go to jail."

We entered the small house through the kitchen. He

had prepared two knapsacks for us. They were both filled with jugs of water.

"This is *sweto*," he said, "water mixed with electrolytes to help us fight off dehydration." He had some energy bars as well.

I nodded and smiled, but he did not smile. "Don't think of this as an adventure or a walk in the park, Delia. Many, many people die crossing this way. Some are not found until they are nothing but bones. They don't have identification, so their families never know they have died and wait forever to hear from them. Real coyotes eat them."

"Stop trying to scare me, Ignacio."

"I'm not trying to scare you. I am telling you this so you will not be surprised at anything and you understand the risks, Delia."

"I want to go home, to Mexico," I insisted.

He looked at my determined face and nodded. "When my father finds out I have taken you with me, he will be so angry the sun won't need to come out. He'll burn bright enough to light the day," he said.

"And when I'm back home, my grandmother and I will write to him, and he will cool down so much it will snow here."

Ignacio finally laughed.

Then I heard the sound of a baby's cry. Surprised, I looked through the doorway into the living room and saw a woman holding an infant. She gazed at me and looked very upset.

"That's my father's friend's wife, Silvia. She was not in favor of her husband hiding me, and now with you here, she is very annoyed. Don't try to talk to her," he warned. "Come with me."

He led me through another door to a small room, where there was a cot on which he had obviously been sleeping.

"We'll wait here," he said, looking out the window. He checked his watch. "He should be here within the hour if he comes."

"What if he doesn't come?"

"Then you'll go back, and I'll take my chances walking and hitching."

Finally, I knew I looked frightened.

He smiled at me.

"What?"

"When I first saw you, met you, and you told me who you were and where you were living, I thought you were just one of those spoiled rich girls, or if you weren't, you would be one soon, and you would not look my way. And now here you are, willing to risk your life with me to get back to what?"

"Happiness," I said.

He laughed. "Happiness? Expect to see dozens and dozens of people heading in the opposite direction and looking at the two of us as if we were crazy. They might think we are mules."

"Mules?"

"People who carry drugs for drug pushers returning to Mexico to get a new delivery."

"How do you know so much about this sort of thing, Ignacio?"

"When you work with some of our people on the landscaping, you hear stories." He grew almost angry. "That is why you should think twice, Delia. No matter how bad things are here, they can't be as bad as they will be if you return to Mexico."

"Believe me, they are," I said.

He stared a moment and then looked out the window. "He's here," he said. "Come on, then."

We returned to the kitchen to pick up the knapsacks and walked out to meet the driver his father's friend had sent. His name was Escobar. Before he could complain about me, Ignacio handed him three hundred-dollar bills.

"For her ticket on the van," he said.

"These are not the arrangements that have been made with the guide," Escobar told him.

"We'll take care of that when we get there."

"Suit yourself. Get in the van quickly," Escobar said, opening the rear doors.

Ignacio got in first and extended his hand for me but held it back just a little.

"This could be your last chance, Delia."

"I know. That's why I'm going," I said, and he seized my hand firmly.

I got into the van, and Escobar closed the door. We sat on the floor. It was already very hot, with the van's engine off and no air conditioning.

"This is nothing," Ignacio said, seeing me wipe my brow, "compared to what's coming."

"You might as well save your strength for the journey, Ignacio. I will not change my mind."

He nodded, and then we heard Escobar open the door and get into the van. He looked back at us.

"It's a very long trip," he warned. "Is it wise to take her?"

"Yes," I said, answering for Ignacio.

Escobar shrugged, started the engine, and slowly drove out of the yard. The van bounced hard onto the road, and he sped up. When we reached the freeway, Escobar turned on his radio, and at least we had music. Ignacio stared at me. His face finally seemed to relax, his eyes warming.

"What is it?" I asked.

"For me, it's like I've been joined by an angel," he said.

I did not feel like an angel. I felt like a fugitive, but for his sake and perhaps my own, I smiled and lowered my head to his strong shoulder. I was tired from not sleeping much the night before, but I didn't want him to know how tired. Nevertheless, my eyes closed. I pictured Abuela Anabela, at first surprised and angry and then filled with happiness. Once again, we would sleep in the same room and say our prayers together. The simple life that had seemed so poor and difficult now looked like the promised land Ignacio thought we were leaving. The music, the drone of the tires on the highway, the bounce in the van as it rolled on composed themselves into a lullaby. In minutes, I was fast asleep.

Ignacio did not want us to eat or drink anything from our knapsacks. Escobar, tired of driving himself, pulled into a roadside fast-food restaurant after three hours. I had slept nearly all the way, and Ignacio had fallen asleep as well.

"We can stop here to get something and go to the bathroom," Escobar told us.

I went directly to the bathroom and washed my face and neck in cold water. Then I came out and ordered a chicken sandwich with fries. We drank lemonades and ate at a corner table. No one paid any particular attention to us. Escobar checked his watch and told us we were on time, but we would have to go all the way without stopping now. We left, and he filled the gas tank before we drove back to the freeway.

It was dark by the time we reached Tucson. We could see the city lights. It was the biggest city I had been in at night, and the illumination both fascinated and frightened me. Escobar made some turns and finally came to a stop on a dark street in front of what looked like an auto body shop. Ignacio started to get up.

"Wait," Escobar said. "Let me see first." He got out and walked to the shop door. It was barely lit inside. He looked through the window, then turned and looked around. Whoever we were to meet was obviously not in there.

"What's happening?" I asked.

"I don't know," Ignacio said.

We saw what looked like a flash of car headlights, and then Escobar walked down the street to a dark automobile. He stood by it and spoke with the driver. After a few more moments, he returned to the van.

"He says his name is Pancho. He is not happy about your bringing the girl. He wants double. I don't like him," Escobar added.

"He's all we have," Ignacio said.

"Don't trust him," Escobar warned. "What will you do about the money?"

"Give me the bracelet," Ignacio told me, and I undid it and handed it to him. "Let me speak with him."

He got out of the van, and they went to the car. I could not see the man called Pancho, but Ignacio was talking and showing him Sophia's bracelet. There was more discussion, and then Escobar returned, opened the door, and told me to come out.

I got out and joined Ignacio.

"Get in," Pancho told us.

"You can go back with Escobar," Ignacio said. "This is really your last chance."

"Let's get in. We're wasting time," I said as an answer.

He nodded, opened the door for me, and got in after me.

Escobar got back into the van, started it up, and drove off.

"This is not a walk in the park," Pancho said. I had barely seen his face, but he looked thin, with a sharp nose and a mouth that looked like a slice cut in his face. His black hair was straggly, down over his ears and down the back of his neck.

"A walk in a park does not cost as much," Ignacio replied.

Pancho grunted, started his engine, and drove away. We wound through city streets to a highway with the number 86, and then he sped up. He did not play the radio, nor did he speak until he turned off the highway into what looked like bushes. They parted, and we were on a hard dirt pathway just wide enough for the car. My heart was pounding. How did we know he wasn't simply going to rob us and leave us out there? I could see the worry in Ignacio's face as well. After all, despite his bravado, this was his first illegal crossing, too.

Pancho drove as far as he could with his lights off and then bragged about it.

"I have saved you a day's walking. No other coyote knows the way I know. When you are back in Mexico and others want to come to the United States, you tell them about me," he said.

"We will," Ignacio said.

"I will park here," Pancho said. "We will begin our

walk now and we will walk all night until we reach a cave, where we will sleep most of the day before continuing. We must keep up the pace, but when I tell you to stop, you stop, and you must do very little talking. The border patrol will be out there, and there are bandits just waiting for fools. You were told how much water to bring. You have enough for both of you? Because I don't have any extra."

"Yes."

"Don't gulp it away the first hour. I have turned back fools that quickly," he said.

"You won't turn us back," Ignacio told him.

"We'll see," he said. "Let's go."

He got out, and we got out. He stood for a moment listening, and then he started to walk straight into the darkness, not looking back to see if we were following. Ignacio took my hand, and we caught up with him. It amazed me that Pancho knew exactly where to put his feet in the darkness, but he did.

We walked for hours without talking. My feet began to ache. I stumbled many times, but I did not complain. I was positive I heard a rattlesnake very close on our right, but either Ignacio and Pancho didn't hear it, or they didn't want to admit to hearing it. Nevertheless, Pancho warned us not to wander too far to the right or the left, and I wasn't about to disagree.

Once he paused and held up his hand, and we waited and listened. I could hear voices off to our left. They were speaking in Spanish. Pancho whispered that this close to the end of the trail, *pollos*—chickens, as the aliens were called—would be stupid to be talking. He said that meant they were police. We stood absolutely still until the voices drifted off, and then we walked on.

The ache in my feet and my legs grew worse, and even though it was cooler, being night, I was growing very thirsty. I was afraid to ask for a drink. I had no idea how long we had been walking. Except for the occasional sound of an owl or the howl of a coyote off in the distance, it was deathly quiet. Above us, the stars were bright and dazzling, with no artificial light to drown out their wonderful glory and promise. The heavens knew no boundaries. There were no borders to cross. The world should be the same way, I thought.

Pancho paused to look at his watch. I was surprised when he said we had been walking for four and a half hours and, by his estimate, at least twelve miles. Neither Ignacio nor I knew enough about it to agree or disagree.

"There is still a good four to five hours of night," Pancho said. "If we keep up our pace, we'll reach my cave before daybreak. Take your first drink of water," he ordered, and we did. He told us to go to the bathroom now if we had to, because we would stop only to avoid bandits or patrols, although he thought we were far enough from the border of the United States now. I was very frightened about going into the bushes. I could think only about upsetting a sleeping rattlesnake, but there was little choice. I knew if I didn't go, I'd suffer for hours.

As soon as we were all done, we marched on. Most of the time, I was able to hold on to Ignacio's hand, but there were narrow passages between rocks and down steep inclines that made it easier and safer for us to go separately, usually with me right behind him, keeping my hand on his waist for balance. Pancho spoke very little and only when it was necessary to give us warnings and directions. I couldn't help but wonder about such a man who made his living sneaking people through the night. In the van, when I had asked Ignacio about it, he told me smuggling illegal aliens had become a very big business. He said his father told him it was all controlled by syndicates and that the coyotes actually worked for someone bigger and more powerful. That was why he was confident that Pancho would take my bracelet. He wouldn't have to report it.

It did frighten me to hear about this. I knew something about the people who suffocated in vans and trucks, who died of dehydration trying to cross the desert. There were always stories about this relative or that, but here I was diving into a sea of sharks myself. How angry Abuela Anabela would be, I thought, but the promise of what would come afterward was too strong to let anything dissuade me. I would go on. I would go home.

Because we were young and strong, perhaps, we arrived at Pancho's cave faster than he said he had anticipated. He complimented us on keeping up with him. The cave itself was not large, but it was an opening in a hill of rocks well hidden by bushes. He said that because it faced north, it would be cool even during the unusually hot spring day. He went in first to be sure no rattlesnakes had decided the same thing.

"It's okay," he said, coming out.

We crawled into the flattest places and fixed the ground the best we could with some brush to make ourselves comfortable. We drank some more water, and Ignacio and I ate one of our energy bars. Then we cuddled. Pancho curled up across from us.

"Usually, you would see and hear many *pollos* tonight," he said. "It's a good time to cross in from Mexico, but as I told you, my route, my way, is my secret, and most don't know how to zigzag about as I do. You are lucky. You are getting across cheaply."

"I don't feel lucky," I muttered.

He heard me. "I don't ask people why they want to go here or there. Usually, I don't want to know too much, but why are you returning? You are not into the drugs, or you wouldn't need me."

"We are both unhappy away from home," Ignacio told him.

He laughed. "I don't care. I was only passing the time. I have learned many things from the desert, one of the most important being that survival makes liars of us all. Remember this, *mis pollos,* the desert doesn't care if you are good or bad. It will eat you up no matter what."

He closed his eyes and squirmed a bit to get comfortable. I was so tired I was sure I would fall asleep quickly, even on the hard ground.

"How are you?" Ignacio whispered, his lips close to my ear.

"I'm okay."

"You are much braver than any girl I have known."

"My grandmother used to say, '*Solamente los valientes tienen miedo.*' Only the brave have fear. She told me that often when I had nightmares and cried. Fear makes you cautious, and caution keeps you alive, she said. Don't be afraid to be afraid."

"No wonder you want so much to return. She is a wise woman. She taught you well."

"And I have more to learn from her," I said.

"Yes." I saw him smile in the budding light of dawn. We kissed, and he held me tighter for a moment. "I was without hope until you forced yourself on me, Delia Yebarra."

"Forced myself?"

"Well, maybe I was a little bit easier to convince than I pretended."

I almost laughed aloud but remembered Pancho's warnings about keeping as quiet as possible. So, instead, I smiled and kissed him again. I am not afraid anymore, I thought. Soon after, safe in each other's arms, we fell asleep.

It was the sound of laughter that woke me. I looked up at the grinning faces of two bearded men, both with teeth missing, one holding a machete, crouching to stand in the cave entrance.

Their bodies blocked most of the sunlight, which made them seem even bigger than they were.

I nudged Ignacio to wake him. Maybe he would not see what I was seeing.

Maybe I was only having a nightmare.

22

Nightmare

Unfortunately, it was real. The man on the left was stocky, with long arms that dangled like the arms of an ape. His companion was taller and as thin as Pancho. They were both so dirty-looking I thought they had been formed from mud. When I looked closer at them, I saw that the man on the right had a piece of his left ear missing. His right eye looked swollen and bruised.

"Stand up slowly," Ignacio whispered.

I didn't think my legs would obey, but I rose with him. Pancho remained in a sitting position. The stocky man nodded at us and then looked at Pancho.

"So, *mi coyote,* how much did you take from them to bring them to the United States?"

"They are not going to the United States. They want to go home," Pancho said. "So it was not as much."

"And where is this not as much?"

"You know it's not here, *amigo.*"

"Something is here," the stocky man replied, widening his smile and turning toward us. "What do you bring home, *muchacho*?" he asked Ignacio.

"Nothing for you," Ignacio said.

The stocky man's smile flew off his face like a frightened bird.

"That's not friendly. I let you use my home," he said, indicating the cave, and his friend laughed. "Now you must pay me my rent." He lifted his machete a little and pointed it at us. "I know you have dollars."

"Give them what you have," Pancho told Ignacio.

"See, *su coyote* is smart and friendly," the stocky man said.

Pancho stood up, and they turned sharply toward him. He raised his arms. Then he opened his knapsack to show that it contained only water and some food.

"You're welcome to any of this."

The stocky man spit. "What else do you have?"

Pancho pulled out his pockets to show they were empty.

"Keep going, *mi coyote*," the stocky man said, waving the machete at him. "Show us you have nothing."

Pancho took off his shirt and dropped his pants. I was shocked to see him lower his underwear, too, but they wanted him naked to be sure he was not hiding anything. The disappointed bandit turned to us, and Pancho put his clothes on quickly. He picked up his sack of water and food and edged toward the entrance. The stocky man turned with him.

"You don't want my poor life," Pancho said. He looked at us. "I'll be outside waiting to take you on your way after you pay the rent," he said.

The two bandits smiled and permitted Pancho to slip past them and out.

"*Sí*, listen to your coyote," the stocky man said.

"The bastard," Ignacio whispered. He turned himself so the two wouldn't see or hear him speak to me. "You can't run with the water, Delia. It will slow you down. When I say, you rush out as fast and as hard as you can, and just keep running." I started to shake my head, and he said, "They won't just take our money. They will rape you."

A chill shot through my heart and nearly took my breath away.

"Throw your sacks this way," the stocky man ordered.

Ignacio nodded at me. He reached down and then tossed the sacks so they fell to the stocky man's left. His companion crossed and knelt down to go through them. Ignacio took my hand behind his back and moved slowly toward the stocky man.

"We have very little," he began. "We will give it to you," he added. "Please don't hurt us," he said, sounding weaker now.

The stocky man smiled and relaxed, and just at that moment, Ignacio charged at him, head down like a bull, and shouted, "Run, Delia, run!"

With his shoulder, he hit the stocky man just below his chest and sent him flying into the jagged walls of the cave. When his companion turned, Ignacio kicked him sharply under his chin, and he fell back. I ran through the opening and then off to my right and down the slope, barely keeping myself from toppling. As soon as I reached the bottom, I stopped and looked back at the cave hopefully, expecting to see Ignacio running out after me. Instead, the stocky man emerged, and I slipped quickly behind a large rock and fell to my stomach. I peered around it and looked again. His companion joined him. They spoke for a few moments, looked around, and then went back into the cave.

"Delia," I heard, and turned to see Pancho, also on his stomach. He was behind a thick bush. "Crawl this way. Quickly."

I looked back at the cave. Where was Ignacio?

"Delia, crawl now, before they come out again."

I did as he said.

He looked back at the cave and seized my hand.

"Quickly," he repeated, and started to run, pulling me along.

"Ignacio!" I cried.

"You can't go back to see. It won't be pleasant, anyway. Run. They won't chase us if we get far enough away."

I tried to stop, but he tugged harder.

"Why did you leave us?" I screamed.

"We would all be dead," he told me. He paused and looked back. "I am sorry for your friend, but he got you out. I have enough to get us through. I will redeem my cowardice by saving your life."

"No," I said. "We must go back for Ignacio."

"And throw away the chance he gave you? That would be a worse sin. It's too late for him. Do you want to die out here? It's a terrible death. You'll get delirious. You'll eat sand. The buzzards and the coyotes will pull your body apart, and no one will ever know you died."

"Oh, *Dios mío*," I cried, and started to sob.

"Don't waste the water and salt in your body, Delia. The desert has no mercy. Come. We'll find a safe, shady place to wait for nightfall. I think we can get to Sasabe after one night and part of the morning. Come," he said, tugging me along.

I looked back as I went.

Ignacio, I thought. I was your hope, your angel, and I'm leaving you behind. I am the coward.

We walked so long in the rising heat that I felt my body softening, my throat parching until it felt as if it was made of sandpaper. It wasn't until Pancho found a place under a jutting rock that he offered me some of his water.

"Drink slowly," he said, and then he handed me some dried sardines to eat.

"What did they do to Ignacio?" I asked.

"There's no way of telling, and it is of no value to think about it. Just think about getting across the border and home."

"Are you going to come back this way?"

"Of course. I will be taking a group of *pollos* into America."

"Will you stop to see about Ignacio? If you do, I'll tell you where to send me word. Please," I begged.

"I might not be going the same way."

"But you said this way was your private way. You said it was the best and fastest way. You said . . ."

"Sleep now, and stop talking. It wastes too much strength," he said, curled up in as much of the shadow as he could, and closed his eyes.

I sat staring out at the hot desert. It looked blurry in the noon sunlight, but I prayed that I would soon see Ignacio hurrying to catch up to us.

"If you don't sleep," I heard Pancho say, "you will not have the strength to walk all night, Delia. I cannot wait. I will have to leave you for the real coyotes." His tone was very matter-of-fact. "Live or die," he added. "It's your choice to make. There is no mercy here."

I tried to ignore what he said, but I was tired. We were supposed to be sleeping during the morning and the hot daylight hours. Our flight from the bandits cut that time short. I knew he was right. I would not have the strength to walk ten hours on this rough terrain.

Forgive me, Ignacio, I thought, as I looked in the direction from where we had come. Maybe you will see us here, I rationalized, and lowered myself to the dirt floor. At least it was cool.

Despite myself, in moments, I was asleep. I slept right into twilight and woke when I heard Pancho say, "Don't move. Don't move a muscle."

I stared at him. He hovered over me, and then, with a quick sweep of his hand, he swept a scorpion off my upper arm and crushed it with his foot.

"I have had *pollos* get bitten, get too sick to walk, and have to be left behind."

"Did they die?"

"Only the desert knows, and she does not tell," he said. "Have some water."

He offered me the jug. It was very warm, almost nauseating, but I knew I had to have it. He gave me some beef jerky and a piece of bread. We ate, drank some more water, and prepared to leave.

"Maybe Ignacio will catch up with us," I muttered. "Or maybe he's just ahead of us."

Pancho started away.

"Stop thinking about Ignacio, and keep up with me," he ordered. "We have to make the distance to our next rest stop before the sun begins to rise."

We walked over rocky ground, through long patches of sand, down and up small gullies. Everything in my body ached, especially around the back of my neck.

I kept praying he would stop to rest, but whenever he looked as if he was slowing down, he sped up. At one point, I was some distance behind him. I thought he would look back, see, and wait, but he never looked back. I knew if I tripped and fell or stopped to rest, he would just go on. He wasn't just a guide through the desert; he *was* the desert, just as unmerciful, as hard and unforgiving. He must have been hatched out there, I thought. What had happened to that redemption he had sworn back at the cave? Was his conscience that short-lived?

It turned out to be my anger that kept me going more than anything. I would not permit him to leave me. I planned to get to someone when we reached Mexico, someone I could tell about Ignacio, someone who might go back to find him.

When Pancho finally stopped to rest, my feet were singing with the pain. I knew I had blisters in places I had never had a scratch or a blemish.

"Drink," he told me, handing me another jug. I seized it as if it were gold and drank. "Slowly, slowly."

He gave me some sardines and another piece of bread. I was still standing. I was afraid that if I sat or sprawled out on the ground, I would not be able to rise again.

"You've done much better than I thought you would," he told me. "We will make it to Sasabe tomorrow night. Tell me where your village is."

I did.

"You will need to take a bus to Mexico City and from there another bus or maybe two. Do you have any money?"

Ignacio had told me to put my dollars in my bra, but I was suddenly afraid to tell Pancho. What if he was asking so he could take it from me?

"I am not a bandit," he said, when I hesitated. "I do not rob from my *pollos*. I make a very good living without being a thief. Do you know how many *pollos* I have brought across just this year alone?"

I was too tired to ask.

"Fifteen hundred," he said. "Not all of them made it, but I was paid for each. My share. Never mind," he said, when he saw that I wasn't going to talk about my money. "We must go on."

He started away. I closed my eyes, prayed, and started after him. About an hour later, he held up his hand for me to pause and be quiet. I could hear voices off to our left. I drew closer to him and waited.

"It's all right," he said after hearing more. "It's a group heading across to the United States."

"Maybe we can tell them about Ignacio. Please," I begged.

"They can't go out of their way. Listen. Don't you hear the *bebés pequeños*? There are families crossing. If they make mistakes because you ask them to look, little children will die. Do you want that?"

"No, but . . ."

"Walk," he said, and started ahead.

I listened to the voices. They seemed closer. For a moment, I debated running to them, but then I would lose Pancho for sure, and if I didn't find them, I would be alone with nothing. I didn't have the strength to walk all the way back to America, either, even if I did find them, and he had made it sound as if we were not that far from our destination. I hated myself for it, but I rushed after him and not after those who might have looked for Ignacio.

Hours later, Pancho said we were at the rest stop. It was another opening in a hill.

"What if more bandits come?"

"You want to sleep out here in the sun?"

He didn't wait for my answer. We entered the smaller cave and settled down for another long day's rest.

"This is the last of the water and food," he said. "We must make it to Sasabe as soon as we can today after the sun goes down."

He gave the water to me and more beef jerky. Then he broke the remaining bread in half, and I saw a roll of bills. Slowly, he unraveled them.

"A little pocket money," he said, smiling. "If those two vermin were hungry back there, I'd have none."

He thought a moment and then handed me some of his money.

"I don't know if you have any money for the buses or not, but here."

"Thank you," I said, taking it.

"Why would a young girl like you, pretty, too, want to risk her life to go back to Mexico? You can tell me now. It will pass the time."

I told him why I had been brought to America and what had happened to me and how Ignacio and his friends had sought to punish Bradley and what had happened. He listened and nodded.

"Ignacio was right to run off, but for you, I don't think it would have been that serious."

"I wanted to go home," I said.

He thought and, for the first time, showed some emotion.

"I have not been home for many years. I do not even know if my brothers and sisters live."

"Why don't you go visit?"

"It's better to remember them than to learn bad things

about them now," he said. "No more talking," he snapped, as if I had peeled off a scab. "Let's go to sleep."

He sprawled out, using his knapsack as a pillow. I wondered what sort of a man made his living guiding desperate people across the desert to work as illegal aliens, knowing that some of them would die trying. Was he doing a good thing or a bad thing? As he had said, he made a very good living doing it, but was he driven by any higher reasons? Did he see himself as someone leading people to a better life, to a better dream, to hope, or did he not care? Was he afraid to know his *pollos,* afraid to feel sorry if one fell too far behind or got injured? How many had died walking behind him? How many would in the future? When would this migration of illegal birds end?

My body was too tired to ache anymore. Even the pain was exhausted. This time, I slept so deeply and so hard it took him a while to wake me, shaking me so hard he nearly broke my shoulder.

"It's time to go," he said. "This is the shortest portion, but it's the hardest, because we cannot stop, and we have no more water. You understand, Delia? Draw upon all the strength in your well."

I nodded, scrubbed my cheeks with my dry palms, and stood up. For a moment, I wobbled. He looked at me, concerned.

"I'll be all right," I said. "Walk."

"Good."

He started, and I followed. Where I found the strength, I do not know. It was as if my legs had developed minds of their own and my upper body was long gone and was simply being carried. Two hours into our walk, we again heard voices. This time, they were very close.

"Wait here," he said, holding up his hand. I stood, but my legs felt as if they were still moving. He disappeared through a bush toward the voices. I waited and waited, nearly falling asleep on my feet. I was too tired even to worry about being deserted.

And then he returned, carrying a jug of water.

"The fools sold it to me," he said. "I offered them too much for them to refuse. They'll be sorry when they run out. Here, drink," he told me.

For a light moment, my conscience complained. I was drinking what might be needed to keep someone else alive, maybe even a child, but the rest of me screamed so loudly against any remorse that I grabbed the jug and began to gulp.

"Slowly, Delia," he warned.

It felt like life itself rolling down my throat and into my body. I took a deep breath and nodded, thanking him and handing back the jug. He drank.

"We're definitely going to make it now," he said. "Let's go."

We walked on. I had long since lost track of time, of when an hour or so had passed, but suddenly, he cried out and pointed, and I looked and saw the lights.

"Sasabe, Mexico," he said. "We're almost there. You're almost home."

I was so happy I couldn't speak. It wasn't until we drew very close that I even thought about Ignacio again. I felt guilty having forgotten about him. Neither I nor Pancho had mentioned him during the night. To Pancho, he was just another *pollo,* I thought, easily forgotten. I wasn't about to forgive him, but it did occur to me that if he didn't forget the ones he lost, he would be haunted and unable to do what he did.

He took us through an opening in the barbed-wire fence at the border crossing and into the village. I stood looking at the lights, the people, the cars, and listened to the noise, the laughter, horns beeping, music from the cafés, and thought I had landed on another planet. How could all of this be going on while we were out there struggling to survive, while hundreds were doing so right that moment?

"There is the bus station." Pancho pointed. "You can find out the schedule."

"Is there no one we can tell about Ignacio?" I asked him.

"You can go, but it will be a waste of time, and you might miss a bus. No one will listen or do anything. No one will want to go out there to search for him, Delia. He is one of so many who are out there, and you don't have enough money to pay anyone. You cannot do any more, Delia. You must do for yourself now. *Buena suerte,*" he said. "So much is luck after all."

I watched him walk off, looked back into the desert from where we had come and where Ignacio might lie injured or dead, and then I walked to the bus station, where I bought a second-class ticket to Mexico City. I had nearly four hours to wait for a bus. I bought myself some tortillas and beef and a cold soda that was to me at that moment what the most expensive wine must be to my aunt, I thought.

After I ate and drank, I sat in the station and fell asleep for an hour despite the hard wooden seat. I was anxious to get onto the bus so I could continue sleeping. I would have plenty of time, since the trip would take more than thirty hours. There was a bathroom on the bus, but there would be stops along the way at terminals where passengers could get off and buy food. No one wanted to guarantee any time, not even the bus driver, when other passengers asked about destinations. At this point, I almost didn't care. I was in Mexico, and soon I would be walking down the street to my family home and my grandmother.

I'm sure I looked pretty bad. My hair was filthy, and so was my dress. I had no money for any new clothes, but I did the best I could cleaning myself in the terminal bathroom. I found a brush someone had left on the bus and cleaned it when we stopped at another station. I was still so tired, however, that I really didn't care how I appeared. Sleep was all I craved. All of the muscles in my body were still very angry. The aches and pains actually grew worse while I was traveling on the bus. I was sure those who saw me wondered how someone so young could sleep so much, but the blessing was that it made the trip seem that much shorter.

When we arrived at the terminal in Mexico City, I searched for the best way to get to my village. The ticket agent told me I would have to change buses three times, but the last bus would take me home. I was anxious and excited, even though I had hours and hours to go.

It was just after midday before I reached my village. As the bus drew closer, my heart started to thump. I wasn't sure how Abuela Anabela would greet me. Would she be so angry that even the sight of me would not calm her? Had my aunt sent word of my running away, with all that had happened? If she had, I was sure she had made me look terrible. Knowing my aunt, she would send it through Señor Orozco, the postmaster, so that everyone in the village would hear the story.

The bus stopped in the square. As soon as I stepped off, I stood gaping at everything. I felt like someone who had been blind for a while and had suddenly regained her sight. Everything looked beautiful; nothing looked too old or in too much need of repair. The church steeple loomed higher than ever, and the elderly people I saw sitting and talking no longer looked pitiful or lost to me. I wanted to run up to each and every one of them and hug him or her.

No one seemed to take much note of me. For a moment, it made me question whether I had actually been away. Had it all been some horrible nightmare? Did I just wake up in the square? The blisters and the aches were quick to tell me otherwise. I started for home, walking the streets I had walked all my life but never noticing as much as I did now.

When I turned the corner for our street, I paused. The great heat had not come there, I thought. It was comfortable. The sun didn't burn, and the breeze was soft and refreshing. In the distance, I saw the smoke spiraling from someone's garbage fire. I smiled at the dogs that lifted their lazy heads while they sprawled in the shade. Their curiosity was not enough to get them to rise to sniff around me. They had begun their siesta, and that was too holy to be violated.

I laughed to myself, eager once again to embrace this simple, unsophisticated, honest life. I gladly would sleep in a room smaller than Sophia's closet. I would lie on a bed she would consider a joke. I would sweep and scrub floors that would never look rich and clean. I would work beside my grandmother, making our traditional foods and never thinking about gourmet cooking, and I would not regret a single moment. I even looked forward to seeing Señora Porres and hearing her warnings about the ever-present evil eye.

"I have looked into that eye, Señora Porres," I would tell her. "I have looked into it as you never have, and I have left it blinded behind me."

My elation filled me with new courage. I walked faster toward our home. No matter what Abuela Anabela had been told or thought, I would soon make her happy again. Tonight, we would say our prayers together, and we would fall asleep listening to each other's breathing and be comforted.

The sight of our dry old fountain and the angels was never as wonderful, nor were the stubbles of grass, the shrubs, and the lean-to of a kitchen. I couldn't take it all in fast enough and again heard Pancho's warning to drink slowly, for this was to me like water in a desert. I was home.

I rushed up to the front door, paused to catch my breath, and then entered my house.

"Abuela Anabela!" I called. It was so quiet. Why wasn't she preparing her midday meal? "Abuela!"

I went through the house in seconds but did not find her. The kitchen looked untouched, not a dish out of place, nothing in the sink, the table clear. In our bedroom, both beds were made. Her nightgown was folded as usual and lying on her bed, something that made me smile. Perhaps she had gone off to deliver some of her *mole,* I thought. I drank some water and pondered what to do. Search for her or just wait?

Then I heard the sound of footsteps and the front door opening.

"Abuela Anabela!" I cried, hurrying to greet her.

I stopped.

Señora Paz was standing there alone. "My sister said she thought she saw you walk up the street," she told me.

Because she wasn't smiling and showing her happiness at seeing me, I assumed I had been right to fear my aunt sending the news back here. The whole village thought badly of me. I would have to work at turning them around.

"Do you know where my grandmother has gone?"

She crossed herself and looked up. "She has gone to God," she said.

Somewhere back in the desert, a coyote was howling over a fallen man, a buzzard was circling, scorpions crawled quickly toward the body, and snakes rattled and hissed nearby.

It wasn't only in the desert where mercy was a stranger. It was everywhere there were hearts made to be broken.

The weight of my struggles, the weight of my dead hope and happiness, was too great to be ignored or resisted.

I folded to the floor like a flag bearer in a great battle, once full of determination, brave and strong, defeated in the end by the enemy he could not see.

His flag floated down over him, burying him under what were once his dreams of glory.

23

Homecoming

"Five days ago, she just didn't wake up, Delia. She passed on in her sleep, dreaming of you, I'm sure," Señora Paz told me.

She had called for her sister, and they had put me on the sofa and placed a cold washcloth on my forehead. The two of them looked down at me with similar expressions of pity and sorrow. They were two years apart, but they were like twins in the way they reacted to things. If one had a headache, so did the other. One didn't laugh without the other joining in, and any complaint one made, the other seconded.

"They're twins, all right," Abuela Anabela would tell me after they left us whenever they had visited. "One was just born later."

It was a funny thing for her to say, but Abuela Anabela used to say neither of the sisters needed to look into a mirror. Each could look at the other and see herself.

"The whole village attended her funeral, Delia," Señora Paz's sister, Margarita, said. "Señor Lopez attended and gave the church a good donation. While you were away, your grandmother often sent him things to eat, her wonderful lemon cakes, her chicken *mole,* or whatever she happened to make that day."

"She was very proud of you and what you were doing in the United States. She read us your letters as soon as she received them," Señora Paz said.

"She read them to anyone who would listen," her sister added, smiling.

"Why did you not know of her passing, Delia? Señor Diaz sent news to your aunt. He sent it through one of those fancy machines," Señora Paz said, those beady eyes of hers filling with suspicion.

"It's called a fax," her sister told her.

"Whatever, it is supposed to be very fast."

"I left before my aunt received it," I told them. It was, after all, the truth.

"Why did you leave?" Señora Paz asked pointedly.

"Since you obviously did not know about her passing, you have come just for a visit?" her sister followed, jumping on my words like a detective.

Grandmother Anabela would tell me they were getting all the information they could so they could spread it firsthand in the square tonight. They were our town criers, the town's radio and newspaper all wrapped into one. It was clear that no news about me having run off had preceded my arrival. No one back in Palm Springs had made much of an effort to find me.

"I have not come back just for a visit. I have come home to stay," I told them.

They both looked shocked, their eyes similarly wide,

their mouths opened equally. I nearly laughed at how perfectly they resembled each other. Then Señora Paz nodded at her sister.

"Margarita said it was odd that a big car didn't bring you here, that you had come back on a bus," Señora Paz said.

"What about *su tía* Isabela? Did she want you to leave?" Margarita asked. "Was she sorry she had taken you in to live with her and her children?"

One thing was absolutely sure about the sisters, I thought. They had to know everything as quickly as possible. It would be terrible for someone else to have even the slightest information ahead of them. I turned away and closed my eyes.

"I need to rest a little and then go to the cemetery," I said.

"Of course. But you should know Señor Diaz has arranged for the sale of this house. Your grandmother gave him the right to do so in the event of her passing," Señora Paz said. "The house was sold to Señor Avalos just yesterday. The money was set aside for you, I'm sure. You will have to see Señor Diaz so he doesn't send it on to your aunt for you."

"The house is sold?"

"*Sí,* Delia," Margarita said. "No one expected you would come back here to live, least of all your grandmother, who was receiving the wonderful letters from you."

I had no more parents, no grandmother, and now no home.

"Maybe you should take your money from the house and go back. Will your aunt take you back?" Señora Paz asked. They would get the nitty-gritty details one way or another, I thought.

"I cannot think about it now," I said, bringing disappointment to both their faces.

"I'm sure Señor Avalos will let you stay here a day or so, but I heard he has plans to do some repairs and changes," Señora Paz said. "We'll let him know you are here. You can come and have something to eat with us when you are ready, Delia," she added. "And until you decide what to do, you are welcome to stay with us as well."

I said nothing. I kept my head turned away.

"No one was loved here more than Anabela. Come to us when you are ready and if you need anything," Margarita said.

"Thank you. I mean *gracias,*" I said quickly. Speaking in English seemed like a betrayal to me now.

I didn't turn around until I heard them leave.

My sorrow and despair turned to anger. Why couldn't God wait for me to get home before taking Abuela Anabela? Why was she permitted to die before learning the truth about my new life? I was just as angry as I was the day my parents were taken. When I sat up and looked around, my anger subsided, and my sorrow returned. How empty the house now seemed. Without Abuela Anabela here, I did not care if it was sold.

I went to the sink and washed away my tears. Then I went to the bedroom Abuela Anabela and I had shared and looked for my clothes. Everything was still here, and in fact, Abuela Anabela had washed and folded my things as if she knew I would return. I quickly changed into clean things and then left to go to the cemetery.

I walked through the village like someone walking in her sleep. I saw nothing, heard nothing, smelled nothing. Despite moving in a daze, I made the correct turns and headed up the small hill toward the cemetery, where my grandmother now lay near my parents. As soon as I reached it, I stopped on the pathway. A cat was lying on my grandmother's freshly dug gravesite. It saw me and sauntered off as if it had been guarding the plot and waiting for my arrival. Although it wasn't a margay, it looked a little like one, and for a moment I smiled, remembering Ignacio's grandmother and her belief in sharing your destiny with an animal. Perhaps my margay had sent this cat to stand in until I arrived.

It really wasn't until I saw her name engraved on the stone that I truly realized Abuela Anabela was gone. I fell to my knees, embraced myself, cried and rocked and cried until I could cry no more. After that, I remained there, picturing her face, her smile, hearing her voice as she sang me a lullaby or said her prayers.

"You will never die the third death, Abuela Anabela, never, as long as I live," I swore. Then I prayed at my parents' graves and pressed my hands to the ground, hoping to draw strength up from their sleeping souls. I stayed at the cemetery until it was almost twilight.

On my way home, I stopped at the square and sat for a while. Señor Hernandez came hobbling along with his painted hand-carved walking stick. For as long as I could remember, he was a regular citizen of the square. It was a rare night without him sitting and smoking his pipe or talking softly with anyone who would stop to pass the time. He was a great storyteller, having once been an actor who played in theaters all over Mexico. Although he didn't look terribly old, I knew he was just as old as Abuela Anabela. She had told me he was getting more and more confused, mixing events from the past with the present, but somehow he still managed to care for himself. He never had a wife, and he never had any children to look after him, so I assumed he was used to being alone. How do you get used to that? I wondered, now that I was alone.

"Ah, Delia," he said, approaching. "Are you on your way home from school?"

"No, Señor Hernandez. School won't be over for at least another hour or so."

"Ah, *sí,*" he said, standing and gazing about. "I don't even look at my watch anymore. When I'm hungry, I eat. When I'm tired, I sleep. What difference does time make for an old man, anyway?" He smiled.

Even now, I thought, looking at his aged face, it was possible to see how good-looking a man he was once.

His question told me he either didn't know or had forgotten that I had left. A realization came to him, however.

"Your grandmother has passed on."

"*Sí,* Señor Hernandez."

"When she was your age, she was the most beautiful young woman here. I would have asked her to marry me first, but her father was not happy to think of an actor as a son-in-law. I can't say that I blamed him. But, alas, I could not give up the stage. It was in my blood. My father was not happy about it, either. Fathers, unless they are actors themselves, are not happy about their sons and daughters becoming actors.

"But you know why I became an actor, Delia? I became an actor because on the stage, you have control of happiness and sadness, life and death. In this hard world, it's better to live in your imagination," he said.

"On the stage, you cry only when you play sorrow, and if you don't want to cry, you don't play sorrow."

He sighed and sat beside me, leaning forward a little on his cane.

"I have played an old man on the stage many times, but when I walked off, I was a young man again. I'm stuck in this part now. Until I walk off," he added, his voice drifting.

He stared ahead, and I could see from the way his eyes moved and his lips softened and then hardened that he was reliving some of his roles, perhaps seeing himself on the stage. I did not speak. I stared ahead with him, reliving my life here in this small Mexican village, the two of us, young and old, caught for a few moments in the same theater.

We were interrupted by Señora Paz and her sister hurrying toward me, shuffling over the cobblestones in synchronization like two parade soldiers, their skirts flapping around their legs.

"There you are," Señora Paz said. "We were worried about you, Delia. You must come to our home to eat and stay. We discussed it and decided you must not be alone. There is to be no argument about it."

I started to shake my head.

"You don't want to be alone in that house now, anyway," she added.

She was right about that.

"Come, dear," Margarita said, reaching for me.

Despite their hunger for gossip, they were kind-hearted, I thought. Abuela Anabela didn't dislike them. They were amusing to her. She would want me to accept their generosity, to find comfort in their company. I stood up.

"*Buenas noches,* Señor Hernandez," I said.

He looked up at me as if he just realized I was there, his eyes dull and quiet and then brightening with his smile.

"Ah, Delia, *sí.* You remind me of a young actress I knew. We were working in a small theater just outside of Mexico City, and . . ."

"She has no time for your silly stories," Margarita snapped. "Don't you know she just lost her grandmother?"

"Ah," he said. "Yes, I heard. I am sorry." He smiled at me. "Nevertheless, you remind me of her."

"Old fool," Señora Paz said, turning away.

"He means no harm," I said, following them.

I looked back at him and remembered how much Abuela Anabela enjoyed talking with him. He was staring ahead again, surely seeing the wonderful people he had known and worked with for so many years, reliving his memories. Soon, I thought, he would step off the stage and be a young man again.

"How that man manages is truly a mystery," Margarita said.

How any of us manages is a mystery, I thought. I knew it was far too bitter and cynical a thought for someone as young as I was, but I had seen too many terrible things.

The sisters made a very good dinner for me, although not as good as Abuela Anabela's dinners. I ate everything they put on my plate. I could see they were surprised at the size of my appetite, but it had been so long since I had eaten a real meal sitting at a dinner table. Their house was much smaller than ours. It had only one bedroom, but it was clean and nicely furnished.

After dinner, I let them prepare a place for me to sleep in the living room. I was very tired, and once they had blown out the candles and I closed my eyes, I drifted off quickly and slept right through the night. Without waking me up, they worked around me in the morning, preparing breakfast.

As soon as I did wake up, I rose, washed, and joined them at the table, anticipating their questions. That was the payment they expected, I thought, and I was ready to give it to them, but they surprised me by talking about my future instead.

"While you were at the cemetery, we met Señora Rubio. You know she runs her *menudo* shop with her son. It makes them a small living, but they have a nice little *casa.* You know her son, Pascual?"

"I know him only to say hello," I said. "We have never had much to say to each other. He is at least ten years older than I am."

"*Sí,* but he doesn't look it," Margarita said.

"His mother would like him to settle with a wife, and we thought maybe with the money you will get for the *casa,* you will have a nice dowry."

"You mean to marry Pascual Rubio?"

"It would be an easier life than a life with a farmer," Señora Paz said.

Pascual Rubio was already balding in his mid-twenties. He was short and heavy and shy to the point of being nearly mute. I was not the only one who rarely had any sort of conversation with him. The very idea of marrying him was shocking. I started to shake my head vigorously.

"You're not going back to your rich aunt, Delia. You've told us so yourself. We don't know why, but our

not knowing why is not important right now. What will
you do here? Go work in the soybean fields?" Magarita
asked. "Or do you want to end up like me, a spinster living with her widowed sister?"

"There has to be another choice," I said. "But thank
you for thinking of me."

They both looked very disapproving of how quickly
I had rejected what they obviously thought was a wonderful, quick solution to my situation.

"You should go see Señor Diaz this morning. We
sent word to him and to Señor Avalos to tell them you
were back," Señora Paz said.

"*Gracias,*" I said.

"Please, Delia, think of what we suggested," Margarita said. "Pascual thinks very highly of you. You should
think yourself lucky. A girl your age with no family to
help her has little future."

I didn't disagree about that. Perhaps I had been too
bold to chase a bigger dream. Perhaps my destiny was set,
and I did belong here married to someone like Pascual.

"It will be a wonderful wedding," Señora Paz said.
"And you will have a home and a business."

"I don't know . . . to be married so soon after my
grandmother's passing seems very wrong," I said, shaking my head.

"She would be the first to tell you, '*No hay dolor de
que el alma no puede levantarse en tres días.*' There is
no sorrow the soul can't rise from in three days."

"Yes," I said, smiling and remembering how she
would pronounce her sayings with the authority of a
priest. "She would."

"Then you will think seriously about this offer from
Señor Rubio?" Margarita asked.

"I'll consider it," I said.

"That's a smart girl," Señora Paz said, patting my hand.

"I'm going to change my clothes and then go see Señor Diaz," I said.

"We'll wait for you to return, and then we'll all go together to see Señora Rubio," Margarita told me. "And we'll let Pascual speak for himself."

I couldn't imagine Pascual saying such things to me in front of an audience of women. If he wanted me so much that he could overcome his great shyness, maybe it was meant to be.

I thanked them for all they had done and went to my house for what could be the next-to-last time. The next time, I would be going to get my things and whatever family possessions remained. After I changed my clothes, I went to see Señor Diaz. He was one of the most highly respected men in the village, having been a judge as well as a lawyer. Few decisions in the village were made without his input, even now. He had an office with a secretary and the most modern communications of anyone, even better than what Señor Lopez had on his large estate and soybean farm.

I had been to Señor Diaz's office only once before, with my father when he went to get some important papers. Señor Diaz's secretary was his sister-in-law. My mother always thought she was an arrogant woman who behaved as if she were the one, not Señor Diaz, who was giving advice. She wasn't a gossip like Señora Paz and her sister, but she had her ways of letting people know she knew important things about them or their families. She held that knowledge like a sword over their heads.

Tall, with a long face that convinced my grandmother

she had a horse in her ancestry, Señor Diaz's sister-in-law had a way of pursing her lips and raising her eyebrows instead of saying *hola*. She spoke to people as if her words were jewels. Few people could make me feel as uncomfortable in their presence as she could.

She knew who I was, but she pretended she didn't when I walked into the office.

"Yes?" she said.

"I'm Delia Yebarra. Señor Diaz knows I am coming to see him."

She stared at me as though I should be telling her much more. Then she got up without saying another thing to me and went to the inner office door. She knocked but did not wait to hear Señor Diaz say to come in. She went in and closed the door behind her.

Not ten seconds later, she stepped out and returned to her desk as if I weren't standing there. She shifted some papers and then looked at me.

"Well, go on in," she said, as if I should have known to do so on my own. I thanked her, but she no longer looked at me or heard me.

"*Hola,* Delia," Señor Diaz said, coming around his desk to greet me. He was a distinguished-looking man with a thin black mustache and a narrow face. He had dark brown eyes and black hair and was no more than five-feet-ten, but because of the proud and confident way he held himself, he looked to be taller. "I am sorry about your grandmother's passing. The deaths of your parents are not yet distant enough of a memory."

"*Gracias, señor.*"

"I'm afraid the money for your family's house is not such a great amount, Delia. It's not going to be enough to live on for long."

"I understand, *señor.*"

"It's more than most houses in the village would get. I'm proud to say I negotiated a fair sum."

"*Gracias, señor.*"

He stared at me a moment, and I knew he had something more to say.

"I knew you would be back here soon, Delia. I was not surprised to hear from Señora Paz that you had returned and were at their *casa.*"

"Oh? *Por qué,* Señor Diaz?"

He stared a moment and then returned to his desk and picked up a manila envelope.

"When your grandmother died, I contacted your aunt in Palm Springs, California. She did not respond, but this morning, this came by special delivery for you," he said, handing it to me.

I looked at the return address. It was Palm Springs, but the name above it was Edward Dallas, not Isabela.

"*Gracias,* Señor Diaz," I said, not hiding the amazement in my voice.

"I have spoken with Señor Avalos since I heard of your return, and he has agreed to permit you to remain at the house two more days, but I'm afraid you will have to take your things and find other arrangements after that, Delia."

"*Sí,* I understand," I said.

"Here," he said, handing me another envelope, "are the proceeds of the house sale. It needs to go to the bank."

"*Gracias.*"

"Do you have a place to go, someone to be with?"

"I will, *señor.*"

"Once again, I am sorry for all your troubles and sorrow, Delia. You had a good family. You must remember them and do only what will make them proud of you."

"*Sí, señor. Gracias,*" I said, and left, clinging to the two envelopes but, for all sorts of reasons, terrified of opening the one from Edward. I didn't even glance at Señor Diaz's sister-in-law, but I felt her beady eyes following me out the door.

I decided to walk back to my house first and to open Edward's mail there. On my way, I saw the children hurrying to get to school on time. I stepped back into the shadows and watched as some of the girls and boys from my class passed in front of the square, talking and laughing. My heart ached with the envy I felt. How I wished I could simply return to that innocent world again, wipe away all the horror of the past with a sweep of my hand, and magically become Delia Yebarra, the fifteen-year-old who had just celebrated a wonderful *quinceañera*. The sight of them and the sound of their voices died away, leaving me alone in the shade.

Not noticing my tears until I was well under way again, I hurried past people who I knew wanted to offer me their condolences. I practically ran up the street to our house and the sanctity that remained inside. As soon as I did, I threw myself onto Abuela Anabela's bed and cried until my throat ached. Then, remembering the letter from Edward, I sat up, ground the tears out of my eyes, took a deep breath, and tore the envelope open.

A money order for five hundred dollars fell into my lap. I looked at it and then read the letter.

> *Dear Delia,*
> *I hope and pray this letter finds you.*
> *Yesterday, my mother received the notice of your*

grandmother's passing. If you're reading this letter, you now know, of course, but there is a lot that's happened that you do not know.

First, we are assuming you ran off with Ignacio Davila. I only hope and pray that you did not suffer the same fate as he did. We learned that his body was found in the desert. Once I heard about it, Jesse and I went to see his father. His family was in mourning. His father told me how he had found out about his son. It seems the man who guided him and probably you through the desert discovered his body when he was returning with a group of what are called pollos, *illegal aliens. He was not able to bring Ignacio's body back, and as horrible as this sounds, he told his father that Ignacio's body was already attacked by coyotes and buzzards, and it was better that he not be brought back. His father has accepted it. The man gave him Ignacio's wallet with his identification.*

Since we heard nothing about you, we have been hoping you somehow got through and reached your village. Of course, my first need was to know why you would run off. I was hoping things would clear up and you could start again. I was upset with my mother when I learned she was not doing enough to protect you. I wanted to protect you even more this time, despite my new handicap. By the way, I'm doing fine. In fact, I'm something of a romantic hero to the girls in my school because I'm wearing this eye patch. Who can explain the mind of a teenage girl?

Jesse and I talked about going to Mexico to find you and bring you back. With Ignacio now gone, the police have moved on with the case. Ignacio's friends have made a deal with the prosecutor. They are being convicted of manslaughter. They will go to prison, but not for as long as they could have gone. No one, and I want to stress this, has any interest in talking with you anymore. It's over and done. In fact, Bradley's father, learning of Ignacio's death, has backed off trying to hurt Ignacio's father.

Sophia tried to complain about your leaving with her bracelet. She told my mother some fantastic story about how you convinced her you were sorry you had hurt her and begged her to be your friend again. Both my mother and I nearly burst out laughing listening to her, and she just ran out of the room. She's back to her old ways and couldn't care less about any of this anymore.

I have enclosed the money order for you to use to pay for your trip back. I had a long talk with my mother about you, and she has agreed to make things easier for you. You will never again be treated as a servant here. With your grandmother gone, we are your closest family. Of course, it didn't hurt that I will be turning eighteen next month and my trust starts to get activated. There are many properties and accounts that she wants me to continue with her. She is now becoming my business partner, or I am hers. My trust activates in stages, and when I'm twenty-five, I'll have even more control.

You have to come back, Delia. I would feel I wasted my efforts and my eye if you didn't. I know that's hitting below the belt or being a little unfair, maybe, to say that in order to get you to return, but in love and war, that's how it goes. Yes, I want to love you as my *cousin. Both Jesse and I believe you are a very good person and belong here. Goodness knows, this family needs someone like you, desperately.*

My mother has even agreed, if you would like, to enroll you in my private school. It will be easier, and your education will go better.

Don't worry about Sophia. We, with you beside us, can handle Sophia. She's too selfish really to care about anyone else, anyway. Maybe your good influence will rub off a little on her, and she'll improve, which is another reason for you to return. Call me. Please.

Come back, Delia.

You'll see. It will be different.

> *Love, your* primo, *Edward*

I folded his letter and sat there feeling sick to my stomach. Ignacio was definitely dead, but the horror of hearing about his body being food for buzzards and coyotes was too much. I went out because I thought I would throw up. The pain was in my stomach, but I just did a little dry heaving and crying. Exhausted from it, I returned to the living room and sat in a daze for a while. Then I looked at the money order again and reread some of Edward's letter.

Go back? Despite all of his promises and what my aunt had told him, I didn't think my life would be much better back there. I certainly didn't believe Sophia would just fade into the woodwork. She was too spiteful, and Tía Isabela couldn't have experienced a sudden change of heart, forgive and forget. In his own words, he was telling me that he was threatening her with some financial matters to get her to be cooperative, just the way he had first threatened her to get me living in the main house after my horrible time with Señor Baker. People back there would always think of me as the girl who caused so much turmoil and sadness. Edward and Jesse, despite their good intentions, could not protect me against that.

No, I thought. I belong here. Fate has insisted on it. The evil eye will have its way.

Besides, I thought, I have no reason to go back. I can suffer enough here.

I rose and went out to meet Señora Paz and her sister and go to see Pascual Rubio and his mother.

24

A New Life

Señora Paz asked to see my check from the sale of the *casa*. I kept Edward's envelope out of sight, because I knew she and her sister would hound me to find out what was in that one, too.

"This is more of a dowry than I thought," she said, when I handed her the check. She looked at Margarita. "Señor Diaz did well. Pascual Rubio is getting more than we anticipated." She waved the check at her. "Let us not look as if we are coming to him with our hats in our hands, begging him to be charitable and take Delia for his wife."

"No," Margarita said. She looked at me. "Don't worry. We'll speak up for you, Delia. Making a good marriage contract is a tricky business."

"How would you know?" Señora Paz asked her.

"I would know. I knew about your marriage contract,

how much our father put into the pot. Your husband's family didn't have much more than Delia. Didn't our father buy the gold ring you wear?"

"At least I wear a gold ring," Señora Paz fired back. Margarita seemed to shrink. "You just don't interrupt me and say something foolish," Señora Paz told her. "Come along, Delia." She threw a reproachful look at her sister, who simply smiled at me as if to say her sister was just being silly.

I told them Señor Diaz had worked out arrangements for me to remain in my house two more days.

"You will stay with us until the wedding," Señora Paz said.

Both she and her sister were very interested in how Señor Diaz's sister-in-law had treated me. I described her, and that set them both off into a tirade about her, spinning stories about her marriage and rumors they had heard about her relationship with her husband. They could have been flies on the wall in her *casa* from the details they revealed. Listening to them was amusing enough to take the edge off my nervousness.

When we entered the *menudo* shop, Señora Rubio froze for a moment and then called for her son, who stepped out of the kitchen, wiping his hands on his already very stained apron. His shirt was open, and the curly dark hairs that grew from the base of his throat and down his chest and stomach spiraled out like thin broken springs. When he saw us, he quickly wiped the sweat off his brow with the back of his hand and smiled. Since the last time I had seen him, he had lost two upper teeth on the left side of his mouth, but because of the thickness of his lips, it was not so visible when he didn't smile. He was trying to grow a beard. His hair was so light brown that it was nearly invisible and was growing in patches rather than in a neat shape.

"*Hola,*" Señora Paz said.

"*Hola,*" Señora Rubio replied, and looked at her son sharply to get him to speak.

"*Sí, hola,*" he quickly parroted.

"We have come to talk about Delia's future," Señora Paz said. She looked at the empty table to our right. "She has no one but us to speak for her."

"Why has she returned from the United States?" Señora Rubio asked immediately.

The negotiation has begun, I thought. She is looking for something negative about me.

"I decided that I did not belong there," I said. "I left before I found out my grandmother had died."

"Nevertheless, she is still more comfortable living here," Margarita inserted. "Just like your son. I don't see him crossing the border to make a better living."

"That's because he has a living here," Señora Rubio said. "A good living."

"Can he keep this good living when you are gone to your maker?" Señora Paz asked. "Can he do all that is required in this shop, cook, clean, be a waiter, and take care of a home?"

Señora Rubio didn't reply. She stared a moment and then nodded at the table, and we went to it to sit. Pascual remained behind the counter. We had yet to say anything to each other.

"Maybe you would offer us a glass of water," Señora Paz said.

Señora Rubio nodded at Pascual, who hurried to pour

water into glasses and bring them to our table. While he did so, he snuck glances at me.

"Where will she sleep in your *casa*?" Señora Paz asked immediately, as if that were the most important consideration.

"I will sleep in the living room, and they will have the bedroom. I don't need much of a bedroom."

"She is a good cook. Her grandmother taught her many things," Señora Paz said. "She can even make her wonderful *mole*, and you could sell it here, maybe."

Señora Rubio nodded. "*Sí*, I was hoping that she could do that."

"Do you expect her to use her meager dowry to help pay for the wedding?"

"How much did she get for the house?" Señora Rubio asked, eyeing me.

"What she got is not important. Where and how it will be used is what's important," Señora Paz said, holding her ground. Traditionally, all wedding arrangements and who would sponsor what were worked out like this.

I had always dreamed of having a beautiful wedding in the church with a good-size group of *madrinas* and *padrinos* attending. The *madrina de arras* would hold the thirteen gold coins my future husband was to present to me as a pledge of marriage. The thirteen coins would symbolize my husband's unquestionable trust and confidence, placing all of his goods into my hands for my care and safekeeping. I had seen it done many times.

Father Martinez would bless the coins and place them in the bride's hands. She would put them in the groom's cupped hands at the start of the beautiful wedding ceremony. He would place them on a silver tray, and near the end of the ceremony, they would be given to Father Martinez to hand to the groom. When he placed it in his bride's hands, it would symbolize his giving her control as mistress of his worldly goods.

"We won't be extravagant on a wedding. The money she has should be kept for other needs," Señora Rubio conceded. "We'll have the reception in our yard. We will provide a simple but traditional menu of spicy rice, beans, chicken and beef tortillas, and *sangria*."

"And the mariachis?" Margarita asked. It was her favorite thing at a wedding.

"Señor Gonzales owes me. He will provide his sons."

Margarita made a face. She was obviously hoping for more.

"That's good. That's sensible," Señora Paz said, however.

"I have always been a sensible woman," Señora Rubio snapped at her.

"She should have a fine dress for the wedding," Señora Paz said. "It would make no sense to use money from her dowry for this. She isn't going to be married every week."

"And new shoes," Margarita added.

"She doesn't have to use her house money for that. She can have my wedding dress. It can be altered easily. We'll find her new shoes," Señora Rubio said.

I thought Señora Paz was keeping her on the defensive in this negotiation well, until Señora Rubio looked at me hard and asked in a low whisper, "Of course, she's a virgin?"

I felt the heat come to my face.

"How could you even ask such a question about Anabela Yebarra's granddaughter?" Señora Paz retorted. "Is
your son a virgin?"

Señora Rubio surprised us by nodding and saying,
"Unfortunately, yes."

Even though he easily overheard the conversation,
Pascual pretended to be occupied behind the counter.

"Your son surely won't fit into your departed husband's *guayabera*," Margarita muttered.

"I think he can afford a new *guayabera*," Señora
Rubio said. The traditional Mexican wedding shirt was
what a tuxedo was to Americans.

"We have yet to hear that Pascual wants Delia for his
wife," Señora Paz said.

Señora Rubio looked back at Pascual, who blushed.

"Pascual," she said. "Have you something to ask Señorita Delia today?"

He came forward to recite the lines he had obviously
practiced with his mother.

"Señorita Delia, I would be very happy to have you
become my wife. I will make you a good husband, and
we will have many children. I will keep you from being
hungry, and I will always keep a good roof over our
heads. I will be faithful and always consider your feelings. Would you be my wife?"

I stared at him. Now that I was really there listening
to him and realizing what it meant, I knew that I had
lost complete control of my destiny. It dulled my brain
and made me numb, but like someone truly trapped, I
did not even consider a refusal.

"*Sí*," I said.

"When?" Señora Paz instantly demanded.

"We have relatives we would want to be here. Let us plan on a week from today," Señora Rubio said. "After we talk with Father Martinez, of course, and confirm the arrangements for the mass."

"Of course," Señora Paz said.

"*Gracias* for agreeing to marry me," Pascual told me.

Everyone was quiet, waiting to hear what he would say next.

"I must go back into the kitchen and complete my preparations for today."

I didn't reply. When he turned away, I realized how big his hips were. How would we lie together in a bed? It nearly made me laugh. I was getting giddy, like someone who had drunk too much tequila. Señora Paz saw it in my face.

"We must go and make plans now," she said, rising quickly. "Come, Delia."

"I have not yet told you how sorry I am about your grandmother's passing," Señora Rubio told me. She looked at Señora Paz and her sister. "I'm sure you miss her more than ever now, but soon you will have a new family to care for and to care for you. You cannot measure this in gold," she added, giving Señora Paz a sharp, cold look.

"*Gracias,*" I said, and eagerly left.

When we stepped out onto the street, it was as if I had been shut up in a closet with little or no air.

"It will be a good marriage," Señora Paz said. "I know Señora Rubio is a thrifty and efficient woman. You will have a good life now, Delia. All your days of sorrow and sadness have passed."

I said nothing.

I had two days yet to spend in my home, and I told

them that I wanted to sleep there at least one more
night.

"But you will eat with us," Margarita said. "We still
have much to arrange for your marriage."

"No, I'll be fine. I need to be alone for a while," I
said. "I will come to see you tomorrow, and we can talk.
Gracias. You are both very generous."

Before they could put up any more arguments, I
started away. When I stepped into the *casa,* I started to
cry again. It felt as if I had just come from a funeral,
and, in a sense, I really had. I had just buried the young,
optimistic, and hopeful Delia Yebarra, who had set out
to find a new and greater life over the border. Crossing
the desert to get here, Delia Yebarra had faded away. I
had left her in that cave with Ignacio Davila. I was no
longer who I had been when I ran off with him. I had
become a stranger to myself.

Just as Abuela Anabela had thrown herself into preparing food after learning of my parents' deaths, I began
to clean the house as a way to avoid thinking and crying
anymore. As I worked, I thought this was what I would be
doing daily now. My school days were over. The dreams
my mother had for me were gone. One day would seep
into another, almost indistinguishable. I would have a
fate similar to those my grandmother looked at and said,
"*Lo que pronto madura poco dura.*" I would ripen fast,
aging with my children and with my work.

But I no longer cared. All I had loved was lost. I
would surrender and obey fate like a mindless slave and
cherish the rare laugh and the rare smile. Right now, I
couldn't imagine when either would occur.

I worked hard, scrubbing the tiles just the way
Abuela Anabela had scrubbed them, getting down on

her knees and putting all of her strength into every swipe of the cloth. I dusted and polished, washed and cleaned, attacking every spot, every blemish in the rooms with a vengeance. Señor Avalos would be surprised at the condition of the *casa* he had purchased. Just as my grandmother wouldn't have let it go any other way, I would not.

I didn't realize how much time had passed while I worked. Suddenly, I looked up and realized it was twilight and I was trying to wash away shadows. I lit some candles, because the electricity wasn't working again, and then began to prepare some tortillas for myself. I would eat because I had to eat. As I made my meal, I recalled Abuela Anabela showing me how to do it, standing beside me. When I closed my eyes, I felt her beside me now.

Afterward, sitting alone in the dark and deadly quiet *casa,* I chewed mindlessly and swallowed. After I cleaned up, I went to bed, but I did not sleep. I lay there staring into the darkness, listening to the breeze toy with the house, whistling through the cracks, scraping over the tin. Abuela Anabela used to interpret every sound for me. She was sure some of them were made by angels dancing around the house. She said she could hear their wings flapping. I listened hard for them, and I heard what were distinctly footsteps at my front door. I waited, holding my breath, and listened harder. I was sure I heard the door open slightly.

I continued to hold my breath. There was no sound for a few moments, and then came footsteps. I sat up. A dark shadow moved across the bedroom doorway, followed by the silhouetted figure of a man. Despite how badly I felt about myself and my future, I was still afraid to lose my life or be raped.

"Who is it?" I demanded.

He did not reply. Could it be Pascual Rubio? Had he come to speak more for himself, to make a stream of promises?

I reached over, lit the candle by my bed, and lifted it to throw light in his direction.

My heart started and stopped.

I gasped.

It was Ignacio.

He laughed at what was surely a look of amazement and shock on my face.

"I am not a ghost," he assured me quickly, and stepped into the bedroom.

He was wearing a blue shirt and jeans, and he looked as alive as ever.

"But how can this be? Your body was found with your identification on it."

He came closer and sat at the foot of my bed.

"I had heard many stories about people crossing the desert illegally into America," he began. "Some were stopped by bandits, as we were, and made to strip, the way Pancho was made to strip in the cave. Their clothes were taken, and they wandered about until they found a corpse and took off its clothes. Identities were lost or exchanged, and many families never knew and still don't know what actually happened to their loved ones.

"Our bandits were only interested in my money. After you escaped from the cave, they stopped me from escaping. We fought and struggled, and one of them hit me hard on the back of my head." He turned to show me the bandaged wound. "When I woke, they were gone. I still had water and food. They left both our knapsacks, so I started out. I got a little lost and spent a night alone, thinking I would surely die. Somehow, I managed to get back on the right path. Saint Christopher was with me, surely.

"I heard voices and headed in their direction, and there, leading a dozen or so *pollos,* was Pancho. He was so amazed at the sight of me he nearly passed out. He told me how he had gotten you to Sasabe, but of course, he was afraid I would tell how he had deserted me. He admitted that he was prepared to tell my father's friend that I had died in the desert at the hands of bandits, but he would surely tell the story so as to make himself look less cowardly.

"It was then that the idea occurred to me to give him my identification and have him tell his story. He explained how I should continue, and I made it to Sasabe and then found my way to your village."

"But your family, they think you are dead. They mourn you."

"They know the truth. Yes, they mourn me anyway, because my identity is dead, and their son is still gone, but I am going back someday, Delia. I will find a way. It might not be for some time, but I swear I will do this."

"I believe you will, Ignacio," I said. Then I told him what Edward had written about his friends and about the police.

"I know about your grandmother dying," he said. "When I reached your village, I stopped at a café to ask where she lived, and they told me she had died."

"Before I got home," I said sadly. "I never got to say good-bye, Ignacio."

"Maybe that was good. She died thinking you were still in the United States living with your rich aunt. So," he said, smiling and taking my hand, "now you have no more reason to remain here. You can go back. Contact your aunt. Perhaps she will send money for you."

"*Mi primo* Edward already has," I said, and showed him the money order I had on the small bedside table.

He looked at it and nodded. "This is good."

"I wasn't going to go back," I said. "My grandmother had arranged for the sale of our house, and it is sold."

"So?"

"Friends of my grandmother have arranged a marriage for me."

"To someone you have always loved?"

"No," I said, smiling. "To someone I have not even liked and rarely have spoken to."

"And you will go through with this wedding, this marriage? You will stay here?"

I didn't answer, and he leaped up from my bed and began to pace.

"You would stay here and condemn yourself to this life? You would have been better off dying in that desert! You would marry someone you do not love? You would . . ."

"Stop, Ignacio," I said, now laughing through my happy tears.

He paused and looked at me, the candlelight flickering over his face.

I picked up the money order and waved it at him.

"Don't disguise yourself so much that I won't recognize you when you go back," I said.

His smile was bigger than sunlight, for it relit my soul to brighten me inside with the reverence of a church candle lit to keep the memory of loved ones alive.

I had escaped the third death, too.

Epilogue

It was very different for me leaving this time. Before, I had been terribly sad, but I had hopes of returning and visiting my grandmother. I had nothing to return to now but my parents' graves, and those of my grandmother and other family members. I would visit, I was sure, but not for some time, and I would carry them with me in my heart, anyway.

Ignacio and I spent the night together. In the morning, he accompanied me to see Señora Paz and her sister and give them the news. They were so shocked they were speechless for once.

"You must give my apologies to Señora Rubio and Pascual," I said.

They simply stared at me and Ignacio.

"I will be eternally grateful for your efforts to help me find a future," I told them. "I'll write to you." Neither had said a word yet.

Margarita started to cry.

"Stop acting like a fool," Señora Paz told her. "She has a better offer."

"I am not crying for her," Margarita confessed. "I am crying for myself. I wish I had run off when I was her age, too."

I hugged her and then Señora Paz. Ignacio and I boarded the same bus to travel together for a while. He would go to Mexico City, too, but there we would part at the bus station, where I was taking a shuttle to the airport. Thanks to Edward, all my documentation would be there for my second crossing into America.

I had called Edward, and he was very excited about my return. He told me he and Jesse would be waiting for me at the Palm Springs airport.

"This time, it will be different, Delia. I promise," he said.

He was sincere, but I had no illusions about it. I was about to begin what might be an even more difficult journey to another future. There were still many ghosts and many demons hovering in anticipation, and I would forever be looking over my shoulder for Señora Porres's evil eye, the *ojo malvado*.

Ignacio stood with me at the bus door until the driver said it was absolutely time to go.

"Don't go rushing into another marriage before I get back," he told me.

"I won't. I promise."

"I will cross again, Delia, even if I have to battle the desert to get to you."

"I'll be waiting," I said, and we kissed.

I stepped up and entered the bus to take my seat by a window.

One time, when I had accompanied Abuela Anabela to the cemetery to be with her when she visited the grave of my grandfather, I asked her if it was not better to forget after all, to suffer less pain.

"No," she said. "He has passed on, but our love for each other has not. The memory of that stops the pain, Delia. Without that, yes, there is less reason to go to the cemetery, less reason not to forget. But what you are left with is an emptiness you will never fill. Love keeps us from living alone."

"*Sí*, Abuela Anabela," I whispered as the bus started away and Ignacio pressed his lips to his hand and waved after me, "I will not be alone. *Gracias, mi abuela.*"

Turn the page for a
preview of the next thrilling novel
in the Delia series.

Delia's
HEART

By V.C. Andrews®

Prologue

Looking down from my bedroom window, I see Señor Casto bawling out one of my aunt's gardeners for doing what he considers sloppy work. Señor Casto is as upset and animated as he would be if he actually owned the estate and not just served as my aunt's estate manager. She is lucky to have such a dedicated employee, but I think his dedication and loyalty are still more to my aunt's dead husband, Señor Dallas, than to her. He talks warmly about him quite often, although usually not in my aunt's presence.

Casto is waving his arms and thrusting his hands in every direction. It brings a smile to my face because it looks like his hands are trying to fly off his wrists but keep being caught in midair and brought back.

The gardener, a short, thin man whose pale corn-yellow sombrero is at least two sizes too big, stares without expression and holds the rake like a biblical prophet might hold his staff. The shadow masks his face. He waits patiently, occasionally nodding. He doesn't try to defend himself. I am sure he is thinking, *Soon it will end; soon it will be time for lunch.* With the other gardeners, he will sit in the shade of my aunt's palm trees and unwrap his taco. They will drink their Corona beers and maybe have some beans and salsa.

Sometimes I watch them talking softly and laughing, and when I do, I'm jealous of their conversation. I know they speak only in Spanish, and they are surely talking about Mexico, their relatives, and the world that they, like me, have left behind. Despite the poverty and the other hardships of daily life back in rural Mexico, there was the contentment that came from being where you were born and raised, being comfortable with the land, the mountains, the breezes, even the dust, because it all was who and what you were.

The weather and landscapes here in Palm Springs are not terribly different from the weather and landscapes in my village back in Mexico, but it is not mine. I don't mean in the sense of owning the property. The land truly claims us more than we claim the land. And it does that for all of us, no matter where we are born. No, I mean that I am still a stranger here.

I wonder, will I ever truly be a *norteamericana*? Will my education, my aunt's wealth, my cousins, and the friends I have made here over the past two years and will continue to make here change me enough? Probably more important is the question, will they ever accept me as one of them, or will they simply treat me as a foreigner, an immigrant, forever? Will they finally see me for myself and not just "another one of them"? What must I give up to win their full acceptance?

Can't I hold on to what I loved and still love about my people, my homeland, my food, my music, and my heritage and yet still be part of this wonderful place? Except for the Native Americans, wasn't that what everyone else who came here had and kept? Italians, Germans, French, and others hold on to their sayings, their foods, and their ancestral memories. Why isn't it the same for us?

Nearly a year and a half ago, I stood by the door of the bus in Mexico City and said good-bye to Ignacio Davila, the young man I loved and thought I had lost forever to the desert when he and I fled back to Mexico. He was fleeing because he and his friends had taken revenge on my cousin Sophia's boyfriend, Bradley Whitfield, who had forced himself on me. During the violent confrontation, Bradley was thrown through a window, and the broken glass cut an artery. He was with another girl he was seducing, Jana Lawler, but she did not call for medical help quickly enough, so he died. Ignacio's friends were found, quickly sentenced in a plea agreement, and sent to prison, but through a friend, Ignacio's father hired a coyote to lead us through the desert back to the safety of Mexico.

A little more than halfway across, bandits attacked us when we stopped to sleep in a cave. Ignacio fought them so I could escape. I thought he had been killed but later discovered he had faked his own death in the desert. Only I, his family, and a few of their very close friends knew he was alive and well, working out a new identity for himself. That day we parted in Mexico City, we pledged to each other that we would wait for each other, no matter how long it took for him to return.

Through our secret correspondence, I knew that Ignacio was doing well and waiting for enough time to pass so that he could return and not be discovered. He had to earn enough money so as not to be dependent on his father and put his father in any more danger. Both his family and I realized that he couldn't come back here, however. It would be too dangerous. Bradley Whitfield's father was an important businessman, wealthy, with connections to government officials and politicians. When the news spread that Ignacio had died crossing the desert, Mr. Whitfield had retreated from driving

Ignacio's family out by destroying his gardener business. The Davilas even had a memorial service that I attended. In a real sense, I imagine they felt their son was dead and gone. Anyway, I suppose Mr. Whitfield believed he had gotten his revenge or what he thought was justice, and was satisfied.

Although Ignacio was just as angry as his friends were about my being raped and Bradley going unpunished for it, he swore to me that when they had gotten to the house that Bradley and his father were restoring and found him with Jana, he did not lay a hand on him. It was mostly his *amigo* Vicente who was so violent. Although Ignacio was technically only an accomplice to what was finally ruled manslaughter, he was afraid that he would not get an even-handed, just punishment. He regretted fleeing; he didn't want to be thought a coward, and he didn't want to leave his family with all the trouble. But his father was worried that Ignacio wouldn't survive in the prison system, and that Bradley's father was so angry he would secretly arrange for some harsher punishment after all.

I had fled with Ignacio so I could return to my little village, hoping to be with *mi abuela* Anabela again, even though I knew it would break my grandmother's heart to see me leave what she believed was a wonderful opportunity for me in the United States. Here, living with my wealthy aunt Isabela, I would enjoy a far better education and have the chance to make something greater of my life. Of course, she knew that *mi tía* Isabela hated our family and had renounced her heritage and her language. She thought it was because Tía Isabela's father had forbidden her marriage to Señor Dallas, a much older American man, but I knew from her own lips that her rage came from my mother marrying the one man *mi tía* Isabela had loved, the man she thought loved her. Grandmother Anabela was hoping my aunt had regret-ted disowning her family and would give me opportunities as a way to repent and relieve her of her guilt.

In my senior English class at the private school I now attended, my teacher, Mr. Buckner, quoted from a play by an English author, William Congreve, to describe how angry someone whose love had been rejected could be. Mr. Buckner was a tall man, with a shock of light brown hair that never obeyed the brush and comb. He was a frustrated actor and enjoyed dramatizing his lessons. He had a deep, resonant voice and took a posture like an actor on a stage to look up at the ceiling and bellow, "Heaven has no rage like love to hatred turned. Nor hell a fury like a woman scorned."

Everyone in the classroom, even my cousin Sophia, roared with laughter—everyone but me, that is, because all I could think of was *mi tía* Isabela's blazing eyes when she described her disappointment and rage at losing my father. She accused my mother of being sly and deceptive and stealing my father from her. Of course, listening to her spout such hatred and anger at my mother and my family, I wondered why she wanted me to come live with her after my parents' tragic truck accident on their way to work. It wasn't long before I realized, as my cousin Edward so aptly put it one day, I had become a surrogate. My aunt couldn't punish my mother, because she was dead, so she transferred her hunger for vengeance to me and wanted to make my life as miserable as she could. She did just that, so I had little hesitation when it came to my decision to flee back to Mexico with Ignacio.

Grandmother Anabela used to tell me, "*Un corazón del odio no pueda incluso amarse por completo.*" A heart full of hate cannot even love itself.

I saw how true that was for my aunt. She flitted from one younger man to another in a determined effort to look pleased with herself and get her friends envious. She flaunted her wealth and was at times ruthless at seizing property, claiming she was protecting her dead husband's fortune for her children, but her children were cold to her and she to them. She had little respect for Sophia, and Sophia was constantly in trouble, doing rebellious things just to annoy her half the time.

Edward was different. I sensed that he wanted to love his mother and, at times, I saw how much she wanted his love, but he, too, did not respect or approve of her actions and lifestyle. He was especially angry at her for the way she had treated me when I first arrived after my parents' deaths. She immediately turned me into another one of her Mexican servants and practically put me into the hands of a known pedophile, John Baker, who was to serve as my language tutor. She forced me to live with him in what he called a "Helen Keller world," in which I was completely dependent upon him for everything, supposedly to enhance and speed up my development of English. But after he tried to abuse me that first night, I fled, and Edward came to my rescue.

For a while, thanks to Edward, my aunt was forced to treat me as her niece and not her house servant. However, she was always conniving, searching for ways to isolate me. She got me to spy on Edward and his close friend Jesse Butler, claiming she was worried that they were falling into a homosexual relationship, when all the while, she knew that was just what it was. What she was really trying to do was drive a wedge between Edward and me.

She nearly succeeded. Edward was very angry at me for doing that spying, but when he learned that his mother had put me up to it, he was at my side again, even after his terrible car accident.

Edward had tried to come to my rescue a second time when he heard what Bradley Whitfield had done to me. In anger, he had chased after him before Ignacio and his friends did. He was going so fast he lost control of his car and got into a terrible crash that resulted in his loss of sight in one eye. For a while, it seemed as if old Señora Porres, a woman back in my Mexican village who believed in the *ojo malvado,* the evil eye, might have been right to predict that it could follow someone anywhere. I thought it was stuck to my back, and all I could do was bring trouble to anyone who wanted to help me.

But in the end, it was Edward who wrote to me in Mexico and sent me the money to return. He and my aunt had learned of my grandmother's death while I was crossing the desert with Ignacio, before I had reached my Mexican village. I was so depressed and lost when I arrived there that if it weren't for Ignacio appearing like a ghost one night, I probably would have married a man in the village, Señor Rubio, and condemned myself to the life of a drudge with a man who was ugly and weak. He owned a *menudo* shop with his mother, who ruled him as she did when he was a small boy. She would have ruled me as well.

With the promise of a future for me once again and the hope that Ignacio would join me in America, however, I returned, willing and strengthened to deal with whatever my cousin Sophia threw at me or whatever my aunt would do to me. Ignacio's love for me and my love for him gave me the courage.

I can't say, though, that my legs weren't trembling the day I deplaned in Palm Springs and met Edward and Jesse at the airport. They were both very happy to see me return, and rushed to my side.

"We'll be your knights in shining armor," Edward promised.

"No one will bother you with us around," Jesse bravely assured me.

It disturbed me that I was accepting their generosity and love and yet would be unable to trust them with the deep secret of Ignacio's existence. Keeping secrets from the people you loved and who loved you was a recipe for a broken heart. I was afraid, however, and out of my affection for them, I also did not want to weigh them down with the burden of such a secret.

There was so much more here in America than there was back in my little Mexican village, so much more opportunity and comfort, but there was so much more deception here as well. Back in my simple village, everyone seemed to wear his heart on his sleeve. Here, most people I met wore masks and were reluctant to take them off and show you their real faces. For me, even with my vastly improved English, I was still like a young girl wearing a blindfold and told to maneuver through a minefield.

However, much had improved for me since my return. As Edward explained in his letter to me when I was back in Mexico, his reaching his eighteenth birthday triggered some financial power and independence through the trust arrangements his father had created before his death. Edward explained that my aunt wanted his cooperation on a variety of investments and properties they jointly owned, and to get that, she relented and granted me many new privileges and benefits. I was, as Edward had predicted, now attending the private school my cousin Sophia attended. Sophia and I were still taken there every morning by my aunt's chauffeur, Señor Garman, and when he wasn't available, Casto would drive us. I didn't know it yet, but Edward was planning to give me a new car someday soon. He was trying to get his mother to do the same for Sophia, because he recognized she would make my life a living hell if I had a car and she did not.

Edward and Jesse had both been accepted to the University of Southern California in Los Angeles, but they were home so often people wondered if they were really enrolled in a college. My aunt continually complained about it to him.

"Why are we paying all this money for you to attend college if you're not there?" she demanded to know.

"I'm there for what I'm supposed to be," he replied.

"College is more than attending classes. It's a whole world," she said.

He didn't reply.

In my heart of hearts, I knew that Edward was worrying about me all the time, how I was being treated, and what new injury or pain my aunt and his sister were planning for me.

I tried to assure him that I was fine whenever he called, but he was still concerned, despite how unafraid I sounded. I did have far more self-confidence now, and I think my aunt realized it. I would never say she accepted and loved me. It was more like a truce between us, or even a quiet respect and awareness that I was no longer as gullible and as innocent as the poor Mexican girl who had just lost her parents. The events of the past few years had hardened me in places I had hoped would always be soft. I didn't want to be so untrusting and cynical, but sometimes, more often than not, those two ingredients were important when building a protective shield around yourself. Here, as everywhere, it was necessary to do so, especially for a young woman my age, whose immediate family was gone and whose future depended not so much on the kindness of others as it did on her own wit and skill.

In one of her softer moments, when she permitted herself to be my aunt, Tía Isabela admitted to admiring me for having the spine to return and face all the challenges that awaited me, challenges that had grown even greater because of the previous events.

But her compliments were double-edged swords in this house, because she often used them and me to whip Sophia into behaving. As a result, Sophia only resented me more.

"Instead of always doing something behind my back or something sly and deceitful, Sophia, why don't you take a lesson from Delia and draw on some of that Latin pride that's supposedly in our blood," she told her once at dinner when she discovered Sophia had been spreading nasty lies about a girl in the school who disliked her, the daughter of another wealthy family. The girl's mother had complained bitterly to Tía Isabela. "Believe me," she told Sophia, "people will respect you more for it. Look how Delia is winning respect."

Sophia's eyes were aching with pain and anger when she looked at me. Then she folded her arms, sat back, and glared at her mother.

"I thought you weren't proud of your Mexican background, Mother. You never wanted to admit to ever living there, because you were so ashamed of it, and you hate speaking Spanish so much you won't even say *sí.*"

"Never mind me. Think of yourself."

"Oh, I am, Mother. Don't worry, I am," Sophia said, and smiled coldly at me. "Just like our Latin American princess," she added.

Frustrated, Tía Isabela shook her head and returned to eating in silence.

Most of the time, silence ruled in this *hacienda* because the thoughts that flew about would be like darts if they were ever voiced. They would sting like angry hornets and send pain deep into our hearts. It was better that their wings were clipped, the words never voiced.

There was little music in the air here as well. Oh, Sophia clapped on her earphones, especially when she went into a tantrum, but there was no music like there was back in Mexico, the music of daily life, the music of families. Here there was only the heavy thumping of hearts, the slow drumbeat to accompany the funeral of love, a funeral I refused to attend.

Instead, I sat by my window at night and looked out at the same stars that Ignacio was surely looking at as well at the same moment, somewhere in Mexico. I could feel the promise and the hope, and vowed to myself that nothing would put out the twinkling in the darkness or silence the song we both heard—nothing, that is, that I could imagine.

But then, there was so much I didn't know.

And so many dark places I couldn't envision.